Dear Re   p

   The n
by such
Rosemary Rogers, Johanna Lindsey, Laurie
McBain, and Shirlee Busbee are accountable to
one thing above all others: Avon has never tried
to force authors into any particular mold.
Rather, Avon is a publisher that encourages
individual talent and is always on the lookout for
writers who will deliver *real* books, not packaged
formulas.

   In 1982, we started a program to help readers
pick out authors of exceptional promise. Called
"The Avon Romance," the books were distinguished by a ribbon motif in the upper left-hand
corner of the cover. Although the titles were by
new authors, they were quickly discovered and
became known as "the ribbon books."

   Now "The Avon Romance" is a regular feature on the Avon list. Each month, you will find
historical novels with many different settings,
each one by an author who is special. You will
not find predictable characters, predictable plots,
and predictable endings. The only predictable
thing about "The Avon Romance" will be the
superior quality that Avon has always delivered
in the field of romance!

Sincerely,

WALTER MEADE
President & Publisher

THE PAPERBACK SH
8000 F. N. Armeni
Tampa, Fla. 33

THE PAP
8000 F.
Ta
THE PAPERBACK SHOP
8000 F. N. Armenia
Tampa, Fla. 33604
Ph. 932-908

THE PAPERBACK SHOP
BEST IN USED BOOKS
1824 W. WATERS AVE
TAMPA, FLORIDA 33604   937.007

Other Avon Books by
Jean Nash

FOREVER, MY LOVE

Avon Books are available at special quantity discounts for
bulk purchases for sales promotions, premiums, fund
raising or educational use. Special books, or book excerpts,
can also be created to fit specific needs.

For details write or telephone the office of the Director of
Special Markets, Avon Books, Dept. FP, 1790 Broadway,
New York, New York 10019, 212-399-1357. *IN CANADA:*
Director of Special Sales, Avon Books of Canada, Suite
210, 2061 McCowan Rd., Scarborough, Ontario M1S 3Y6,
416-293-9404.

JEAN NASH

SURRENDER THE HEART

AVON
PUBLISHERS OF BARD, CAMELOT, DISCUS AND FLARE BOOKS

SURRENDER THE HEART is an original publication of
Avon Books. This work has never before appeared in book
form. This work is a novel. Any similarity to actual persons
or events is purely coincidental.

AVON BOOKS
A division of
The Hearst Corporation
1790 Broadway
New York, New York 10019

Copyright © 1985 by Jean Nash
Published by arrangement with the author
Library of Congress Catalog Card Number: 84-091826
ISBN: 0-380-89622-2

All rights reserved, which includes the right to
reproduce this book or portions thereof in any form
whatsoever except as provided by the U. S. Copyright Law.
For information address Sanford J. Greenburger Associates,
Inc., 825 Third Avenue, New York, New York 10022.

First Avon Printing, June 1985

AVON TRADEMARK REG. U. S. PAT. OFF. AND IN OTHER
COUNTRIES, MARCA REGISTRADA, HECHO EN U. S. A.

Printed in the U. S. A.

WFH 10 9 8 7 6 5 4 3 2 1

For my husband,
again and always,
with love and gratitude

SURRENDER THE HEART

Prologue

IT WAS COLD on the deck of the R.M.S. *Britannia*. The spring night was clear; a silver-white moon and a brilliant array of stars cast a phosphorescent glow on the ebony surface of the North Atlantic sea. A lone passenger stood at the rail, a young woman in mourning, a portrait in black, the only contrast her cameo face, upon which a recent and profound grief was most intensely, exquisitely etched.

Nearby, a gentleman was watching her, a tall, slender, dark-haired man with eyes that were startlingly blue beneath a brush of dark lashes. Impeccably clad in evening clothes, he had left the first-class dining saloon a quarter of an hour earlier in need of a cigarette. Catching sight of the lady, so aloof and alone in the still, icy night, he had extinguished his smoke lest its light alert the object of his interest to his scrutiny.

The woman intrigued him and that she did so surprised him. There was little about women that Jason Carradine, at the age of thirty-six, did not know. Wealthy, charming, attractive, a bachelor by choice, he had had more than his share of relationships. He had loved some, had hurt some, and had been loved and hurt in turn, and by the time he reached thirty, he had been reasonably certain that he had discovered all there was to learn about the opposite sex.

But the woman in black loomed a mystery to Carradine, and a mystery, above all things, intrigued him. He had caught glimpses of her several times since boarding the *Britannia* at Southampton four days earlier. Clothed always in black, and always alone, she had attracted his attention from the first day he saw her making her way gracefully up the gangway. Since she was never escorted on the occasions he noticed her on deck or in the ship's library or in the spacious first-class lounge, he had assumed that she was traveling alone, which was not done in the year 1910.

In light of this flaunting of the laws of accepted conduct, it occurred to Carradine as he watched the young woman at the rail that she might not be an American. Her clothes and her bearing were decidedly Parisian: the cashmere coat furred at the collar was closely fitted to her frame; the turban hat overlaid with a veil enhanced the pale beauty of her face. On that basis, on impulse, Carradine formed an opening statement and decided at last to approach this attractive enigma.

"Mademoiselle." He spoke in French. "Your pardon if I disturb you, but I believe we met in Paris last month at the château of Emile Laducer."

He presented his card.

She accepted the card, read it, returned it, and replied in the same tongue, "You are mistaken, monsieur. I know who you are, but we have certainly never met."

"You know me?"

"Yes," she said distantly. "The 'Prince of Wall Street' is not an anonymity."

He smiled, amused. She was younger than he had thought. Her eyes, in the moonlight, were a soft velvet brown, fringed heavily with lashes as dark and as lustrous as the wisps of sable hair that escaped her black turban. Her nose was charmingly upturned over a petal-pink mouth, and her face, although haughty, was the angel-sweet face of a soul as yet unstirred.

"I see," he said smoothly. "Then my celebrity precedes me."

" 'Celebrity,' monsieur? I would more say 'notoriety.' The countless investors who have lost fortunes as a result of your ruthless stock manipulations stand as testimony to your insatiable thirst for money and power."

His assured smile faded; he regarded her soberly. Such hard words from soft lips gave him pause. His dealings in the stock market were detrimental to some, that was true, but "ruthless" seemed an excessive description of his methods.

"Mademoiselle," he said at length, "I admit that others lose when I make gains, but unfortunately that is the way in this capitalistic society of ours. In light of your obvious disapproval of such a system, I would venture to guess that you have socialist leanings."

She gave him a look of such unmitigated scorn that for a second time he was taken aback. And then, before he had a chance to gather his wits about him, she said cuttingly in English, "No, Mr. Carradine, I am not a socialist—and neither am I French. You are mistaken this evening on all counts."

And with that cold rebuff she left him standing at the rail, as thoroughly bereft of dignity as if she had boxed his ears.

He looked after her, scowling, as a sudden surge of rage and an unaccustomed embarrassment quickened his pulsebeat and splashed color in his cheeks. Impudent brat! What she needed was a sound thrashing, administered by himself with consummate pleasure. She was rude and uncivil, and though her face was angelic, she had the tongue of a boorish barbarian.

But then he shrugged and softly laughed. No woman in his experience had ever so totally disarmed him. She was young, a child really, and with the ease of a seasoned soldier she had brilliantly outmaneuvered him and had counterattacked his every advance. What a delight she was, and what a refreshing change from the compliant companions who had lately been occupying his time.

He laughed again softly and set off toward the dining saloon. The young lady in black had been even more intriguing than he had imagined.

One

As THE R.M.S. *Britannia* approached harbor a full fourteen hours ahead of schedule, Adrian Marlowe stood at the ship's rail, and in spite of her recent grief, she caught her breath in awe at first sight of New York's towering skyline. She had witnessed this spectacle before, having been abroad several times in the past. But to watch the city appear, rising like an ethereal length of stalagmites from some subterranean grotto, never failed to stir her.

Overhead shrieked the gulls, their gray-tipped wings wide, dipping, and swooping, in search of a meal as the great ship, with its entourage of tooting tugs, glided gracefully toward port. The harbor was alive with traffic: steamers, freighters, ferries, and barges; and directly aport Lady Liberty beckoned to the homeward-bound, both resident and alien alike, her pedestal proudly proclaiming, "I lift my lamp beside the golden door!"

It was a clear April morning with cloudless blue skies. Radiant sunshine smote Adrian's eyes as she disembarked at the White Star pier on West Fourteenth Street. A thick crowd milled at dockside: friends and relatives waved a greeting; journalists and photographers lay in wait to accost and detain a newsworthy traveler. Adrian welcomed the chaos, the excited babble of voices, the endless line at customs, anything to distract her mind from her crushing bereavement: the death of her aunt and the demise of the last of her dreams.

Her beloved Aunt Meg. Her sudden passing in Paris had been a blow from which Adrian wondered if she would ever recover. Meg Marlowe and her husband Harry had been mother and father to Adrian, whose natural parents had died in a train accident when Adrian was two.

Her uncle, who had formally adopted her, had died of heart failure three years earlier. Harry Marlowe's fortune had been lost in the Panic of 1907. His brokerage firm, along with that of Otto Heinze & Company, had collapsed in the United Copper debacle. Heinze and Marlowe had conspired to corner the market on United Copper shares, drive up the price, and then sell at the proper time, thus making a hefty profit. Unfortunately for them, other stockholders caught wind of their scheme and began selling their stock in great blocks, thus driving the price down to virtually nothing, beggaring the firms of Marlowe and Heinze in the process.

The resulting furor in the stock market caused a panic that was nearly as devastating as the one that had rocked Wall Street in 1893. Other investors, frightened by the United Copper failure and suspicious that their brokers might devise similar schemes as had Heinze and Marlowe, began to dump their stocks on the market in damaging quantities. For Harry Marlowe this further devastation did not much matter. His firm was finished; he was totally bankrupt and without credibility. Shortly after the United Copper failure, he suffered a severe heart attack, lived for three days in a stupor of excruciating pain, and then quietly and gratefully died.

Marlowe's death and his failure in the stock market was a shock of such magnitude to Adrian that she would never be quite the same thereafter. She was barely eighteen years old when he died; she had grown up a pampered pet, the adored daughter of a man who had thought he would never be blessed with a child. Adrian had been loved by Harry Marlowe as totally and as fiercely as if she had been his own.

Not her slightest wish had ever been denied. She was the center of his universe, as he was of hers. No one was as noble as Uncle Harry, no father as kind or as wise. No child was happier than Adrian, no daughter more loved or secure.

But when his brokerage firm collapsed, when his name became a vile thing on Wall Street, Adrian's unshakable faith in her uncle received a stunning blow. This could not have happened to the man into whose keeping she had placed her utter trust. Uncle Harry was too honorable, too powerful to have failed not only himself but those he loved. When he died shortly thereafter, Adrian's shock at his business failure was compounded by the trauma and grief of losing him. "I can't bear it," she said to her aunt when Harry Marlowe was laid to rest. "How can we go on? On whom can we depend now?"

Gently but firmly her aunt replied, "On ourselves, Adrian. For we are all we have left."

Curiously those simple words were a great comfort to Adrian. Yes, she had her aunt, but more importantly, she had herself. And of one thing she was sure: She would never fail herself. With a courage and self-confidence she had not known she possessed, Adrian vowed on that day that henceforth she would be her own strength, her own support. How much better to rely on oneself than on someone who might ultimately prove a disappointment. Never consciously did Adrian consider that her uncle had disappointed her; that was too disloyal a thought. Nevertheless, because of the devastating failure of one whom she had considered invincible, Adrian was determined, in the future, to rely on the resources of no one but herself. Sooner than she realized, that determination was put to the test.

After Marlowe's death, upon settling his estate, Adrian and her aunt learned that he had been deeply in debt to his banker, J. Carradine & Company. To diminish, if not satisfy, that debt, everything had to be sold: the house on Fifth

Avenue; the summer cottage in Connecticut; the paintings; the sculptures; even the most personal items of both women, such as silver combs and brushes and enameled jewel cases. To make good the balance of the debt Adrian and her aunt soon found it necessary to seek some means of income. Adrian, from a young age, had had both a talent and an inclination for fine needlework and design. She suggested to her aunt that a dressmaker's shop might be the solution to their problem, which indeed it turned out to be, for within a year after Marlowe's death, his wife and his niece had totally discharged his debt and had begun to make a small success of their business.

This success, although moderate, encouraged Adrian greatly. She and her aunt had overcome an adversity that might have proved too much for some. Everything they were used to had been lost to them: the opulent town house on Fifth Avenue; the furs; the jewels; the accoutrements of prosperity that had ornamented their lives. But oddly, working for a living pleased Adrian. The independence appealed to her; the creativity of designing excited her. She was now responsible for her own well-being, for her very existence. And that she was doing so by her own wits and intelligence and courage further convinced her that her only source of strength should be herself.

This conviction motivated her desire to do more. Why just eke out a living in a little dress shop when the great couturiers of Europe lived like potentates on the earnings from their designs? Adrian said to her aunt one day, "Let's expand. Let's go to Europe and learn what we need to open a fashion house here in New York."

"Money," her aunt said dryly. "That's what we need to open a fashion house."

"Plenty of money," echoed Tessa Keller, their seamstress, a good friend to Adrian and who had been with the Marlowe women since their initial foray into business.

Adrian looked at the two people who were closest to her in all the world. Her aunt, still beautiful at thirty-nine, with her curling brown hair and her no-nonsense brown eyes; and Tessa, petite, blond, and green-eyed, an indefatigable worker despite her small size, who possessed an enormous talent for transposing her employer's designs from sketch pad to cloth. Adrian felt she could wholly depend on these two, women like herself who stood alone, who did not rely on the questionable strength of men.

"Aunt Meg," she said, "do you remember telling me about your mother's cousin, the Earl of Bedford?"

"Yes, of course I remember, but what—"

"If we go abroad," Adrian said, excitement quivering in her voice, "we could kill two birds with one stone. First of all, we could ask the earl for a loan—at the prime rate of interest, naturally—and then we could go on to Paris, to the houses of Poiret and Worth, to see for ourselves precisely what we need to do to open a fashion house here. I doubt any bank would be willing to finance us, but with the earl's assistance—"

Meg Marlowe laughed and regarded her niece with renewed admiration. "Dumpling," she said fondly, "you never cease to amaze me."

"Then you'll do it?" Adrian urged. "Tessa, you could handle the dress shop for a few months while we're gone, couldn't you? Oh, Aunt Meg, we're going to succeed, I just know it!"

But expectation and realization, Adrian soon learned, are two different matters. Scraping together every last cent of their small savings, she and her aunt set out for England with the highest hopes. Those hopes were quickly dashed when they arrived at the Bedford estate in Sussex to learn that the old earl had died and that his heir had no wish to render financial assistance to a distant cousin he had never before set eyes on.

"And besides," young Bedford had said, pulling at his mustaches with a supercilious snort, "whyever would you want to open a fashion house in America?"

And before Adrian could offer a reply, the earl's wife had added scornfully, "Yes, Miss Marlowe, indeed? I was of the impression that the colonists attired themselves in buckskin and beads. Surely a couturiere would be superfluous in such society."

Bristling with indignation, Adrian left the Bedford estate with her aunt and had gone on to France. The Channel crossing had soothed her ruffled feathers. By the time she reached Paris, her spirits lifted, and a good night's sleep at the St. Gervais Hotel had further buoyed her natural enthusiasm.

The following day, clad in their finery, Adrian and her aunt had visited the fashion houses of Revillon, Worth, and Paquin where, much to Adrian's dismay, they had seen little, only the outward trappings of haute couture as shown to the patrons of these soigné establishments. But at the House of Poiret, armed with a letter of introduction from one of Monsieur Poiret's favorite patrons, an acquaintance of Meg Marlowe's, Adrian and her aunt had been treated to a personal preview of the master's fall line.

And what a showing it was, as live mannequins glided about the art nouveau salon, dressed in a delicious array of peacock-blue silk and Nile-green brocade and ruby-red velvet and silver lamé. Adrian had been delighted and astonished by the revolutionary designs, a startling change from the "pouter pigeon" silhouette of recent years, which twisted the torso into an unnatural thrust of bosom and derriere. Poiret's creations were slim and free-flowing, much in the manner of a Greek garment, gathered beneath the breast and falling to the feet in a sinuous draping of elegant simplicity.

The models were rapier-thin, and it was obvious to

Adrian, from the fit of their gowns, that Monsieur Poiret had them discard their S-shaped corsets and had supplied them with an innovative undergarment of his own design which enhanced rather than exaggerated the natural form. Adrian had read about this new corset in *Vogue* magazine and had been disappointed to learn that none of the New York department stores carried them. So she gave strict attention to the line of the mannequins' figures, and after carefully questioning Monsieur Poiret, she was sure she could duplicate the garment, thus creating the proper foundation for the new line of dresses she had already begun to design in her mind.

When the Marlowes left the salon, the Rue de la Paix was a spectrum of spring color: eggshell-blue skies; yellow and green budding trees; pale violet and fragrant pink blooms. The Parisian ladies strolling by were a rainbow of hues, butterfly-beautiful in a dizzying variety of Gainsborough-blue voile, India pongee of lemon chiffon, and the softest of willow-green crepe. Dazzled and inspired by this stunning display, Adrian eagerly confided her plans to her aunt. But then, remembering their setback in Sussex, she said with a groan, "But where are we going to get the money?"

"Don't worry, dumpling," the aunt soothed. "We'll get the money somewhere."

"How?" Adrian grumbled.

"We'll speak to Evan Colby," said Aunt Meg, referring to a childhood friend of Adrian's who had been in love with her for years. "He's been at Carradine and Company for almost a year now, selling new stock issues. I'm sure by now he has enough influence to secure a loan for us."

But Adrian balked at the suggestion. "No, Aunt Meg," she said decisively. "We will not speak to Evan. I won't use him in that manner. We'll do it on our own. And besides," she added, frowning, "I prefer not to do business with Jason

Carradine. Evan told me that it was he who was largely responsible for the failure of Uncle Harry's firm."

"That's nonsense," the aunt said. "It was Harry's own imprudence that was responsible for the failure." Her voice was brisk as she spoke of her husband, seemingly without emotion. But her eyes were suddenly very bright, and her lips trembled almost imperceptibly.

Adrian reached out compassionately and squeezed her aunt's hand. She wanted to contradict her, to assure her that Evan was in a far better position than she to know whether or not Jason Carradine had contributed to Harry Marlowe's downfall. Evan had related to Adrian many incidents of Carràdine's unscrupulous dealings on Wall Street, dealings that had netted great profits for Carradine at the expense of some unfortunate victim.

But as her aunt's eyes grew brighter with memory and pain, Adrian only said gently, "Don't worry, Aunt Meg, we'll get the money somewhere. We needn't speak to Evan. We'll do it on our own."

"Adrian, be sensible," Meg said, composing herself. "We must speak to Evan. We haven't a sou for collateral. No bank will give us a loan unless someone like Evan undertakes responsibility."

"Please, Aunt Meg," the girl said patiently. "I cannot do that. I know Evan still loves me, and I don't want to take advantage of his feelings."

Her aunt retreated and said nothing else on the subject, but Adrian was not appeased by this easy acquiescence. She knew her aunt well, and she was willing to wager that when they returned home, Meg Marlowe would take it upon herself to speak to Evan Colby and to solicit his help.

But she never did.

On April first, shortly before they were due to sail home, Margaret Wilson Marlowe contracted a virulent and painful infection, the cure for which eluded the finest French doctors, and a few days later, with merciful swiftness, she was dead.

"Adrian. Adrian, wait!"

The girl had finally stopped a taxi on West Fourteenth Street and was just about to enter it when she heard her name called. She turned to see a young man pushing through the dockside crowd, hat in hand, his sandy hair tousled, his hazel eyes alight in a flushed, boyish face.

"Evan!" she exclaimed. "What are you doing here?"

With a grin he responded, "I just happened to be in the neighborhood."

The lie did not deceive her, but she smiled as Evan dismissed the taxi she had flagged down and then instructed the porter to load her luggage into his auto, standing curbside nearby. Adrian was delighted to see him, intensely grateful that a dear friend had been so thoughtful as to meet her at the end of a long, lonely journey. She was so fond of this young man with the fresh-scrubbed good looks of a choirboy. Two years earlier she had thought she might marry him, but she realized, as time passed, that although he was kind and loving and thoughtful, everything any woman could hope for in a husband, he was not the man she wanted. In truth she was not sure what she wanted or needed. But it wasn't Evan. Of that much, at least, she was certain.

"I'm truly sorry about your aunt," said Colby after they had settled in the backseat of the Pierce-Arrow and he had directed his chauffeur to drive on. "I wish you had let me know."

"But how did you learn of it, Evan?"

She lifted her veil and turned in her seat to face him. Her pallor, Colby noted, served only to heighten the sheen of her sable hair and the velvety depths of her splendid, dark eyes.

"The obituary notice was in the *Times*," he explained.

"Someone must have cabled the newspaper from Paris. I had thought it was you."

"No." She shook her head. "It never crossed my mind to let anyone know. It was such a shock . . ."

She trailed off and looked out the window at the city. How familiar it looked with its small parks, a verdant surprise amidst a jungle of colorless concrete, and yet how different it seemed now, how lonely. She was going home to an empty house, an empty life. Aunt Meg was gone, buried on foreign soil. The fashion house of which they had both dreamed seemed destined to perish in the cold light of reality. If Adrian was to survive—and she must—she had to do it alone. For a moment she wondered if she was able.

She turned then to Evan and was startled to see him watching her with a look of compassion and concern. Embarrassment surged through her; her cheeks flamed. If her plight inspired compassion, could pity be far behind? She straightened her spine and spoke, determination firm in her tone.

"Evan, I must advertise for help at the shop. With Aunt Meg gone I shall need someone to do the accounts and perhaps another seamstress or two. I dislike dealing with the patrons, but it is necessary now that I do. Aunt Meg had a great deal more patience and diplomacy than I have. I must try to emulate her as best I can."

Evan's boyish face grew stern. "You can't be serious."

"Of course, I'm serious. Why are you scowling?"

"Adrian, for heaven's sake, you must forget all that nonsense now. You can't possibly operate the shop alone; it's too heavy a burden for a young girl alone. Marry me, Adrian. Marry me and I promise you you'll never have another worry as long as you live."

Impulsively, ardently, his hands covered hers protectively. Adrian looked down at those hands, hard and competent and strong, and for just a fraction of an instant she

envisioned a life without worry or care, the golden insouci-
ant fairy-tale life to which her uncle had bred her. Like that
carefree, golden life, Aunt Meg, too, was gone, a source of
strength on which Adrian now realized she had depended
more than she knew. In the end, she thought, there was no
one but oneself. Having a husband did not insure a life free
of care. Aunt Meg had a husband, yet she had spent the last
few years of her relatively short life working and struggling
to achieve a measure of security. For Adrian to marry Evan,
therefore, was not the solution to her problem. She realized
she had no alternative but to strengthen her own position and
resolution.

"Evan," she said, withdrawing her hands from his, "it's
very sweet of you to want to look out for me, but I'm really
capable of doing so on my own."

"To look out for you?" he echoed, stung. "Adrian, I
love you. I want to marry you."

"Yes, I know you do," she said gently, "but I don't want
to marry anyone just now. I have the shop to consider; I
won't abandon it. We worked hard, Aunt Meg and I, to establish Marlowe's, and if I turn away from it, if I let all our
work go for naught, it would be a terrible disloyalty, both to
my aunt and to myself. Can you understand that, Evan? Can
you see that this is something I must do?"

"No," he said angrily. "I can see nothing past your incredible willfulness. This is all your uncle's fault. He
spoiled you outrageously since the day he adopted you, and
as a result you think that anything you desire is yours for the
asking. Well, the real world's not like that, Adrian. The real
world is a man's world, and women like you stand little
chance of surviving in it without a man's hand to guide and
protect them."

It was difficult to dispute the logic of his words. It *was* a
man's world, and Adrian realized, with a dart of fear, that if

ever she was to succeed in that world, she must work ten times as hard as any man.

"Evan," she said softly, laying a hand on his sleeve, "please don't criticize my uncle. Perhaps he did spoil me, but more importantly, he taught me to have a mind of my own. I don't want a man's hand to guide me; I want to make a success of my business by myself."

"But you can't!" Evan protested. "You and your aunt barely eked out a living from Marlowe's. If you engage an accountant and more seamstresses, how do you propose to pay them?"

"I don't know!" she cried, and her voice had gone sharp with a sudden, swift panic. Evan had aroused in her all the doubts she had valiantly tried to suppress. She was alone; she needed money. Did he honestly think she was unaware of those facts? "I don't know how I'll pay them," she said again, "but I will do it!"

"Adrian, Adrian." Once more he took her hands in his. "You must be reasonable. You cannot do this alone. Give it up; let me take care of you."

She did not answer; she could not speak. Her expression was stony, and her hands, still in his, felt like ice. But it was fear of the future that hardened the contours of her face, fear of a future that loomed darkly before her like the inescapable certainty of the death of all she loved.

Two

SHE WAS ASHEN and still when the Pierce-Arrow drew up to her house. Too late, Evan realized that his clumsy attempt to give her comfort had instead done the opposite.

"I'm sorry," he said in a low, rapid voice. "I'm desperately sorry if I've upset you. Adrian, let me come in, let me stay with you awhile. I don't want you to be alone just now."

She regarded him silently: his clean-shaven face; his expressive hazel eyes; the apologetic curve of his sensitive mouth. In the midst of her own misery she was nonetheless moved by his. By sheer will she managed to collect herself, and at length she said with effort, "No, don't come in. I'm all right, truly I am. And I think it would be better if I spent some time by myself."

She looked toward the house, a dark brownstone, flanked on both sides by identical buildings, and she doubted, momentarily, the wisdom of her decision. But she had to face it alone. To put it off, to invite Evan in, thus delaying the moment when she would be truly alone, would be simply delaying the inevitable.

"I'm all right," she said again when he grasped her hands to detain her. "Please, Evan, let me go in now. I'll telephone you later . . . yes, I promise I will."

Reluctant, concerned, Evan escorted her to her door. She accepted his kiss—a brotherly brush of his lips on her cheek—and for a moment, for just an instant, she held on to him tightly. When at last she released him and turned into the house, she had to struggle against the impulse to drag him inside with her.

The chauffeur had carried the trunk and portmanteau upstairs, which was just as well, Adrian reflected as she shed her hat and gloves. The heavy work in the house was attended to by the day man, whose duties included maintaining the coal furnace and carting out the ash cans but whose services would now have to be terminated.

She would also have to think about dismissing the cook and the charwoman. Servants would be a luxury now, an extravagance she could ill afford. The house, fortunately, was small: three rooms on the first floor; two rooms and bath on the second. Adrian was perfectly capable of doing the dusting and mopping herself, and the cooking, too, if need be; or else she could eat at the Horn and Hardart on Broadway, which was clean and inexpensive and only one block away from the dress shop.

She removed her cashmere coat, laid it on the hall table, then went into the parlor where she drew back the heavy curtains, letting the afternoon light spill into the cluttered room. Adrian and her aunt had leased the house furnished. Adrian had never cared for the sofa and chairs upholstered in maroon horsehair, the black marble-topped tables, and the assortment of bric-a-brac that reposed on the mantelpiece and on the tulip-tree étagère, but the monthly rental rate had been within her means, and the neighborhood was safe, if no longer fashionable.

To a girl reared on Fifth Avenue amidst the most opulent surroundings, this small, graceless house might have seemed an ugly prison, a humiliating comedown. But to Adrian, inherently pragmatic, essentially realistic, it was a place to live, nothing more, nothing less, and that it suited her needs was all that concerned her.

The dining room and kitchen were as dull and uninspired

as the parlor. Adrian inspected the rooms, found them dusty but neat. She picked up the small valise she had left at the foot of the stairs and carried it up to the second floor.

She went first into her aunt's bedroom, a gloomy chamber with bulky mahogany pieces and papered walls the color of dried mud.

"Dumpling, I'll take this room," her aunt had said when they first leased the house. It was like Aunt Meg to see that Adrian always had the best, although the second bedroom, with its tatty lace curtains and pseudo-French furnishings, could hardly be called the "best" of anything.

At the thought of Meg Marlowe—the first concentrated thought Adrian had given her aunt since the funeral—her facade of stoicism dissolved; her eyes blurred with tears, and she turned away from the silent, empty bedroom and went into her own.

She dropped the valise, kicked off her shoes, and sank wearily onto the chaise as bittersweet memories flooded her mind, memories of happier days, safe, carefree days, when all those she loved had lived. She remembered the ballroom in the house on Fifth Avenue, the sparkling chandelier, the silk-papered walls, and Uncle Harry's smile when he led her in her first waltz on the night of her debut. She had been wearing white satin with a lace bodice, and rosebuds of white had encircled the crown of her glossy sable curls. The ballroom was resplendent with elegantly groomed guests. Diamonds and sapphires had glimmered upon fair breasts; sleek broadcloth-clad kings had hovered solicitously at the elbows of their queens. But no one had been more regal than her uncle; no one, to Adrian's mind, had been handsomer or nobler.

"You look enchanting," he had told her, his dark eyes adoring her. And her own eyes had worshipped the man she most loved.

She remembered other times, simpler times, the long,

lazy summers at their cottage on the coast of Connecticut. With a painful nostaglia she felt the sun, saw the blinding blue skies and the tranquil verdant hills that stretched endlessly in the distance. She remembered, as a child, running barefoot through the open meadow, clutching her skirts in her dimpled hands, her chubby legs pumping as fast as they could go. The sea-dampened air would whistle keenly past her ears, its clean, tangy scent the most heady intoxicant. Heart pounding, blood racing, she would fling herself to the ground and linger luxuriously in the sweet masses of clover.

''Adrian!'' her aunt would scold when she saw her. ''Your dress is ruined with grass stains, and your face and hands are a catastrophe. Go into the house and bathe at once. Wash twice, do you hear me? What a vagabond you are!'' But then she would laugh and give Adrian a quick embrace.

Adrian's throat ached with the memory. Why had Aunt Meg died? She had not been old; thirty-nine was not old. And Uncle Harry—he had been three months short of his forty-fifth birthday when his heart gave out.

Alone in the house she had shared with her beloved aunt, Adrian succumbed to her misery and shed bitter tears for the first time since Meg Marlowe had died. How she would miss dear Aunt Meg, how terribly she had missed Uncle Harry for the past three years; but now, with both of them gone, the pain was unendurable. She had loved them so deeply, had felt herself more their daughter than she might have felt with natural parents. She had been ever aware that the love her aunt and uncle gave her was a precious gift, the special love that parents give when their child is specifically chosen by them.

As these thoughts filled her mind Adrian reflected dimly on how fortunate she was to have been blessed with such a family. Her aunt and uncle were gone, but they had left her a legacy of love. She had that, at least, though she no longer had them. And, as her tears ebbed, she began to think less of her loss and more of the many assets the Marlowes had bestowed on her: immeasurable love; a strong sense of worth and independence; an ambition from Uncle Harry that only death could have stifled; an optimism from Aunt Meg that even now, in the depths of her gloom, shed a rising light of hope and expectation.

She sat up on the chaise and brushed away the last of her tears. Their legacy to her lived on. If she was to be true to it she could not permit herself to succumb to despair. She had lost the family who loved her and nurtured her, but she had not lost everything. She had her youth, she had the shop, she had herself. Very well, her plans for a fashion house of her own had been temporarily thwarted, her expectations for financial assistance had been dashed, and Aunt Meg, her beloved mentor, was gone. But Adrian could do it alone; she knew she could. She was young, she had talent, and the will to succeed was her strength and her inspiration. And so far as money was concerned, Adrian was confident that there were bankers in New York who were sure to look on her venture with a far less jaundiced eye than had the contemptuous Earl of Bedford and his condescending wife.

She went to the dress shop later that day. Tessa Keller was there to welcome her.

"My deepest sympathies," said Tessa.

"Thank you," said Adrian with a warm, grateful smile. She had napped earlier and now felt strong and refreshed. A late lunch at the Automat and a brisk walk to the shop near Union Square had further restored her. She had no wish to dwell on her loss. She was grateful for the support of a good and trusted friend, but it would not do to indulge her grief. She must think of the future; it was now all she had.

"Tessa," she said, running her hand over a bolt of blue satin, "we did not get the money."

She went on to recount the disappointment in Sussex. She looked around the shelf-lined back room as she spoke, at the great bolts of cloth, the boxes of buttons, the rolls of ribbon, the sheaves of designs that lay helter-skelter on table, chair, and floor, and at Tessa, finally, seated at the sewing machine, listening sympathetically.

They had met ten years earlier at Losanti's School for the Dance. All the young ladies and gentlemen of wealth attended Losanti's and were instructed in the finer points of ballroom etiquette and in the rudiments of social behavior. Although Adrian had been born to wealth, Tessa's had been newly acquired. Her father, a miner from Colorado, had discovered a vein of gold, which changed him overnight from a barely surviving prospector to a man worth more than three hundred thousand dollars. In possession of this fortune Mr. Keller moved his family at once to New York, in hopes of increasing his windfall in the booming stock market. For a time he prospered, and Tessa, his only child, enjoyed the fruits of his lucrative dealings. But in 1907, along with countless other investors, Mr. Keller lost everything he owned. Destitute and disgusted, he returned to Colorado with his devastated wife. Tessa remained in New York; she had been offered a position by a very good friend.

"But I'm not worried," Adrian said, concluding her account of her meeting with the earl. "I'll get the money somewhere, I know I will. Tomorrow I intend to make the rounds on Wall Street. There has to be at least one bank willing to finance us. I'm not giving up on my idea for a fashion house, Tessa." And, Adrian added silently, I have to insure that I shall never have to depend on anyone again.

"Why don't you try Carradine's?" Tessa suggested. "Surely Evan can be of some help to you there."

Adrian smiled at her friend. Tessa's feelings for Evan Colby were clearly evident in the tone of her voice when she mentioned his name. It was ironic, Adrian thought, that

Evan should be so devoted to someone who did not love him, when Tessa's love was so touchingly available.

"Yes," Adrian replied, "that's what Aunt Meg said, too. But I'll tell you the same as I told her: I have no intention of using Evan that way."

"Nonsense," said Tessa with a gesture of impatience. "You wouldn't be using Evan if you asked for an introduction to his employer. Mr. Carradine is quite the entrepreneur, I understand. He has financed, and sometimes managed, many a risky venture, and is ever the richer for it. It was his backing that made Standard Steel Car the leading railroad manufacturer in the country, and it was he who supplied Florenz Ziegfeld with the capital to produce his first Follies three years ago. If anything, Adrian, Jason Carradine would be using *you,* your talent, your future success, to increase his own wealth and the revenues of his bank."

Adrian's face flushed with anger. That man—his very name—was anathema to her. Jason Carradine had ruined her uncle; Jason Carradine, that venomous viper, had dared to approach her aboard the *Britannia* with the intention of seducing her with his specious charm. How she had ached to strike him when his dark-lashed blue eyes had regarded her with amusement. Even now her palms itched to lash out at him, *tingled* to wipe the smile from that dark, handsome face.

"That snake in the grass," she said bitterly. "He's the last man on earth I would ask for a favor. You know what I think of him; you know what he did to my uncle."

Tessa sighed and shook her head. "Adrian, my father lost everything in the Panic, too, but I rather doubt that Jason Carradine, or any one man for that matter, was responsible."

"I don't know about that," Adrian said, bristling. "It was Carradine who hoarded those United Copper shares, then delivered when the brokers couldn't possibly pay him.

That's the reason Otto Heinze collapsed. And when my uncle went to the bank, desperate for help, Jason Carradine had the gall to refuse to extend him more credit.''

"Yes," Tessa conceded. "But Carradine did agree not to call in your uncle's loan. When my father was in difficulty, the Mercantile Trust demanded their money on the spot. Repaying his loan was what actually bankrupted him. At least Carradine had the generosity to waive his right of call.''

"Generosity?" Adrian said, her voice more bitter than before. "That word does not exist in his vocabulary. Apart from what he did to my uncle, I've heard stories about him from Evan that would curl your hair. The bank was his father's, you know; an honest and respected man, Evan told me. But Jason Carradine, with his shady stock manipulations, is another man entirely.''

Tessa sighed again, rose from the sewing machine, and slipped an arm around her friend's waist. "Adrian," she said, "very well. If you don't want to go to Carradine's, that's your decision. It just seems a great deal more sensible to ask Evan's help than to go traipsing up and down Wall Street with no results. Offhand I can't think of a bank that would be willing to lend money to a woman. Can you?''

"No, I can't," Adrian admitted, still seething at the thought of Jason Carradine. "But you have my solemn promise, Tessa: I'm not going to rest until I find one!''

Three

IN THIS SAME frame of mind Adrian set out to storm the citadel that was Wall Street. The following morning, a fine, warm spring day, she rose with the sun and girded herself fittingly for battle. After donning a creation of her own design, a simply styled walking suit of royal blue mohair, she tilted her straw boater at the most becoming angle, fluffed up the ruffles of her ecru silk shirtwaist, and with a final flick of the comb and a splash of French perfume, she sailed out of the house on a tide of youthful arrogance.

She had purposely chosen to discard her mourning clothes. The pale, helpless orphan was *not* the image she wished to project. There were already two marks against her as a prospective borrower: she was young, just twenty-one; and she was a woman. To advertise the fact that she was alone in the world would only further hinder her chances of securing a loan.

The streetcar to Wall Street was crowded and noisy. Young office workers, both male and female, chatted animatedly and made arrangements to meet that evening at either the beer garden on Canal Street or at Maury's Lobster Palace on Mott. Adrian watched these cheerful wage earners and felt herself a part of them. The girls frankly reveled in the glances of their admirers; the young men teased and flattered and were rewarded with coquettish smiles. They were vital and spirited and supremely self-assured. Adrian's own spirits soared in such confident company, and by the time she reached Wall Street, she was ready to beard even the fiercest lion in his den.

She had mapped out her strategy the previous evening. Her first stop would be the Hanover Bank on Nassau and Pine, and if she failed there she would next try the Manhattan Trust across the street. If Manhattan declined there was the Merchants' National Bank, N. W. Harris, the Metropolitan Trust, the Bank of New York, and, of course, the elite but plain establishment of Mr. J. Pierpont Morgan. There was also the great pillared palace of J. Carradine & Company at the corner of Broad and Wall streets, but Adrian, when she passed it, did not even glance at it.

"Good morning, miss. May I help you?"

Within the high-ceilinged rotunda of the Hanover Bank, Adrian sat at the desk of the senior loan officer, an elderly gentleman wearing a style of apparel that had gone out with the bustle and high-buttoned shoes. His frock coat was black, his cravat wide, and the winged collar he sported had not been seen in many a year. Adrian smiled at this reminder of another, simpler age. How sweet he looked, like a loving old grandfather, with his wire-rimmed spectacles and his luxuriant growth of white side whiskers.

"Yes," she said, encouraged. "I hope you can help me. I require a loan."

"A loan," he said, nodding. "Well, you've come to the right place. For which concern are you applying?"

"Concern?" she said, puzzled. "I don't understand."

The old gentleman gave her a look of benevolent patience. "Your employer, young lady. Whom do you represent?"

"Oh, I see." She smiled again, more encouraged by his kindness. "I represent myself. I own a dress shop on Union Square—Marlowe's—and I want to expand, to have a showroom and mannequins, as do the fashion houses abroad. I shall need seven thousand dollars at the outset. Here is my estimate of proposed initial expenditure. I've already chosen a location on Broadway; it's the old Graham Building near Herald Square. With renovation of the interior and a new facade, it would house an excellent showroom on the first floor, with plenty of space for seamstresses and storage on the second.''

"Your proposal seems sound," he said approvingly after looking over her list. "And have you any collateral to offer against the loan?"

"Collateral?" Adrian's hands tightened on her purse. "No."

"Well, then," he said, still kindly, "have you someone willing to act on your behalf as cosignatory?"

She thought fleetingly of Evan, then quickly dismissed him from her mind. "No," she responded, "I haven't."

The old gentleman sighed. "I'm so sorry, miss. I should be more than happy to assist you if I were able, but under the circumstances . . ." He sighed again regretfully and returned her proposal. "My hands are tied, you see. I'm terribly sorry."

Dismayed but undaunted, Adrian left the Hanover Bank and went on to the Manhattan Trust across the street. The loan officer there was not nearly as congenial. Younger, in his fifties, with a thin black mustache and a shock of black hair fairly saturated with Macassar oil, he merely raised disinterested eyes to the young applicant and told her laconically, "We do not transact business with women."

It was the same wherever she went: some were kind, some were rude, some sympathized, some scoffed; but in the end the answer was no—unequivocally, decidedly no. By half past three she was ready to concede defeat. She was tired and hungry, the back of her shirtwaist was damp with perspiration, and her confidence had all but disappeared.

Weary and dispirited, she paused near the steps of the United States Sub-Treasury. The day had grown hot and humid. Although the narrow streets were shaded, the tall, close-knit buildings blocking out the rays of the sun, Adrian felt as though she stood in the midst of the steamy equator. She could barely draw breath, and black spots began to dance before her suddenly blurring eyes.

Dear God, she prayed silently, please don't let me faint.

Her legs felt like rubber; she fanned herself languidly with her purse. The streets were deserted. An eerie unreality pervaded her senses. She was totally alone in a still, deadly landscape. The surrounding buildings seemed dark-breasted birds of prey preparing to swoop down on her and devour the last of her fast-waning courage.

"Adrian! For heaven's sake, is that you?"

That pleased, surprised voice was an instant restorative. Adrian looked up, revived, into Evan Colby's delighted face.

"Adrian, what on earth are you doing here?" He was smiling broadly, his hat in his hand, and under his arm he carried a leather portfolio.

"Oh, Evan," she blurted gratefully, "I'm so glad to see you!"

She clutched his arm as if it were a lifesaving buoy. How happy she was to have found an amiable ally within the hostile environs of this bleak, unfriendly place.

"Why are you here?" he asked again. Then, noting her pallor: "My God, but you're pale. Are you ill?"

"No," she said slowly. "I'm not ill. I'm just tired . . . and hungry. I haven't eaten all day."

"Come along," he said sternly, taking her arm.

"Where are we going?"

"To Havermeyer's. I'm buying you some lunch. You look ready to faint. For God's sake, Adrian, what are you doing on Wall Street, anyway? After what you've been through you should be at home, resting, conserving your strength. What am I going to do with you, you reckless child?"

She smiled at his concern and let him lead her. "Child?" she said, her good spirits returning. "Really, Evan, you're only five years older than I. You can hardly consider me a child."

"Sometimes you act like one," he retorted, ushering her into the dimly lit café.

An indignant waiter showed them to a table; it was, after all, long past lunchtime. "What will you have?" he asked crossly.

"Steak and potatoes for the lady," Evan ordered. "I'll just have coffee."

The waiter left. Adrian set down her purse on the checkered tablecloth and regarded Evan with a puzzled look. "Evan," she asked, "why do you say such a thing? I don't act like a child."

"You do sometimes," Evan said, scowling. "What in blazes are you doing on Wall Street, for example? No, wait; let me guess. You've come begging for money for your great fashion house. Now, if that isn't childish—not to mention unrealistic—I don't know what is."

For a moment she stared at him, harsh words on the tip of her tongue. But then it occurred to her that he spoke out of love, not out of rancor. Her expression softened; she reached out to touch his hand. "Evan, you're very sweet to worry about me—"

"Sweet?" He snatched his hand from hers. "Is that how you see me, the sweet, harmless suitor who doesn't have brains enough to know he's been rejected?"

"Oh, Evan . . ."

"Listen to me," he said sharply, his young face contorted with anger and hurt. "I love you. I want you to be my wife. And if you had even half the sense God gave a goat you'd chuck this crazy dream of a fashion house and marry me."

"Crazy dream?" she cried, affronted. "Evan, *you* listen to *me!*"

She stopped suddenly, drew a deep breath, and checked the impulse to tell him to go to the devil.

"Evan." Her voice now was gentle; she reached for his hand again and held on to it firmly. "Evan, you must, please, try to understand how important this is to me. It's not a crazy dream; it's a well-thought-out undertaking. The women in this city want to wear fine clothes. Where do they buy them? A continent away. Now wouldn't it be wiser, simpler, cheaper, to just hop in one's auto or onto a streetcar and find the same fine clothes right in the heart of their own shopping district? And I'm not only concerned with wealthy clients. It's my plan to design an inexpensive line so that department stores can sell them at affordable prices. Think of it, Evan! Mrs. Astor can wear a Marlowe original, and her maid can purchase an Adrian skirt and shirtwaist at Macy's or Hearn's."

"Yes, all right," he said grudgingly. "You've explained it all to me before, and I admit it's a good idea; I'm not denying that. All I'm saying, Adrian, is that I think you'd be happier with a husband and a home and children to take care of."

With a sigh she released his hand and leaned back in her seat. "Evan, I suppose I shall want that too someday, but it's not what I want now."

The waiter approached with a steaming tray and a surly expression. As he set out the lunch and coffee Evan stared at the table, his face set in obstinate lines.

"Evan, please," Adrian said when the waiter had left, "don't be angry. I've had the most appalling day. No one wants to lend me the money; I'm at my wits' end. If you turn against me, too—"

Evan raised his head abruptly; his hazel eyes blazed. "I'll never do that," he said vehemently, "never! I may disagree

with you, but I'll never turn against you. As much as I op-
pose what you're doing, I still admire and respect it. I've
even gone so far as to—''

He broke off in mid-sentence and gave her an odd look,
half-angry, half-embarrassed. She returned his gaze curiously as her steak and potatoes cooled, untouched, on her
plate. "Evan, you've even gone so far as to do what? What
were you going to say?"

He shrugged uncomfortably. "Forget it. It doesn't matter. Eat your lunch."

"Evan, tell me," she insisted.

He watched her a moment, his expression defensive. An
inner struggle was evident in the depths of his eyes, and
Adrian watched him in turn, her curiosity heightened. At
last he said shortly, "I've spoken to Mr. Carradine about
your ideas. He seems interested. He said he'd like to meet
you."

Adrian stared at him in silence. "Jason Carradine?" she
said at last. "But, Evan, after all you've told me about him—"

"What of it?" he said curtly. "If he can help you what
difference does it make if he's an unprincipled scoundrel?"

Evan's bitter epithet served to intensify Adrian's own
feelings toward Jason Carradine. Under those circumstances
how could she even consider putting herself in debt to the
man who had ruined her uncle?

And yet, she thought in frustration, what choice had she
now? No one else on Wall Street was willing to finance her. If
she allowed her personal aversion to stand in the way of her
dream, it would go unrealized; unrealized, it would perish.

Her gaze fell from Evan to the steak on her dish. Globs of
grease had congealed on the meat; the potato in its jacket
was crumbling and cold. With a shudder of distaste she
picked up her knife and fork and cut into the meat. To Evan
she said grimly, "When can I meet him?"

Four

AN APPOINTMENT was scheduled for the following Friday. In the interim of three days Adrian changed her mind a dozen times. She would meet him; she wouldn't—she wouldn't; she would. Deciding finally that to meet with Jason Carradine was in her own best interest, she determined to show to him her most contemptuous face.

"I wouldn't do that if I were you," Tessa Keller advised when Adrian announced her intention.

They were dining together at Tessa's flat on Bleecker Street. The flat was small—three tiny rooms—but the sparse Eastlake furnishings and the Currier and Ives prints on the wall were harmonious and tasteful and pleasing to the eye.

"If you're hostile," Tessa went on, "or the least bit scornful, Mr. Carradine will simply tell you to take your proposal elsewhere. And then what? Where will you go? To whom will you turn? Remember, Adrian, in matters of finance Jason Carradine invariably holds the upper hand."

Adrian poked listlessly at her lamb chop instead of answering. It was insufferable, she thought in frustration, that she was forced to seek the help of such a man. Evan, Carradine's own employee, never had a good word to say in his behalf. Adrian herself had seen Carradine only twice in her life, and both times he had aroused in her the most unruly emotions. On the *Britannia* she had ached to expose him for the low fraud he was, but her well-chosen insults had only seemed to amuse him.

32

"I don't know if I can go through with it," she said, laying down her fork. "From the first day I saw that man I disliked him intensely."

"Did you?" said Tessa, sipping calmly at her wine. "I was with you that day, and as I recall, it did not seem to me that you disliked him."

Tessa's soft-spoken words awakened a memory in Adrian's mind. Adrian had to admit, if only to herself, that the first time she saw Jason Carradine, on the day her uncle was buried, he had aroused in her an emotion quite unrelated to antipathy.

The funeral had been held at Green-Wood Cemetery. Of the scores of mourners who stood at the site of the Marlowe mausoleum, Carradine was the last to arrive. So as not to disturb the proceedings, he stood apart from the congregation, near the gravel drive, beneath the low-hanging branches of a wind-twisted elm. He could not have been more conspicuous.

He held his hat in his hands, and he was as soberly attired as all the mourners present, but to Adrian, heavily veiled, benumbed by her grief, there was a look about the man that set him distinctly apart from the crowd. In his excellent black broadcloth and impeccable linen, he seemed an eagle among sparrows, a god among mortals, as superior to his fellows as is a diamond to glass. Tessa's head had turned when he appeared, and as Adrian followed the direction of her curious stare, she found that she, too, despite her bereavement, could not take her eyes from that elegant figure.

She whispered to Tessa, "Who is that man?" And Tessa replied, "It's Jason Carradine, the banker. I'm always reading about him in the *Times* and the *Herald*. He has a yacht and a summer house in Tuxedo Park and a mansion on Madison Avenue. The newspapers have dubbed him the 'Prince of Wall Street.' "

What an apt description, Adrian remembered thinking,

unaware at the moment that this was the man who had ruined her uncle.

Jason Carradine did indeed seem regal, with his commanding height and the patrician perfection of his aristocratic face. Unaware that Tessa was watching her, Adrian stared at him openly, at the curve of his jaw, the hard line of his mouth, his midnight-dark hair, and those Irish-blue eyes, a stunning surprise in a lean face burned brown by a benevolent summer sun. She had never seen anyone so devastatingly attractive. Even motionless he radiated an electric aura of irresistible physical magnetism.

When the service ended, Carradine left the cemetery without approaching the widow and her niece. And Adrian finally realized who he was. She remembered him at last from photos she had seen of him in the Sunday rotogravure section of the newspapers. That she had even momentarily admired the man raised a flush of guilty rage in her pale ivory cheeks.

Even now, three years later, Adrian's resentment burned hot in her breast. She stared at her dish with mutinous eyes while Tessa rose and began to clear the table. She *would not* meet with him; she had made up her mind. Despite the fact that Aunt Meg had pronounced Carradine blameless of Uncle Harry's ruin, Adrian remained convinced of his guilt. Evan agreed with her, and Evan, of all people, ought to know the truth. Therefore, to ask Carradine's help, to be in his debt, was unthinkable, a compromise of principle.

And yet, Adrian realized, when common sense prevailed, the alternative was failure. If she was to succeed, if she was to give substance to her dreams, she must swallow her pride, subjugate her feelings, and do business with a man she found utterly dishonorable.

She raised her gaze to Tessa, who had resumed her seat and was watching her quietly. Tessa's sweet face was grave, but her green eyes were gentle with understanding.

"Very well," Adrian said grudgingly, "I'll go to him. I have no choice. But it's a dear price to pay for the prize I most want."

"Yes," Tessa agreed, "it is, Adrian. But then again, nothing worth having is easily won."

The day of the meeting dawned radiant and warm. Again, as for her first visit to Wall Street, Adrian dressed with care. But this time she chose less businesslike garb, a lemon-yellow tunic over a black skirt so narrow that it delineated every curve of thigh and calf and daringly exposed her black-stockinged ankles. Instead of a hat, she twisted a length of yellow silk around her head, bandeau-style, in the manner of the mannequins she had seen in France. In her ears she wore dangling, black jet, a slender jet necklace completing her costume.

When she inspected herself in the mirror, she was pleased with the effect. She looked confident and poised, a woman of the world, a match for even the likes of the black prince of Wall Street. But inside she was shaking with impotent frustration. How she dreaded this meeting; she wished she had the courage to call it off, to tell Jason Carradine to keep his money—she didn't want it. But she couldn't, of course; she had nowhere else to turn.

His bank, as she had anticipated, was the last word in opulence. On the first floor marble walls housed a spacious lobby dotted with large clawfoot tables surmounted by antique vases filled with dew-fresh flowers. Underfoot, a tesselated floor echoed the cadence of Adrian's nervous step. How like him, she thought, gazing around critically, to create an entrance worthy of an Oriental potentate.

A uniformed guard approached her. His look was suspicious. Ladies rarely, if ever, crossed the pillared threshold of J. Carradine & Company.

"Good afternoon," he said unsociably. "May I be of assistance?"

His attitude rankled. Adrian drew herself up and responded in her firmest voice, "I'm Adrian Marlowe. Mr. Carradine is expecting me. Will you kindly direct me to his offices?"

The guard's demeanor changed instantly. "Mr. Carradine? Yes, of course. This way, Miss Marlowe. His offices are on the second floor."

She followed the guard up a wide marble staircase, her gloved hands clenched tightly around her purse. Her momentary display of hauteur had done nothing to quell her dread. If she had been on her way to the gallows she could not have felt more panicked. Her hands were shaking, her mouth and throat were parchment-dry, and her heart beat so furiously that she feared she might faint.

"Here we are, Miss Marlowe." They stopped at a great oak door. "Just go inside. Mr. Carradine's secretary will announce you."

The guard left. Adrian stared after him, then turned with trepidation toward the door. She depressed the silver latch and peered cautiously into the room. A young man sat at a paper-strewn desk. Beyond him was another door, marked J. CARRADINE in gold.

The young man looked up as Adrian entered.

"Yes?"

His smile was genuine. Adrian felt herself relax. She stated her business in a clear, steady voice, then waited as he went into the inner office to announce her arrival.

"You may go in now," he told her a moment later, holding the door open for her to pass through.

Her nervousness returned. At a grand mahogany desk carved with cherubs and nymphs, Jason Carradine was making notations in a leather-bound journal. Behind him, the afternoon sun streamed through three leaded windows that rose to the ceiling. The room was large and simple; bookshelves lined the walls, and on the polished oak floor an Isfahan carpet muffled Adrian's footsteps as she moved warily to the desk.

Closing the journal, Carradine looked up at last. With the sunlight behind him and shining in her eyes, Adrian was unable to make out his features.

"Ah, Miss Marlowe," he said, rising, "you're right on time. Won't you sit down?"

He held a chair for her, then resumed his seat. With a measure of apprehension Adrian watched his shadowed figure, squinting her eyes against the rays of the sun.

"Forgive me," said Carradine, noting her discomfort. He rose once more and drew the rose-colored curtains against the offending light. "There, that's better." He sat down again and regarded her amiably across the expanse of his neatly appointed desk.

As her vision became accustomed to the rosy-toned dimness Adrian's nervousness began to fade, and she studied the man in silence. He was clad impeccably in dark blue, which enhanced the vibrant color of his Irish-blue eyes. His hair, which had appeared black when she last saw him, was actually a warm shade of brown. His hard mouth was curved in a frankly admiring smile, and he leaned back in his chair as if pleasantly surprised by the appearance of so attractive a visitor.

"Well, Miss Marlowe," he broke the silence, "I'm most anxious to listen to your proposal. Evan Colby tells me that you're talented, ambitious, and extremely determined. Those qualities intrigue me, especially in a woman. Tell me your plans, and I'll see if I can help you."

I must control myself, Adrian thought cautiously as she planned how best to begin. If he knew her true feelings he would show her the door and then slam it behind her, thus shutting out forever her chance of success.

"My plans," she repeated consideringly. "Well, I wish to establish a fashion house in the city."

"Yes." Carradine nodded. "So Colby told me. But Madame Keily and Madame Borel already do a thriving business among the social set. Do you see yourself competing against those eminently successful ladies?"

"Without a doubt," she said confidently, warming to the subject and forgetting, for the moment, her dislike of this man. "Those establishments are not houses of haute couture; Keily and Borel are, quite simply, dressmakers who design to the specifications of their patrons. What I have in mind is a departure from this practice, a line of apparel of my own design that would be presented seasonally, in the same manner as Worth and Paquin and Poiret."

"Interesting," he said. "Please go on."

"And also," she continued, leaning forward in her chair, "it is my intention to introduce a ready-made line for department store sales. In this way," she explained, "I capture two markets at once, and my profits are doubled."

"And your expenditures?" he suggested. "Are they not also doubled?"

"No, not really," she told him, extracting from her purse a long list of expenses and estimated profit. "Look here," she said, drawing her chair closer to his. "I'll pay rental on one place of business, the Graham Building near Herald Square. The seamstresses I employ will be proficient in fine needlework as well as commercial. They will work where necessary, on whichever line is busier at the time. This will prevent seasonal layoffs and encourage steady workers, the best in the field. Most difficulties in the clothing line, I've learned, arise from a lack of skilled and available seamstresses."

Carradine's interest was evident in the long look he gave

her. Glancing down at the list in his hand, he asked, "May I keep this for further study?" And when Adrian nodded eagerly, he said, "You appear to have a keen understanding of business, Miss Marlowe. What remains to be seen now is your talent."

Heartened by his approval, and quite forgetting that she disliked him, Adrian dug into her purse for a batch of small sketches. "Take a look at these," she urged. "They're my newest designs, inspired by the work of Monsieur Poiret in Paris. They're not copies," she hastened to add. "I have merely adapted the line of Poiret's dresses to a version of my own interpretation."

Carradine went through the sketches with careful attention while Adrian watched him in barely concealed excitement. He was going to finance her; she sensed it, she was sure of it. Dimly she wondered why he should be willing to finance a woman when virtually every other banker on Wall Street had refused to do so. It was such a daring, unusual, *fair* thing to do. She had never before associated the word *fair* with Jason Carradine. But now . . .

In this state of bewilderment she continued to watch him. His face was downturned, his brow faintly creased as he studied the designs. His blue eyes were hidden by the dark brush of lashes that threw shadow on his cheek, and from his crisp, warm brown hair there was a pleasantly clean, fresh-washed fragrance. He was vitally attractive, and she stared at him silently while a curious warmth began pervading her senses.

"I like them," he said, looking up at her suddenly with those vivid blue eyes. "You have talent; there's no doubt of it. And there's a certain Parisian flair to your designs that will capture the fancy of even the most fashion-conscious patron. You're not French, by any chance?"

The question awakened in both of them a recent shared experience. Adrian remained sheepishly silent while Carradine peered at her curiously, searching his memory for that particular experience which apparently, at the moment, eluded him.

"Good Lord!" he said finally with a delighted laugh. "You're the woman on the *Britannia.*"

And when she nodded, chagrined, he told her, still laughing, "What an assault you launched on me that night. My God, I'm still nursing my wounds!"

Discretion, she decided, was the better part of valor. In an effort to maintain his goodwill, she said with caution, "You were a stranger to me, Mr. Carradine. I was uncertain of your intentions, and I was, therefore, perhaps less courteous than I might have been."

"Indeed," he said wryly. "I have seldom met anyone less courteous. I believe you said I was 'ruthless' and 'insatiably thirsty for money and power.' Correct me if I am misquoting you. I was so taken aback by the ferocity of your attack that I may have forgotten the exact wording of your insults."

He was smiling good-naturedly, but his eyes were keenly alert. It was obvious to Adrian that he was trying in his mind to connect the prospective businesswoman who sat before him to the poison-tongued shrew on the *Britannia* who had coldly denounced the fundamentals of business.

With a great deal of effort she managed to return his smile. "Mr. Carradine, I cannot recall what I said that night. If I offended you I'm sorry."

He watched her in silence as if he didn't quite know if he believed her or not. Adrian held her breath, maintained her pleasant smile, then, after a moment said, to divert his thoughts, "Mr. Carradine, you were saying you like my designs . . ."

"Ah, yes," he said, looking down at the sketches in his hand. "Tell me more about your plans, Miss Marlowe."

Her voice was clear and steady as she launched into detail, but inside she was shaking with enormous relief.

Five

WHEN SHE LEFT his offices an hour and a quarter later, she
felt as battered and bruised as if she had been run down and
trampled by a team of runaway horses. Her head pounded
frightfully; the afternoon sunlight affronted her eyes. By
sheer effort of will she dragged herself to Broadway where
she hailed a passing streetcar and staggered aboard. When
she finally arrived home, she crawled up the stairs, tottered
weakly to her room, and collapsed in a heap, fully clothed,
on her bed.

Dear God, how was she going to do it? Where would she
find the strength to go on with this devious charade?

Carradine had said at the end of the interview, "I can't
give you a definite answer at this time; I should like to study
your proposal and then make a few inquiries on Herald
Square. But I'm almost certain," he had added with an encouraging smile, "that this is the beginning of an extremely
profitable venture for both of us."

"Oh, how wonderful!" she had gushed, while inside she
had fumed at the helplessness of her position.

"Let's talk further next Thursday evening," he had said
when he escorted her to the door. "I'm having some people
in for dinner whom I think you'll enjoy meeting. I should
also have an answer for you by then. Shall I call for you at
eight?"

She started to say no; she couldn't possibly. But just then

his telephone had rung, and he had ushered her out the door and closed it politely but firmly behind her.

Dinner. At his house. She shuddered and groaned and burrowed her head into the pillow. How could she endure an entire evening in his company, talking, listening, smiling, laughing, when she would much prefer to show him the sharp side of her tongue? She groaned again softly and drew up the bedspread to cover her head. And when eventually she drifted into an uneasy sleep, she dreamed she was drowning in a cold sea the color of money.

The telephone awakened her a few hours later. Groggy and out of sorts, she dragged herself out of bed, tramped downstairs to the hall, and snatched the receiver from the switch hook.

"Hullo," she said grumpily. "Who is it?"

"It's Tessa," said a startled voice. "Adrian, where have you been? I've been ringing you for hours."

"I've been sleeping," she said more sharply than she intended.

Tessa's aggrieved and sudden silence brought Adrian instantly to her senses. "Tessa, I'm sorry," she apologized. "Don't mind me, please. I've had the most dreadful day imaginable."

"Oh, Adrian, no! He refused to lend you the money?"

"No, no. He said yes. Well, he didn't actually say yes, but I'm sure he's going to."

There was a pause on the line and then a sigh of relief. "Thank goodness for that. Tell me everything that happened."

After Adrian related the particulars of the interview Tessa said, "But that's marvelous news, Adrian. Why do you sound so glum?"

"Because it's *him*," she said irritably. "Because of all the bankers in New York, only that unprincipled rogue is willing to finance me."

"For heaven's sake!" Tessa exploded. "What does it matter who lends you the money? You'll have what you want now. That's the main thing, isn't it?"

Tessa's no-nonsense attitude restored Adrian. Tessa was right: she had the money. What difference did it make who supplied it? In Adrian's absorption with her antipathy toward Jason Carradine she had quite forgotten that her dream of a fashion house was nearly at hand.

"Tessa," she said ruefully, "that *is* the main thing; thank you for reminding me. I know I sound like a childish ingrate, but I've been in such a muddle this week. I've been so worried about getting the money, and I've been thinking about Aunt Meg and Uncle Harry. I've had to let the cook and the charwoman go, and . . ." She paused and drew a shaky breath. ". . . and everything has just seemed so hopeless, do you know what I mean?"

"Yes." Tessa's tone gentled. "I know what you mean. But it's over now, Adrian. All the bad times are ended. You can start making plans now, real plans, for the House of Marlowe. Do you remember telling me once that you would put Worth out of business?"

"I remember," said Adrian with a brief, nostalgic smile.

"Well, now's your chance!"

"Tessa," she said, laughing and feeling more like her old self, "what would I do without you?"

Tessa dryly responded, "I shudder to speculate."

Adrian laughed again heartily, her optimism restored, then told Tessa good-bye and replaced the receiver. Humming "The Maple Leaf Rag," she went off to the kitchen and raided the icebox. She was all at once ravenously hungry.

The days that followed were busy and productive. Since Jason Carradine's offer of financial assistance had not been definite, Adrian could make no major plans regarding the fashion house, but she did begin making tentative overtures to several seamstresses whom she had employed on occasion, and she spent long nights till dawn at her drawing board, designing a spectacular line of apparel to launch her new enterprise.

Coincidentally, business at the dress shop was improving daily. In the three years since Marlowe's inception, Adrian had been steadily making a reputation for herself. Her designs were distinctively classic yet with enough modish concession to appeal to the adventurous as well as the conservative ladies who patronized the shop. The cut and fit of the garments, thanks to Tessa's skill, was without parallel. In the comparatively short period of time Marlowe's had been in existence, there was a host of satisfied customers who would shop for their clothes nowhere else.

Meg Marlowe, of course, had been chiefly instrumental in attracting this clientele. It was her friends, the women of the social set to which she had belonged before her husband's death, who had first bought at Marlowe's and then had spread the word. Adrian missed her aunt sorely; she missed her love, her good sense, her unflagging confidence, her unwavering faith in her young niece's talent. "We're going to do it, dumpling," Aung Meg had been fond of saying. "It's only a matter of time. With your gift and my connections, Marlowe's is going to set the fashion world back on its heels!"

And now, three years later, it appeared that Meg Marlowe's ambitious prediction was soon to become a reality. Like her aunt, Adrian had always had every confidence in the future of her fashion house. Opportunity and money had previously been the only obstacle, but now, with financial support, nothing stood in the way of Marlowe's success. Adrian wished with sad regret that Aunt Meg could have lived to share this triumph.

* * *

Jason Carradine called for her at the stroke of eight o'clock, six days following their initial meeting. With Tessa's stern admonitions in mind, Adrian was determined to be at her most charming. When she answered the door, clad in an ethereal webbing of white lace and tissue silk, she greeted him brightly. "Mr. Carradine, good evening! Won't you come in for a moment while I get my wrap?"

He looked especially regal in evening clothes. His black broadcloth was elegant, and his pearl-studded white shirt was a startling contrast to the lean sun-browned contours of his aristocratic face. He had the grace of a panther and the same cool, dark beauty. As he smiled and walked past her into the hall Adrian stared at him, unmoving, momentarily mesmerized by his physical magnetism.

"Miss Marlowe?" he said when she continued to stare at him in motionless silence. "Is something wrong?"

He regarded her questioningly with those arresting blue eyes, and Adrian was vaguely reminded of an August sky turned brilliant blue after a summer storm. And then, oddly, she thought of a line from a half-forgotten poem of her childhood: "The devil came, wearing the form and brightness of an angel."

Giving herself a quick mental shake, she crossed to the side bench where her purse and cloak lay, picked them up, and said rather curtly, "No, nothing's wrong. Shall we go?"

In the backseat of the car she regretted her lapse of control and sought at once to correct it. Carradine's smile had faded at the sharpness of her tone, and he had helped her on with her wrap and had escorted her to the car in a wary and bewildered silence.

"Mr. Carradine," she said engagingly as the chauffeur directed the Rolls-Royce past the Washington Square Arch, "I am most anxious to see your house. Is it true that your art collection surpasses the combined collection of the Louvre and the Prado?''

His eyes lost their wariness; they were aglow now with enthusiasm. His collection, Adrian had read, was his passion in life.

"I wish it were true," he said. "I should dearly love to own the *Mona Lisa* and Velasquez's *Las Lanzas.*"

"I have read," she went on artfully, "that all the museums clamor for the loan of the paintings in your possession."

"They do," he admitted. "And I have lent some on occasion. The Metropolitan is currently exhibiting my Flemish collection. Perhaps you have seen it. *The Crucifixion* by Rubens is my favorite. I've been told that Sir Joshua Reynolds, upon first seeing it, ranked it as one of the finest pictures in the world."

"I have not seen it," Adrian answered, gazing down at her gloved hands with feigned regret. "If only I had the time. I haven't been to the museum in ages; I've been so busy of late—making plans and decisions for the fashion house, you know."

She looked up at him then with an ingratiating smile. She had managed—rather neatly, she thought—to allay his suspicions and to bring the topic of conversation around to her loan.

"Ah, yes, your fashion house," he said as the Rolls-Royce slid smoothly to a halt outside his house. "Let's talk about that after dinner. There are a few details I need to discuss with you."

"Details?" she said anxiously. Was he going to say no?

"Minor details, Miss Marlowe; nothing to worry about. Come along now," he said as he helped her out of the car. "My friends are looking forward to meeting you."

His house on Madison Avenue was magnificent. As they entered the great Painted Hall, of which Adrian had read much, she was nonetheless unprepared for the dramatic impact of color and light that blazed radiantly from the Louis Laguerre murals that decorated the walls and domed ceiling of the room. A double staircase, separated by an archway, rose to a second-floor balcony, and on the banisters, stately candelabra sporting twinkling electric lights illuminated the ceiling mural, which depicted in all its glory a pastoral scene from the first act of *Tannhäuser*.

"Incredible," Adrian whispered, quite stricken with awe. No newspaper account or grainy photograph even conveyed the breathtaking grandeur of this veritable palace.

The drawing room, also, was majestically appointed, but Adrian had no time to study those surroundings. When she entered on Carradine's arm, she saw, to her surprise, that the room, although immense, was filled wall to wall with guests. It seemed the whole of the city's notables were present: bankers; industrialists; actors and actresses; an opera star; a senator; and even a prince of the Catholic Church, resplendent in scarlet and black.

"Come," Carradine said as Adrian gaped at this glorious assemblage. "Let me introduce you to a few of your future patrons."

Future patrons. Adrian's heart gave an excited thump. Then he *was* going to finance her. She accompanied him into the crowd, acknowledging introductions in a delirium of joy.

Mrs. Astor, Mrs. Goelet, Mrs. Morgan, Mrs. Frick. Adrian knew all the ladies' names though she had never before met them. These were the leaders of Society, the trendsetters, the fashion-makers. As Adrian shook gloved hands and exchanged social pleasantries she could only think happily that with such an elite clientele, the success of the House of Marlowe was unquestionably assured.

"My dear Miss Marlowe," said Fanny Lindquist, the wife of a financier, a slim middle-aged woman with a shock of red hair and merry brown eyes in an astonishingly youthful face, "how soon may we see your fashions? Jason tells me your creations are extraordinary, and if that dress you're wearing is your own design, I must admit I agree with him completely."

"Thank you," Adrian answered jubilantly. "I did design my dress. And Mr. Carradine is very kind to compliment my efforts. I'm afraid I don't know how soon my house will be ready. But if you like, in the meantime you can visit my shop on Union Square. I'm sure you'll find something there to your liking."

"Indeed I will visit it!" Mrs. Lindquist declared, then she left with an apology when her husband called her name from across the room.

Carradine bent his head to Adrian's ear and told her confidentially, "Fanny has a great many devoted friends. If she decides to wear your designs, all those friends will surely follow suit."

Adrian gazed up at her benefactor with dark, shining eyes. In the excitement of the moment she had quite forgotten that she disliked him. Breathlessly she whispered, "I don't know how to thank you."

"We'll think of something," he said with a smile. And then, tucking her hand through his arm, he began to introduce her to another group of guests.

Dinner was a delectable blur of fine French cuisine, stimulating conversation, and extravagant compliments. Seated on Carradine's right at a seemingly mile-long refectory table, Adrian found herself the center of attention as the gentlemen made toasts to her success and the ladies plied her with questions about her plans. She ate enormously from every one of the twelve courses and drank glass after glass of Mouton-Rothschild '64. She knew she ought not to drink so much—she was unused to wine or spirits—but the company was so convivial, the food so exquisitely spiced, and she so incomparably, deliriously happy that she simply felt it her duty to keep up with the hard-drinking crowd.

Carradine was the perfect host. Although attentive to all who addressed him, it was his young guest of honor to whom he paid the most heed: "Is the duck to your liking, Miss Marlowe?"; "More truffles, Miss Marlowe?"; "Higgins, fill Miss Marlowe's glass, if you please." And in the drawing room, over coffee, he lingered by her side most often, as if proclaiming to his friends that this particular young lady was deserving of special attention.

When the festivities came to an end at last, close to midnight, Adrian felt that the evening had only just begun.

"You'll stay a moment, won't you?" Carradine asked her as he was bidding his other guests good night. "There are a few matters I'd like to discuss with you before making the final arrangements tomorrow morning."

"Yes, of course," Adrian said readily, brimming with joy and slightly tipsy from the wine.

There had never been such a night, she was thinking ecstatically. A dozen ladies had promised to shop at Marlowe's, and still more had admired her gown and had expressed a genuine interest in her design ideas. Without even opening the doors of her fashion house, Adrian had acquired the very *crème de la crème* of Society patronage within one evening.

She owed it all to Carradine, of course. Despite her feelings about him, she had to admit that his money and connections were the source of the evening's success. In a haze of euphoria, Adrian felt extremely grateful and not in the least antagonistic toward him. In fact, as she watched her elegant host, cool and aristocratic, shaking hands with his friends and kissing their wives' proferred cheeks, she thought in a wine-soaked fog, He really is the most deliciously attractive man.

Six

THEY WERE FINALLY ALONE in a small, charming room Carradine wryly referred to as his "den of sweet solitude." He bade Adrian be seated on a deep leather couch, and filled two glasses of brandy from a tray on the side table.

When they had entered the den, Adrian had shivered slightly, and Carradine immediately summoned a servant to lay and light a fire. Basking now in the fragrant heat and radiance of the crackling cedar logs, Adrian watched her host dreamily as he handed her a glass, then raised his own in a toast.

"To a successful relationship," he said. "And to a happy one."

Adrian tasted the brandy and found it pleasantly warming. She felt wonderfully relaxed, almost boneless, as she curled up snugly against the cushions of the couch. The dimness and quiet of this room was a curious comfort after the kaleidoscopic activity of the past few hours. She felt calmed to her soul, a profound, peaceful repose from which she wished never to arise.

As if reading her thoughts Carradine commented, "No one enjoys a party more than I, but I have to confess that when the guests finally leave, I'm most grateful for the quietude that follows."

She looked up at him, surprised, with a sudden and genuine smile. "Why, yes," she exclaimed. "That's exactly how *I* feel."

51

He was standing at the fireplace, his glass in one hand, his arm resting lightly on the mantelpiece. The light from the fire threw flickering shadows across his face. His expression was unreadable, his blue eyes half-veiled by sooty lashes. Adrian gazed at him silently, unable to look away. His eyes, his lean cheek, the hard curve of his jaw, all were a mesmeric force from which she could not tear her gaze. Her mind, her very essence seemed captive to his. Only he and she existed in that dim and fragrant room, only he and she and the strange enchanted silence that stretched and shimmered between them like an inescapable bond.

"More brandy, Miss Marlowe?" His voice broke the spell.

With the greatest of effort Adrian forced herself to respond. "No . . . thank you, no."

She put aside her empty glass and attempted in vain to gather her wits. Her mind was beclouded, her reason impaired. She had been staring at Carradine like some awestruck adolescent. She was exceedingly embarrassed and somewhat confused. He was attractive, that was true, and she was grateful for his help; but those were surely no reasons for the nameless emotions that stirred restively in her breast, emotions that quickened her pulse and sent languorous waves of warmth through every fiber of her being.

"Evan Colby is quite excited about your prospects," said Carradine, interrupting her thoughts. "He's been in and out of my office all week on one pretext or another, but his real mission was to learn whether or not I decided to grant you the loan."

By sheer effort of will Adrian directed her thoughts to the matter at hand. "Evan, yes. Evan has worried about me for years. I'm very fond of him."

"Really?" said Carradine casually, but his gaze was oddly intent. "Are the two of you affianced . . . or keeping company, perhaps?"

"Oh, no," she assured him while puzzling over the intensity of his gaze. "We're just good friends."

"Good friends?" he repeated as if commanding her to elaborate further.

And, in unconscious response to that unspoken command, Adrian heard herself say, "There was a time, though, that I had thought . . ."

"Yes, go on, Miss Marlowe. What had you thought?"

"Well, I had thought we might marry, but then . . ."

She paused again, disconcerted by her host's steady scrutiny.

"Yes?" he urged. "But then?"

"I decided not to."

"May I ask why?"

The question was an impertinent one, but Carradine's gaze was so compelling and Adrian's mind was so benumbed by the excitement of the evening and the amount of wine she had consumed that she answered involuntarily, "I discovered he was not the sort of man I could love."

A fleeting expression crossed Carradine's lean face, but it was gone before Adrian could determine its significance.

"I see," he said. "Please forgive my curiosity, Miss Marlowe, but I was under the impression that your relationship with Evan Colby was a closer one than friendship. And if you're wondering why that relationship should concern me—"

"Yes," she said, baffled. "I *am* wondering why. I'm also wondering where you got the impression that Evan and I are more than friends."

"Why, from Colby," he answered. And then, anticipating the protest that rose to her lips, he added hastily, "Colby said nothing to me along those lines, I assure you. His feelings for you, however, are more than evident, and I merely thought that you reciprocated those feelings. I can see now that I was wrong, which is fortunate for both of us."

"Fortunate?" she echoed, her bewilderment increasing.

"Well, you see," he explained, taking a cigarette case from his inside coat pocket, "I should not want to invest many thousands of dollars in your fashion house only to have you marry in a year or two and then abandon your career." He paused and opened the cigarette case. "Do you mind if I smoke?"

"No, not at all. Go right ahead."

While he lighted his cigarette Adrian began to wish desperately that she had not had so much to drink. She had the strongest feeling that Carradine's questions about her relationship with Evan had nothing whatever to do with the security of his investment. But she couldn't be sure. Her thoughts were a jumble; she simply could not focus her mind on what he was saying. As she watched him she could only think irrelevantly, His eyes are so blue, so incredibly blue. And his mouth—his mouth is hard, almost severe. Yet, when he smiles . . .

"Miss Marlowe." He was smiling now, in sudden comprehension and amusement. "Are you all right?"

"Yes." The word was a whisper. She cleared her throat and said more distinctly, "Yes, I'm fine."

"Are you sure?" he persisted, his eyes dancing. "I think, perhaps, that you may have had a little too much to drink tonight."

Her cheeks flamed. In a fever of embarrassment she denied vehemently, "No! Not at all. Please go on with what you were saying."

He snuffed out his cigarette, laughing softly. "I'm afraid," he said wryly, walking toward her, "that whatever I say to you tonight will fall on deaf ears. Why don't we talk tomorrow morning? If you agree to my terms I shall have my attorneys draw up the necessary papers for your signature later in the day."

"No, please," she insisted, gazing up at him imploringly. "I'm perfectly all right. Tell me your terms now. I'm sure I'll have no objection—"

She broke off in embarrassment. What was wrong with her? She was behaving like a fatuous child. If only she hadn't drunk so much; if only she could think clearly; if only he wasn't so devastatingly attractive . . .

"Very well," he conceded, eyeing her with some doubt. "If you're sure you feel up to—"

"Yes, yes," she said rapidly. "I couldn't be better, I assure you."

She faced his gaze squarely, but inside she was cringing with mortification. Fool! she upbraided herself. Of all nights to drink like a fish! What an idiot he must think her to be, and what a poor risk besides. She hoped against hope that her ridiculous behavior had not given him second thoughts about financing her fashion house.

"Now, Mr. Carradine," she said, straightening her spine as she summoned the last trace of her badly damaged dignity, "what was it you wanted to discuss with me?"

He gave her one more dubious look, then settled opposite her in the Morris chair. "I'm somewhat concerned," he said at last, "about the question of management. You see, Miss Marlowe, although your business sense is keen, your involvement with the creative aspect of your endeavor will leave you little or no time for anything else. You need a manager—more accurately, you need a partner—someone whose main concern is the financial stability and growth of Marlowe's."

An unpalatable suspicion took form in her mind, and the alcoholic haze that had numbed her thoughts began to dissipate. "A partner?" she echoed warily.

"Let me anticipate your reservations," he said obligingly. "The fashion house is your brainchild, exclusively yours. It's easy to see why you would be reluctant to share it. But you must try to view the situation from my standpoint. I'm prepared to extend to you a great deal of money, and naturally I'm concerned about the future of my investment. My faith in your talent is not at issue here; I trust you implicitly when it comes to designing clothes. By the same token I must ask you to place equal trust in my ability—and desire—to protect my interests."

"In other words," she said slowly, his intention at last made clear to her, "you want part ownership of my fashion house."

"Precisely."

"And if I refuse?"

"Now why would you want to do that?" he asked pleasantly.

But his meaning was unmistakable: no partnership, no loan.

She was suddenly sober and as alert as a cat. Carradine was watching her, his long legs crossed comfortably, his lids lowered lazily as he surveyed her with a smile. Adrian was thoroughly disgusted that she had, even for a moment, admired this man. While he had wined her, dined her, and plied her with compliments, he had been planning all along to purloin a piece of her business. She stared at him narrowly, yet some remnant of inner logic kept her hard thoughts unspoken. She had to tread this perilous path carefully; the future of her fashion house depended on her discretion.

As her silence continued, she raked swiftly through her mind for a rebuttal to his insupportable proposal.

Carradine regarded her questioningly, and when long moments passed and she still did not speak, he said, his smile fading, "Miss Marlowe, apparently my suggestion does not meet with your approval. But I can't help thinking that you're displeased with me for a reason other than that. When we met on the *Britannia,* your attitude toward me seemed more than coolness toward a stranger. If I have inadvertently offended or angered you, I should very much like you to tell me in what way you think I have done so.''

''You are mistaken,'' she said cautiously. ''I have already explained to you the reasons for my behavior on the *Britannia.* I am not in the habit of speaking to strangers.''

''Forgive me,'' he contradicted, ''but I don't think you're being entirely candid.''

''Mr. Carradine,'' she said hotly as a swift surge of anger propelled her to her feet, ''my aunt died while we were abroad. I had to bury her in Paris and then return to America alone. When you approached me on the *Britannia,* the last thing on my mind was social amenities. If I was less than courteous to you, I apologize—which, by the way, I have already done—and if you choose to read something else into my conduct that night, you are certainly at liberty to do so. However, I really don't see why you keep referring to that incident. It has nothing whatever to do with our present business relationship—''

She broke off abruptly as she suddenly realized the harshness of her tone. What was she doing? She had promised herself that she would be on her best behavior this evening, and here she was, screaming like a fishwife at the man who held her future in his hands.

But, to her utter disbelief, Carradine's smile returned. He rose from his chair, poured two glasses of brandy, then handed one to Adrian and drank his own.

''Miss Marlowe,'' he said while she watched him in bewilderment, ''I can't begin to tell you how much I admire you. You're a woman who not only knows her own mind but who is also not the least bit shy about speaking it. How refreshing you are! I just know we're going to get along famously.''

She thought scornfully, You wouldn't admire me so much if I told you what I really thought of you. But aloud she said evenly, "Yes, I'm sure we're going to be the greatest of friends."

Carradine poured another brandy and raised his glass in a toast. "To our partnership then, Miss Marlowe?"

"To our partnership, Mr. Carradine."

But to herself, she said bitterly, And to my monumental capacity for hypocrisy and deceit.

Seven

THE LAST THING she wanted was a relationship, business or otherwise, with Jason Carradine; but after the partnership was formed and the loan at last approved, she realized grimly that she had had no other choice. As Tessa had once so accurately pointed out to her: "In matters of finance, Jason Carradine invariably holds the upper hand."

What Adrian liked least about the arrangement was that she was no longer working on her own. With Carradine as a partner, the independence she craved was now a mockery, a joke. She was figuratively under his thumb and that she disliked him only worsened the situation. And yet the more she was thrown into proximity with him, the more she was struck by the irresistible allure of his extraordinary good looks.

As a designer, an artist, a lover of the aesthetic, Adrian was exceptionally appreciative of beauty in any form. And as much as she hated to admit it, Carradine was beautiful. There was a sleek animal grace in the way he looked, the way he walked, the way he moved. He was always impeccably dressed, fastidiously clean, with the pleasing masculine scent of fresh soap and starched linen about him. His face was perfection: the high brow; the straight nose; the curved jaw; the hard mouth; and those fine, dark-lashed eyes, so expressive, so arresting, and so incredibly, astonishingly blue.

She found herself thinking about him at the oddest times:

at her drawing board; on a streetcar; at the dress shop; in her bath. Of course, it was difficult *not* to think of him; she saw him almost daily. There were always papers to sign or decisions to be made jointly. He telephoned her at least once a day, whether they had seen each other or not.

Adrian had the feeling that he went out of his way to foist his presence upon her. For example, when it came time to sign the lease on the Graham Building, Carradine insisted on accompanying her. "I know that you and the owner have already agreed on the monthly rate," he told her, "but I'd like to see if we can lower that figure if we lease the building a few years longer." And to Adrian's mingled gratitude and annoyance, he was successful.

When she was planning the renovation of the building, Carradine said, "Don't worry about that; let me take care of it. I have a friend, an architect, who owes me a favor. He'll be happy to draw up some designs for your approval. After you've decided what you want, let me know, and I'll put you in touch with a trustworthy contractor."

She could hardly refuse his help. He was, after all, her partner, and she had to admit that his intervention saved her a great deal of effort and time. She had so much else to do. There were mannequins to interview and suppliers to deal with. The finest fabrics could now be purchased: mousseline de soie; crepe de chine; silky, soft cashmere; chiffons and brocades; and the most delicate of hand-fashioned lace. With her newly acquired funds Adrian was able to do all this and more. With Carradine's help she was free to devote her time to those aspects of her business that most interested her. But, oh, how she resented him! He was a thorn on the rose of her flowering success.

During the months of June, July, and August, while the contractors were working on the downstairs showroom, Adrian was occupied on the second floor with Tessa and the seamstresses, designing, cutting, sewing, and fitting the new spring line that would highlight the fashion house's grand opening in December. All the month of September, Adrian had perfected the new lightweight corset that would free American women from the restraints of the past. To complement this garment she had also designed a *soutien-gorge,* or "brassiere," a slim strip of cotton to support the breasts and give a firm, attractive line to the close-fitting bodices of her gowns.

"Try it on," Tessa said, holding up the fragile wisp for Adrian's inspection. And after Adrian had fitted the brassiere to her breasts and had slipped on a clinging silk shirtwaist, Tessa exclaimed, "Good gravy, it's indecent, it's decadent— Adrian, it's wonderful!"

Adrian peered into the mirror, turning this way and that to afford her the full effect of the scandalous garment. She did indeed look indecent beneath the silk. Every line of her breast was distinctly evident, from the sweet, youthful curve to the soft, rounded tip. She felt suddenly vulnerable, oddly defenseless, and delectably feminine.

"It's perfect," she decided, turning to Tessa. "Now women can look like women instead of like overfed pigeons. Make up a dozen more in varying sizes. Once our patrons try these on, they'll never go back to concealing their figures with those hideous cast-iron corsets."

But despite her incisive confidence, Adrian had her doubts about her design. What if her patrons rejected this innovation? Worse yet, what if their menfolk disapproved of the symbolic freedom? It might be wise, she decided, before presenting the brassiere for public scrutiny, to first gauge its impact upon a man she knew.

Her first thought, peculiarly, was Jason Carradine. He was her partner, after all, and he would naturally be interested in every facet of her work. But when she gave the idea more thought, when she imagined Carradine's eyes resting appraisingly on the curve of her barely covered breast, her face grew hot, and she was suddenly assailed with those curious emotions she could not define. She decided to gauge the reaction of another man instead.

"Well, Evan," she said that night, "what do you think?"

She had invited Evan Colby to dinner, a hastily thrown-together affair of cold ham, a salad, and fruit for dessert. He had been unusually quiet throughout the meal, watching her covertly as she bustled from buffet to table. At last, over coffee, Adrian was forced to ask him outright what she knew had been on his mind all evening.

He looked up when she spoke and muttered morosely, "What do I think about what?"

They were in the gloomy parlor. The maroon rug was dull; the gimcracks and geegaws were filmy with dust; a five-day accumulation of newspapers lay untidily on the coffee table. Adrian had had neither the time nor the inclination to clean house in recent weeks. She felt vaguely guilty that she had not fussed for Evan's visit, but she rationalized sensibly that a little dust and disorder never killed anyone.

"About the way I look," she said impatiently. "Come now, Evan, you've been stealing glances at me all night. Surely there's something you want to say to me."

"As a matter of fact," he said, his glum tone reproachful, "there is much I'd like to say to you, but it's certainly not my place—"

"Evan, please," she said, sighing, "don't go all grumpy and pompous on me. You've been playing big brother ever since I was in pinafores and you were in knickerbockers. Just be my friend, won't you? Don't judge me, encourage me."

"Adrian," he scowled, setting aside his coffee cup, "how can you expect me to encourage your . . ." He paused and gestured angrily in the direction of her bosom. "Have you looked in a mirror?" he demanded. "And, if you have will you kindly tell me where you got the courage to show yourself in that manner?''

"Evan . . ." She sighed again.

But before she could go on, he jumped to his feet and pulled her up from her chair. "Look at yourself," he snapped, and directed her roughly to the mirror over the mantel. "What self-respecting woman would exhibit her body like that? You wanted to know what I've been thinking all evening? All right, I'll tell you: I've been trying to restrain myself from carrying you upstairs and making violent love to you. Is that what you *want* me to think? Is that why you're half-naked? Do you want every man who sees you to want to think about raping you?''

"Evan!" she gasped. His arms were crushing her ribs. His face, inches from hers, was dark with anger and suffused with another emotion held tightly in check. "Evan, let me go!''

But his arms held her fast, and when he turned her to face him, pressing hard against her body with his own, she realized dimly that she had made a serious error in judgment this night.

This man was in love with her. For an indeterminate number of years Evan had wanted her, while she had blithely used his love and need for her own purposes. To have shown herself to him "half-naked," as he pronounced it, had been a grave mistake. She should have sought out Jason Carradine's opinion as she had originally intended. Carradine, at least, had no interest in her as a woman.

"Evan, please," she said, struggling as his arms around her tightened. "Stop it now. You're frightening me."

"I want to frighten you," he said harshly. "I want to scare some sense into you. Do you know what you do to me? Do you know what you would do to any man by showing your body to him in that way?''

"Evan, stop it!" she insisted, enraged now that she was

helpless against his superior physical strength. "You're not looking at me objectively. You've *always* wanted to make love to me. It has nothing to do with what I'm wearing. Now turn me loose before I really lose my temper."

He released her abruptly and slumped disgustedly on a chair. Sweat poured from his brow; he pulled a handkerchief from his pocket and wiped his face with a trembling hand. "You think you know everything, don't you?" he said bitterly. "Well, the truth is, I *have* always wanted to make love to you. And it *is* because I love you, not because you are indecently dressed. But what the devil are you trying to prove in that skimpy thing? That you're beautiful, desirable? You needn't go around half-naked to prove that."

"Evan," she said, sinking shakily onto the couch, "I'm terribly upset with you. And I wish you would stop saying I'm half-naked. Men don't wear layers of undergarments, do they? And nobody thinks the less of them for not hiding their bodies under tons of linen and whalebone. Why must women suffer? Where is it written that a woman's not fully dressed unless there's at least three inches of underclothing between her skin and her dress?"

Although her tone was hot and indignant, she was cringing inside with remorse. Evan loved her, and she had hurt him, and she sorely regretted the pain she had caused him.

He rose, pocketed his handkerchief, and moved toward the door, his face ashen and grim. "I'm leaving," he said. "There's just no sense at all trying to talk to you."

"Evan, wait!" She flew to his side and put a hand on his arm. "Don't leave; don't be angry."

"Let me go," he said dully, shrugging off her hand.

"Evan, please," she implored. "Don't leave here in anger. You're my dearest, oldest friend. I don't want to quarrel with you."

She gazed up at him beseechingly, her dark eyes fervent,

her mouth slightly parted in silent appeal. Evan stared at the cameo purity of her sweet, heart-shaped face, at the dark-fringed eyes, the rose-soft cheek, the clean, youthful line of her ivory throat; his hand shot out, and he grasped her wrist in an iron hold. "You little witch," he ground out fiercely. "I don't want to be your friend, I want to be your husband. I want to share my life with you. But *you*—you want only to prove to the world that you can stand alone, that you're as strong and as independent as a man. Why?" he demanded sharply. "Why is it so important to you to prove who you are?"

She stood silent beneath his hard, accusing gaze. His emotional vehemence surprised and subdued her but not nearly as much as his unexpected question. She had never consciously asked herself why she strived to attain her goals. It never occurred to her that she felt the need to succeed because her uncle had failed her. She loved Harry Marlowe too much to ever allow such a disloyal thought to surface in her mind. Why did she wish to stand alone? The question intrigued her. And as she reached deeper into her most secret thoughts, she told Evan Colby the truth as she perceived it. "Because in the end," she said at last, her voice hesitant and low, "we all stand alone, man or woman."

"I don't understand." He let go of her wrist and took a step backward. Now he was the one who regretted his harshness. "Adrian, tell me what you mean."

"If I were to marry you . . ." Her voice was still low and distant, as if involved in some inner dialogue. She turned and moved slowly to the open window and looked out toward the dark, deserted square. "If I were to marry you, as you wish, and you were to die—ten, fifteen, even fifty years later—and I survived, I would then have to stand alone. Having depended on you all those years, how could I survive without you? How, in the twinkling of an eye, could I become a woman dependent on no one but myself?''

"Adrian . . ." Puzzled, he followed her and turned her to face him. "Adrian, that's nonsense. You *would* survive. Women have gone on without their husbands. Look at your aunt.''

She shook her head and continued to gaze out at the still, summer night. "After my uncle died," she said quietly, "my aunt's life was a constant struggle to survive. The dress shop barely supported us. It was a makeshift existence at best. Aunt Meg was unprepared for life, Evan, don't you see that? Without my uncle's wealth behind her she was scrambling every minute of every working day just to keep her head above water. I don't want that ever to happen to me.'' Her voice shook.

"Adrian," he said, "those fears are baseless. You're still not over the shock of your aunt's death. You can't go through life thinking that everyone you love is going to die and desert you.''

"It's not that," she said in despair. "Oh, Evan, can't you understand that this is something I must do? I have to insure my own future. I can't leave something so important in someone else's hands.''

"All right, stop it now," he soothed, taking her gently in his arms. "I tell you, you're still reeling from your aunt's death; you're not thinking clearly. Your future in my hands would be even safer than in your own. Do you think I would ever let anything or anyone harm you? Don't you know how much I love you? Adrian, marry me. Be my wife, be mother to my children. Find your happiness and security with a husband and children who love you.''

She let him hold her, and when he raised her face to his and kissed her mouth, she did not resist. She thought of what he said about finding her happiness and security with a husband and children. But that was not what she wanted. She wanted her happiness and security to be built on the foundation of her own strength. Couldn't he understand that?

His kiss was tentative, gentle, worshipful. He had kissed her before, several times, and then, as now, Adrian felt nothing but a comfortable warmth, an emotion little different from being kissed by an uncle or brother. She wondered curiously why this should be so. She wasn't in love with Evan, but surely a man's kisses should be more stirring than this.

Her meandering thoughts took another turn. As Evan murmured endearments against her lips, Adrian thought of Jason Carradine with his Irish-blue eyes, his hard curving mouth, and the sensuous grace of his tall, slender form. If it was his mouth on hers it would be anything but gentle; his arms around her would be forceful and strong. Dimly she realized that it was highly irregular to be thinking of Jason Carradine while Evan was kissing her. But if it was Carradine's mouth, and Carradine's arms holding her, urging her, demanding a response, she had the strongest suspicion that, as much as she disliked him, she would be thinking of no man but him.

Eight

THE NEXT MORNING she telephoned Carradine—something she had never done before—and told him that she needed to see him.

"I'm so sorry," he said in his low, pleasant, courteous voice. "I am engaged all day with Mr. Ziegfeld. Is it important? Can it wait?"

"No, it can't wait," she answered. Her words surprised her. Her intention was to present the brassiere for his inspection to elicit the opinion of a man whose judgment was undistorted by his love for her. But in the back of her mind she sensed a more profound reason to see him, a reason that, though it was unclear to her, still managed, oddly, to alarm her.

Despite that, she said firmly, "I want your opinion on something I've designed. And it *is* important. I need to see you as soon as possible."

"Tomorrow morning?" he suggested. "Will that be all right?"

"No," she said so adamantly that she was startled by the fleeting notion that her need to see him was unrelated to his professional opinion. "Today . . . or tonight at the latest. I must see you immediately. I tell you, it's important."

He was silent for a time, and his silence enraged her. *She* had to jump whenever he demanded it; *she* was expected always to be at his beck and call. Well, if this was a partnership, then, by all that was holy, she would exercise her

68

rights. "Today," she said firmly when he did not speak. "I insist, Mr. Carradine. I will see you today."

"Very well," he said at last, and in his voice she detected an amused curiosity. "I am dining this evening at Rector's with Mr. Ziegfeld and his wife. It might be a good idea for you to join us. If you were to persuade Mrs. Ziegfeld to patronize Marlowe's you'd have another ready-made endorsement for your fashion house. Let me call for you at seven. We can talk then and go on to Rector's afterward. Does that suit you, Miss Marlowe?"

Have I a choice? she wanted to say. But instead, she said simply, "I'll see you at seven." And with a brief farewell, she severed the connection.

But immediately after she replaced the receiver she thought, What have I done? Why did I telephone him? Last night's fiasco must have upset her more than she realized. She knew in the back of her mind that Evan would disapprove. And why had he asked her those disturbing questions? What difference did it make why she was ambitious? If she were a man no one would think twice about it. Carradine never questioned her about her motives. He, at least, had the decency and the sensitivity to accept her as she was.

Decency. Sensitivity. Odd that she should ascribe those attributes to a man whose very presence raised the hairs on the back of her neck.

I've been working too hard, she thought irritably. I'm not thinking clearly. Jason Carradine is neither decent nor sensitive. He merely sees me as a dollar sign, another way to increase his ambiguous fortune. The fact that I'm a woman couldn't matter less to him.

She picked up the telephone again and called Tessa at the showroom. If she were to meet this evening with that fabulous showman, Florenz Ziegfeld, and his beauteous wife, Anna Held, she needed at least a full day to prepare herself.

"I won't be in today," she said when she heard Tessa's greeting.

"Why not?" Tessa asked in a harried tone. "Adrian, we have tons of things to do today. Mr. Lester is coming this afternoon with the trimmings and fastenings, the painters are due this morning, and we still haven't decided on the color for the dressing rooms. The chandeliers are hanging crookedly, and the electrician says—"

"Tessa, please," Adrian stopped her. "I need a free day. Mr. Carradine has invited me to dine with him tonight—with the Ziegfelds."

"The Ziegfelds?" Tessa exclaimed. "Adrian, how exciting!"

"Yes, it is, isn't it?" Adrian said slowly. But she was thinking, strangely, that it was not the thought of dining with the Ziegfelds that excited her as much as . . .

"Tessa," she said, giving herself a mental shake, "please take care of things for me today. Telephone Mr. Lester and postpone until tomorrow. Tell the painters to use the same shade of dusty rose for the dressing rooms as they used in the downstairs powder room. As for the electrician, let him know in no uncertain terms that if he doesn't straighten those chandeliers he'll have to whistle for his payment."

To Adrian's gratitude Tessa agreed to shoulder these burdens alone. Adrian thanked her friend warmly and, after concluding the conversation, began to give serious thought to raising Tessa's position from dressmaker to one she more richly deserved.

After an uninspired breakfast of oatmeal and coffee Adrian felt the weight of her unaccustomed freedom settle about her shoulders like a cloak of chain mail. She wandered around listlessly, regretting her decision to spend the day at home. As she gazed without interest at the three downstairs rooms she became unpleasantly aware of the condition of the house.

Dust puffs lay everywhere on tables and floors; cobwebs hung accusingly from ceilings and lamps. The kitchen floor was grimy and sticky from cooking grease, and in the dining room, the remnants of last night's meal lay soggy in dirty dishes upon a wrinkled and food-soiled cloth.

Good grief, she thought distastefully. What if Carradine notices this filth when he comes here tonight?

Seizing a cloth, a broom, and a dustpan, she went into the parlor and began to straighten up the clutter. It took her most of the morning to set the room to rights. After the parlor she cleaned the dining room, then went into the kitchen, scrubbed and waxed the floor, and polished the bloated black stove. When she was finished, the house shone. It did not occur to her that she had done something for Jason Carradine she had not thought worth doing for anyone else.

A long nap and a leisurely bath took up the remainder of the day. At seven forty-five the doorbell rang. It was just as well Carradine was late, for Adrian was still in her bedroom, putting the finishing touches on her toilette.

Her gown, of ice-blue silk, was deceptively simple. The sleeves were short and shirred; the bodice was low but modest, banded beneath the breast with a ribbon of peacock velvet; and the skirt, plain and narrow, falling to the silver buckle on her blue satin shoes, was slit to the knee, exposing a shocking expanse of her silk-stockinged leg.

More stunning than that, however, was the effect created by her undergarments. In her new lightweight corset and her wisp of a brassiere, Adrian looked totally uncovered beneath the blue fall of silk. When the doorbell sounded a second time, she had the strongest urge to ignore it. But then she remembered that the only interest Jason Carradine had in her was monetary. After a final inspection in the mirror she picked up her ostrich-feather fan and descended the stairs with a mutinous curve on her mouth.

"I'm sorry I'm late," he said when she ushered him into the hall. "I had to— Why, Miss Marlowe, you look absolutely riveting! Is that the design you wanted to show me? I heartily approve!"

"No," she said coolly, laying aside her fan and gesturing for him to follow her into the parlor. "The dress is not what I wanted your opinion on."

"Well, what then?" he asked, settling himself on the cushion-strewn sofa.

She did not answer at once. She went to the cellarette and poured a glass of sherry, then handed it to him, saying, "I'm sorry I have nothing stronger to offer you."

"Sherry will do," he said, accepting the glass. "Aren't you joining me?"

"No." She shook her head. "No, I don't want to drink tonight."

He tasted the wine and refrained from commenting. Adrian couldn't be certain, but she had the distinct impression that she had amused him.

"Well, then," he said when she perched stiffly on a chair across the room, "what was it you wanted to discuss with me?"

For a moment she watched him, affected, as always, by the flawless, hard contours of his lean, patrician face. His face was browner now from the Indian summer sun, and his eyes, in stunning contrast, were a deeper, more arresting shade of blue.

She felt a growing unease. The bodice of her gown seemed uncomfortably tight. The material pulled silkily against her breasts, and a feeling, vaguely alarming but oddly pleasurable, brought a faint flush of color to her suddenly warm cheeks.

"I've designed a brassiere," she announced abruptly.

"A what?"

"A brassiere," she repeated, and in a swift, breathless voice, she explained to him its function.

"Oh," he said.

"Well, what do you think?"

He glanced at her bosom. "Are you wearing it?"

"Yes." She reddened. "What do you think of it?"

"It looks fine," he said, smiling, obviously entertained by her obvious discomfort. "It's about time women started dressing sensibly."

She stared at him in astonishment. "Do you mean that?"

"Of course, I mean it. I'm sure you know better than I the countless ills women suffer because of the unhealthful construction of their undergarments."

"Yes, I do know it, but . . ."

"But what, Miss Marlowe?"

"But, as a man, don't you think it's immoral for a woman to be so scantily dressed?"

"Miss Marlowe," he said with a gravity she suspected concealed a high degree of amusement, "I rarely judge a woman's morals by the amount of clothing she chooses to wear. You look charming—and perfectly virtuous. Now, do you mind if we leave? I promised the Ziegfelds that we'll meet them at eight o'clock."

His intense blue eyes regarded her steadily, openly.

She was curiously pleased by his words, but she found it impossible to admit the reason. She had not previously cared about Jason Carradine's opinion of her physical appearance, but she knew he was commenting on more than just her design innovations. Yet, she could not take exception to what he said; he had concurred with her own feelings and gave her the confidence to face meeting strangers. She decided to ignore the undercurrents and enjoy the evening.

* * *

Rector's restaurant, alternately referred to as "The Court of Triviality" and "The Cathedral of Froth," was the last word in epicurean dining. Located at Times Square, between Forty-third and Forty-fourth streets, it was the first establishment in New York to feature a revolving door and was so internationally famed for its exquisite cuisine that no name was ever engraved on the Greco-Roman facade. Instead, a fierce griffin, electrically illuminated, proclaimed to the public that therein dined the world's most illustrious citizens.

Adrian had never before been to the noted restaurant. As she entered on Carradine's arm they were escorted to a choice table by the punctilious maître d'hôtel. She gazed at the floor-to-ceiling mirrors, the crystal chandeliers, and the green and gold Louis Quatorze decor, and was pleasantly gratified by all that she saw. At the flower-banked table she said to Carradine, "It's huge, so much bigger than Delmonico's, and yet every table is occupied."

"There are seventy-five more tables on the second floor," he told her, "and four private dining rooms. And they, too, I imagine, are occupied every night."

"It's very elegant," she remarked, glancing around at the notables present. Across the room Charles Frohman, the impresario, was dining with his current protégée, the sloe-eyed actress Maxine Elliott. Rudolf Friml, the Bohemian composer, was also at their table; and not far from them sat Richard Harding Davis, whose attractive virility had been captured to perfection by the very handsome sketches of Mr. Charles Dana Gibson.

As Adrian's gaze turned from Mr. Davis to her likewise attractive escort she found herself thinking that Jason Carradine's striking looks could only be captured artistically by a Titian or a Rembrandt. He was far handsomer than Mr. Davis; indeed, Adrian could not recall ever seeing a man whose physical perfection equaled Carradine's. His eyes were so incredibly blue, and their azure light seemed to reflect an inner beauty, which struck Adrian as odd in view of his ruthless reputation.

"Mr. Carradine," she said abruptly, dismissing these unsettling thoughts, "you did mean what you said before? You don't find my attire objectionable?"

He regarded her again with that facade of gravity that ill concealed his amusement. "Objectionable, Miss Marlowe? By no means. However," he added wryly, "I do wish you wouldn't hide yourself behind that fan. Since you've gone to the trouble of designing such a spectacular gown, you may as well let everyone see it."

Embarrassed, she lowered the fan and placed it, folded, at her side. "I wasn't hiding," she denied, coloring. "The fan happens to be an important part of the ensemble, Mr. Carradine."

He leaned back and smiled, his gaze openly admiring. "Will you do me a favor?" he asked.

"If I can," she said warily.

"Will you call me Jason? At this point in our relationship formality becomes superfluous, don't you agree?"

She eyed him suspiciously, but his blue gaze was candid; his face revealed nothing but amiable sincerity.

"Very well," she said reluctantly. Then, as an added concession, "And you may call me Adrian."

He nodded silently and continued to watch her. She chafed beneath the scrutiny of those admiring blue eyes. She felt the tightness of her bodice against her breasts; again that feeling, half-pleasurable, half-alarming, brought a fresh wave of color to her cheeks. Disconcerted, she said abruptly, "The Ziegfelds are late."

"I'm not surprised," he said. "Mr. Ziegfeld has a deathly aversion to clocks."

"To clocks? How extraordinary."

"Flo Ziegfeld," he said, "is an extraordinary man. Despite a number of other eccentricities, he is one of the few true geniuses I know. Ah, there he is now.''

Adrian turned her eyes toward the door, as did almost everyone else in the room. At Ziegfeld's side, his stunning wife waited while a violinist positioned himself at the sweeping train of her gown. When the musician broke into a lilting Strauss waltz, Anna Held, in a luscious creation of dove-white satin trimmed with tiny white rosebuds, undulated across the room to Jason Carradine's table.

''Monsieur,'' she purred as Carradine rose to greet her.

''Madame,'' he murmured.

''A pleasure to see you again.'' She gave him a gloved hand, which he raised to his lips. ''Florenz, *mon coeur* . . .'' She turned to her husband, a tall, handsome man, satanically dark and somberly silent. ''Monsieur Carradine awaits us. We are late, as usual. Can you forgive us, monsieur?''

''Seeing you in the flesh, madame,'' said Carradine smoothly in French, ''is worth waiting an eternity of lifetimes.''

She laughed charmingly, her piquant face and dark eyes a Gallic delight. ''You are too kind, monsieur, *très galant*. But we must speak in your language, *n'est-ce pas?* Your French is perfection while my English, I fear, bears improvement.'' She turned again to her husband with a coquettish toss of her saucy black curls. ''Florenz, is not Monsieur Carradine's pronounce without flaw?''

''Yes, my dear Anna,'' said the saturnine showman. ''His pronunciation is indeed exceptional.''

He was very tall, Adrian noted, although not as tall as Carradine, and his brooding good looks were not nearly as polished. He seemed the very antithesis of the woman at his side: a dark bird of prey hovering gloomily silent over the bright shining dove who was his wife.

Carradine urbanely performed the introductions, and

when all were seated, the Frenchwoman went into ecstatics over Adrian's attire.

"What excitement! What verve! Mademoiselle, who is your dressmaker?"

"Mademoiselle Marlowe," explained Carradine, "is a couturiere, Madame Ziegfeld. The gown she is wearing is of her own design."

"But I am stun!" cried Anna Held, her fiery dark eyes fairly flashing with admiration. "Mademoiselle, you are so young, so . . . decorative—have I speak the right word?" She turned to elicit her husband's confirmation. "Florenz, are you not impressed? Observe the fall of the fabric, the wonderful cling of the . . . the . . . how you say, *corsage?*"

"The bodice," supplied Carradine, his eyes resting there for an instant.

"Oui!" the woman exclaimed. "The bodice. Florenz, *regardez-vous!"*

But Mr. Ziegfeld was already observing the sensuous cling of Adrian's gown, and his quick, active, artistic mind was envisioning a line of showgirls, tall and shapely, voluptuously clad in several different versions of this clever young lady's very special designs.

"Miss Marlowe," he said, inclining his sleek falcon's head toward her, "would you consider designing a line of costumes for next year's Follies?"

"For the Follies?" Adrian echoed, her heartbeat accelerating. "Mr. Ziegfeld, are you joking?"

"I never joke about business," he said somberly. And indeed Adrian suspected that this dour, reserved, eccentric genius never joked about anything. "Of course," he added, "I shall have to see more of your designs before making a final commitment. But I generally trust my instincts, Miss Marlowe, and my instinct about you is that you've an uncommon talent for eye-catching style. And that," he con-

cluded with the barest trace of a smile, "is what the Ziegfeld
Follies is all about."

Adrian digested his words in silence while Ziegfeld
turned his attention to Carradine. "You were right about
this child, Jason," he said. "If that dress is an indication of
the caliber of her skill I've found myself a jewel of a designer. My thanks for your invitation tonight. And to think
that I almost refused you."

Adrian looked swiftly toward Carradine, who regarded
her quietly with those eloquent eyes. "You arranged this,"
she said, astounded.

He smiled briefly. "In a manner of speaking."

"You knew," she persisted, unmindful of the Ziegfelds,
aware now of only one man as her giddy thoughts spun.
"You knew he would ask me if he met me. You arranged
this meeting so that he could . . ."

She trailed off self-consciously and lowered her gaze as
she became suddenly aware that the Ziegfelds were watching her in interested amusement.

It had all been prearranged, she thought, trembling with
excitement. Carradine had invited Mr. Ziegfeld to dinner
with the express intention of exhibiting her talent. He had
been so determined, if fact, that he had had to persuade—
perhaps coerce—Mr. Ziegfeld into coming.

She was breathless with appreciation; her gratitude knew
no bounds. It was indisputable that without Jason Carradine's assistance her life might have taken a very different
turn.

She looked up at him silently, her eyes scanning his
face as if she were seeing him for the very first time. His
features seemed somehow finer, nobler; his eyes, thickly
lashed, were a more subtle, yet vibrant, blue. His smooth
brow and straight nose seemed a classic Greek rendering,
and his mouth was as sensuous as a passionate Greek
god's.

Adrian had the strongest desire to run a slow, trailing finger along the smoothness of his jaw. But more, so much more, she wanted to hold that lean face, to feel his flesh beneath her hands, and to press his dark head against the curve of her suddenly quivering breast.

Nine

THAT EVENING at Rector's became a vivid and shining memory she would treasure forever. The meal was perfection: green turtle soup; succulent lobster; boned baby chicken stuffed with rice and *foie gras;* and a full complement of wines that included Amontillado, Pommery Sec, and Charles Heidseck Brut. Adrian sampled them all in great quantity despite her earlier decision not to drink.

Anna Held was a delight, regaling Adrian with accounts of her appearance at the Palace Theatre in London, her first marriage which had produced a daughter—"Liane, *ma petite bijou!*"—and her legendary milk baths, which had brought both applause and censure from a disbelieving public. Ziegfeld, surprisingly, set aside his reserve to recount several humorous incidents connected with the current year's Follies. But despite the fine fare and the scintillating company, Adrian's gaze fell most often on Jason Carradine, and her thoughts remained fixed on him.

At evening's end, as the Ziegfelds prepared to leave, Anna Held said to Adrian, "You must inform me of the opening of your fashion house, mademoiselle. I am much eager to see your designs. I shall be marvelous in one of your dresses, yes?"

"Yes, madame," Adrian laughed. "But I think you are marvelous no matter how you are attired."

"*Chérie!*" the woman exclaimed, and saluted Adrian in the French manner, with a kiss on both cheeks. And then, turning to Carradine, she likewise favored him. "We shall see each other soon, *n'est-ce pas, monsieur?* Make the engagement with Florenz. We are both at the disposal of you and your enchanting protégée. *Bon soir, bon soir!*"

And with a dazzling smile and a wave of a gloved hand, Anna Held, at the side of the world's greatest showman, made an exit no less flamboyant than her carefully staged spectacle of an entrance.

In Jason's car, riding home, Adrian lounged in cozy comfort against the elegant upholstery. Was there no end to his surprises? she wondered drowsily. At the restaurant he had said to her, "Flo has signed Lillian Lorraine, Fanny Brice, and the Dolly Sisters to appear in next year's Follies. I happen to be acquainted with those ladies, and I'm more than certain that they can be persuaded to attend the grand opening of Marlowe's."

He said this in the most conversational of tones, as if those luminous stars of the Broadway stage were no more than four unknown country misses from the hinterlands of New Jersey. Lorraine, Brice, the Dolly Sisters! And the incomparable Anna Held! Every salesclerk, stenographer, and working girl in New York clamored to copy what they wore. Not only had Adrian garnered a Society clientele because of Jason Carradine's seemingly illimitable influence, but also she could now anticipate a multitude of enthusiastic customers for her ready-to-wear line.

She said to him in the car, trembling with an excitement whose source, she dimly realized, was other than gratitude, "I don't know how to thank you for all you've done."

He turned to her and smiled. His eyes in the dim light were a deep, delicious blue. "You've said that once before," he reminded her. "And as I told you then, we'll think of something."

His voice, too, was low, with a soft, slow, sensual timbre that started a curious tingling sensation in the pit of Adrian's stomach. She was numb from all the wine she had drunk, yet her sensory perception had never been keener. She was acutely aware of the purr of the motor as the Rolls-Royce sped quietly through the night. She could feel the leather upholstery, smooth and supple beneath her hand. The crisp whiteness of Jason's shirt was dazzling to the eye. The scent of soap and linen, mingling with the lingering aroma of excellent tobacco, tantalized her sense more beguilingly than the sweet smell of late-summer roses.

When the car halted in front of her house, she asked politely, "Will you come in for a moment? For coffee?" she added at once. But even as she issued that courteous invitation, she realized with astonishment that she had asked him to come in because she simply could not bear the thought of his leaving her.

Her heart was beating in the most peculiarly erratic fashion. Her breath kept catching in her throat, and the feeling in the pit of her stomach was radiating through her veins, languorously warming the flow of her blood.

Jason was watching her as if debating in his mind an insoluble problem. His eyes were grave; his mouth was compressed in a hard, thoughtful line. At last he responded, when she feared he might refuse her, "Yes, I'd like some coffee."

And, handing her from the car, he escorted her in silence into the house.

"I'll just be a moment," she said, taking his hat and gloves and laying them on the hall table alongside her fan and her blue, beaded purse. "Will you wait in the parlor?"

He was watching her again with that faintly questioning gravity, but Adrian was aware of only her own disturbing thoughts. She wanted to touch him—odd, since previously she could not bear even to be in his company—and yet now she wanted to touch him as she had never before in her life wanted anything.

''Why don't we forget the coffee?'' he said quietly. ''I'd prefer to have sherry; that is, if you'll join me.''

She knew she should not; she already had had more than enough to drink. His quiet gaze seemed to see to the depths of her soul. Her legs began to tremble, her heartbeat grew chaotic, and she realized, with a thrill of alarm, that tonight she would refuse this man nothing he asked.

On shaking legs she preceded him into the parlor. A small lamp shone dimly on the table near the sofa. As Adrian reached for the wall switch to give the room more light, Jason's hand closed on hers, and softly he said, ''No. Leave it off.'' Then his hand moved away, and, like hers, she noted numbly, it was trembling.

She stood motionless before him. His brief touch had reawakened in her those same languorous emotions that oddly quickened her pulse. How desirable he looked, with his strong sun-browned cheeks lending brilliance to the color of his dark-lashed blue eyes. She was standing so close to him that she could feel his warm breath on her face, could smell the clean, fresh, male scent of shaving soap and starched linen. She wanted to touch him; she ached to touch him. Never in her life had she wanted anything more.

Every emotion she felt was reflected in her face. Her eyes were wide and dark and lustrously bright with a half-fearful wonder. Her ivory cheeks were flushed, her sable lashes trembled, and her soft lips were parted as if awaiting the invasion of a hard, demanding mouth.

''My God,'' he uttered softly, staring down at her. ''Do you know how beautiful you are?''

''Jason,'' she whispered as if tasting the sound of his name on her lips. ''Jason.''

She leaned pliantly toward him, impelled by a force she was powerless to control. She raised her face to his. He stared down at her unmoving, and then, slowly, hypnotically one arm went around her and one hand cupped her cheek. He drew her against him, and his warm mouth closed gently on hers.

His kiss was a narcotic, sapping all of her will. Both his arms encircled her now, a sweet, ecstatic bond. She moved closer against him as if to fuse her flesh with his and, as his gentle kiss deepened and his arms around her tightened, she could feel the core of his passion, throbbing hotly against her, lending fuel and fire to her own.

All strength left her limbs; all sanity deserted her. She knew only sensation as his mouth explored hers. Her newly discovered passion became an inferno in her veins. She wanted to feel each line and contour of his body next to hers, to submit to his desire, to give vent to her own, to quell the fierce emotions that, like a turbulent tempest, she only half-understood and was helpless to control.

When at last he lifted his head, she clung to him blindly. She was dizzy and faint. His face, inches from hers, was a featureless blur.

"Kiss me," she whispered in a sensual daze. "Kiss me again."

The heat of his body sent a dark thrill through hers. She had no strength but his. She was captive to his whim, and slave to the desire that brought a moan to her lips and set her heart pounding wildly in her breast.

"Where's your bedroom?" she heard him say over the tumult that was her passion.

"My bedroom?" she whispered faintly. "Why?"

"I want you," he said hoarsely, his arms crushing the breath from her lungs. "I want you now. Where's your bedroom?"

"Upstairs. It's upstairs."

She could barely speak, could hardly breathe. He directed her up the stairs, his arm tight around her. She felt driven by a force outside her knowledge, outside her will. He wanted her, wanted her. She forgot how much she had loathed him and how, in her heart, she had scornfully reviled him. What she knew now was only sensation: the taste of his mouth; the heat of his hands; the strength of his passion pressing urgently against her. She knew only desire, like a torment in her soul; she knew only that she wanted him, and she wanted him at once.

The bedroom, like the parlor, was dimly lit by a lamp. But she saw nothing of the room, sensed nothing of her surroundings, save for the man at her side who pulled her into his arms and pressed fierce, burning kisses on her hot, compliant mouth.

Her fledgling passion responded to his like a new bud unfurling. She was all warmth and yielding, a willing flower in his arms. When he drew her to the bed, she acceded without reluctance. And at the side of the bed, when he unfastened the buttons at the back of her gown, she stood breathless against him, her dark eyes fixed on his, her heart beating violently in anticipation of the touch of his hands upon her flesh.

"I have wanted you," he breathed, his voice shaking, "since the first night I saw you."

She quivered and watched him; she could not speak.

He slipped the gown from her shoulders; only the thin wisp of cotton now covered her breasts. He regarded the device in frowning concentration, and at length he said impatiently, while she trembled beneath his gaze, "How do you get this thing off?"

Without a word, without thought, she freed her breasts of their scant covering. Oddly she felt no shame, no compunction. It seemed natural and right that she should bare herself for his scrutiny. And when he touched her at last, sending shivers of sensation through every part of her body, she took his face between her hands, and with an age-old and inborn instinct, she directed his mouth to the rounded pink tip of one quivering breast.

"Jason," she moaned as his mouth and his tongue blazed a slow, burning trail from one breast to the other. "Jason." A will, not her own, arched her body close to his. A being, not hers, touched his hair and pressed his mouth ever closer to her hot and yearning flesh.

As he kissed each trembling curve, each quivering rise, his experienced hands adeptly divested her of the rest of her clothing.

"Lie down," he said, shaking, drawing away to remove his own clothes. "Adrian, lie down."

"No," she said insistently, unwilling for even a moment to part from this man who had awakened in her an intense, fierce desire she could barely endure. "No," she moaned, and bound her eager lips to his, clinging to him tightly. His mouth answered hers, and his hands grasped her bare hips and pressed her against him, so that even through the barrier of his silky black broadcloth she was acutely aware of his hard, aching need.

"Lie down," he said again, his voice hoarse with passion, and with firm commanding hands he compelled her to comply.

She lay on the bed, quivering, aching, as he shed his coat and collar, tore off his tie, shrugged free of his shirt, and began to unfasten the buttons on his trousers. Fascinated, she watched him: the play of muscle in his arms; the dark, curling hairs that glistened wetly on his chest; the hard, narrow hips; his passion unfettered as he lowered his trousers and kicked off his shoes.

Unclothed he was magnificent, a slender Greek statue, lean of torso, hard of limb, with grace and natural beauty in every contour. She wanted to touch him, to embrace him; she wanted to feel the heat of his passion against her own scorching skin. She wanted his hands on her body, his mouth on her mouth, his hard, lithe body pressing so close to hers that nothing, not even a sigh, could come between them.

With a knee on the bed he bent down to caress her. "Beautiful," he murmured, his hands at her thighs. "You're too beautiful for words."

"Kiss me," she whispered, wanting him, needing him, as a new surge of longing left her breathless and limp.

His hands brushed the skin at the soft, tender curve at the inside of her thighs. He bent his head, and with a feather-light movement, his warm mouth caressed her, beguiled her, inflamed her, till she was writhing and helpless beneath the magic of his touch. She was drowning in passion, adrift on a sea of desire and need. With his mouth he enslaved her; with his hands he commanded. She was his, solely his, and as his warm, demanding mouth traveled upward to hers, she received him with a sigh and a heart-pledging kiss that bound soul, mind, and body to the man who had shown her the meaning of love.

When he parted her thighs, she eagerly received him, her inborn instinct her conduct and her guide. She could feel the strength of his passion pressing firmly to gain entrance. When he encountered resistance and stopped and looked down at her, she returned his puzzled gaze, then with that unerring and urgent instinct, she arched up against him and locked her legs tightly around his.

The pain she felt as he fully entered her was allayed by the pleasure of her flesh enclosing his. She felt him, hard and hot, within the confines of her body; she felt the exquisite intrusion of his unrestrained desire, expanding, increasing, igniting her own.

"Dear Christ," she heard him utter, his lips against her throat. "You're a virgin. Adrian . . ."

He tried to pull away, but she would not let him go. His words had no meaning; only his hands and his mouth and his touch mattered now. "Jason," she breathed, her breast aching, her senses reeling. "Jason, kiss me, love me."

As she writhed beneath him, his fullness filling her, thrilling her, she groaned involuntarily. He slipped a hand beneath her hips, and with slow rhythmic probing, he ignited the fire he had started within her, ignited it, fueled it, raised it higher, ever brighter, till at last it exploded, sending showers of sensation, sparks of emotion, through every last molten region of her shuddering body. Then and only then did his own passion crest. As she quivered beneath him, her arms still around him, he pressed into her deeply, his hard mouth claimed hers, and with one fierce forceful thrust, he spilled himself, moaning, inside her.

Ten

As SHE LAY by his side in the aftermath of loving, not touching, not speaking, but intensely aware of him, she thought calmly and rationally, I love him. I have loved him for months under the pretext of hating him. I love him because he knows me, because he sees me without illusion and accepts me as I am. That's why I could never consider marrying Evan. Evan doesn't know me; he loves someone unreal, a figment of his imagination, a woman who doesn't exist. But I am real, I do exist. And only Jason, of all who know me, accepts me for the woman I am.

That she had held him responsible for her uncle's misfortune lay dormant but not forgotten in her mind. She might have been unjust, she admitted to herself for the first time. He might not have been the sole cause of Harry Marlowe's ruin. Tessa thought not, and even Aunt Meg had held him blameless. Adrian decided that she would ask him about it outright. Yes, that was what she would do; it was the right thing to do. But not now, she thought dreamily as she remembered his mouth and his hands and his love. Not now. She would talk of it later.

Drowsy and satisfied, her body still tingling from the lingering sensations of her first taste of passion, she turned her head and regarded the man who had awakened her to the reality of love. He was on his back, a hand covering his eyes. When he felt her move, he turned his head and returned her

silent gaze with a look she could not decipher. At last, he
asked softly, "Are you all right?"

"Yes." Her voice was warm. She smiled. He did not.

"Did I hurt you?" His voice was tense.

"No . . . no, you didn't." She touched his hand, deciding to tell the truth as he watched her and waited in
disbelieving silence. "Well, yes," she admitted. "But only
at first, and then not. Honestly, Jason."

He sighed and looked away from her.

"What's the matter?" She was vaguely unsettled by his
unlikely quiet and by the hard, somber set of the mouth that
had thrilled her in a manner undreamed of. "Jason, what's
wrong?"

"I wish you had told me," he said at some length, and his
voice, she realized with a start, was filled with anger and
bitterness and self-condemnation.

"Told you what?" she asked, bewildered.

"That you were a virgin."

Incredulous, she stared at his averted face. "You didn't
know? You didn't assume . . ."

"By your actions tonight," he said curtly, and still he did
not look at her, "I was foolish enough to assume just the opposite. You should have told me!"

Her astonishment faded at the terseness of his tone and
was replaced by a resentful irritation. "I should have *told*
you?" she retorted. "How might I have broached the subject, pray tell? Should I have said to you when we met,
'Good afternoon, Mr. Carradine. I'm here to inquire about a
loan. Oh, and by the way, I'm a virgin.' Is that what I
should have done?"

"Don't be absurd," he snapped, turning his head swiftly
to stare at her severely.

"Absurd? You're the one who's absurd, Jason."

He scowled forbiddingly and raised himself on an elbow.
"Listen to me, you insolent little innocent. I don't make a

practice of seducing virgins. I have never, in point of fact, made love to a virgin. You might have told me, Adrian; you *should* have let me know in some way.''

''Why?'' she demanded, her irritation increasing. ''What difference does it make? You wanted to make love to me, didn't you? If you had known I was a virgin would it have stopped you?''

He stared at her a moment longer, his eyes cobalt blue in the dim light. Then, with an angry sigh, he slumped back against the pillows and laced his fingers tightly together over his head. ''No,'' he said grimly, ''it would not have stopped me. Nothing could have stopped me from making love to you tonight.''

His words thrilled and pleased her, and oddly, they alarmed her. She put a tentative hand on the tangled dark hairs on his chest, and warily she asked him, ''Why, Jason?''

He seemed suddenly aware of her trepidation. ''Come here,'' he said, turning to her once more and bringing her gently into his arms.

She thrilled to his touch again, to the warmth of his skin, the strength of his hands, to the strong, clean male scent that was so distinctively, wonderfully his.

''Let me tell you something,'' he said with a recollective smile that was curiously grave. ''The first time I spoke to you, on the deck of the *Britannia,* I wanted at the same time to kiss you and to turn you over my knee. No woman of my experience had ever angered or aroused me as much as you did that night. Then, when you came to the bank, when I realized who you were, I said to myself, 'This one again. By God, I'll have her dancing to my tune before I'm finished with her.' Yet in the back of my mind I wanted to take you to bed, I wanted to teach you to love, for I was convinced that you had never—''

"But you just told me you thought I wasn't a virgin," she interrupted him.

"Be quiet, minx," he said mildly, "and let me finish. At first I *was* convinced that you were a virgin. For one thing," he said dryly, "you were such a haughty little horror that I was certain no man on earth would be brave enough to approach you."

"Jason!"

"Quiet," he hushed her. "Hear me out. You must admit that you were aloof, to say the least. There were times, in fact, that I could swear you despised me."

He lifted her chin, and with his eyes, he defied her to deny it. She could not, of course.

"At any rate," he went on, drawing her closer in his hold, "your aloofness, your disinterest, your downright disdain piqued my interest to no end. You made me so angry at times that I wanted to throttle you. But the more angry you made me, the more I wanted to have you, and the more I wanted to have you—"

"Jason," she interrupted again, thinking guiltily of the reasons for her coldness and disdain, "I think I should tell you something."

"What is it now?" he said with affectionate impatience. "Can't you let me finish what I'm saying?"

"No." Her voice was rueful. She huddled against him, an arm across his chest, as if his very nearness, which she had once despised, was now her sole source of comfort and courage. "I have something to tell you, and I know it's going to make you angry."

"My dear girl," he said, laughing, "almost everything you say to me makes me angry."

"This is serious, Jason. You're going to hate me."

He looked down at her bent head and smiled. Hate her? Hate this little she-devil with the tongue of a viper and the face and the body of a Tintoretto divinity? He kissed her tumbled curls. "Tell me," he said softly. "I promise not to hate you."

"Well, you see," she began, and burrowed closer against him, "my uncle's business failed in the Panic of 1907. . . ."

"Yes, I know," Jason said. "I was his banker."

She raised her head and stared at him. "You knew? You knew all this time who I was?"

"I've only known," he explained, "since shortly after you came to me for the loan. Naturally I made inquiries about you, and—"

She moved out of his arms and sat upright against the headboard. "But why did you never say anything, Jason?"

"Say anything about what?" He moved up alongside her. "What was there to say that we both didn't already know? I was his banker; you were his niece. His brokerage firm collapsed because of the United Copper mess—"

"Yes," she said slowly as her resentment and distrust momentarily resurfaced. "And you profited nicely from that mess, didn't you?"

"Good Lord!" He laughed as he realized at last the origin of her antipathy. "That's what's been gnawing at you all these months. You think I had something to do with your uncle's failure."

"Well, did you?" Her tone was accusing.

"No," he said truthfully. "A thousand times no! Adrian, listen to me. Without going into a lot of boring details, let me assure you that Harry Marlowe's own less than shrewd judgment was responsible for the failure of his firm. He and that gang of vultures at Otto Heinze tried to corner United Copper shares, at the risk, I might add, of plunging a good many firms into bankruptcy. When your uncle and his cronies miscalculated, it was their own two brokerage houses that failed. Now, how in the name of heaven can you fault me for something in which I took no part?"

"But, Jason, you delivered those shares at the precise moment when my uncle and Otto Heinze couldn't pay for them."

"Yes," he conceded. "I and a hundred other shareholders. Adrian, none of us knew what your uncle was up to. I delivered in good faith; so did the others. Harry's burning and unwise desire to turn a fast dollar is what did him in. I give you my word: I had nothing to do with the failure of his firm."

"Honestly?" she pursued, wanting desperately to believe him.

"Honestly," he said. "Now come here; let me hold you."

"No, wait." She kept her distance. "When my uncle came to you afterward for a loan, you refused him."

With a great deal of forbearance Jason permitted the indignity of this insulting inquisition. "Yes, that's right," he said wearily.

"Why?"

"Why, Adrian? Come now; you're not ignorant of financial matters. Would you lend money to a man who almost single-handedly caused a panic in the stock market? And besides," he added bluntly, "not only did your uncle already owe the bank a staggering sum, but his reputation was ruined as well. He was finished on Wall Street; he was finished, in fact, in the State of New York. A loan would not have helped him, and we both knew it."

He allowed her to digest these unpleasant but vital facts. She said nothing but only plucked at the sheet in disconsolate silence. At length he said in a different tone, "In any case, after your uncle's death I was prepared to write off his debt, but then your aunt came to see me. An exceptional woman, Meg Marlowe. You're very much like her, Adrian, although her manners were far superior to yours."

She threw him a dark look, which he pretended to ignore.

"Your aunt," he went on, "insisted on repaying the loan. She told me in no uncertain terms: 'I won't have it said that a Marlowe defaults. I'll pay my husband's debt; just tell me how much he owes.' I could see that she was determined to make good the balance. I also knew she was woefully short of funds, so I named a figure high enough to impress her but low enough to be within her means if she took a year or two to pay. The true balance I wrote off. I had intended to do so, anyway."

"You did that for my aunt?" said Adrian, touching his hand, discovering in this man a new, unexpected, admirable grace.

"I did it," Jason qualified, enclosing her hand in his, "for a valiant lady whom I happened to respect. I like a fighter—and your aunt, God rest her soul, was a champion."

Adrian's heart swelled with gratitude and with a fresh surge of love. How she had misjudged him! How different he was in the flesh from the villainous portrait she had painted of him in her mind.

"Jason," she said remorsefully, "I owe you an apology."

"Do you mean it this time?" he asked with a smile. "You have apologized to me before—with resentment, I've no doubt, and without sincerity."

"Yes, yes," she assured him. "I'm sorry; I do mean it. I had thought the most awful things about you. I had accused you in my heart of the most despicable treacheries."

His smile grew grave. "You're not the first person who's ever had those thoughts."

"Jason, you *will* forgive me?"

He reached out an arm and gathered her close to him. "Of course, I forgive you, imp. Now kiss me once more. I have to be leaving."

"Oh, don't go!" she cried, clutching his arm, then

blushed to the roots of her hair when she realized what her protest implied.

"My little temptress," he murmured, pressing his lips to her rose-colored brow, "do you mean to say you want me to spend the night? I'm afraid I can't—much as I'd like to. The proprieties must be observed, you know."

"Jason . . ." Her arms crept around his neck. ". . . when will I see you again?"

"On Friday," he said, his fingers brushing lightly at the base of her spine. "We're meeting with the decorators; had you forgotten?"

"No," she said, her voice dropping to a hesitant whisper. "I didn't forget. But that's not what I meant. When will I . . . be with you?"

"Why, Adrian," he said with a delighted laugh, "I do believe you're inviting me to share your bed again. I couldn't be more flattered."

She wrenched out of his hold in a tangle of hands and arms, and glared at him fiercely. "Don't laugh at me, Jason! You want it, too; I know you do."

"I certainly do," he said agreeably. "And I shall be most happy to oblige you at your earliest convenience."

She glared at him still, embarrassed by her disgraceful lack of modesty and infuriated by what struck her as an inordinate amount of conceit on his part. Fuming, she said to him, "It's a matter of supreme indifference whether or not you ever make love to me again."

"I believe you." He laughed and, swinging out of bed, began to dress. "All the same, I shall take you to the theater Saturday evening and then for a late-night supper at Sherry's. And then afterward . . ."

She turned her back on him in a huff and stared in stony silence at the wall. Arrogant devil! She didn't care if she never saw him again. She had not misjudged him after all. He was every bit as vile and loathsome and totally self-serving as she had thought him to be. If she never saw him again it would be too soon. If she never saw him again she would be the happiest woman in the world.

But, presently, she felt his hand on her shoulder, his hand, warm and strong, that had touched her in secret places, that had aroused her, thrilled her, burned her, scorched her, and had awakened in her soul a conflagration of desire that even now began to kindle and fan a fever in her blood.

"Adrian." His voice was a caress. "Turn around; let me look at you before I go."

She obeyed as if mesmerized by his low voice, by his touch. He was fully dressed, as impeccably turned out as he had been at the start of the evening. She raised her gaze to his; he laid a hand against her cheek. "Kiss me," he said softly. "Kiss me once before I leave."

She slid slowly to her feet, unashamed of her nakedness, and with a deep, contented sigh, she put her arms around his neck. His hands at her hips drew her close to his passion. He was aroused again—she felt it—and the knowledge aroused her, too.

"Jason," she whispered as he moved her against him, "stay . . . just a while longer. Stay."

"No," he said gently. "Not tonight. I don't want to run the risk of . . ."

He paused, said nothing more, and then he moved her away from him. He reached around her to pull the sheet from the bed, and without looking at her, he draped it around her shoulders. "Good night," he said briskly. "Go to bed now. I'll telephone you tomorrow."

His abrupt change of mood and his unfinished sentence was puzzling to say the least, and she could hardly ignore it.

"What do you mean?" she asked curiously, rearranging the sheet by tucking it snugly under her arms. "What risk are you talking about?"

"The risk of pregnancy," he said plainly, and now he faced her squarely. "A first encounter is not likely to have done it, but in future, Adrian, I shall have to take precautions."

Pregnancy? Pregnancy? That had not once entered her mind. What if she . . . ? What if he had . . . ? The possibility gave her pause, and she stared at the floor in disconcerted contemplation of the consequences.

"Adrian," he said, easily reading her thoughts, "don't concern yourself. If you do become pregnant because of tonight—which I doubt—we'll simply be married."

"Married?" Her head shot up at the unexpectedness of the suggestion. Without thinking she blurted, "But I don't want to get married!"

"Neither do I," he concurred with a quickness that, surprisingly, irked her. "But if I've gotten you pregnant we *will* marry. Do you think I'd want a child of mine branded a bastard?"

Frowning, thinking furiously, she took a step backward. No, no. It was impossible. This was not a decision to be made on the spur of the moment. She loved him—there was no question in her mind about that—but she wasn't ready to marry yet, not Jason or anyone.

"Jason," she said sensibly, drawing the sheet more securely around her breasts, "I couldn't marry you—even if I did become pregnant. I have my fashion house to think of; I can't give that up. And don't try to convince me that nothing will change if we marry. I know the male mind. The instant you slip a ring on my finger you'll insist that I stay home and devote myself fully to being a wife and mother. Well, I won't do it, I tell you. Even if I do become pregnant I will not marry you."

He regarded her thoughtfully for a moment as if reading a hidden meaning in the intensity of her protest. At length he said pleasantly, "Look here. If by any chance we should be forced by circumstance into marrying, I wouldn't dream of denying you your career, no more than I would expect you to ask me to give up banking. Your fashion house comes first with you, Adrian. Don't you think I know that? At any rate we don't have to think about that now. As I said, I doubt that I've gotten you pregnant. If I have, however, you will have no other choice but to marry me.''

"I won't do it," she maintained.

"Yes, you will, Adrian."

"I won't," she said mutinously.

"Oh, no?" he said, drawing her back into his arms with one deft, easy motion. "We'll see about that."

Eleven

IN THE WORK-FILLED weeks that followed, Adrian was far too busy to worry about an unwanted pregnancy. The fashion house would soon be having its grand opening celebration; only Adrian's design for the wedding dress, an apparently simple but vexatiously complicated variation of a Greek garment, was as yet uncompleted.

She was seeing Jason on a regular basis—two, sometimes three nights a week—in addition to the daily business meetings she had formerly detested. Besides, she would think on those few occasions when she considered the possibility of having conceived a child that Jason had said it was highly unlikely, and he, of all people, ought to know about those things.

She was happy with her new relationship, happier than she had ever thought she could be. An empty part of her life had been abundantly filled. Jason had awakened her to a need that she had not known existed, and then he had proceeded to sate that need in the most exquisite manner imaginable.

And apart from the physical side of their relationship, Adrian had discovered in Jason all she had ever wanted in a man. He was thoughtful and caring, intelligent and witty. His diverse interests and investments were a marvel to Adrian, whose professional inclinations lay in only one direction. Jason, on the other hand, was as diverse an individual as Adrian had ever known. He was the staid and stately

banker, the daring entrepreneur. He was invested in a myriad of enterprises: fashion, entertainment, industry, ship-
ping, a silver mine, a diamond field, and even an airplane
manufacturing firm in Billancourt, France.

He was a paradox, an anomaly in an age of monotonous
consistency. He was rock-firm dependable yet the most ex-
citingly unpredictable man Adrian had ever encountered.
On nights when she yearned for a cozy evening in bed he
would hustle her into the waiting car, direct his chauffeur to
drive on, and off they would go to the Hippodrome Theater
to watch *The Ballet of Niagara* and *The Earthquake*, two
lavish productions complete with a breathtakingly realistic
depiction of the Niagara cataract and a full-scale reproduc-
tion of an ancient Aztec village.

On the nights she preferred to see the bright lights of the
city, Jason would plan an evening at home, dinner *à deux*,
catered from Sherry's. Three white-coated waiters would
serve, impeccably, silently, and throughout the meal Jason
would be the correct and punctilious host, addressing
Adrian as "Miss Marlowe," touching on only the ritual
topics of dinnertime discourse: the weather, the theater, or
the timeless classic novels of the past. But when dinner was
over, when the waiters had packed up their accoutrements
and vanished like silent wraiths, Jason would sweep Adrian
into his arms, proclaiming his ardor like a lovesick swain,
vowing that he could not wait another moment to ravish her
fair white body. And, lifting her off her feet, he would carry
her up the stairs, huffing and puffing and complaining of her
weight, finally depositing her, with a groan of relief, in an
ignominious heap on her bed.

Yes, she was happy with Jason, indescribably happy, but
she wondered at times, with a jealousy that astounded her,
how many women he had made love to before her. He was
thirty-six years old, and a man of that age—attractive, desirable, and utterly unattached—must have had hundreds of

lovers. Not that it mattered, Adrian would tell herself sensibly. *She* was his lover now. From here on in he would neither want nor have anyone else but her.

Or would he?

At times his attitude baffled her. Although an interested business associate, an attentive escort, and the most sensuously passionate of lovers, Jason never truly revealed to Adrian his innermost feelings about her. She doubted that he loved her, and though she loved him deeply, with an intensity and loyalty of which she had thought herself incapable, she was somewhat relieved that he only seemed fond of her.

She was glad in a way that he did not love her, because his love would entail a commitment and responsibility she was not yet ready to undertake. As he had said, the fashion house came first with her. She simply could not allow anything to displace it in her priorities. Someday perhaps, when she was thirty or thereabouts, she would think about marrying Jason, having his children, devoting herself to home and hearth as a good wife should. But in the meantime she was content with things as they were. Only . . . only . . . she would sometimes find herself wishing that he *did* love her—even a little. It would be ever so much nicer if he loved her.

She never once stopped to wonder, in the midst of these random musings, why she had so easily surrendered her virginity without sanction of marriage. The reason was simple, had she only thought to examine it. Although she was convinced Jason did not love her, she loved him so completely and without reserve that giving herself to him seemed, in retrospect, as natural as breathing, as inevitable as the sun rising daily in the east. It never occurred to her that she was married to him in her heart. The commitment she sought to avoid had already been made. She belonged to Jason more totally, more irrevocably than if their union had been solemnized a dozen times over. And, for the rest of her life, she knew she would never love any man but him.

* * *

Shortly before her fashion house was to open, the door-bell rang one morning as Adrian was dressing for work. Her heart gave a thump. Jason, she thought. Hastily knotting the tie on her dressing gown, she slipped into a pair of mules, then descended the stairs with a happy staccato clatter. But, when she opened the front door, Evan Colby answered her expectant smile, obviously delighted that she seemed so pleased to see him.

"Evan!" she said, concealing her disappointment. "How nice to see you. What brings you here at this hour?"

"May I come in?" His hat was in his hands; his eyes held an apology. "I need to talk to you. I won't keep you long. We both have jobs to go to."

The last was spoken with a trace of irony, and Adrian chose to ignore it. "Yes, of course," she said at once. "Come in. There's some fresh coffee in the pot. I'll heat it up."

She took his hat and coat, and he followed her to the kitchen. The room shone. Fresh curtains hung at the windows; the black stove gleamed from a recent polishing. A bowl of shiny apples graced the small circular table, which was covered with a spotless lace cloth.

"What a change," Evan said, seating himself as Adrian heated the coffee. "Have you rehired the servants?"

Adrian laughed, placing cups and saucers on the table. "No. Believe it or not, I'm doing the housekeeping."

"You?" He eyed her askance. "Where do you find the time?"

She was searching for the sugar bowl in one of the cup-boards. She paused momentarily, her back to Evan. With a smile he did not see she said softly, "When something is important to me, I make the time."

"Since when has a tidy house been important to you?"

Adrian had located the sugar; she brought it to the table.

"Oh, I don't know." She poured coffee, then sat down. "I suppose I've come to the conclusion that a house in order keeps one's life in order."

Evan said nothing to this but continued to regard her with skeptical curiosity. Finally he tasted his coffee, found it too hot to drink, then set the cup back in the saucer.

His behavior, to Adrian, was both puzzling and unlike him. He obviously had something on his mind that he was reluctant to disclose. This was not the Evan she knew, the man who had no qualms about speaking his mind to her.

"What's wrong?" she asked gently, laying a hand on his. "Why did you want to see me? And why are you upset?"

He had been staring at his cup; he raised his eyes abruptly. "Who said I was upset?"

"Evan, please," she said with a sigh. "We've known each other far too long to try to deceive each other. Tell me why you're here; tell me what's bothering you."

Almost against his will, it seemed to Adrian, he asked, "Is it true what I've been reading in the scandal sheets?"

A thrill of alarm darted through her. Slowly she withdrew her hand from his. "What have you been reading?" she asked, although she was more than certain that Evan, like the whole of New York City, had been reading about her gay whirl of all the posh night spots in town in the company of Jason Carradine.

Evan's hazel eyes reproached her. To Adrian's annoyance and chagrin she felt her face color. Evan said in a stern voice, "I thought we were going to be honest with each other."

She regarded him in silence. Jason had warned her about this: "The gossip hounds and yellow journals will have a field day with the fact that you're being seen about town with me. Facts don't much matter to those people. They'll conjure up all manner of titillating news about us. They'll have me drunk in Delmonico's or you doing the

Highland fling on a table at Rector's. Will that bother you, Adrian?''

"No, why should it?" she had asked.

"Then will it bother anyone you care about?"

Thinking at once about Tessa, and knowing Tessa's loyalty, Adrian had answered with certainty, "Not at all."

But now, face-to-face with Evan's protective disapproval, she wished she had given better heed to Jason's cautionary words.

"Evan," she said with a smile designed to placate, "don't you know better than to believe what you read in those dreadful newspapers?"

"Then you haven't been seeing Carradine?"

She realized her smile had not had the slightest effect on him. "Evan, yes, I've been seeing him. But I haven't been behaving like a hoyden in public as those newspapers would have you believe."

"How could you?" he said so sharply that she jumped. "How could you dine with that man, attend the theater with him, hang on his arm and 'gaze up at him adoringly'?"

Despite his anger, she could not suppress a smile. "I see you've been reading the *Tattler.*"

"Adrian, you seem to think this all a great joke. I can accept the fact that you must work with Carradine, but to willingly socialize with him—my God, it's inexcusable!"

His vehemence took her aback, though it did not much surprise her. She should have known that when Evan learned she was seeing Jason, he would not take kindly to the idea. But the truth of the matter was that for the past few months Adrian had given little or no thought to Evan Colby.

"Evan," she said reasonably, "I can understand your concern. I used to be under the same misconceptions as you about Jason. But he's not at all the rogue we thought him to be. And the truth of the matter is . . ." She paused, reluctant to hurt Evan but determined nonetheless to make clear to him once and for all that his longtime romantic pursuit of her was truly a hopeless quest. "The fact is," she went on resolutely, "that I'm in love with Jason Carradine."

"In love with him? Are you mad? You know what he is; you know what he did to your uncle."

"He did nothing to my uncle," she said quietly. "Jason explained what happened with United Copper—"

"And you believed him?" Evan cried. "Adrian, the man lies as easily as he breathes. How do you think he gained his reputation as the 'Prince of Wall Street'? When his father was alive, Carradine's was a respectable banking house. When Jason took over, he turned it into a circus, financing every outlandish venture that took his fancy. He's nothing more than a P. T. Barnum, for God's sake. He hoodwinks and deceives to make his enormous profits; he cheats and steals and—"

"Evan, stop it," she said firmly. "None of that is true."

His face was white with rage. Adrian strongly suspected that jealousy had motivated his tirade, jealousy of her and of Jason's wealth and success. Jason's methods were unorthodox—that much was true—but Adrian knew enough now about his work to know that Evan's envy-induced accusations were totally inaccurate.

"I know what this is all about," she said when Evan assumed a semblance of calm. "You're angry that I'm seeing him, and you're determined to tarnish his image in my eyes. But I know Jason too well to—"

"How well do you know him?" His voice shook.

"That's none of your business, Evan."

"Are you sleeping with him?"

She flushed and did not answer. Evan's face went even whiter.

He rose slowly as if in pain. Adrian watched him in silence, regretting the profound injury she had inflicted on him.

"You're a fool, you know," Evan said. "You've merely added your name to a long list of conquests. Carradine changes women like he changes his shirts. If you're hoping to marry him you'd better forget about it."

"I don't *want* to marry him," she said, her face flaming.

"If you believe that," Evan said bitterly, "then you're a bigger fool than I think you are."

He turned abruptly and left the room. Presently Adrian heard the front door open and close. She stared at the apples shining brightly in their china bowl. They seemed to mock her with their cheerfulness. The entire kitchen in its pristine cleanliness, seemed to taunt her for causing pain to a dear friend she loved. Evan had hurt her as well by suggesting that Jason was merely toying with her; but that didn't seem nearly as important. She had deliberately hurt Evan by revealing her relationship with Jason. Evan had only told Adrian something she already knew. Jason did not love her, nor did he wish to marry her. Adrian should have been relieved, since she herself had no wish to marry at this time. Why, then, did she suddenly want to weep?

Twelve

ON DECEMBER 3, a bracing, cold day brightly lucent with winter sun, the House of Marlowe opened its gilded doors to the public. The grand opening celebration had a Christmas motif. Sprigs of mistletoe and aromatic pine wreaths decorated the showroom; liveried footmen, serving canapés and wine, wore small sprays of holly on their satin lapels. On a raised platform in the center of the showroom an enormous fir tree stood in stately splendor, its spreading branches laden with jaunty red bows, sparkling, jeweled ornaments, and virtually hundreds of tiny electric bulbs casting pinpoints of diamond light against the emerald-green darkness of the tree.

Adrian herself paid tribute to the season in a medieval-style gown of red panne velvet cut low in the bosom and trimmed at bodice and sleeves with a delicate banding of blond Venice lace. In her sable hair she wore a velvet rosette nestled cunningly on lace, and a matching band of lace encircled the slender span of her ivory throat.

Her dark eyes sparkled; her lips and cheeks glowed with a color of their own. As she greeted her guests—society matrons, debutantes, Broadway actresses, deep-breasted divas from the Met—she radiated an aura of electric anticipation that added to the charm of her youthful vitality. She had never felt better, she had never been happier, nor had she ever looked more beautiful than she did on this day.

The unveiling of her spring line, a dazzling parade of

breathtaking color and fabric in rose-hued organza, saffron crepe, periwinkle gauzes, and clingy silk-metallics in silver and gold, was an undisputed triumph. Her live manne-quins—the first New York City had ever seen—were a sensation: four young ladies, all dark-haired, tall and whip-pet-slim, with kohled eyes and vermilion lips, slid slinkily across a lighted runway, showing Adrian's avant-garde de-signs to their most striking advantage.

The ladies present were entranced; their escorts gaped, awestruck.

"Miss Marlowe," said Heinrich von Hapsburg, the patron and escort of the superb Nellie Melba, "forgive me, but your mannequins appear to be . . . unclothed beneath their gowns. Am I imagining . . ."

"It is an illusion, Herr von Hapsburg," said Adrian, at her most charming. "I have designed a form of foundation garment that permits the female contour its own natural line. Many medical men have strenuously advocated that women should discard the unhealthful constriction of tight linen and whalebone. May I assume, from your interest that you agree with them?"

"Indeed, yes!" he said emphatically. "A lady's health must come first. Most judicious, most wise! I cannot wait to see madame so attired."

And off he went to induce the luscious Melba to place an immediate order for the "judicious" and delightfully titillating underpinnings.

As the showing proceeded Adrian gazed around at the as-sembled crowd. She smiled at Helen Frick, Henry Clay's lovely daughter, and waved a greeting to Grace Vanderbilt and her husband. All of New York's most elegant citizens had turned out for the grand opening of her fashion house. Ziegfeld's ladies were there, and his irrespressible wife. Ava Astor, newly divorced from Jack, had come with an at-tractive and much younger man. The junior Morgans were present, and the ethereally beautiful Maude Adams. They, and so many more like them, were her friends now, courtesy of Jason. Adrian's life, in less than a year, had taken a spectacular turn down a new and exciting path she had only dreamt she would ever travel. With Jason's help the dream had become a reality.

It was sadly ironic then that Jason was not here with her today to share her glory. He was currently in Albany with the governor, discussing bond issues for new state roadways, badly needed now because of the increasing popularity of the automobile. Adrian missed him; she missed him sorely. Somehow, because he was not here to share it with her, her sense of triumph and accomplishment was greatly diminished.

When the showing ended, Adrian drifted around the pine-fragrant salon, receiving plaudits and praise with a gracious nod, a grateful smile, and a personal word to each patron present. Her fashions were an unqualified success. The ladies were already asking the date of her next showing, and several young debs commented blushingly that they had most liked Adrian's wedding dress design with its elegant and timeless Hellenic silhouette.

A full contingent of journalists and photographers from every newspaper in the city were on hand to report the grand opening for their Sunday editions. At the show's conclusion Adrian was interviewed at length by the various reporters; some were complimentary, some highly impertinent.

"Miss Marlowe," said a brash young man, wearing a green checkered suit and a yellow bow tie, "don't you think your designs are a little risqué?"

"Risqué?" Adrian said sweetly, as if the word were unfamiliar to her. "In what way?"

"Well, they're revealing, aren't they?" he pointed out suggestively. "They leave nothing to the imagination, if you follow my drift."

"My designs," said Adrian with care while the other journalists listened avidly, pencils poised, "are modest to the extreme. You will note that not one gown even hints at
décolletage. I believe a woman's charm should come from
within and not from an overabundance of overexposed
flesh."

"But what about the underclothes?" the young journalist
asked, smirking. "Or rather, the lack of underclothes.
Those mannequins were naked as jaybirds under those
'modest' dresses. Now how do you think the city's clergy is
going to react to that, Miss Marlowe?"

Pencils scribbled at a breakneck pace. A few of the journalists pressed closer for Adrian's answer. She took a deep breath,
and in a controlled voice, she responded, "Mr. Crandall, if
you and the other gentlemen will accompany me to the dressing room, I'll be happy to give you all a firsthand look at what
my mannequins were wearing under their gowns."

The journalists followed eagerly, nudging one another
with winks and leers. The photographers readied their
equipment. In the dressing room the mannequins, in silk
robes, were relaxing on the cushioned divan or at the vanity,
chatting excitedly about the success of the showing.

"Dolores," said Adrian to the tallest and most attractive
of the group, "would you mind showing these gentlemen
what you're wearing under your robe?"

The mannequin turned sultry, kohled eyes to the hovering
journalists; then, uncoiling herself from the depths of the divan, she rose to her feet and slowly began to untie the knot at
her sash.

The journalists moved closer excitedly, eyes bulging.
The photographers positioned themselves for a sensational
"shoot."

Dolores, in the best tradition of one of Ziegfeld's showgirls, dropped the sash that secured her robe, slipped the material from her shoulders, then draped the garment behind

her so that her white underclothing was dramatically high-
lighted against a sensuous background of shimmering black
silk.

A buzz of excitement burst forth from the newsmen; pencils scribbled furiously. As the photographers fired their
magnesium troughs, the room lighted brilliantly, then filled
with an acrid cloud of smoke. Dolores posed serenely, her
kohl-smudged eyes fixed on her audience with the aloof de-
tachment of an Egyptian deity. Adrian watched her in quiet
admiration. She had chosen well this former Floradora girl
to be the first and the finest of the House of Marlowe mannequins.

"As you can see, gentlemen," said Adrian when the last
picture had been taken and every extravagant adjective had
been expended, "my mannequins were indeed clothed beneath their gowns. Now, if you'll all be good enough to excuse me, I think I should be seeing to my guests."

She thanked each journalist and photographer individu-
ally, gave a grateful nod to Dolores, then returned to the
salon with a qualm of misgiving. She hoped she had done
the right thing. Publicity was what she wanted, but it had to
be favorable. The press, as a whole, had been supportive
and encouraging, but there had been one or two skeptics, especially that wretch from the *World* in his atrocious checkered suit. His reports, Adrian feared, would be less than
complimentary. Well, it was too late to worry about that
now. What was done was done, and she would have to face
the consequences, good or bad.

The salon, when she returned to it, was aglow with color
and beauty. The patrons were milling around, sipping
French wine and chattering excitedly about the fashions.
Evan Colby, Adrian noted, had put in an appearance and
was conversing in a corner with Tessa. He was watching
Adrian even though he was apparently listening intently to
Tessa. Adrian moved through the crowded room in his di-

rection, thinking hopefully that his presence here today signaled an end to his anger with her.

"Congratulations," Evan said as she approached him. "You're the town's newest celebrity."

His tone was sincere, but his hazel eyes were bitter. His anger, Adrian guessed, had not altogether left him.

"Thank you, Evan," she said, and laid an affectionate hand on his sleeve. "I'm really glad you came today."

"I wouldn't have missed it for the world," he said. But although he was making all the correct comments, the expression in his eyes was impossible to ignore.

Adrian wished they were alone and that Tessa were not standing alongside them watching Evan curiously, apparently aware of the anger he strove unsuccessfully to conceal. Tessa knew of her relationship with Jason, but she did not know that Evan knew of it. Knowing Tessa's feelings for Evan, Adrian could not bring herself to tell her how profoundly she had hurt him.

"Tessa," she said brightly, attempting to ease the tension, "the Vanderbilts alone have placed an order in excess of ten thousand dollars!"

"I'm not surprised," said Tessa complacently. "I always knew you were going to succeed. *You* were the one with all the doubts."

Adrian smiled at her valued colleague and gave her slim waist a hug. Tessa looked enchanting in one of Adrian's new designs, a sea-foam green sheath that intensified the color of her elfin green eyes and brought out all the golden lights in her honey-blond hair. Evan was watching the two women, a curious, hard look on his face. Abruptly he said to Tessa, "If you're free later on I'd like to take you to dinner."

Tessa stared at him for a moment, then turned with a questioning look to Adrian. Adrian, looking at Evan, said, "That's a splendid idea. Why don't you go to the Lobster

Palace? Tessa's mad for seafood.'' But her eyes said, Please don't hurt her, Evan. *I'm* the one who has disappointed you, not she.

"Tessa?" Evan said, his hazel gaze still on Adrian. "Does that suit you?"

"Why, yes," Tessa said uncertainly. "I'd love to eat at the Lobster Palace."

He turned to her at last. His eyes, Adrian noted with relief, gentled somewhat as Tessa smiled up at him expectantly.

"Good," he said, his hard mouth relaxing. "Perhaps afterward," he added, glancing once more at Adrian, "we can go to the theater."

Adrian excused herself and left her two friends. Evan's intention was clear: He was trying to rouse Adrian's jealousy. She could only hope that his ploy would prove beneficial in a way he had not calculated. Tessa loved him; she loved him deeply. Perhaps once Evan realized this, his hopeless obsession with Adrian would end.

"Miss Marlowe, may I have a word with you, please?"

Adrian turned to see the brash reporter from the *World* lounging against a pillar, his hands in the pockets of his atrocious checkered trousers, his battered felt hat pushed to the back of his head, exposing an uncombed riot of carrot-colored hair.

"Yes, Mr. Crandall?"

She left the matrons and gave her attention to this very unpleasant man. His young, freckled face was incongruously predatory: he had a short, upturned nose and a small childish mouth; but his eyes, gray and narrow, were ageless, and they rested with lascivious insolence on the curve of Adrian's breast.

"Miss Marlowe, I was wondering . . ." His eyes traveled upward with insulting insinuation. ". . . would you care to take supper with me when you're finished here?"

His invitation was unmistakable; it was more than supper he wanted. Adrian shuddered distastefully, but in her most courteous voice she answered, "I'm so sorry, Mr. Crandall. I am engaged this evening."

"Perry," he said.

"What?"

"My first name is Perry."

"Oh, yes, well, I'm sorry. I can't have supper with you tonight."

"Tomorrow night then?"

"I'm sorry." She managed a smile. "I can't."

"Miss Marlowe," he said, his gaze lowering once more to the curve of her breast, "let me explain to you the reason for my invitation. Perhaps then you might think it well worth your while to spend some time with me. I'm planning to do a series of articles on you and your fashion house. I find you unique, and I think my readers will, too."

"Mr. Crandall," she said impatiently, "I'm complimented by your interest, but I couldn't possibly—"

"You don't seem to understand," he interrupted, and although his tone was conversational, it was undeniably threatening. "I *must* do this series on you; it's my job, you see. And I shouldn't want to submit a report to my editor without fully investigating all the facts of my story."

Adrian faced him, unwavering. Bullies had never intimidated her. And this man was a bully of the very lowest kind. He was the kind of man she had always despised, the man who saw women as mere objects, mindless toys, who were put on earth solely to be submissive to a man's every whim.

"Mr. Crandall," she said, "you have your facts. There is nothing more I can tell you."

Crandall shifted position against the pillar and fixed her with his lewd, gray gaze. "Miss Marlowe," he said in that softly threatening voice, "let me tell you how I see you. You're a woman who's worked hard to achieve success.

You like to think for yourself—one can see that right off from your"—his eyes, like a slimy caress, slid over her breasts—"designs. I would imagine that you dislike the ordinary, the commonplace. In other words you're like myself: We both of us have little or no use for convention."

"Mr. Crandall," she said stiffly, "I have guests I must attend to. Will you kindly get to the point?"

"The point is this," he responded with an odiously suggestive smile. "I want to discover more about you; *all* about you, in fact. I think your work, dealing as it does exclusively with women, leaves you—shall we say, 'hungry'?— for a man's companionship. Come to supper with me tonight, and then afterward we'll go to my flat. To be perfectly frank, Miss Marlowe, I want to see for myself if those bouncy little breasts of yours are half as seductive naked as they are beneath that extremely enticing undergarment."

Adrian's face flushed with insult and a hot, killing rage. "You'd better leave," she said in a shaking voice. "If you know what's good for you you'll leave here right now and never set foot in this salon again."

She turned to walk away, but with a lizard-swift movement Crandall's hand shot out of his pocket and fastened, like a claw, on her arm. "Don't refuse me," he said ominously. "You'll regret it if you do."

Adrian's skin prickled at his touch. She had known he was dangerous; she had felt it in her bones. Beneath that Huck Finn mop of hair and that spattering of boyish freckles, this man was a cesspool of malevolence and filth.

She wrenched out of his hold and had to forcibly restrain herself from cracking him across the jaw. "Stay away from me," she warned, choking with rage, "or *you'll* be the one with regrets."

He took a step toward her. She backed away as if scorched.

"Stay away from me," she said again. "Or I swear to you, I'll have the law on you."

He stopped in his tracks and regarded her narrowly, his hostile gray eyes pledging harsh retaliation. Adrian braved his hard gaze, her courage greatly bolstered by a roomful of people. It was Crandall who then yielded, although Adrian's victory was dubious, for she knew that this was far from the end of the matter. Crandall doffed his hat and made a low, mocking bow; but before he took his leave, he said with a vengeful smile, "Miss Marlowe, you're going to eat those words."

Thirteen

CRANDALL'S HARD, sneering face and his soft-spoken threats frightened Adrian more than she realized. For days afterward she did not leave the house without first peering out the windows and the front door. On the streetcar to Herald Square and on the crowded midtown streets, she constantly looked over her shoulder as if expecting at any moment the smirking wretch in his checkered suit to leap up at her from the stinking sewers whence he had likely been spawned.

The brilliant triumph of her first showing was thus twice eclipsed: Jason had not been present, and Perry Crandall of the *New York World* was planning revenge.

He had already begun to do damage with his venom-tipped pen. The *World*'s coverage of the grand opening of the House of Marlowe was an inflammatory piece, maliciously designed to depict Adrian as a woman of questionable virtue whose aim, via her fashions, was to seriously impair the morals of American women. Joseph Pulitzer, the editor, although ailing and nearly blind, wrote a scathing denouncement of Adrian and her designs, instigated no doubt by his vengeance-bent reporter, whose own virtue and morals were ironically nonexistent.

At the salon Adrian was edgy; she could not keep her mind on her work. Tessa noticed Adrian's preoccupation, and when she questioned her, Adrian gratefully poured out the entire sordid episode. "I'm frightened," she admitted.

"Crandall's dangerous, I know it. The matter is not over as far as he's concerned."

"Do you want to stay at my flat for a while?" Tessa offered.

"No," Adrian said. "I don't want you involved in case anything should happen."

Alarmed, Tessa asked, "What do you expect to happen?"

"I don't know." Her voice was tense. "But I'm afraid."

"Adrian . . ." Tessa rose from the sewing machine and slipped a comforting arm round her waist. "Do you want me to speak to Evan? Perhaps he can think of something to do."

Adrian smiled at her friend, momentarily forgetting her worries. In her fear of Crandall's reprisal she had completely forgotten that Evan was now seeing Tessa on a steady basis. "How are you two getting on?" she asked. "I've been so wrapped up in my own concerns that I haven't given your relationship a thought."

Tessa gave Adrian's waist a final squeeze, then returned to the sewing machine. "I think he's serious," she answered. "He keeps talking about 'the future.' Not *our* future, but he keeps telling me what his plans are, how many children he would like to have when he marries, his idea of a social life, and so forth." Tessa laughed lightly. "He's terribly old-fashioned, you know. He says women who choose to work are doing themselves a great injustice. Any wife of his, he says, wouldn't *want* to work because he would provide for her amply, and treat her like a queen besides. I find him endearing, Adrian, despite his antiquated beliefs." Tessa paused momentarily and lowered her gaze. "I love him so much," she added softly.

Adrian smiled at her friend and gave an inward sigh of relief. Evan obviously cared for Tessa. He would not otherwise be making plans for the future.

"Tessa," she said sincerely, "I'm very happy for you.

Evan needs someone to love him. I couldn't be happier that it's you.''

Tessa looked up and returned her smile. Then, sobering, she said, ''Adrian, about Crandall . . . do you want me to speak to Evan?''

Crandall. His very name gave Adrian the shudders.

''No,'' she said. ''Don't worry him unnecessarily. Jason will be home soon from Albany. He'll know what to do about Perry Crandall and his threats.''

Several nights after that, the doorbell sounded as Adrian was preparing for bed. She glanced with a frown at the bed-side clock. It was close to midnight. Who could be calling at this hour? And then she thought joyously: *Jason!*

She stole a quick glance at the long mirror. She was still dressed, in a work dress of navy blue wool, but her hair was unbound, falling in tumbling waves against her suddenly flushed cheeks. She debated momentarily about pinning it up but then decided not to because Jason so loved the sable length of her luxurious hair.

Instead she merely straightened her white collar, tugged at her cuffs, then, with a heart thumping wildly with happiness and love, she flew down the stairs and flung open the front door.

But it was not Jason who stood on the steps in the icy night air. It was two policemen, their faces ruddy from the cold and the breath from their nostrils flaring whitely like puffs of dragon smoke.

''Miss Marlowe?'' said the older of the two, an unmistakable Irishman with the brogue of County Meath still thick on his tongue. ''Miss Adrian Marlowe?''

''Yes?'' It took her a moment to answer, so surprised and disappointed was she by the sight of these two strangers. ''I'm Adrian Marlowe.''

"You are the proprietress of the House of Marlowe, situated in the Graham Buildin' on the Sixth Avenue?"

"Yes, that's right," she said, puzzled, and now shivering from the cold. "What is it you want from me?"

"Miss Marlowe, you're under arrest. Would you get your things and come with us, please?"

"Arrest?" She shivered again. "Is this a joke? On what charge are you arresting me?"

The officer drew out a warrant from his tunic pocket. "For lewd and lascivious conduct," he read in an impassive monotone. "For the possession of lewd and lascivious goods. For the sale of lewd and lascivious—"

"Stop!" she demanded, and snatched the warrant from his hand. "This is insane. I know who's responsible for this, and he won't get away with it. I have my rights; you can't arrest me!"

"We can, miss," the policeman contradicted, "and we will. Now, if you'll kindly come quietly and not be makin' a fuss you can telephone your attorney from the station house, and if it's a mistake someone's made, sure and you can discuss it in the mornin' with the judge."

"In the morning?" she ejaculated. "Do you mean to tell me I have to spend the night in jail?"

"I'm afraid so, miss."

"I won't!" she cried. "I won't! I refuse!"

But she had no choice. The policeman made it clear to her that if she did not comply peaceably, he and his partner would have no recourse but to carry her bodily to the patrol wagon.

She complied but not silently. On the way to the station house she assured the hapless arresting officers that if it was the last thing she did, she would sue every city employee from the lowliest sanitation man to the mayor himself. What kind of city was this, anyway, hauling innocent citizens off to jail in the middle of the night? She had done nothing,

nothing, and here she was, being treated like the most despicable of criminals while *real* criminals—lunatics, murderers, rapists, and thieves—were running loose about town, committing crimes.

At the station house she was no less vociferous. After telephoning her attorney, who was not at home, and leaving a message, she demanded of the desk sergeant to be set free.

"I've done nothing!" she shouted, awakening a burglar on a bench and the vagrant to whom he was manacled. "I design dresses, for heaven's sake! You have no right to detain me. I insist you release me. I will not stay here; I will not spend even one minute in this jail!"

But she did. She spent, in fact, an entire night as a guest of the city, a night she would not soon forget.

Her cell was called a holding tank, for it was here that prisoners were held while awaiting transport or disposition to courts or other confinement. It was a damp, filthy, unheated room, with mildewed stone walls, a cracked concrete floor, two cots with mangy blankets, and a chamber pot in the corner that smelled abominably.

There were six or seven women in detention, of various professions—pickpockets, prostitutes, drunkards, and "shills" —and they, too, smelled abominably in the cramped airless confines of the cell. Most of the inmates were grouped near the one narrow window in the room, breathing deeply of the outside air, and they ignored Adrian's entrance. But one, a middle-aged woman with an enormous bosom and a broad, rosy face, introduced herself as Gertie the Grifter, and she introduced also a heartbreakingly young prostitute named Annie Laurie Higgins, who had a thatch of straw-colored hair and a tubercular complexion. She lay hunched on one of the cots with the blanket pulled up to her childishly rounded chin.

"Hey, dearie," said Gertie as Adrian was locked in, "ain't I seen your pitcher in the newspapers?"

"Perhaps," said Adrian warily, standing stiffly by the bars.

"P'raps!" Gertie laughed. "Well, you must be a grand duchess at least with such hoity-toity language. Annie, look here. Don't she look familiar? Who is she, love? One of the Astor bunch?"

"Who cares?" said Annie Laurie, and burrowed her thin child's body more deeply under the blanket.

The cell stank unbearably. Adrian pulled a handkerchief from her sleeve and held it to her nose. As she did so a fat rat scurried across the floor, and she screamed. The other inmates ignored the scream, but Gertie laughed uproariously and sank down on the cot beside Annie, who promptly gave her a whack on the back of the head.

"Get on your own cot!" the child said, coughing.

"Ah, Annie," the woman coaxed, "let Lady Astor have the other. You and I can double up. Lord knows we done it plenty a times afore."

Gertie horselaughed again as if this were the funniest of jokes. Annie shrugged and settled down, gazing listlessly at the ceiling with feverish, dark eyes. Adrian stared at them both as if they were creatures from another planet.

"Sit down, girl," Gertie told her. "Tell us how a social-ite like you happens to be penned up with low lifes the likes of this bunch here."

"I am not," Adrian began nervously, "a socialite. I work for a living. I'm a dress designer. And I'm in here because—"

"That's who you are!" Gertie exclaimed. "You're that coo-too-ree-ay who's been in the newspapers all week. Annie, we've got a celebrity with us! This is that woman who designs them fancy clothes. Ain't you read about her?"

"You know I can't read," Annie answered disinterest-edly. But then, glancing at Adrian's white face and rigid body, she propped herself up painfully on an elbow, and with a touching attempt at courtesy, she asked, "What're you in for, sister?"

This had to be a dream. Adrian was not in jail, exchanging social pleasantries with a confidence woman and a prostitute. She was not standing here with the cold sting of metal bars pressing hard against her back; she was not casting wary glances around the cell, waiting to see if the cat-size rat reappeared. This was a dream . . . no, a nightmare. She would wake in a moment and find herself snug and warm in her bed on Washington Square.

But it was not a dream, she realized grimly as the endless night wore on. She was in jail, where she would likely rot forever. She knew who had put her here, and she would have loved to get her hands on him. Perry Crandall, damn his hide, had exacted his revenge.

Oddly, she was never thereafter able to clearly recall all the details of that night. She would only remember standing for hours—she was afraid to sit down—and Gertie's stentorian laugh and poor Annie's wracking, insistent cough. She would vaguely recall the other inmates as a silent, ghostly group, standing massed at the window, their matted hair and filthy clothing exuding a revolting odor that was hardly worse or better than the fetid fumes of the uncovered chamber pot.

Near dawn, when she thought she could bear it no longer, when a thin, gray light struggled weakly through the window and cast a wan, sickly glimmer on the vermin-infested floor, the cell door was unlocked, and the turnkey told Adrian, "You're free, miss. Pick up your things at the desk, and then you can go home."

She stumbled out of the cell in an insensate daze. Gertie and Annie had fallen asleep; the other women still stood with pallid faces lifted to catch a ray of the pale winter sun. Adrian took one last look at the cell that had housed her for six hours but had seemed like so many years, then she went down the hall to collect her personal belongings.

At the sergeant's desk Charles Harrison, her attorney, awaited her. He was Jason's attorney actually, and he was attired in evening clothes, Adrian's message apparently having reached him at the end of a long night's entertainment. He was just Jason's age, dark-haired, attractive, and a bachelor as well, but he lacked Jason's flair and his electric vitality. He was an excellent attorney, though, and Adrian trusted and respected him.

"Adrian!" he greeted her. "I'm awfully sorry about the delay. I came as soon as I could."

She nodded dully as he helped her on with her coat. "It doesn't matter, Charlie. You're here now. I just want to go home; they said I could go home."

"Yes, you can," he assured her. "This has all been a most unfortunate mistake. Jason is on his way here now. He's just left Judge Lorimar—"

"Jason?" she said as she collected her things from the desk sergeant, "He's back from Albany?"

"Yes," Harrison answered. "I telephoned his house as soon as I got your message. He had only just arrived home when I called. I told him what had happened, and he told me to get right down here and that he'd speak to Lorimar and straighten everything out, which obviously he's done, because the charges have been dropped."

"Dropped?" she said as he escorted her from the building. "But, Charlie, why was I arrested in the first place? I know who's behind it all; it was that wretch from the *New York World*, Perry Crandall. But how did he—"

"Adrian," he said soothingly as he handed her down the steps, "you're not to worry about it anymore. Jason has taken care of everything. The charges have been dropped, and Perry Crandall, I daresay, is now on his way to Venezuela. A stupid man, Crandall. Oh, well, I suppose he didn't realize who he was dealing with. Ah, there's Jason now.''

The Rolls-Royce, long and black and dotted with early-morning dew, drew up to the curb just as Adrian and Harrison reached the sidewalk. Immediately the car stopped; Jason opened the door and stepped out onto the pavement. He merely nodded at Harrison. His prime concern was for Adrian. ''Are you all right?'' His tone was low, worried; he reached for her hands.

She moved away from his grasp, her face colorless. ''Don't touch me,'' she said in a choked voice. ''I feel like I'm crawling with lice. Just take me home; take me home quickly. I want to bathe and wash my hair. Take me home, Jason.''

He watched her a moment, taking in at a glance the revulsion and shock and extreme agitation she was striving valiantly to hold in check. She was trembling and pale; her eyes were unnaturally bright. He wanted to take her in his arms and press her close to his heart, and at the same time he wanted to seek out that journalist from the *New York World* and grind his face to a pulp beneath the heel of his boot.

''Charlie,'' he said gruffly, ''I'll telephone you later.'' Then to Adrian, more gently, ''Come along, I'll take you home.''

On the drive to Washington Square she did not speak, and he, in deference to her state of mind, kept silent as well. When they reached home, Adrian opened the door and scrambled out of the car, fairly racing up the walk to the house.

Dismissing the chauffeur, Jason followed her. When Adrian dropped her key, fumbling at the keyhole, Jason picked it up without a word and unlocked the door. Opening it wide, he stood aside to let her enter.

Once inside the house, Adrian shed her coat, letting it drop to the floor, then mounted the steps swiftly, unbuttoning her dress as she ascended, hardly aware that Jason was close behind her. She was in a fever to undress, to bathe, to wash the stench of the jail from her body and her hair. Her skin itched, her scalp prickled; she felt vile, contaminated, unspeakably befouled, as if she had spent a lifetime of nights in that desolate hellhole.

"Let me help you," said Jason carefully as she stood at the bathroom door, tugging furiously at her stockings, which seemed plastered to her legs.

"No!" she cried, and looked up at him fiercely through a veil of waving hair. "Don't touch me, Jason. I'm filthy, filthy!"

"All right," he said calmly, though his concern deepened at the look in her eyes. "All right, darling, go on and bathe. I'll wait for you in your room."

Not listening, not thinking, only desperate to be clean, she flung off the last of her clothing, went into the bathroom, slammed the door, and turned on the taps in the tub.

As the room filled with steam she searched frantically through the cupboard. Pulling out towels, wash cloths, sponges, and brushes, she pushed aside the various jars and bottles until she found the thick brown bar of Octagon soap at the back of the shelf. Only this pungent laundry soap was strong enough, harsh enough, to scrub clean the smell of putrefaction and decay that hung on in her nostrils like the stench of death itself.

When the tub was almost filled, she turned off the taps and went, by force of habit to the mirror to pin up her hair. But as she gazed at her white-faced reflection, at the abundant fall of hair that to her mind seemed overrun with vermin, she went back to the cupboard, opened the top drawer, and took out a large pair of shears. Returning to the mirror, without a second thought, she cut and cut and cut until there was almost nothing left of the glorious sable splendor that Jason so loved.

When she was done with her hair, she stepped into the tub, sat down with a groan, and began to lather her skin. The soap burned, but she welcomed the pain, for it was this burning acidity that would cleanse her skin at last, and her mind, too, it seemed, of malodorous filth. She soaped and scrubbed methodically until every last inch of her was tingling and red. It was only when she doused her head and touched the soap to her shorn tresses that she realized what she had done. And it was then and only then that she bowed her head, covered her face with trembling hands, and wept.

Fourteen

WHEN SHE EMERGED from the bathroom an hour later, Jason was not in her room, nor was he anywhere upstairs. Donning a cashmere robe and a pair of slippers, Adrian covered her hair turban-style with a clean towel and went downstairs to seek Jason out on the first floor. His hat and greatcoat were on the hall table, but he was nowhere in sight. Bewildered, Adrian stood in the kitchen, wondering where he could have gone, and then she heard his footsteps on the cellar steps.

"What were you doing?" she asked as he emerged from the cellar, coatless, tieless, his shirt sleeves rolled up and his face and hands grimy with soot.

"I burned the clothes you had on," he said, crossing to the sink where he briskly washed and toweled. "I burned everything"—he turned to face her—"including your coat and shoes. They weren't costly, I hope. I shall replace them if you like."

She regarded him in silence, too moved to speak. She depended on this man more than she ever had on anyone. At the moment this thought did not penetrate her consciousness. She did not think of how she had vowed at her uncle's funeral to depend on no one but herself. All she could think of now was how grateful she was to Jason and of how well he knew her. She had been planning to burn her clothing as soon as she finished in the bathroom, and Jason had spared her that distasteful task.

"Are you feeling better?" He leaned against the sink, one polished boot crossed over the other, his arms folded loosely against his lean middle. His face shone from its recent washing; a lock of damp hair clung to his brow, and his lids were half-lowered as he surveyed her with a smile. "You look very fresh and clean," he observed. "May I touch you now?"

"Yes," she whispered, drinking in the dear sight of him. "Yes." She flew to him joyously and threw her arms around his neck. And as he held her close and pressed his lips to her brow, she could only think over and over again how good he felt, how warm and hard and strong, and how very much she loved him, of how she loved him more than life.

Dimly she realized that she was behaving in a manner she had previously thought unacceptable: the loving, clinging woman, totally dependent on the strength of a man. Under other circumstances, if she were thinking clearly, she would have laughed with self-contempt at the picture she made. As it was, she could think of nothing else now but the warmth of Jason's nearness, infusing her with love and contentment.

"I missed you," he murmured as his hands caressed her back. "I missed you terribly while I was away. Did you miss me at all?"

He held her away from him to wait for her answer, and as he did so, the towel slipped from her head, exposing a tousled riot of short sable curls.

"My God," he said, shocked. "What have you done to your hair?"

Her chin came up with a mutinous jerk. She faced him defiantly, daring him to upbraid her. But beneath her show of bravado Jason sensed remorseful tears perilously close to the surface, and quickly he amended, "You look delightful, Adrian! Like a charming boy. Step back; let me have a good look." And after viewing the curling locks with a practiced eye, he said thoughtfully, "Do you know something? You just might set another trend with this coiffure. The Gamine Look, you could call it. No," he said, reconsidering. "Better yet: The Emancipation Bob. Yes, that's it! I like the idea. Think of it, Adrian. More freedom for women. No more hairpins, no crimping irons, no false switches—"

"Oh, Jason," she said anxiously, "do you mean it? It's not awful? I don't look hideous?"

"Hideous?" He smiled and pulled her back into his arms. "You couldn't look hideous if you tried."

She relaxed against him, warm and secure in the haven of his hold. How could she ever have thought she hated this man? She had never loved or needed anyone more. Yes, she needed him, she realized with a start. And that was odd, because she had always before thought, with the arrogance of youth, that she needed no one in life but herself.

"Adrian." His voice was low; his hand rested comfortingly at the nape of her neck. "Do you feel up to talking about it now? Do you want to tell me what happened?"

She shuddered at the memory, but drawing strength from his nearness and support, she moved out of his arms, sat down at the kitchen table, and told him the story from beginning to end.

He listened without a word, but his eyes, as she spoke, grew dark with a restrained, deadly rage. When she finished, he said in a rigid voice, "He never touched you? You've told me the truth? He never came near you after that day at the salon?"

"No," she said swiftly, for in his voice and his eyes there was a murderous intensity. "He never did, Jason!"

He took a deep breath. His gaze softened, and his voice gentled, too. "Very well, it's over then. Put it out of your mind. He won't bother you again; I give you my promise."

She did not doubt his word for a moment. She knew she had seen the last of Perry Crandall, and she could not have cared less how Jason had accomplished this. But one thought persisted.

"Jason, how did he do it?" she asked. "How did Crandall arrange to have me arrested?"

"A simple matter," he explained, leaning back against the sink, "and thoroughly devious, which doesn't surprise me in light of what you've told me about him. When Charlie Harrison telephoned me, he told me your warrant had been signed by Judge Lorimar. I telephoned Lorimar, who told me that Perry Crandall had presented him with a petition signed by a number of prominent clergymen in the city. The petition demanded legal action against the 'pernicious influence' of your designs."

"A petition?" she said, stunned. "Signed by *clergymen?*"

"Wait," Jason said. "Let me finish. After I spoke to Lorimar I telephoned the city editor of the *New York World*—he's a friend of mine who owes me a favor—and asked him for Crandall's address. I then paid a visit to Crandall, and we had a friendly chat."

"A friendly chat?" she said suspiciously.

"Yes." Jason smiled. "Crandall admitted to me—after a little persuasion—that the petition was a fraud, that he had had in his possession a legitimate petition to which was affixed a list of clergymen's signatures. This petition—to abolish prostitution, by the way—was given to him several months ago by one of the clergymen who asked Crandall to publish the names along with a front-page article on the subject. Crandall complied, I understand, and then kept the list of signatures. Yesterday he went to Judge Lorimar with those signatures attached to a petition Crandall himself had drawn up, a petition denouncing you and your designs."

"Oh, that wretch," she said bitterly. "And that puny weakling of a judge!"

"The judge," Jason explained further, "was merely hon-

oring the wishes of his constituency. A good number of the
men whose signatures were on that list lead congregations in
Lorimar's district. He was only acceding to the demands of
the community. When I proved that Crandall's petition was
a fraud, he immediately rescinded the warrant.''

Adrian was tempted to ask Jason exactly what manner of
''persuasion'' he had used to induce Crandall to confess his
foul deed. But then she decided not to. It was over; Crandall
was out of her life, and that was all that mattered to her now.

She looked up at Jason, her strength, her protector. Never
had he looked more desirable, never had his grace and
beauty been more arrestingly evident than it was at this moment. He was watching her quietly, his arms still folded
loosely, his eyes azure blue in the pale morning light. There
was the faintest trace of stubble on his jaw, but somehow it
only added to his beauty and to his extreme desirability.

Adrian wanted him physically; her desire to have him
now was more profound than anything she had ever experienced. She could feel his mouth on hers, his hands on her
body. She could feel the very joining of his flesh with her
flesh and the sweet consummation of his fierce, exquisite
love.

''I want you,'' she whispered, the words barely audible.
''I want you right now.''

''Do you?'' he said softly with a slow, lazy smile. ''Show
me, darling. Show me how much you want me.''

She rose from the table and went to him and wound her
arms around his neck and kissed his brow, his cheeks, his
chin, and took his face in her hands and kissed his warm
mouth. He stood passive yet alert, beneath her ardent aggression. She had never made love to him before; it had
been he, always, who set the sensuous pace of their love.
But it was she now who wooed, she who touched, caressed,
enticed, and enchanted with her hands, with her body, and
with her soft, searching mouth.

Beneath her passionate quest she could feel his quick arousal. She could feel the steady beating of his heart, the outline of his ribs, the lean line of his hips as she traced them, embraced them, with her hands and with her lips. She could feel his flesh quiver as she slipped off his shirt, kissed his throat, his shoulders, his lean, hard middle; and then his sharp indrawn breath as she loosened his trousers and slipped to her knees and wound her arms around his legs.

His hands were in her hair; she could feel his pleasure in the pressure of his fingers, could hear it in the short, aching, almost painful intake of his breath. His pleasure became hers, his desire fired her own. With infinite love and an unconstrained passion she possessed him absolutely, and she, in loving passion, was possessed absolutely by him.

She sank deeper and deeper into a sensual spell. Every nerve in her body vibrated with passion, and when he lifted her to her feet and his arms tightened around her, she melted against him, contentedly his captive, and gave herself up to the rapture of his kiss.

Still clinging, mouth on mouth, they sank to the floor, and then, easily, smoothly, he parted her robe, mounted her, entered her, then lay motionless, quivering, as her spell-binding passion radiated wave after wave of sensation through her own quivering form.

She strained toward him hungrily; she writhed in breathless ecstasy as he began to move inside her. His movements were slow, lingering, as if he wished to prolong both her pleasure and his. But she wished only release— swift, immediate, delicious release. She groped for his hips, and with hot, insistent hands, she altered the tempo of his tantalizing strokes. With her hands she demanded, with her mouth and her tongue she bewitchingly persuaded him to take her, possess her, with the same fierce desire that ignited a raging fire in her body and her soul.

His arms pressed her closer; his movements quickened

with a sudden, passionate intensity that matched her own. His mouth ravaged her, thrilled her, and the power of his passion fanned the fire of desire that blazed higher, uncontrollably, inside her. She felt driven to celestial heights of indescribable rapture. Locked in his embrace, entwined limb on limb, she felt that he and she were an inseparable entity, spiraling as one toward a glorious goal, which, when it came, bound them indivisibly together in a radiant starburst of an almost unendurably thrilling consummation.

For an interminable time afterward they neither stirred nor spoke nor uttered a sound. They remained in a tight embrace, his head on her breast, her fingers entwined in his damp, tangled hair. It was as if time had stood still and, with it, all reality. Only this was reality, she was thinking with drowsy content. Jason was reality; her love for him was reality. She belonged to him completely, and he . . .

To whom did Jason belong? she wondered with a sudden concern. She stirred restively beneath him as the thought displaced the sweet tranquillity of her drowsy content.

Jason looked up at her after a moment and shifted his weight. "Am I hurting you?" he asked.

"No." With her arms she detained him. "Don't get up. I want to ask you something."

"What is it?"

"How many women have you made love to?"

The question surprised him, and it obviously amused him. He smiled and bent his head and kissed the tip of her breast. "At last count," he considered, "it was six hundred and fifty-seven."

"Jason, be serious!"

"My darling girl," he laughed softly, "*you* be serious. I haven't the vaguest idea of how many women I've had. Why do you ask?"

"I want to know." She avoided his gaze.

"Why?" He took hold of her chin and forced her to face him.

Thus challenged, she could not respond. It was too humiliating to have to ask him outright if he thought of her as "just another of his women."

"I was curious," she finally answered.

"Why?" he asked again.

"I don't know, Jason." She buried her face in his chest. "I was wondering, that's all."

"How intriguing you are," she heard him say, and there was a smile in his voice, and his arms around her were loving and gentle. She felt his lips in her hair, and his hand stroked her thigh, her hip, and lingered with languorous leisure on the curving rise of her abdomen. For one wonderful moment she thought he was going to make love to her again, but he only kissed her brow briefly and rose and began to dress.

She rose, too, with a trace of disappointment, then she fastened her robe and ran a hand through her tumbled curls. As Jason donned his shirt and trousers he kept glancing over at her with a strange, searching look that somehow unnerved her.

"What's the matter?" she asked. "Why do you look at me like that?"

"I like to look at you," he answered lightly. "It gives me pleasure. Do you object?"

"No, of course I don't object. Only . . ."

"Only what?" he said, tucking his shirttails inside his trousers.

"Only you looked as if you were . . . sizing me up."

" 'Sizing you up'?" He laughed. "Good Lord, Adrian, where did you learn that appalling expression?"

"Jason, don't change the subject. Why did you look at me like that?"

The laughter faded from his eyes. He faced her directly,

his expression suddenly sober. "Well, you see," he said, "I was wondering something, too."

"What was it?" she asked.

"I was wondering," he said quietly, "if you're pregnant."

Pregnant? The question took her aback. "No, of course not," she said. "I mean, I don't think so. I mean . . ."

The truth of the matter was, she was not at all sure. Her menstrual cycle had always been erratic. She had never thought to monitor its regularity—there had previously been no need—and in the past few months she had been much too busy to even think about that monthly nuisance. But now, confronted squarely with the implication of its absence, she was forced to admit that the possibility that she was pregnant did indeed exist.

"Maybe I am," she said reluctantly, and she would not meet his gaze. "I can't be sure."

"I want you to make sure, Adrian."

His low tone was peremptory. She looked up, startled. His mouth was stern, his brow faintly creased in authoritative command.

His attitude irked her. "What if I am pregnant?" she said defiantly. "I won't marry you, you know."

"That's what you think."

"Jason, I won't, I tell you. This is my body. I'll do with it what I choose."

"Meaning what?" he said placidly, but in his eyes there was a tempest. "An abortion?"

"No! No, never!"

"Then what, Adrian? What is it you plan to do with my child's life?"

"*My* child, Jason!" she flung back at him. "If I am pregnant, *I* shall carry the child for nine months. *I* shall give birth to it."

"And my seed conceived it," he reminded her.

''I don't care!'' she cried wildly and glared at him furiously. ''I won't be forced into marriage; I won't be made a slave of! If I'm pregnant it's my affair and no one else's. Do you understand me?''

She faced him in a trembling fury. The effects of the long night had finally taken its toll on her. All the color drained from her face, and she swayed unsteadily on her feet and clutched at a nearby chair for support.

In an instant Jason was beside her, his arms folding protectively about her. ''All right,'' he said softly, pressing her close to his heart. ''All right, my stubborn little mule. Let's not talk of it now. Come upstairs, I'll put you to bed. And then later, perhaps tomorrow, we can discuss it more rationally.''

''Jason,'' she said wearily as he turned her toward the stairs, ''I won't marry you. I absolutely refuse.''

''Yes, very well, darling. But let's not talk of it now.''

''I won't do it,'' she maintained as they mounted the steps.

''Whatever you say, Adrian.''

''Jason,'' she insisted as they approached her bedroom, ''you can't force me. I won't marry you, no matter how you try to convince me.''

At the door to her room he stopped and looked down at her. In his eyes she detected a curious indecision, and at length he said slowly, ''What if I were to tell you that I love you and that I can't live without you?''

She was absolutely stunned by his unexpected words. Of all the persuasion he might have chosen to employ, this was the last she would have expected. But then it dawned on her that his startling admission was simply that: a ploy, a persuasion to induce her to marry him. Evan had told her that Jason changed women like he changed his shirts. Not for one moment did Adrian believe Jason would discard her as he had his other women, but neither was she going to take a chance on marrying him—which she didn't want to do in the first place—and then have him cast her aside when he was tired of her.

"I wouldn't believe you," she said, and glared up at him stubbornly.

Jason sighed and shook his head. "I didn't think you would," he said.

Fifteen

WITH THE RESILIENCY of youth and by virtue of her superb physical health, Adrian soon was able to put behind her the memory of Perry Crandall's treachery and the disturbing experience of her brief incarceration. What she was not able to forget as easily was the probability that she was carrying Jason's child.

During the day, when she was busy, she could block it from her mind. The House of Marlowe was now a beehive of activity. Because of the large number of orders placed on the day of the grand opening, along with subsequent orders that came in daily, Adrian had to employ more seamstresses. The sewing machines buzzed day and night to keep pace with the ever-increasing demand for Marlowe fashions.

While her employees were thus occupied under Tessa's able supervision, Adrian began to design her fall line, which she planned to unveil at a public showing in August. At the same time she was working closely with Mr. Ziegfeld, sketching gowns, headdresses and accoutrements for the Follies of 1911, and she was preparing as well a full line of skirts and shirtwaists for the Adrian label, which would appear in the city's major department stores in time for the 1912 holiday season.

It was a heavy load to carry, but Adrian bore it happily. The success she had dreamed of for three long years was at last a reality, and the labor generated by this success was a burden she most willingly endured. What did it matter if she slept only four or five hours a night? She awoke wide-eyed, refreshed and eager to greet the day. What difference did it make if she was forced on many occasions to miss breakfast or lunch? Her fashions demanded a slender silhouette. She was thinner now, yes, but she felt better and stronger than she ever had before.

Tessa, though, was worried.

"Adrian, you must slow down. You're wearing yourself to a frazzle. Delegate some of your work. You can't keep up this pace; you're going to make yourself ill."

Adrian would laugh and promise to slow down, but nothing would change. She would work even harder and get less sleep and eat less meals; and Tessa's worries would continue to grow.

Evan Colby, too, expressed concern when he happened to meet Adrian one day in February on the polished marble staircase of Carradine & Company.

"Great Scott!" he gasped, catching sight of her and stopping dead in his tracks, almost dropping the mountain of reports he held precariously in both arms. "What in the name of God have you done to yourself? You look bloody awful!"

Adrian laughed, unperturbed. "Oh, you mean my hair? Don't worry, you'll get used to it. Some people think it makes me look like a charming boy."

"I'm not talking about your hair," he said, juggling the burden in his arms. "You're a skeleton, for God's sake. Tessa told me you'd lost weight, but I never dreamed—"

"Tessa?" Adrian teased him. "Ah, yes, you've been seeing a lot of Tessa lately, haven't you?"

Evan's boyish face turned hard. "Yes, I've been seeing her," he said, his tone a challenge. "What of it? I'm very fond of her."

Taken aback by that look, Adrian asked, concerned,

"Are you really fond of her, Evan? You're not just saying that, are you?"

"Yes, I'm really fond of her," he said with a trace of bitterness. "Does that surprise you?"

"No," she said warily. "Why should it surprise me? Tessa's a wonderful girl. I couldn't be happier that you're seeing her. I only hope . . ." She paused, then said quietly, "I only hope you're sincere when you say you're fond of her."

"Believe me, I'm sincere." But his harsh tone worried her. "Tessa's the kind of woman any man would be proud to call his. She's different from you, Adrian. She's not so wrapped up in her bloody career that she would sacrifice having a husband and family."

"Evan, that's not fair," she countered, wounded by his hostility.

His hard look vanished. She had leaned back against the banister, and her upturned face seemed to Evan to be exceptionally weary and pale.

"Adrian, I'm sorry." He took a step toward her, but encumbered as he was by the pile of papers in his arms, he could not even reach out to touch her in a conciliatory gesture. "Forgive me, please," he said earnestly. "I have no right to snipe at you like that. It's just that when I saw you looking so tired and thin, it worried me—and then it angered me. Why do you have to drive yourself so? You've got what you wanted; you've made a success of Marlowe's. Why can't you ease up a bit? Take some time off, take a vacation. You really look awful. You're going to make yourself ill if you continue in this way."

She smiled up at him, touched as always by his protective possessiveness, and she gave his arm a grateful squeeze. "I do love you, Evan," she said sincerely. "And I love Tessa, too, for worrying about me. But please don't be concerned. I feel wonderful, honestly. It's my hair that's shocked you;

and I know I'm thinner, but I had been thinking of shedding a few pounds, and now nature's done it for me.''

"Adrian, it's more than that—''

"Evan.'' She stopped him and gave him a quick kiss. "I'd love to talk more, but I must see Jason for a moment, and then I'm off to the drapers. Come to my house for dinner Saturday evening—and bring Tessa, of course. Now I really must go.'' With another quick kiss she skipped lightly up the stairs, leaving a very troubled young man staring after her.

But despite her reassurances, despite her carefree jauntiness in the face of Evan's concern, Adrian paused a moment outside the door to Jason's offices. Was it true that she looked awful? And was her weight loss that noticeable, and unattractive besides? As is sometimes the case when one is bombarded on all sides by negative criticism, Adrian began to wonder if she was indeed working too hard or if she truly felt as hale and hearty as she thought she did.

When she greeted Frank Robbins, Jason's secretary, her voice was so distant and her manner so subdued that Robbins asked, with a solicitude that only heightened her doubts, if she were ill.

"No, I'm fine,'' she said at once. And then, to forestall further inquiries on the state of her health, she asked briskly, "Is Mr. Carradine free, Frank?''

"Yes. Go right in, Miss Marlowe. He's waiting for you.''

Jason, it turned out, had been waiting for her most impatiently. He had planned a surprise: a catered luncheon of poached eggs in aspic, chicken mousse with mushroom sauce, soft-shell crabs *meunière,* a chilled bottle of Chateau Lafitte '69, and a delicious-looking strawberry truffle for dessert. The meal was elegantly arranged on a linen-covered table set with fine crystal and china and Georgian silver, and there was even a fragrant spray of hothouse gardenias in a silver bowl in the center of the table.

"Jason, it's lovely!" she exclaimed. "What's the occasion?"

"It's my birthday," he said, a boyish excitement in his eyes.

"Your birthday? Oh, Jason, why didn't you tell me? I would have got you something."

"There's no need for that," he said, taking her hat and coat and putting them aside. "Don't you read the newspapers? I'm 'the man who has everything.' "

He held her chair as she sat down, then bent to kiss her curls. Nuzzling the nape of her neck, he murmured, "You're looking inordinately desirable today. Would you mind very much if we forgo lunch and make love on the floor instead?"

"Jason!" She laughed delightedly.

"Very well," he said, straightening up with a great air of mock disappointment. "I shall try to control my ardor until tonight. But now," he said dramatically, "since you were so insensitive as to not have gotten me something for my birthday, I shall increase your guilt by presenting *you* with a gift."

"Oh, Jason, you shouldn't have . . ."

"Hush. Not another word. Take a look at this. Tell me if you like it."

From his inside coat pocket Jason produced a small blue jeweler's box, which he placed in Adrian's hand. "Open it," he urged her, then sat down across from her and eased the cork from the bottle of wine.

When Adrian opened the box, she saw nestled on white silk a diamond so large, so brilliantly beautiful in its icy perfection that for a moment she could only stare at it in awestruck silence.

"Jason," she said at last, her eyes still on the ring, "it's incredible . . . magnificent.'' She looked up then, apologetically. ''But I couldn't possibly accept such a gift.''

''But you must accept it!'' He poured the wine, then returned the bottle to the cooler. ''I want you to have it.''

''I can't,'' she maintained. ''People would think . . .''

''What would they think?''

''Well, that you're keeping me.''

''Nonsense,'' he said. ''In a year or two you're going to be richer than I am. Men don't 'keep' women who have more money than they do.''

She smiled and shook her head. ''Jason, be serious. You know as well as I that a gift of this nature is entirely unsuitable between friends.''

''We're not friends,'' he said, and his voice had gone very low. ''We're lovers, Adrian.''

Her heart skipped a beat. Beneath his unsmiling gaze she sensed a smoldering passion that raised a hot splash of color in her cheeks.

''Jason, don't,'' she said faintly. ''Don't look at me like that.''

''Why not?'' he asked, and still he continued to watch her with that sensuous gravity. ''Does it arouse you to know that I want you?''

''Yes,'' she whispered, ''yes.'' And helplessly she lowered her gaze.

''Adrian, look at me.'' His hand encircled her wrist, and with his thumb he stroked the place where her pulse raced and leaped. ''I want you to have the ring. I want you to wear it—to please me. Will you do that for me? Will you, Adrian?''

She looked up at him slowly, her senses benumbed yet exhilarated by his touch. She was putty in his hands. How often she had heard that phrase, and how she had scoffed at it. But whenever Jason touched her, she became malleable, eager to be molded into whatever shape he chose to fashion

her. She saw him as Pygmalion, and herself as Galatea, the
cold, ivory statue to whom Pygmalion had given life. Jason,
she felt, had given her more than life. He had given her freedom and understanding and unequivocal support; he had
given love and joy and meaning to her very existence.

"Yes," she said at last, for she could refuse this man
nothing when his warm flesh touched hers. "Yes, I'll wear
it."

"Good!" He released her abruptly and began to fill her
dish. "Let's eat," he said with an odd blend of relief and
excitement in his voice. "I'm absolutely famished."

"Jason." She eyed him curiously. Now that she was free
of his mesmerizing touch, she was alert to his mood, which
was bewilderingly unlike him. "What is it? Why are you
acting so peculiarly? I've never seen you this way."

"What way?" he said, attacking his chicken with gusto.
"I'm happy, that's all. I've reached the venerable age of
thirty-seven, the House of Marlowe has already turned a
tidy profit, and the most intriguing woman in New York has
consented to become my wife."

"What?" She dropped her fork with a clatter. "What are
you talking about?"

"Why, about our marriage, darling," he said, and saluted her with his wineglass. "You've accepted my betrothal ring—"

"Betrothal ring?" She leaped to her feet, almost upset-
ting the table as she did. "Is that what it is? In that case,
you'd best return it to Tiffany's or Cartier's or wherever you
bought it, or you can throw it in the gutter for all I care!"

"Adrian—"

He rose and followed her as she snatched up her hat and
coat and headed for the door.

"You sneaky snake!" she said hotly, and flung off the
hand he had placed on her arm. "What do you take me for?
Did you think you could *trick* me into marrying you? Did

you think you could blindfold me and march me up the aisle? Well, you have another thing coming, Jason Carradine! I've told you before, and I'll say it one last time: I'm not going to—''

She broke off in mid-sentence as a loud, insistent buzzing sounded suddenly in her ears. The room dimmed; bright spots began to dance before her eyes. She felt herself falling. Jason's arms went swiftly around her, and as if from a far distance, she heard his frightened voice calling her name.

Some time later, when she struggled feebly to consciousness, she found herself on a sofa in the small room that adjoined Jason's office. A stranger was kneeling beside her, holding a vial of sal volatile to her nose. She averted her face weakly as the pungent odor assaulted her nostrils.

"Just once more," the stranger coaxed. "Breathe deeply, Miss Marlowe."

Numbly she obeyed, because his voice was so kind and because she hadn't the strength to do otherwise. He smiled when she took a deep breath and grimaced at the smell; some color began to return to her cheeks.

"That's better," he said approvingly, then he reached behind him and extracted a stethoscope from a black leather bag on the coffee table.

"You're a doctor," Adrian mumbled as he unbuttoned her shirtwaist and placed the flat piece of metal to her heart.

"Yes, that's right," he said genially. "My name is Ned Garvey. I'm an old friend of Jason's. My offices are just up the street on Broadway."

She regarded him docilely as he made his examination. He looked much younger than Jason. He was slightly built, like a boy in his teens, and his curly brown hair and merry brown eyes only added to this illusion of youth.

"Where is Jason?" she asked, glancing lethargically around the room.

"He's in his office, pacing the floor like a caged tiger. You gave him quite a scare before."

"What happened?" she said dully. "I know that I fainted, but—"

"Quiet, please," he said, moving the stethoscope and listening intently. After a moment he withdrew the instrument and returned it to the bag, then rose from his kneeling position on the floor.

"Well, your heart and lungs are sound," he commented, perching on the edge of the coffee table and leaning forward, elbows on knees. "As to your other symptoms—"

"What other symptoms?"

"Jason tells me he thinks you're pregnant."

"Oh!" she cried softly, and turned her head away with a shudder of embarrassment.

"Now, now," Ned Garvey said gently. "Don't be ashamed, Miss Marlowe. These things happen. Jason assures me he's very much in love with you and that he wants to marry you as soon as possible."

"He's a liar," she said, thinking dully of Evan's words.

"A liar? Oh, no, Miss Marlowe. He told me he's most anxious to set a wedding date—"

"Yes, I know," she said wearily. "He *is* anxious to marry me, but he doesn't love me. That devious devil would say *anything* to have his way. But he won't, you know. I refuse to marry him, and you can tell him I said so."

"Miss Marlowe," said Garvey, nonplussed by her extraordinary pronouncement, "I think you yourself should discuss your feelings with Jason. At any rate, I should like to see you tomorrow morning at my offices. If you are pregnant a program of prenatal care should be started as soon as possible. Jason was most insistent about this, and, of course, he's right. One can't be too careful with one's first child."

Later that day, after Jason had taken her home and personally tucked her in bed like a fussing mother hen, he said to her sternly, "You brought this on yourself, you know, refusing to accept the inevitable. If you weren't such an unreasonable stubborn mule you would simply recognize the fact that you're carrying my child and that your only alternative is to marry me."

A child, she thought despondently after Jason left. It was true; she was carrying his child. And now he would be after her with a vengeance, urging, persuading, conniving or browbeating her into marrying him. She had to do something; she simply could not let herself be trapped in a union that would enslave her, that would change her from a creative, productive, individual human being into a chattel, a possession, a mere extension of someone else.

Evan Colby had impressed upon her the status of a wife: a woman devoted exclusively to husband and family. It was what Jason wanted, too, despite his reassurance that he wouldn't think of asking her to give up her career. Ha! she thought bitterly. How quickly he'd change his tune once they were married. "Don't go to the salon today, Adrian; the baby has a toothache." Or, "Can't you work on your designs another time? I want you to make up the guest list for the masquerade ball."

Yes, Adrian could see that a marriage with Jason Carradine would be no worse or no better than a marriage with Evan Colby. Men were men, and in the final analysis, they wanted only two things from their wives: unwavering devotion and absolute obedience. Well, that was fine for some women, but it was far from fine for Adrian. Adrian was devoted unwaveringly to her work, and she pledged absolute obedience to no one but herself.

Let Jason plot and plan all he liked. She was not going to marry him, and that was all there was to it. She knew what she had to do; it couldn't be simpler. For some weeks now she had been considering a trip abroad to review the new fashions of Creed and Renfrew and Paquin and Poiret. Now was as good a time as any to get away from New York. She could work on her designs in London and Paris and then mail them off to Tessa. If Adrian's calculations were correct the child was due in late June. This would give her enough time to board a homebound ship in early August and be back in New York just before the fall showing.

Full management of Marlowe's was a hefty burden to lay on Tessa's shoulders, but Adrian trusted her implicitly, and she knew that, if anything, Tessa would welcome the added responsibilities. Tessa would understand once Adrian explained her predicament. She simply could not marry Jason at this time; she loved him with all her heart, but marriage was out of the question. If she stayed in New York she knew that by hook or by crook he would somehow induce her to change her mind. If she were a continent away, however, there was no way on earth he could exert his influence on her. She would miss him, of course; she would miss him unbearably. But that was a small price to pay when she considered the alternative of losing her freedom to the man who had taught her the meaning of the word.

Sixteen

SHE WAS COOL and methodical in planning her great escape. With Jason she was quietly submissive, neither agreeing to nor rejecting his suggestions for their wedding. To further allay any suspicions he might entertain, she visited Ned Garvey. Her primary purpose in seeing the physician was to ascertain if her calculations had been correct, which they were: The child was due in late June or early July—and to determine if she was truly at death's door as Tessa and Evan had frightened her into believing.

Dr. Garvey pronounced her in excellent health, but he cautioned her strongly against overwork. "You are much too slender," he admonished. "I suspect you've been overdoing it. That fainting spell was nature's way of warning you to slow down. I prescribe a long holiday, Miss Marlowe, to restore the strength and energy that is vital at this time to your baby's health and yours."

Adrian nodded and said nothing. A voyage across the Atlantic was just the ticket, she thought. Six days and nights to rest undisturbed aboard an ocean liner would be more than sufficient time to restore and revitalize her flagging energy. She was admittedly tired now, but she attributed this new lassitude to the strain of making her stealthy preparations, along with a gnawing guilt whenever she stopped to think of how cruelly she was deceiving the father of her child.

Jason was so happy these days. "Adrian, think of it," he would say. "I waited thirty-seven years to take a wife, a wait well worth it, I might add, for I am going to marry the most beautiful, the most exciting, the most exasperating woman in the world!''

And then he would sweep her into his arms and cover her face with kisses. He made love to her with a new tenderness, an almost reverential awe that within the precious vessel of this body he held dwelt a tiny human life, a renewal of himself and of the woman he loved.

"I do love you, you know," he would tell her with increasing frequency. "I know you don't believe me; I can hardly believe it myself. You're stubborn, pigheaded, opinionated, and spoiled. God alone knows how I could possibly love such a woman. But I do, and you're stuck with me, whether you like it or not."

At times like these her decision would waver. She would say to herself, I can't leave him. I love him. I can't bear even the thought of being away from him for five or six months. But then she would think of Evan and his impassioned tirades on a wife's duties and responsibilities, and with renewed determination she would close her mind against all of Jason's persuasion. She closed her heart as well to the sweet possibility that he did indeed love her quite as much as she loved him.

She booked passage for the twentieth on the White Star Line's *Majestic*. To Tessa she said, "Under no circumstances are you to tell Jason where I am. If he even suspected I was in Europe he would turn the continent upside down trying to find me."

"Adrian," Tessa said bluntly, "you're being an absolute ass. Stay here and marry him. It's obvious you're both head over heels in love with each other. And more to the point, how in heaven's name are you going to explain the baby to everyone when you come home?"

"Oh, that's simple," Adrian said airily. "I have it all worked out. While I'm in France I shall lease a small house in Chantilly, and I'm going to tell everyone that an infant was left in a basket on my doorstep. I couldn't resist the little darling, so I adopted it."

Tessa snorted scornfully. "And how many people do you suppose are going to believe that fairy tale?"

"I don't really care." Adrian shrugged. "They won't be able to prove otherwise, will they?"

"What about Jason?" Tessa persisted. "How do you imagine he's going to react to this charade?"

With a shiver of guilt Adrian lowered her gaze. "I don't know," she said uneasily. "And I don't want to think about it."

Naturally she could think of little else. As her sailing date drew nearer she became so noticeably tense and distracted that Jason said to her one evening, "I'm worried about you, darling. You're thinner than you ever were, and you haven't been eating enough to keep a bird alive. Why don't you do as Ned suggested? Come away with me on an extended holiday. The yacht's moored in Florida; I can alert Captain Peterson to collect us on Friday, and we can cruise the Caribbean for as long as you like. Adrian, look at me. What are you thinking about?"

They were dining at Delmonico's; that is, Jason was dining. Adrian had merely been pushing her food around on her plate and gloomily pondering her imminent departure.

"Nothing," she said, looking up at him reluctantly. "I wasn't thinking of anything. Jason, your offer is very tempting, but I can't leave New York right now. Let me think about it a while, and perhaps in a week or so I'll have a better idea of when I'll be free to get away."

He took her at her word, which only sharpened her guilt to a razor-keen edge. Oh, where would she find the strength to go on with this painful deception, even for only a few more days? She loved him so much, and she was finding it easier and easier to believe he loved her. And it *was* his child, after all. He certainly had the right to want to insure the child's future by giving him a mother, a father, a home, and a name.

Adrian almost relented, especially on her last night home as she lay in Jason's arms. His kisses seemed warmer and sweeter than they had ever been. When he made love to her with that gentle tenderness, when he touched her with loving hands and whispered her name and moved slowly, deliciously inside her, she wanted to lock him into her heart until the end of eternity, she wanted to tell him over and over again that she loved him more than life, that she would never leave him, never, and that if he wanted marriage, she wanted it, too. She would fight him no longer; she was his to command.

She wanted to say all those things and more, but she said nothing at all. Instead, after he tensed above her and shuddered with pleasure, then grew still in her embrace, she began to cry, bitterly, soundlessly, at the thought of her treacherous cruelty. And when he tasted her tears on his lips, when he felt the tortured heaving of her breast, he raised himself on an elbow. His face went white at the sight of her tear-drenched eyes. He eased himself off her quickly and asked in a swift, frightened voice, "Adrian, what is it? Did I hurt you? Darling, for the love of Christ, answer me. What's wrong?"

"It's nothing," she managed to say, her breast aching with misery. "I'm just blue tonight. I don't know why."

"Adrian . . ." He took her in his arms, and his voice was hoarse with his lingering fear. "Darling, for God's sake, don't do that. If you only knew what a fright you gave me." He pressed her closer as if to ward off whatever dangers might threaten his beloved. "Adrian, you're blue because of your condition. Ned says it's common for pregnant women to be weepy and weary. When he told me that, it surprised me, because you're never tired, and I've never seen you cry— Darling, don't, please!'' he begged when the tears gathered again in her eyes.

But she couldn't stop crying, as much as she wanted to, because she knew that on the morrow she would be leaving him, hurting him, and she could not bear the thought of it.

''Adrian, listen to me,'' he said in an effort to lift her spirits. ''This will all be over before you know it. When our daughter is born—''

Adrian raised her head abruptly and regarded him through tear-kissed lashes, and for the moment her misery was forgotten. ''How do you know it's going to be a daughter?''

''I know,'' he said with confidence, and his lips brushed her cheek where a single tear trembled, then vanished, beneath his kiss. ''I can see her in my mind, Adrian. She'll have cherubic dark curls and mischievous dark eyes. Her nose will be tilted haughtily, just like yours, and she'll be a perfect little horror because I intend to spoil her thoroughly.''

''Jason''—she smiled tearfully, enchanted by his charming imaginings—''you mustn't spoil her.''

''Oh, but I want to. I'm looking forward to it, don't you see? Since the day I knew for certain you were going to have a child, I've been visualizing her entire life. I've been thinking of her birth, her christening, her first step, her first beau, her debut, her wedding day.''

''Honestly?'' she said, adoring him. ''Have you really been doing that?''

''Yes, I have,'' he answered gravely. ''And I've been thinking, darling. Would you mind very much if we named her after my mother? She died when I was twelve, and I've always promised myself that if I had a daughter I would name her Elyse.''

''Yes, all right,'' Adrian agreed softly, and she wound her arms around his neck and kissed his chin and his throat and laid her cheek against his heart. "We'll name her Elyse, if you like. I'll do anything you ask."

Oh, how could she leave him? she thought as he stroked her tumbled hair and murmured loving endearments against her quivering mouth. How could she endure being thousands of miles away from him, not seeing him, not touching him, deprived of his love? It was too much to bear; she couldn't go through with it.

"Jason," she whispered in a compulsion of love and longing, "Jason, can we be married right away? I want to marry you at once. I won't spend another moment away from you. Do something," she urged him. "You have your sources. Arrange it so that we don't have to wait. I want us to be married as soon as we can."

"Darling!" he said, and his arms tightened around her. He kissed her so fervently, so passionately that she thought she would surely expire from ecstasy and lack of breath. "Of course, I can arrange something. I'm busy all day tomorrow, but first thing Tuesday morning we can go down to City Hall and be married there. There are a few people at the Health Department and License Bureau who owe me favors. I'm sure they'll be more than willing to waive the waiting period."

"Oh, Jason." She sighed as a great sense of well-being filled her. "I'm so happy. I'm doing the right thing, I know I am. I feel ever so much better now."

And she did feel better. She felt wonderfully at peace and free from all anxiety. When Jason left her an hour or so later, she burrowed contentedly under the covers, planning her wedding day, reflecting joyously that Jason would never again have to leave her bed. Now he could make love to her and sleep with her and awaken the next morning with his strong arms around her and his head pillowed lovingly against her breast.

But early the next morning, when she awakened alone,

without the warmth of Jason's body distorting her logic, she realized clearly that she could not remain in New York; she simply could not marry him. It was a momentary insanity that had weakened her will, that had made her think she could be happy solely in the role of mother and wife.

She rose from her bed, went downstairs, and telephoned for a taxi. Her trunks were packed and waiting behind the locked door of Aunt Meg's room. She dressed quickly, bolted down a piece of toast, and was ready when the cabbie rang the doorbell. Within an hour she was luxuriously ensconced in her stateroom on the A deck of one of the White Star Line's finest vessels. The ship sailed on schedule. At 10:30 A.M., Adrian was on her way to Southampton, England, and Jason, in his Wall Street office, was picking up the telephone to call her and tell her how much he loved her and missed her.

Seventeen

THOSE MONTHS AWAY from Jason, the time spent in England and France where she designed, bought fabric, visited the fashion houses of the great European couturiers, and awaited the birth of her baby, were the longest, hardest, loneliest months Adrian had ever endured.

The crossing alone had been enjoyable. Adrian had sorely needed a respite from work and worry, and the superb ocean liner *Majestic* was the perfect environment in which to rest and renew both body and spirit. Aesthetically gratified by the ship's elegant surroundings and physically invigorated by the salubrious sun and bracing sea air, Adrian was soon feeling her old self. She spent the first two days at sea on a comfortable deck chair, wrapped in a blanket, watching the parade of passengers out for a leisurely stroll on the promenade deck. At mealtimes she ate like a trencherman. The tangy sea air had revived her waning appetite, and she stuffed herself sinfully on the great ship's delectable French cuisine.

On the third night out she was invited to dine at the captain's table. The dining saloon on the *Majestic* was a great two-tiered room, decorated in the Louis Seize style, with gilt-traced painted walls and satinwood tables and chairs, all lighted magnificently by crystal chandeliers. Adrian chose a gown carefully to grace this fabulous setting, a coffee-brown metallic threaded with gold, fashioned in the Empire mode, which concealed the slight rise of her abdomen, and which set off her ivory skin to perfection.

The dinner was festive, presided over by the White Star Line's senior officer, Captain Thaddeus Blake of Bristol, England, a great bear of a man with a fierce golden beard and unexpectedly gentle blue eyes. As the ship's staff served course after course of tempting delicacies, Captain Blake spun sea yarns at length, much to Adrian's delight, and to the enthrallment of her smartly attired tablemates.

After dinner in the first-class lounge, the ladies complimented Adrian on her charming coiffure and said they wished they had the courage to follow suit. The gentlemen eyed her admiringly, wondering how it came to be that such an attractive package was traveling alone, and wondering as well if there were other conventions she might care to flout. Adrian, however, while gracious, ignored all overtures, both friendly and otherwise. She was traveling under the name of Mary Spencer, a pseudonym she had assumed to throw Jason off the track should he think to check the passenger lists of all outgoing ships. She wisely decided that the less she encouraged intimacy with her fellow passengers, the less likelihood there was of Jason learning her whereabouts.

England, when she arrived, was foggy, dismal, and cold. Adrian stopped off at Sussex to visit Aunt Meg's cousin, the pompous Earl of Bedford, and despite a cool reception and an uncomfortable two-day sojourn, she was grateful for the impulse that had sent her to the nobleman's estate. There she met and subsequently purloined a young servant of Bedford's, one Molly Brewster, a spirited redhead, just eighteen years old, with a tart tongue and impudent brown eyes, who would serve nicely, Adrian thought, as companion, personal maid, and, eventually, as nursemaid to baby Elyse.

Adrian accepted with utter faith that the child would be a girl. Jason indicated he wanted a daughter, and more than anything in the world, she wanted to give him what he

wanted. It was the least she could do, she would think with
an ever-increasing guilt. She had hurt him, betrayed him,
and with each day that passed, she regretted more profoundly the unforgivable wrong she had done him.

Daily, almost hourly, she wondered what he had done
when he learned she was gone. Had he ranted and raved at
Tessa? Had he cursed a blue streak and vowed he would
make Adrian pay for her treachery? Was it possible he might
call in her loan, dissolve the partnership, take Marlowe's for
himself, or, even worse, close its doors and leave Adrian
with nothing after all her hard work?

No, no, no, she would think as she went about her business in London and Paris with an aching heart and a remorseful guilt. Jason could not be so brutal; he would never
close Marlowe's doors. He was so proud of her accomplishments; he had supported her from the start, and it was his
help, his encouragement, that had insured her success.
Without Jason's support . . . both financial and moral,
Adrian knew she might still be selling dresses from her shop
on Union Square. Jason had brought her to the peak of her
profession. And it was her lucrative success, achieved in
part through Jason's influence, that had afforded her the
funds to turn her back on his love and leave New York.

"There's a letter for you, Miss Marlowe. It's from America, from your manager friend, Miss Keller."

Adrian and Molly were installed in the little house in
Chantilly, near Paris. Almost a month had gone by since
Adrian had left New York, and she had been both longing
for and dreading a letter from Tessa.

She ripped open the envelope that Molly handed to her
and hastily scanned the five pages. Most of the letter was devoted to business matters: the orders continued to come in;
more seamstresses had been employed; Mr. Ziegfeld had
been pleased with the final batch of sketches Adrian had sent

him from London; and would Adrian consider designing a line of children's clothing, because the patrons had been pressing Tessa for weeks now to pose the question to her employer.

On the fourth page Adrian caught sight of Jason's name, and with a pounding heart, she sank onto a chair and braced herself for the worst. Tessa had written:

He's in a fine rage. On the day you sailed he had telephoned you at home, and when he received no answer, he came to the salon and inquired about your whereabouts. I told him as gently as I could that you had gone away and that you wouldn't be returning until after the baby's birth. He wouldn't believe me at first. He kept telling me I must be mistaken, that you had promised to marry him and that you couldn't possibly have gone away under those circumstances. Did you really tell him you'd marry him, Adrian? That wasn't very nice of you.

Anyway, he finally realized I was telling the truth. I cannot describe to you the emotions that crossed his face. One moment I thought he was going to choke the life out of me, and in the next instant I could have wept for the shock and hurt and disbelief I saw in his eyes.

Adrian, it's not too late to change your mind. *Please* come home. His pain, though he tried to hide it, broke my heart. He did his very best to get me to tell him where you were, but when he saw it was no use, he said in a helpless rage, "Be damned to her then; I wash my hands of her."

But he came back the next day and tossed an envelope containing three thousand dollars on my desk. He asked me in a cold voice to see that you received it and to let him know if you needed more (I've cabled the money to LeGrange et Cie in Paris), and then, before he left, he said bitterly, "Tell her she needn't fear that I'll continue to press her to marry me. If she wants to be free of me, by God, I shall oblige her.''

He left then, and I haven't seen him since. He sends one of his staff now to attend to business; it appears he wants nothing more to do with the House of Marlowe. I wish I could close this letter on a happier note, but I can't. You've hurt that man badly, Adrian. And the saddest part is, I'm convinced he's still in love with you.

Adrian dropped the letter to the floor and burst into tears. Molly, who had been mending a petticoat across the room, leaped to her feet and flew to her mistress.

"What is it, miss? Is it bad news? Oh, please don't cry so; you'll harm the baby. Miss Marlowe, please stop crying.''

The girl knelt at Adrian's feet and distractedly patted her wrists, and after a time, Adrian's guilty tears ebbed, and she lifted a woeful face to her sympathetic companion. Early in their relationship, Adrian had confided to Molly the entire sordid story of her inexcusable flight from Jason, and now she said miserably, "He's angry and hurt, Molly. Miss Keller says he's terribly, terribly hurt.''

"Ah," said Molly, rising with a sigh of relief, "so that's it. I was afraid a loved one had been murdered.''

"Mr. Carradine *is* my loved one," Adrian whispered in anguish. "And I might as well have murdered him for the monstrous hurt I've done him. Molly, he'll never forgive me.''

Molly clicked her tongue and settled a pillow behind Adrian's back. "Never forgive you, miss? That's hardly likely. Don't forget, it's his child you're carrying. When you return to America, I'm willing to wager that he'll be standing on the dock, a bouquet of flowers in one hand and a diamond necklace in the other. When a man waits thirty-seven years to give a woman his child, you may rest assured he's not going to turn his back on that woman at the drop of a hat.''

But Adrian did not share Molly's confidence. Jason had not only been hurt by her cruelty, he had also been used and betrayed, and Adrian very much doubted he was ever going to forgive such treachery. There was no way to explain to him that she had had to run away, that if she had stayed she would have given in to him; she would have married him and gladly. But she couldn't marry him, not now, not yet, not at least until she had proven to herself inconclusively that she could stand alone, that she, as well as any man, needed no one but herself to survive, to *succeed*.

Paris, in the spring of 1911, was looking its loveliest. Adrian, despite her gloom, was not unaffected by the immortal city with its graceful blend of the old and the new, its arching bridges, ancient winding roads, its rivers and canals, its monuments and gardens. The intoxicating scent of new flowers and budding chestnut trees was sweet in the air. As Adrian walked the colorful streets from one great house of couture to another, she could only wish longingly that Jason were here to share with her the most beautiful of all seasons in the City of Light.

At the houses of Paquin and Poiret Adrian's guilt-laden thoughts of Jason were temporarily suspended as she viewed with some excitement the newest Paris fashions. The most startling change was the new and narrower skirt, which was scandalously shorter and so close-fitting at the ankle that the mannequins were forced to hobble as they walked the salon runways, much in the manner of Oriental geisha girls. Adrian found the style most attractive and made a quick mental note to write to Tessa, directing her to alter all the skirts of the gowns that were now being readied for the fall showing.

She also admired the daring peasant blouses of Madame

Paquin. Over the narrow skirts the mannequins wore collarless tunics, belted at the waist, with long, flowing sleeves, which to Adrian seemed the essence of femininity. In her mind she was already sketching eight or nine versions of the style. Some were simple white batiste, some were elegantly beaded, others embroidered or trimmed with lace. She made another mental note to revisit the factory at Chantilly. She had seen there some smart lace bandings that would be perfect on the tunics and that she must add to the order she had placed just last week.

The months spent in Paris were busy and productive, but they were arduous and lonely as well. At the end of April, when Adrian was finally forced to retire to the little house in Chantilly to await the birth of her baby, she was enormously relieved. Soon thereafter she would be going home at last— and going home meant seeing Jason. He *would* see her, she was sure, if only to see his daughter. What would happen afterward she could not guess. She knew she had to explain to him her reason for leaving him. Would he accept as the reason her need for independence? Would he even understand it? Men so much took for granted their own freedom, their spiritual liberty and strength. Could Jason be objective enough to realize that Adrian, though she loved him, still could not marry him, that to marry would mean the end of independence as Adrian defined it?

Her labor pains began on the tenth of June, rather earlier than either she or Ned Garvey had anticipated. Dr. Armand Mitterand, the physician who had cared for Aunt Meg at the time of her illness, was in attendance. He was a tall, thin gentleman with a small, neat goatee, piercing dark eyes, and an aristocratic mien that was daunting. Adrian saw beneath his imperious manner a soft heart and a loving and sympathetic nature.

When Adrian had first called on him at his offices in

Paris, Mitterand had welcomed her warmly. When she told him of her pregnancy, he had not questioned her marital status, nor had Adrian enlightened him. He continued to address her as Mademoiselle Marlowe, and his only interest seemed in the state of her health and the well-being of the child she carried.

He had exhibited this same kindness and understanding at the time of Aunt Meg's death. It had been Mitterand who had sadly informed Adrian that because of the nature of her aunt's illness, her remains would not be allowed to be transported back to America. He had arranged the burial at the Pére-Lachaise Cemetery in Paris, and he, the sole mourner besides Adrian, had held her arm at the grave site and had bid Margaret Marlowe a final adieu.

Now, as he sat at Adrian's bedside, awaiting the onset of hard labor, he said to his apprehensive patient, "You are not to worry at all, mam'selle. My examination has indicated that the birth will be a normal one. You will, of course, experience some pain, but that is the will of *le bon Dieu* Who grants us nothing in this life without extracting His little payment, yes?"

Adrian smiled weakly at the physician and tried not to think of the pain that was radiating from her swollen abdomen to every extremity of her body. She had labored for nine hours before sending Molly to fetch Mitterand at his home in Pontoise. The pain then had been unbearable; now it was near to excruciating.

"Monsieur le docteur," she gasped as a sudden spasm tore through her, "will it be much longer? I am in a good deal of discomfort."

"Let us see," he said calmly, and rose to examine her.

He found, to his surprise, that the cervix had greatly dilated since his last observation. He said to Molly, who waited alertly at the foot of the bed, *"Ah, bien,* it begins now, the birth. Your assistance, *s'il vous plaît,* Mademoiselle Brewster.''

The nature of Adrian's labor suddenly changed, intensified, so that she could hardly breathe for the viselike pain that gained control of her body. It was as if giant hands had taken hold of her insides and were forcing them outward.

She moaned involuntarily as wave after wave of contractions knifed through her. Dear God, she was going to die. No one could be in this much pain and survive. She was going to die on foreign soil, as Aunt Meg had died. Jason would never forgive her now; she would die without ever having told him how much she loved him and needed him. Yes, she *needed* him! In the grip of mortal pain, her mind unfettered by the chains of her own distortions, she was finally able to admit to herself that she needed Jason—just as much as he had shown her, without fear or shame, that he needed her.

It seemed she remained in the throes of this agony for a time without end, a merciless eternity. And then, just when she was sure she was on the very threshold of death, her body gave one last great shuddering heave, the pain was somehow arrested, and dimly she heard Mitterand say, *"Félicitations,* Mademoiselle Marlowe! You have a beautiful and perfect baby girl.''

As if by magic, the pain she had suffered ceased abruptly. In a sweet, joyous fog Adrian held out her arms to receive the living proof of Jason's love.

''In a moment, miss,'' Molly said cheerily while the doctor attended to his weary patient. ''Let me spruce her up a bit before you have a look at her.''

When at last the child was laid in her arms, Adrian looked down at the pink-and-white bundle, and tears of happiness and love filled her eyes. How beautiful she was, how incomparably lovely. She had a tuft of dark hair and a tiny button nose, and her little mouth was a miniature rosebud that already was seeking an immediate source of nourishment.

Adrian guided the searching mouth to her breast, and at once the infant began to suck with loud, hungry noises that brought a smile of pride and love to her lips.

"See how strongly she nurses," she said to Molly and the doctor. "She's going to be a fine, healthy girl. Her father will be thrilled at having produced such a daughter."

"That he will," Molly agreed. "And he'll be seeing her very soon. Are you looking forward to that day, Miss Marlowe?"

Adrian gazed at her daughter, the physical pledge of Jason's love, and with renewed courage and unwavering certainty, she answered, "More than anything else in the world."

Eighteen

SHE WROTE to Tessa as soon as she was able.

> I've had a daughter. She's the most beautiful, most
> wonderful baby on the face of God's earth. She's per-
> fectly formed; her hair is dark, and I think her eyes are
> going to be blue, like Jason's. I can't wait for you to see
> her. She'll be christened when we come home, and I
> would be happy and in your debt if you and Evan would
> consent to be her godparents.
>
> Only eight more weeks till I'm home—I'm counting the
> hours! Please tell Jason my ship, the *St. Louis*, docks in
> New York on August 4. Do *not* tell him he has a daughter.
> I want to tell him myself. I know he hasn't forgiven me,
> but when he sees Elyse, I think he may find it in his heart
> to remember that he loves the woman who has presented
> him with such an extraordinary child.

Her recovery was rapid. The very next day after the birth
she was ravenously hungry, and within two weeks she was
feeling as good as new. The baby was a constant source of
awe and delight to her. How could she and Jason have produced this incredible creature? Elyse was surely one of
God's angels, sent down from above to give celestial happiness to her ecstatic and doting mother.

The last weeks in Europe passed quickly. Adrian was enchanted with her daughter, and she knew that when Jason

saw her, he, too, would fall under her spell. To Adrian the simple acts of feeding her, bathing her, and dressing her were the most blessed of chores. Just looking at the child and touching her soft skin reminded Adrian that this precious scrap of humanity was the living embodiment of the love she bore for Jason.

When the day finally came to board the *St. Louis*, Adrian was in a fever to be home, to see the father of her child. The voyage was pleasant. Every day becalmed seas shone sapphire-blue beneath a brilliant sun. The fare on the *St. Louis* was equal to all the White Star Line's cuisine: pâté, escargot, and cornets of smoked salmon would be followed by duckling in Cointreau, veal Milanese, roast baby lamb, with dessert choices of parfait apricotine, marrons aux Kirsch, or an irresistible bombe Vesuvius.

Adrian ate enormously of each and every course that was served, and afterward, in her stateroom she would complain to Molly, "I'm going to be big as a house when we reach New York. None of my clothes will fit me, and when Mr. Carradine sees me, he will probably retch with disgust at my gargantuan figure."

Molly, who, like Adrian, had no living family, and therefore had eagerly accepted Adrian's offer to come to New York, would smile at her mistress and shake her head at her complaints. Adrian had never looked more beautiful, more womanly, more desirable than she did now. Her figure was fuller but alluringly so, and her ivory face glowed with a radiance and color that might have been tinted by Raphael's brush. Mr. Carradine, Molly was sure, would take one look at this glorious masterpiece and whisk her off to his bed, where he would most likely endeavor to give her another child with the greatest of passionate pleasure.

When Molly confided as much to Adrian, Adrian blushed and laughed and said with unabashed enthusiasm, "I certainly hope he does!"

But he was not on the dock when the ship arrived in New York. He was not at her house (to which he had a key), and later in the day, when she went to the salon, he was not there, either.

Hiding her disappointment, Adrian greeted Tessa with a bear hug, a kiss, and a long, rhapsodic description of her daughter. She toured the salon and the upstairs workroom, delighted at the progress Tessa had made in her absence. The fall showing was two weeks off, and already the alterations to the skirts had been made, and the tunics Adrian had sketched were near completion, needing only her final approval as to trimming and fit.

"Tessa," she said as they walked into her office on the second floor, "I can never thank you enough for what you've done for me. I intend to give you a huge bonus, and I should like you to think about becoming my partner—"

Tessa waved her hand in a gesture of protest. "Please don't," she said somewhat sheepishly.

"Don't be silly." Adrian frowned. "You deserve it. Why should you refuse?"

"Because," Tessa said, glancing guiltily away, "I won't be working here much longer."

"What?" Adrian dropped the satin tunic she had been examining. "Don't you dare say such a thing, Tessa Keller, not even as a joke!"

"It's no joke, Adrian. I'm leaving Marlowe's."

"Why? Why?" Adrian's voice rose in panic. "If it's a question of money I said I'd raise your salary. And if it's—"

"It's not money, Adrian. I'm getting married."

"Married?" Relief flooded Adrian like a drenching of rain on a hot sun-scorched desert. "Oh, Tessa, is that all? Thank God! I thought for a moment I was really going to lose you. So Evan has finally popped the question. I'm delighted! But that doesn't mean you can't continue to work."

"Adrian." Tessa's voice was somber and low. She bent

to pick up the tunic Adrian had dropped, then folded it neatly and placed it on the desk. "I cannot continue to work. I want to—believe me, I want to—but Evan is adamant on this point. He wants me to make a home for him, to be a wife and mother, which means leaving my job at Marlowe's. It's unfair perhaps, especially since he knows how much I enjoy my work. But I love him, and if that's what he wants from me, that's what he shall have."

For a long while Adrian stared at her and said nothing. It couldn't be true; she couldn't be losing Tessa. It would be like losing her right arm. They had been through so much together. Tessa had been with her from the very start; she had shared every hope, every disappointment, every triumph with Adrian. And now she was leaving? Just like that? No, it couldn't be true, it simply couldn't.

"Tessa," she said when at last she could speak, "there must be some way you can convince Evan to . . ."

She trailed off and fell silent again as Tessa regarded her with a helpless regret. Both of them knew there was no way of convincing Evan to permit his wife to work. It was almost a point of honor with him: the woman he married must devote herself fully to her husband and children. He had given Tessa the same choice he had given Adrian. Tessa, unlike Adrian, had chosen to abnegate her needs in deference to the needs of the man she loved.

"Adrian, listen," said Tessa gently, "I can put it off for a while. Evan wants to be married next June. I had planned on leaving in a month or so. But I might as well stay until shortly before we're married. That will give us a year, Adrian, almost a full year before I have to leave."

Adrian could not speak; she could hardly think. Tessa was leaving her. Tessa, her friend, her comrade-in-arms. It was unthinkable, intolerable. What would she do without her?

"Tessa," she said finally, her voice breaking, "it won't be the same without you."

"I know," Tessa answered, and her eyes filled with tears. "I don't want to leave, I really don't . . ."

Tessa turned away, her throat aching with emotion. Adrian touched her shoulder lovingly, comfortingly, and in an instant they were in each other's arms, sobbing their hearts out, mourning the finale of a relationship neither of them wanted to end.

"Oh, Tessa," Adrian said, holding on to her friend as if she were never going to see her again, "it's not fair. Just when everything is starting to go so beautifully you're going to leave. It's not fair."

"Yes. Well." Tessa moved out of Adrian's arms and attempted to achieve some semblance of control. "I've always said that nothing worth having is easily won. I've wanted to marry Evan for a long time, and if I have to sacrifice some happiness for the greater happiness of having him, I'll do it gladly. Perhaps," she added meaningfully, "you should consider doing the same with Jason."

Adrian pulled a handkerchief from her sleeve and dried her wet cheeks. "Tessa," she said, swallowing the last of her tears, "you can't seriously be suggesting that I should give up my career to make Jason happy."

Tessa shook her head impatiently, reached into her apron pocket, and took out a packet of cigarettes. "Certainly not, Adrian. I never said that giving up your career would make Jason happy."

"Tessa, cigarettes?" said Adrian, shocked, as Tessa expertly lighted a Sweet Caporal and blew out the match. "Does Evan know?"

Tessa smiled ironically. "Of course, he doesn't know. Do you want to try one?"

"Yes," Adrian said eagerly with a guilty excitement. "Show me how to do it."

Their immediate problems were forgotten for the moment as Tessa attempted to teach Adrian to smoke. Watching herself in the wall mirror, after the first few experimental puffs, Adrian decided that although she disliked the taste of tobacco, she very much liked the picture of sophistication she made with a cigarette held between two fingers.

"I'm going to do it!" she declared, admiring her soigné image in the mirror. "Do you have an extra packet? I'll practice tonight, and when I see Jason—"

She broke off and turned to Tessa, realizing suddenly that she had been home for almost five hours, and as far as she knew, Jason had not tried to contact her.

"Tessa," she said, "have you spoken to Jason? Did you let him know I was coming home today?"

"Yes," Tessa answered. "I telephoned him last week."

Adrian was worried by the tone of Tessa's voice. "What did he say?" she asked with gloomy foreboding.

"Nothing, really." Tessa doused her cigarette in a china candy dish. "He thanked me for telephoning, and said he hoped I was doing well."

"And then?"

"And then he said good-bye."

"Good-bye? That's all?"

"That's all, Adrian."

Adrian moved dejectedly to the desk, crushed out her cigarette in the candy dish, and regarded her friend with doleful, dark eyes. "He hasn't forgiven me then. He's still angry. He didn't even ask about his baby."

"No," Tessa said softly, "he didn't."

"Tessa," she cried abruptly as all her guilt and remorse resurfaced to torment her, "is it over, do you think? Does he hate me?" She was firm in her resolve; she needed her independence. But could Jason understand this? Would he *want* to understand it?

"Hate you?" Tessa put an arm around Adrian's waist.

"I've never known a man who loved anyone as much as Jason loves you."

"But, Tessa, he's angry. I've hurt him."

"Yes," Tessa agreed, "you have. And now it's up to you to make amends for that hurt, to prove to him you love him just as much as he loves you."

"By doing what you did?" demanded Adrian, suddenly frightened. "By sacrificing myself, by giving up my career? I love him, Tessa, but I cannot give up my independence for him."

"Adrian," said Tessa, taking her by the arms and giving her an exasperated shake, "you really can be obtuse at times. That isn't what Jason wants from you at all. When in heaven's name are you going to realize that?"

Nineteen

ADRIAN NEVER HAD a chance to ask Tessa to explain her startling words. Just then a seamstress burst into the office with the distressing announcement that one of the stockboys had been knocked unconscious in the storeroom by a falling bolt of fabric. Tessa telephoned at once for an ambulance, and when it arrived, both she and Adrian accompanied the unfortunate boy to nearby St. Anthony's Hospital.

Luckily his injury was slight. "A good bump on the head," the intern told Adrian after his examination. "No fracture, no concussion. He'll have a headache for a few days, but otherwise he's sound as a dollar."

Adrian talked to the boy to ascertain for herself his condition after he regained consciousness and had been moved from the emergency room to a bed in one of the wards.

"Sam, are you sure you're all right?" she asked as Tessa looked on sympathetically. "Do you want to contact your father?"

"No, don't do that," the boy said morosely. "If you disturb him at his work he'll be madder than hell—I beg your pardon, Miss Marlowe—mad as hops. As it is, he's going to tan my hide for being so clumsy. I should have stacked those bolts more secure."

"Now, Sam," Adrian said sternly, "it wasn't your fault. An accident like that could have happened to anyone. Your father will understand."

Sam shook his head painfully. "Miss Marlowe, he won't

175

understand the loss of a week's wages. The doc told me I'd
be here overnight and then to stay home a few days to be
sure no problems crop up.''

"Don't worry about it," Adrian soothed him. "You'll be
paid for your time off. And if you like, I'll speak to your father and explain to him that you were entirely blameless for
what happened."

"Miss Marlowe," the boy said, brightening, "you're a
peach! And I'm sure glad you've come back. We all missed
you in the shop, and we're mighty happy you've come
home."

"Thank you, Sam," she said gratefully, softly. "It's
good to be home."

And she wondered with a doubtful pang if Jason had
missed her and was as happy as her employees that she was
back in New York after half a year's absence.

When she left the hospital shortly afterward with Tessa,
she said, "Would you mind very much if I don't go back to
the salon with you? I want to go home and telephone Jason.
Perhaps he's forgotten I was to arrive today."

Tessa nodded understandingly. "Yes, go on, call him.
You know how busy he is. I'm sure it slipped his mind."

They regarded each other gravely on the steaming city
street. Jason never forgot anything, and they both knew it.
At length, because there was nothing more that could be
safely said on the subject, they parted with a hug. Adrian
hailed a passing taxi, settled gloomily in the backseat, and
was suddenly reminded by the aching fullness of her breasts
that she had a child at home, waiting to be fed.

As the cabbie maneuvered his vehicle slowly crosstown
on the congested streets, Adrian's gloom deepened as she
reviewed the day's events. Jason had not met her ship; Tessa
was leaving Marlowe's; and poor Sam Johnson was in the
hospital. Her first day back in New York had been an unmitigated disaster. Under those circumstances she wondered if

it was a good idea after all to telephone the man who had said, "I wash my hands of her." Surely he wasn't still angry. She had been home since early morning, and he had not as yet attempted to contact her.

When she arrived at the house on Washington Square, and had fed her little glutton of a daughter, she buttoned up her shirtwaist, surrendered the sated child to Molly's expert care, and marched resolutely downstairs to the telephone. She was not going to sit at home like a coward, waiting for a call that might never come. She would confront Jason openly and explain her reasons for leaving. If he was hurt and angry, so be it. It was up to her to make amends for that hurt and to bear the brunt of the anger she so richly deserved.

She picked up the receiver, gave the number to Central, and when the connection was made, she said in a clear, determined voice, "Adrian Marlowe for Mr. Carradine."

She was transferred at once to Jason's secretary, who greeted her enthusiastically.

"Miss Marlowe, what a pleasure to speak to you again! Yes, he's in. Please hold on. I'll let him know you're calling."

Some of her courage deserted her. What if he wouldn't speak to her? What if he gave Frank some flimsy excuse, or even worse, what if he said to him, "I am not in for Miss Marlowe—not now or ever"?

But her fears were quickly put to rest when she heard his voice. At that long-awaited sound her heart leaped joyously, and she sank to a chair as her knees went weak beneath her.

"Adrian." His tone was low, without inflection. "Welcome home."

"Jason." She could barely speak. The intensity of her emotions was such that to draw even a breath required a superhuman effort. "Jason, I had thought to hear from you before now. Tessa did tell you I was coming home today?"

"Yes." His tone had not changed. "She told me."

Adrian willed herself to speak evenly and slowly. The tempo of her heartbeat caused a tremor in her voice she could not control. "Jason, I know you're angry with me. I realize how I hurt you by leaving you as I did, but I thought at the time that it was the only thing to do. You must try to understand my viewpoint, and you must, please, understand that I'm mortally sorry for any pain I may have caused you."

He was silent for so long a time that she thought he had rung off.

"Jason," she said, alarmed, "are you still there?"

"Yes, I'm here."

"Please," she said, her hand gripping the receiver till her knuckles showed white. "Please say something, anything. Tell me you're angry, tell me you despise me, but don't shut me out. I know what a cowardly thing I did. I should never have run away from you. I should have stayed and fought for what I wanted."

"Fought for what you wanted?" he said quietly, bitterly. "What exactly did you want, Adrian?"

"My freedom!" she blurted. "All I ever wanted was to be free to live my own life, to pursue my career. I never, *never* wanted to be free of *you*, Jason. You must believe that."

"You'll have to forgive me," he said, and his tone was even more bitter, "but I find it extremely difficult to believe that the freedom you desired was not from me. You did not leave New York to escape anyone else, did you? It was from me that you absconded like a thief in the night; it was my marriage proposal you pretended to accept—"

"Jason," she whispered, "Jason . . ."

"Listen to me," he said coldly. "I don't want to hear any more of your feeble explanations. I don't want to hear anything at all you have to say. I do, however, want to see my child. I shall come to your house on Sunday at three, and I expect you *not* to be there.''

''Oh, but—''

''Don't be there, Adrian!''

And without another word he rang off.

She replaced the receiver with a shuddering sigh. He hadn't forgiven her, but he still loved her, of that she had no doubt. He would not fear a face-to-face encounter if he did not love her. It was painfully clear to her that Jason was afraid to see her.

She was somewhat heartened by the fact that he had insisted on seeing his child. A renewed hope awakened in her breast, and with it, a sudden plan occurred to her. Jason would see his baby, she decided, but he would see the baby's mother, too, whether he wanted to or not. And as the plan grew in her mind, expanded, took shape and substance, she rose from the chair with a lighthearted smile and swept briskly up the stairs to talk to Molly.

On Sunday at three o'clock, Adrian was impatiently awaiting Jason's arrival. Molly, with the whimpering child in her arms, paced the floor of Meg Marlowe's room, which had been converted into a nursery, complete with rocking chair, cradle, little blankets, tiny underthings, assorted talcum tins, and a mountain of folded diapers.

''Miss Marlowe,'' Molly said worriedly, ''Mr. Carradine had better hurry up and get here. This baby is hungry, and she's going to be screaming her little lungs out in a moment.''

Adrian, at the mirror, looked over apologetically at her fretting daughter. She knew the baby was hungry—her aching breasts told her as much—but Elyse would just have to wait until her father arrived.

''Molly,'' she said, glancing anxiously at the bedside

clock, "are you sure you remember everything you're supposed to do? Let's go over it one more time."

Molly rolled her eyes heavenward. "Miss, I know my part letter-perfect. There's no need to—"

"Molly, please!"

"Oh, all right," the girl relented, jiggling the restless bundle in her arms. "When Mr. Carradine arrives, I answer the door and say, 'Won't you go right upstairs, sir? The baby is asleep in Mrs. Marlowe's old room. I'll be up with you in a moment. But first there's something I must attend to in the kitchen.'"

"Yes, yes," Adrian urged. "Go on, Molly. And then?"

"And then," Molly recited, "I wait until I'm sure he can't see me, and I let myself out of the house, real quiet. Then I take a taxi to Miss Keller's flat at number fifty-one Bleecker Street, and I stay there until you telephone to tell me it's all right to come home."

"Yes, good!" Adrian said. "Now don't forget; he mustn't suspect I'm in the house. If he asks for me you're to say I'm at Miss Keller's and that I won't be back until later this evening."

"Yes, miss." Molly sighed. "I won't forget. How *could* I forget when we've been over it at least a thousand times in the past two days?"

The doorbell sounded.

Adrian turned rapidly again to the mirror to check her attire. "Molly, he's here! How do I look?"

Molly smiled at her mistress's excitement, which was dizzyingly infectious. Adrian looked ethereally lovely in a delicate wrapper of ivory challis with a trimming of ivory lace at the low neckline and sleeves. Her hair, newly cropped and freshly washed, was a charming, feathery frame around her radiant face, and her dark eyes glowed brilliantly with expectation.

"You'll do," Molly said wryly. "Here, take your baby.

And start feeding her, for pity's sake, while I go down to let her father in.''

Adrian took the child from Molly's arms, sat in the rocker, and hastily fumbled at her bodice. Elyse was beginning to wail, and it was absolutely imperative that she be quieted so that Jason would think she was asleep. With a gentle but adamant hand Adrian directed the child's mouth to her breast. Instantaneously the hungry mouth clamped on Adrian's nipple and began to suck greedily.

Jason found them thus a few moments later when he appeared in the doorway. He stopped stock-still, at the sight of this beatific tableau. They looked like a Della Robbia rendering of mother and child: Adrian, indescribably beautiful, bathed in a golden shaft of afternoon sunlight; and the baby, a Botticelli angel, nursing contentedly at her mother's breast.

For an endless time Jason stared first at the woman he loved and then at the child she had borne him. His sun-browned face and his lean, graceful form were as still as a Greek statue and as classically beautiful. All his love and need and hurt and anger were painfully evident when he raised his eyes again to Adrian. She returned his gaze in a passion of love and longing. Her heart swelled; her mouth began to tremble. "Jason," she whispered, "come. Come look at your daughter."

He came slowly into the room as if compelled by a will not his own. Adrian watched him, unmoving, afraid to say more, afraid to break the sudden spell of enchantment that took hold of her senses and shimmered before her vision like some vivid and palpable presence.

When Jason reached her at last, he did not speak. He knelt at her feet and touched his daughter's hand. On his face was a look of utter love and wondering awe that brought tears to Adrian's eyes. He touched each tiny finger, then turned up the tiny palm and brought it gently to his lips. The child, sated now from her feeding, turned her head and gazed drowsily at this new presence. Jason stroked her pink cheek, her rounded pink chin, then traced the tender line of her sweet, milk-stained mouth.

"She's so small," he finally said, his head bent, his voice rough with emotion.

Adrian longed to reach out to him, to touch his dark hair, to feel it crisp and warm beneath her hand, and to smooth the waving thickness from the curve of his brow. But she only asked softly, "Does she please you, your daughter? Is she truly as you had imagined her?"

"She is more," he said, his voice very low. "Even in my wildest imaginings I could not have envisioned such beauty and perfection."

Adrian drew the wrapper closed around her breast as Jason stroked the fluffy tuft of his daughter's dark hair. Under his soothing touch the child nodded drowsily, then fell fast asleep in her mother's arms. Jason stood and assisted Adrian as she rose with the child and placed her in her cradle.

"She is beautiful, is she not?" murmured Adrian, gazing down at the sleeping form. "God has never made a more perfect child."

At her side Jason was silent. She turned to look up at him, and it was she he now watched and not the child she had given him. His eyes were a deep, dark blue; his lean face was elegant, beautiful, the same dear face she had been longing for, yearning for, seeing each night in her dreams for five long, lonely months.

She spoke his name softly. Still he said nothing but only continued to watch her as if he could not have his fill of her fair ivory beauty. His hand reached up to touch the curve of her cheek. Her eyes closed; she leaned toward him pliantly. She felt an arm encircle her waist, and she was drawn close against him. The hand on her cheek moved slowly, enticingly to the nape of her neck, and then she felt his fingers in her hair, tightening almost painfully with a trembling and passionate restraint.

"Look at me." His low voice shook. His hands in her hair drew her head up and backward. "Open your eyes, Adrian. Look at me."

She complied with a dreamy languor. He was looking down at her intently, his eyes narrowed hungrily, his mouth a hard line of desire and reproach.

"Why?" he said roughly, and the roughness was his pain. "Why did you leave me? What manner of madness prompted you to put an ocean between us when you knew how much I love you and want you? How could you go, knowing how I felt? How could you leave with a child inside you that was mine as much as yours?"

"Jason," she said, remorseful, "I was wrong. You must forgive me."

"Forgive you?" His eyes were a tempest; his arms crushed her ribs. "I shall never forgive you, never; just as I shall never stop loving you. Now, why did you leave me? I insist that you tell me."

She endured his fierce gaze and his brutal embrace with a rapture so ecstatic it took her breath away. To be close to him and touching him was the fulfillment of a need that had long burned within her. In the curve of his arms, with his mouth so close to hers, she was back where she belonged. Her will was his and not her own. And when again he demanded to know why she had left him, her captive heart answered, "Because I love you."

Twenty

IF SHE HAD told him she despised him he could not have looked more astounded. His arms fell away from her; he took a step backward and stared at her with a scowl that was part bewildered, part disbelieving, and totally enraged.

"Have you gone mad?" he demanded. "Or am I the one who has lost his reason? Did I hear you correctly? Did you say you left me because you love me?"

"Jason, hush," she said, flustered. "You'll wake the baby. Come," she beckoned, and held out a hand to him. "Let's go to my room."

He ignored her hand and strode past her out the door. She followed him swiftly, regretting the passionate impulse that had bade her speak her heart. Of course he thought she was mad. What sane person crosses an ocean, putting thousands of miles between herself and the man she professes to love?

He awaited her in her room, arms crossed forbiddingly, his dark face a thundercloud. As she attempted to collect her thoughts and present her defense, he commanded curtly, "Explain yourself."

"Jason," she appealed to him, "if only you will calm down . . ."

His scowl grew more intimidating. "I am perfectly calm, Adrian. Now, if you will be good enough to tell me—" He stopped abruptly and fixed her with his severest gaze. "You *do* love me? I did not misunderstand you?"

"Yes," she said anxiously, "I love you, but—"

184

"Then why in the name of Christ Almighty did you leave me?"

She looked up at him helplessly, feeling miserable, guilty, and trapped. He was forcing the issue, demanding she tell him a truth she knew he would not accept. With misgivings she explained, "I had to, don't you see? I wanted so much to stay, to marry you as you wished. But I knew I couldn't. I knew that marrying you was a mistake, a temporary solution that, in the long run, would create an insoluble problem. You have said that you would never ask me to give up my career, but, Jason, I know differently. I know that a man wants a wife who is devoted solely to him. I know that despite what you may say now, you will eventually come to resent my work, to see it as a rival, and then ultimately you will insist that I—"

"God damn you!" he blazed. "How dare you presume to think you know my thoughts? Have I ever shown resentment of your work? Have I ever once given you the slightest indication that I felt your career interfered with our relationship?"

"No, but—"

"Do you think I would have invested hundreds of thousands of dollars in your fashion house, only to have you abandon it on the day you marry me?"

"No! No! You don't understand!"

"I don't understand. Of course not, how stupid of me! But *you* understand my convictions, my motives. *You* know exactly what goes on in my mind at any given moment—"

"Jason, please," she stopped him. "When you put it like that, it sounds ridiculous."

"Adrian, it is ridiculous. *You're* ridiculous if you truly believe I would ever force you to give up what means most in the world to you."

"Jason," she said desperately, *"you* mean most in the

world to me. I love you with all my heart, but I won't give up my work, not for you or anyone.''

"Jesus· Christ!" he cried in an impotent rage. "Have I *asked* you to give up your work?''

"No," she said stubbornly, "not yet. But you will. Eventually you will.''

He drew a deep breath, and Adrian watched guiltily as he struggled to gain control of the patience and understanding she had tested to the limit. What a fool she had been to have admitted she loved him. If he had been angry with her before he was a hundred times more so now.

"Adrian," he said, and his voice was unsteady as he strove to bring to order his unruly emotions, "let's try to discuss this rationally, shall we? Why won't you believe me when I say I would never stop you from pursuing your career?''

He had slipped his hands into his pockets but not before Adrian had noted their trembling. He was angrier than she had ever seen him, yet he was attempting for her sake to appear calm and controlled when she knew without doubt that he would like nothing more than to turn her over his knee and give her the thrashing of her life. She was moved beyond words by this further demonstration of his unqualified love for her.

"Oh, Jason," she cried softly, and flew across the room and flung her arms around his neck. "It doesn't matter," she said, covering his startled face with kisses. "Nothing matters except that we're together again. I don't want to quarrel . . . not now, not today. I've waited so long to see you. I cannot tell you how much I missed you while I was away. I dreamed of you every night. I longed for you unbearably. Oh, Jason, hold me, kiss me. I dreamed of your kisses, I ached for your kisses—''

She pressed her lips to his, and a wild thrill went through her as his arms, with a sudden fierceness, went hard around

her. He groaned softly as her mouth parted beneath his; his
arms tightened, and she strained against him, feeling his
hard desire already full with the need of her.

"Make love to me," she whispered urgently, tearing her
mouth from his. "Now. Hurry. I love you, I want you."

She fumbled at his tie while he shrugged out of his coat.
The few moments it took to undress were to her an eternity
of waiting. She wanted him, wanted him; she had waited so
long. When they were in bed at last, she went eagerly into
his arms, smothering his face with kisses, running her hands
over the body she so loved. He felt so warm and hard and
wonderful and strong. His desire equaled hers; he could not
have enough of touching her. She thrilled to his touch, to the
warmth of his hands and the heat of his mouth as he kissed
each quivering breast; then he rose over her and entered her
and kissed her waiting mouth as he pressed deep inside her.

She moaned with excitement as he grasped her hips and
drove into her with a passion that was beyond his control.
Never had his love been so violent, so fierce, and never had
consummation come so swiftly and intensely. She cried out
with pleasure at the same moment he pressed hard against
her, releasing his passion. But he had not had enough of her,
nor she of him. He remained inside her, his mouth against
her cheek, his breathing harsh and ragged near her ear. His
sweat-covered body lay heavily upon her, but his weight
was a rapture she joyously endured. She wanted him again,
though the tingle of satisfaction still hummed in her nerves.
She wanted more of him, all of him; she wanted to drain and
deplete him, to absorb his very essence through the sweet
and savage passion of his love.

After some time, he stirred above her, and she felt the
fullness of his reawakened desire deep within her. She
turned her mouth to his and kissed him deeply, possessively,
her hands moving sensuously over his hard, narrow hips. He
began to move inside her with a long, slow, tantalizing

rhythm that seduced and enticed her and sent spasms of sensation to the furthermost regions of her body. His skin against hers was a silky fire that reignited her passion, fueled it, fanned it, drove it to brilliant heights as he loved her and touched her and kissed her burning mouth. He was her love, her spendid lover; she loved him with all her soul. Wrapped in his arms, his desire deep inside her, she knew nothing, wanted nothing but Jason, only him. Consummation came again, breathtaking and dazzling. And when he filled her again with the essence of his passion, she surrendered her very being to his all-consuming love.

An hour might have passed, or an endless eternity. Time ceased as she lay in his embrace, her head near his heart, one arm wrapped tightly around him as if she feared he might vanish. A delicious contentment stole over her. She was at rest and at peace for the first time in months. In the arms of her lover she knew love and serenity and utter completion such as nothing else had ever afforded her.

He spoke first, breaking the silence that had wrapped itself around her like a dreamy cocoon.

"Your servant," he said, ever the practical man, "she won't come upstairs?"

Adrian smiled and looked up at him with passion-drowsy eyes. "She is not here. I sent her to Tessa's."

"Good God," he exclaimed softly. "You had this planned."

"Of course I did." She kissed his shoulder and then nuzzled her cheek against its sinewy hardness. "I have thought of nothing else since the day I came home."

He laughed and hugged her closer. "My sincerest congratulations on a plan well executed."

She basked in the glow of his admiring approval. Her contentment deepened, and she kissed him again on the throat, on the cheek, and then, with slumberous passion, on his hard, curving mouth. He returned the kiss with ardor, but then, moving her head away, he said with another laugh, "No more, my little seductress. You have destroyed me completely. My strength is at such a low ebb, I fear I shall have to spend the rest of my life in this bed."

"Good," she murmured. "That was the second part of my plan."

With a chuckle he reached down on the floor for his coat, extracted a silver case, then sat up against the headboard and lit a cigarette.

"Let me have one," said Adrian, sitting up alongside him.

Jason raised a dark eyebrow, then held out the open case to her and watched with interest as she drew a light from the burning end of his cigarette.

She leaned back against the headboard and inhaled deeply as she had been practicing for two days. "Ah," she said, exhaling, "just what I needed."

"Since when," Jason asked, suppressing an amused smile, "have you taken up cigarettes?"

"I've been smoking awhile," she said airily. "I can't remember for how long." She hazarded a glance in his direction. "You don't object, do you?"

"Why should I object?"

She shrugged and inhaled again. "Oh, I don't know. Some men are so unreasonable when it comes to a woman enjoying the same things they do. For example, I know I shouldn't enjoy making love as much as I do. From all I've heard, women are supposed to lie back and think of better things. But when you make love to me, all I can think of is how delicious you make me feel."

He choked with laughter on a lungful of smoke, then when he recovered, he drew her across his lap and dropped a kiss on her brow. "You are the most astonishing woman! But do you mind if we turn the conversation to a less erotic topic? Tell me about my daughter; what have you named her?''

"Why, Elyse, of course. Did you think I would do otherwise?"

"My dear girl," he said sardonically, "I so seldom know what to think where you're concerned. But thank you for naming her after my mother. It was very important to me."

She snuggled closer against him. "Why is that, Jason?"

He sighed reflectively and stroked her bare arm. "My mother was extraordinary," he explained. "She was a loving wife, a devoted parent, an upstanding member of the community, and she was also a hellcat of a militant suffragette. I remember meetings at our house—loud, raucous affairs attended by the likes of Susan B. Anthony, Lucy Stone, and Anna Howard Shaw. And I particularly remember one bitter-cold day in January when my mother and her cronies paraded up Fifth Avenue carrying placards that demanded the vote, and I, a shivering six-year-old, holding on for dear life to my mother's skirts as she harangued a curbside crowd of jeering dissenters."

Adrian sat upright excitedly and crushed out her cigarette in a small tin tray on the night table. "A suffragette? How wonderful!"

"Yes," he agreed with a pensive smile, "my mother was wonderful. By the way," he added dryly, "she, too, enjoyed an occasional smoke in the privacy of her bedroom."

He leaned over to snuff out his cigarette, then continued thoughtfully, "She was amazing, Adrian. Her fight for the vote was her passion in life, yet even while she was engaged day and night with her fellow suffragettes, she could arrange a banquet for two hundred people with an ease and perfection that was astounding, and then appear at that banquet looking as lovely and as purely ornamental as any society matron."

His eyes warmed with memory. Adrian watched him

quietly, discovering yet another facet to this many-faceted man. "She sounds marvelous, Jason. I wish I could have known her."

"You would have liked her," he said, smiling. "You remind me of her in many ways. You have that same stubborn, unyielding determination I remember so well in her. Besides her work for the vote, she was also an early advocate of anticonception, and she distributed instructive pamphlets, much to my father's displeasure. She and he had many a ferocious battle and almost separated more times than I care to recall. They never did, though. He loved her utterly, you see, absolutely—the way I love you."

"Jason," she said, touched by his words but not fooled for a moment by his recollective meanderings, "I'm beginning to think that you're telling me all this with a specific purpose in mind."

"Which purpose, Adrian?"

"You're trying to show me that I can be a wife and mother as your mother was and still pursue my career."

"Is that what I'm doing?"

"Yes, it is, Jason. And I appreciate that you're trying to understand my position. I love you for it. I shall never love any man but you. But I can't marry you. I know it's what you want, but I simply can't."

He regarded her soberly and brushed the hair from her brow. His eyes bespoke a grudging admiration, but they were adamant, too, with that severe, authoritative look Adrian knew so well. For a moment she feared a quarrel, for his face was very still and his hard mouth unsmiling. But at length he said quietly, "You *can* marry me, my stubborn little mule, and eventually you will."

Then he took her in his arms, and despite his earlier comments on his waning strength, he made passionate love to her for the rest of the afternoon.

Twenty-one

MORE THAN A YEAR went by with the speed of a month, and still she continued to refuse to marry him, and still he continued to say with a calm and a certainty that bewildered her, "You will, Adrian, you will."

In no way did he force the issue; in fact, he accepted her repeated refusals with a good-natured equanimity that was deeply puzzling to her. Also puzzling was his absolute tolerance of all decisions she made regarding their daughter's upbringing. When she weaned Elyse at the age of three months because feeding the child interfered with her work, Adrian fully expected Jason to register a vehement protest, but he surprised her by saying, "I have already talked to Ned Garvey about a replacement formula. If you'll make an appointment with him for some time next week, he should have two or three suitable substitutes ready for you."

When she purchased a house, a grand, palatial three-story affair on East Fifty-ninth Street, she anticipated that now Jason would say to her, "Why buy a house of your own? Marry me and move into mine." But he only said helpfully, "If you're thinking of having it professionally decorated let me know. I have a friend, an interior designer, who owes me a favor. I know she'll be more than happy to be of whatever service she can."

There seemed no end to the friends who owed Jason a favor, and there seemed no end as well to his baffling patience. Adrian said to him once in a fit of frustration,

"You're an enigma if ever there was one. You keep insisting I'm going to marry you, and yet no matter what I do to resist you, you simply smile and say nothing."

He smiled and said nothing.

Jason's passivity was a great source of consternation to Adrian. It had been easier to deal with him when he had actively sought to coerce her into marriage. But in the past year he had changed his tactics—much like a military strategist, Adrian would think sourly—and during this deceptively tranquil cessation of aggression, Adrian worried even more about the strength of her defenses.

She did want to marry him; that was the difficult part. She loved him so deeply, and with each day that passed she grew to love him more. He was the perfect lover, a loving friend, an invaluable business partner, and he was the most wonderful of fathers. For Elyse's first birthday he bought her an exquisite assortment of porcelain animals: a bear; a giraffe; a horse; a zebra; a unicorn; a lion; and many more, all of which had to be housed in a separate display cabinet, so large and so precious was the collection. He also instituted a trust fund for the child which, upon her twenty-first birthday, would surely establish her as one of the wealthiest young women in the country.

It was an open secret among New Yorkers that Jason was Elyse's father. As Tessa had predicted, no one believed Adrian's basket-on-the-doorstep story, and moreover, the child so much resembled Jason with her warm brown curls and her splendid blue eyes that the question of paternity was easily deduced.

Anna Held, no longer married to Ziegfeld but still a dear friend to Adrian, said to her often, "Chérie, you must marry your lover—if only for the child's sake. You cannot want little Elyse to be known as a bâtarde."

No, Adrian did not want that, but neither did she wish to destroy the beautiful relationship she had with Jason. And marriage, she was convinced, would do just that. Marriage, Adrian felt, was the end to independence, and to Adrian the end to independence was a living death. She would not marry Jason, as much as she wanted to. She had made up her mind, and nothing was going to change it.

While her private life continued to play havoc with her peace of mind, her social life and her career could not have been more satisfying. Adrian was the new darling of the fashion world, and her fame even had begun to reach across the Atlantic. At the fall showing of 1911, she had intoduced the V-neck blouse, a daring departure from the strangling, boned collars of the past. *Punch,* the renowned English weekly, called it the "pneumonia blouse," but by the spring of 1912, these comfortable garments were seen everywhere: on Bond Street, the Rue de la Paix, and the Via Veneto, as well as on American streets from the east coast to west.

For the spring showing of 1912, she introduced a children's line. Inspired by her beautiful daughter, she designed an irresistible collection of smocked charmers, cossack-style tunics, low-sashed dresses trimmed with Valenciennes lace, and embroidered christening gowns of linen lawn. For Tessa's wedding on June 1, 1912, she designed a most loving tribute to her friend, a classic and exquisite creation of ivory peau de soie, with a simple slim skirt and a bodice of delicate hand embroidery.

When Tessa walked down the aisle on her father's arm, wearing that gown, Adrian, the maid of honor, could not contain her tears. She wept both with joy and with the pain of losing her beloved colleague. Adrian had been so busy in the past year, working, enjoying her daughter, socializing with Jason at the fabulous homes of his affluent friends, that she had not had time to think that her working days with Tessa were numbered. Even when they went out as a foursome—to the theater, the opera, or if they dined at the roof garden of Stanford White's magnificent Madison Square Garden—Adrian could not conceive of her working relationship with Tessa coming to an end.

She would tease Evan, "Surely you're not going to force Tessa to give up her work when you know it means so much to her?"

Evan would answer meaningfully, "*Tessa* knows a wife's duty and expects to perform it."

She would look at Jason then, as if to say, That's why I won't marry you.

Later, when they were alone, Jason would say in response to her unspoken words, "When are you going to realize that I am not Evan Colby?"

Adrian thought of that now as she watched the Reverend Lewis unite Tessa and Evan as man and wife. No, Jason was not Evan. It was a simple fact which, for the past few years, Adrian had known but not really understood. Jason, unlike Evan, would never dream of denying her the independence she craved. Why, then, this stubborn refusal to marry him? Did independence mean more to her than the happiness of the man she loved?

At the champagne breakfast at Sherry's restaurant Adrian clung to Jason's arm as they greeted and chatted with the elegantly clad guests. Many patrons of Marlowe's were in attendance, people who admired Adrian's creativity while fully aware of Tessa's talent for transposing that art to reality.

Ava Astor, always outspoken, said to Adrian, "How *can* you let her go, my dear? Tessa's an absolute wonder, you know. Aren't you afraid your designs might suffer in the hands of someone less gifted than she?"

Yes, Adrian feared exactly that. She would sorely miss Tessa's skill, her unparalleled genius for interpreting ideas. But much more than that, Adrian would miss Tessa's presence at the salon; her friendship, her love, her spiritual support.

And what of Tessa? Adrian wondered. Wouldn't Tessa miss the work that had become as much a part of her life as it was part of Adrian's? Hadn't Tessa labored as long and as hard to perfect her art, to raise Marlowe's from a shop around the corner to a fashion house on a par with the great houses of Europe?

"Would you excuse me, Ava?" Adrian had to talk to Evan. She had to try to convince him to allow Tessa to remain at Marlowe's, to share in the fruits of its success.

She sought out the bridal couple, who stood partially hidden by a gilded column, toasting each other in conspiratorial solitude.

"Forgive me, you two," she said as she approached them. "I hate to intrude, but I must speak to you both."

"Yes, what is it?" Tessa smiled, her cheeks flushed with a delightful, happy glow.

Evan, at her side, looked uncommonly dignified in his morning coat and striped trousers. In one hand he held a glass of champagne; in the other, as if claiming ownership, he held his wife's slender arm.

"Evan," Adrian began, "I'll be candid—"

"One of your most admirable traits," he interrupted her.

His irony was not lost on her. Since the day Evan had learned of her relationship with Jason, his attitude toward her had never been quite the same. At times Adrian found it easy to believe that he thought her contemptible. Other times, she would catch him watching her with a curious intensity. It was her imagination, of course. Tessa was the only woman he now loved.

"Evan," she went on, "perhaps this is not the right time to bring this up, but I must ask you to reconsider your refusal to let Tessa work."

"Adrian!" Tessa exclaimed.

Evan said deliberately, "I'm sorry, Adrian, I cannot do that. In any case, Tessa is quite willing to give up her work and devote herself fully to being a wife and a mother. Isn't that right, Tessa?"

He glanced at his wife for confirmation. Tessa said, upset, "Yes, that's right, Evan." Then, to Adrian, "Why are you asking this now? I've told you my decision; this is what I want to do."

But the vehemence of Tessa's confirmation made Adrian doubt her sincerity. This was not what Tessa wanted; it was what Evan wanted.

"Tessa, listen to me," Adrian said. "If you really want to work you should be honest with Evan. Perhaps he feels that your career doesn't matter that much to you, and that's why he wants you to give it up."

"Adrian, please," Tessa said stiffly. "I must ask you not to interfere in matters that don't concern you."

"Don't concern me?" Adrian said, stunned. "Tessa, your happiness concerns me. Everything about you concerns me. We're more than friends, you and I. We've created Marlowe's together; I want you to share in its success. I want—"

"Adrian," Tessa said quietly, "it's not what *I* want anymore. Can't you understand that?"

Adrian was silenced. No, she couldn't understand how Tessa could so easily toss aside something for which she had toiled so long and hard. Marlowe's was a symbol, as much to Tessa as it was to Adrian; a symbol of their struggle to succeed in a so-called man's world. They *had* succeeded, that was the beauty of it all. And yet Tessa could turn her back on that success without a second thought. No, Adrian could not understand it.

At last she said, defeated, "Very well, Tessa. If that's your final decision I won't bring up the subject again. I did not mean to interfere."

"Oh, Adrian," Tessa said, and remorsefully embraced her. "I didn't mean to snap at you. I know you care about me, but I've made my choice, and I don't regret it."

She pulled away from Adrian and linked an arm through Evan's, as if reinforcing her decision. But still, she said to Adrian, "This won't alter our friendship, will it?"

"Never!" Adrian said at once. But when she turned to Evan to tender an apology, she could not help reflecting on how marriage had irrevocably altered the course of her friend's life.

Twenty-two

ON THE EVE of Elyse's second birthday, an unusually cool June night, Adrian was in the sumptuous bedroom of her new house, with the fireplace blazing as though it were January, awaiting Jason's arrival. He had been away for almost two months on one of his frequent business trips to Europe. He was in Berlin now, where he had witnessed the trial run of the Prussian-Hessian Railways' diesel locomotive. The locomotive's performance, he had written her, had been less than impressive, but the concept intrigued him, and he was sure that with certain modifications diesel-powered trains were a worthy investment.

His arrival in New York early that morning aboard the *Teutonic* had gone unnoted by the journalists and photographers who hounded the docks. According to all the newspapers, Jason was expected home later in the month, but unbeknownst to the press, he had changed his plans when he remembered his daughter's birthday. When he had telephoned Adrian at noon at the salon, she had been pleasantly surprised to hear his voice. And when he explained the reason for his earlier arrival, she had asked him, "What time will you be coming to the house? Shall I keep the baby up for you?"

"No," he had said. "I might be late. I'm having dinner with Neily Vanderbilt. He's been pressing me to join his syndicate for next year's America's Cup race. When he

spotted me this morning on Wall Street, he insisted I meet
with him tonight to discuss it.''

"How late will you be, Jason?"

"I'm not sure. Wait up for me—and give the servants the
night off.''

"You're in luck!" She had laughed. "This *is* their night
off.''

Awaiting him now in her gilt-and-ivory bedroom, she ad-
justed the folds of her rose-colored peignoir and dabbed a
few drops of French perfume behind her ears, at her throat,
and at the curve of her breast. As always, when she had been
separated from Jason for any length of time, she was in a fever to see him. It astonished her at times how much she
loved him and wanted him. They had been lovers for three
years, yet each time he made love to her was as thrilling and
as delicious as the first.

Her one complaint was that their time together was somewhat limited now. Since moving into her house almost a
year ago and acquiring a full staff of servants, Adrian was
only able to share Jason's love on Thursdays, the servants'
night off, and sometimes on Sundays when the servants
were at church. Here again was another inducement for her
to lower her defenses and accept his proposal. But as much
as the idea appealed to her, as much as she daydreamed of
being snugly married and free to spend night after lovely
night in Jason's bed, she refused to give in.

When she heard footsteps on the stairs, her heart began a
happy pounding. He was here at last—and earlier than expected! She rose from the vanity and went to her bedroom
door, a radiant smile lighting her face, a smile that died a
sudden death when she threw open the door and found herself staring at Perry Crandall, that wretch from the *New York
World*.

He lounged against the door frame, his freckled face as
boyish as ever and his narrow gray eyes more lascivious

than Adrian remembered them. He wore what looked like the same checkered suit and yellow bow tie in which she had last seen him, and the overpowering stench of cheap liquor emanated from his person.

"What are you doing here?" she gasped. "How did you get in?"

"A good reporter," he answered, stepping insolently into the room, "has ways and means of gaining access to even the most heavily guarded of fortresses."

"Get out!" she commanded, too angry to be frightened. "Leave here at once or I shall summon the police—"

"You threatened me once before with the law," Crandall reminded her, unmoving, "and your threat backfired, as I recall. How did you enjoy your stay in jail, Miss Marlowe? A pity it was so brief. Thirty days in the cooler might have taken you down a peg or two. God knows you could use a lesson in humility."

Now she was frightened. Now she fully realized the position she was in. This man was drunk and very possibly deranged; otherwise, he would not have broken into her house and be standing here, hands in pockets, surveying her lightly clad form with that revoltingly lewd gaze.

"If you don't leave," she said, steeling her spine, "I shall call a servant and—"

"Your servants are off tonight," he said, stopping her. "Oh, don't look so surprised, Miss Marlowe. I've had you and your household under surveillance for months. I can recite your every move from one hour to the next. You rise at seven, breakfast at eight, and you're at your salon no later than eight-thirty. You work until six or seven, then you return home, have a light supper, spend some time with your daughter if she's still awake, and retire at ten, unless you have plans for the evening."

"How do you know all this?" she demanded, but in her voice there was an unmistakable tremor.

"It's very simple." Crandall smirked. "You have a young parlormaid whose acquaintance I happened to make back in December. She finds me very attractive, Miss Marlowe; in fact, I think she'd like to marry me. Anyway, during the course of our loving relationship I have questioned her at length about her work and her employer, questions she's only too eager to answer. There are other things about you I have had to find out or surmise for myself. For instance, I know that on Thursday evenings you entertain your lover, the great Jason Carradine, and sometimes on Sunday mornings he stops in for a quick roll in the hay while the servants are at services."

"Get out!" she cried as a bloody rage exploded within her. "Jason will be here any minute, and when he comes, he's going to kill you!"

"I doubt that," said Crandall, unperturbed by her outburst. "Your lover's in Germany, and unless he sprouts wings, he's not going to be here until long after I'm done with you."

Now she was terrified. Crandall's intention was clear. He was going to assault her; his lust was disgustingly evident in those leering gray eyes. And Jason . . . dear God, where was Jason? Why wasn't he here? When would he come? Would it be in time to prevent this slimy pervert from exacting a further and unspeakable revenge?

"Stay away from me," she choked when he began to walk toward her. "If you take one more step I'll scream."

"Scream all you like," he said with a shrug. "The windows are closed; no one will hear you. By the way, Miss Marlowe, you look very lovely tonight. Are you wearing your brassiere? It doesn't look like it. Come here; let me see if you have it on."

He reached out a hand and she slapped it away. Then she made a dash for the door, but he was upon her in a moment.

"Not so fast," he snarled, twisting both her arms behind

her back. "I've come here with a specific goal in mind, and I'm not going to leave until I've achieved it. Do you know what your lover did to me two and a half years ago? Do you know he came to my flat one night and near broke my arm until I told him I had given Judge Lorimar a bogus petition? And do you think that satisfied him? No, Miss Marlowe. He then had me discharged from the *World* and further arranged it so that no newspaper in town would hire me. I've been out west all this time, working at the most menial and degrading positions. But I never forgot you or your precious lover. I simply bided my time and saved up my money till I had enough to come back and settle the score with both of you. Do you understand what I'm saying, Miss Marlowe? Do you see why I'm not going to leave here until I get what I want?"

"Yes, yes," she gasped, her throat dry, her mind working furiously. She had to stop him somehow; she had to divert him. If she could just play along with him until Jason . . .

"Turn around now, Miss Marlowe, and give us a kiss. But first promise me you won't try to run away. If you refuse," he threatened softly, "I'll break your arm."

"Yes, all right, all right," she gabbled desperately. "I promise. I won't run away."

His grip loosened, but he did not release her. He stood quietly behind her holding on to her wrists, and after a time he pressed her hands to his body and groaned softly as he forced her fingers to close about his hardening passion.

"No!" she cried and wrenched away from him in disgust. "Let me go! Stay away from me!"

Her glance darted wildly about the room. A weapon, she needed a weapon. Her eyes fell on the poker near the fireplace. She made a move to go for it, but Crandall was quicker than she. He grasped her wrists, flung her onto the bed, and advanced toward her with a menacing glare, unbuttoning his trousers as he reached the bed.

"All right, you bitch, we'll do this your way."

She leaped to her feet, her heart hammering against her ribs, but he captured her easily and forced her down on the bed. He knelt over her, pinning her arms above her head with one hand and lifting her peignoir over her thighs with the other.

"Dear God, no," she cried, struggling. "Don't do this. Don't!"

"Shut up!" he said savagely, and covered her mouth with his.

His breath reeked of liquor; his tongue pushing past her lips was a foul intrusion. He kissed her brutally, obscenely; she wanted to vomit in his mouth. His hand was on her thigh, squeezing, hurting, and she could feel the hard length of him pushing to gain entry as his fingers poked and prodded with slimy insistence between her legs.

With a sudden burst of strength she freed her arms from his hold and brought her nails raking viciously across his cheek. He cried out in pain, half lifting himself from her body. Panting, struggling desperately, Adrian pushed at his chest, but in the next instant, she was knocked almost unconscious by a blow of his fist to her jaw.

She lay beneath him in a daze. Her head was swimming; the pain in her jaw was devastating. In a stupor she heard his rasping breaths, felt his lips on hers again, his tongue in her mouth, his hands between her legs. But just when she felt he was ready to enter her, he was jerked suddenly from her body. Adrian turned her head weakly. She saw Jason, his eyes like death, land a close-fisted blow on Crandall's disbelieving face.

She watched in helpless shock as Crandall scrambled to his feet, only to be knocked down again. Blood spurted from his mouth; his narrow gray eyes were wide with fear as Ja-

son picked him up by the collar and pummeled his face until
the features were unrecognizable.

"Jason!" she screamed, coming swiftly to her senses.
"Jason, stop!"

He was going to kill him. Nothing but murder would satisfy the bloodlust that Adrian saw in Jason's eyes. She
stumbled from the bed as he bent over the moaning Crandall
and put both hands around his throat and began to choke the
life from his body.

"Jason, no!" she screamed, pulling at his shoulders.
"Don't kill him; you'll go to prison. Jason, he's not worth
it. Oh, dear God, please stop!"

Perhaps her terror restored his sanity; perhaps his own
morality intervened. He loosened his grip and rose slowly,
looking down at Crandall as if he could not believe what he
had been about to do. He turned to Adrian, his face ashen,
his body shaking. He was about to speak, when with a
lightning-swift movement, Crandall was on his feet and running out the door.

As Jason turned swiftly to pursue him Adrian cried, "No,
Jason. Let him go!"

But he was out the door before the words were out of her
mouth. She heard pounding footsteps on the stairs. She ran
out into the hall and looked over the banister just as Jason
went out the front door, following closely on Crandall's
heels. In the next instant she heard a screech of brakes, a
man's scream, a sickening thud. And then she heard nothing
as her vision dimmed, her mind reeled, and she sank to the
floor in unconscious oblivion.

Twenty-three

SHE STRUGGLED SLOWLY to consciousness as if fighting her way out of a clinging black mist. She was on the bed in the guest room, outside of which she had fainted. Standing over her, watching her gravely, was Ned Garvey, flanked by a very frightened-looking Molly. Adrian's jaw ached intolerably; she felt dizzy and sick. As she gazed dully at the two watching over her she asked in a tortured whisper, "Jason? Where is Jason?"

"He'll be here as soon as he can," Garvey answered. "He's gone down to the police station to answer a few questions."

"And . . . Crandall?" The name was almost inaudible.

"He's dead," said Garvey grimly. "Run down by an auto. He won't bother you anymore, Adrian. You rest easy now."

Hot tears stung her eyes, and she reached out to Molly, who immediately grasped her hand and held it tightly in hers. "The scum is dead, miss," Molly said vehemently. "Mr. Carradine told us what happened here, and if you ask me, Crandall's end was too good for him. That filthy—"

"Molly," cautioned Garvey mildly, "we needn't be reminding Miss Marlowe of something she would rather forget."

"Oh, to be sure!" Molly agreed, and patted the hand she held. "We're going to put this out of our minds, miss. We won't ever think of it again."

"Molly," Adrian said weakly, "why are you here?
How—"

"Mr. Carradine sent his chauffeur to fetch me in the mo-
torcar," Molly explained. "He was worried about the tyke,
but she slept through it all, God love her. She's sleeping
peacefully now; I looked in on her just a moment ago."

Adrian shuddered and closed her eyes as the memory of
Crandall's attack swept over her. Dear God, what if the
baby awakened, what if Jason hadn't come when he did,
what if Crandall had . . . ?

Her eyes flew open and she clutched at Molly's hand. "I
want Jason," she said fiercely. "I want him now. Ned!"
she cried. "Please get him for me. I want him. I need him."

"Adrian, calm yourself," Garvey said sternly, then
picked up her wrist and checked her galloping pulse. "You
must be patient. Jason will be here as soon as the police are
done with their questioning. Sleep now if you can."

"No," she said feverishly. "I can't sleep, I won't. Not
until he's here. Don't you understand, Ned? If it hadn't been
for Jason . . . Crandall would have . . . would have . . .
Oh, don't you see? I need Jason to be with me. I won't feel
safe until he's here with me."

She knew she was babbling like a madwoman, but she
couldn't stop herself. Her nerves felt drawn tight as bow-
strings, her heart was beating a staccato tattoo, and she
swallowed continuously as if a foreign presence were
lodged in her throat. She had never been more frightened in
her life, yet she was perfectly aware of the fact that the danger was past. But she couldn't stop shaking, and her pulse
felt treble its normal tempo. "Molly," she said, crushing
the girl's hand, "you'll stay with me until he comes? You
won't leave me?"

"Of course not, miss," Molly answered, glancing anxiously at the doctor. "We'll both stay with you—all night if
necessary."

"Adrian," Garvey said, mixing a draft into a glass of water, "drink this. It'll steady your nerves."

She stared at him violently. "It won't put me to sleep? I don't want to sleep."

"No," he said soothingly, "I promise you. It will only steady your nerves."

She took the glass and drank unwillingly, afraid he might have tricked her into taking a sleeping potion. But as he had said, the mixture did not induce sleep; it only loosened her knotted nerves so that the anxiety she felt was to a small degree relieved.

Garvey settled on the chaise longue, and Molly, on a bedside chair, held on to Adrian's hand with a warm, loving grip. Garvey spoke to his patient gently, questioning her about the upcoming showing. Adrian answered automatically, knowing that he was attempting to divert her mind from the horror of the evening. But even as she told him half-heartedly about her new designs and about the hectic rush that always precedes a public showing, she was seeing in her mind Crandall's lust-swollen face above hers and feeling his probing fingers touching her in places that still ached and prickled sickeningly with the memory.

Finally, close to midnight, Jason returned. At the sound of footsteps in the hall Adrian's eyes darted to the door, and when he entered the room, weary, his face drawn and ashen, she had to restrain herself from leaping out of bed and flying into his arms and never, ever letting him go again.

"Are you all right?" he asked, approaching the bed, his eyes so dark a blue, they looked black.

"Yes," she said faintly, "I'm all right."

The expression on his face brought a chill to her heart. He looked tired to the bone, but more than that, when his eyes fell on her bruised jaw, Adrian sensed in his anguished gaze a torment that surpassed her own.

"Ned, thank you for staying," he said, turning with effort to his friend.

"Yes, of course," said Garvey, rising. "Molly, would you mind showing me out?"

The two left, leaving Adrian alone at last with her lover, her savior. If he had not come at the moment he did, if he had not pulled Crandall from her inert body . . .

"Jason," she whispered, tears clouding her eyes, "oh, Jason, hold me."

He went to her at once and sat on the bed, took her fiercely in his arms, held her tightly, and pressed shaking lips to her hair. "My God," he said hoarsely. "Adrian . . ."

His arms were hurting her, but she did not care. She was safe now; Jason was here, holding her. Nothing would ever harm her as long as he was holding her.

For a long while they held on to each other, sharing their separate fears, easing them in the sharing. At length he drew slightly away from her, lifting her chin with a finger, and looked deep into her eyes. "Adrian." His low voice shook. "He didn't . . . ? Crandall did not . . . ?" He could not speak the words; they were a torment in his throat.

"No," she whispered, her lashes lowering against her flaming cheeks. "He did not."

She felt him draw a ragged breath, and then he held her close again, stroking her back with hands that shook with relief. Her own trembling increased. Safe in Jason's arms, she was even more aware of the fate she had narrowly escaped.

"Jason," she said, her words muffled against his chest, "promise me you'll never leave me. Jason, give me your word."

"Yes, of course, you have my word." His voice was hoarse, aching.

"You won't leave me? Ever?"

"No, never," he promised her, kissing her fevered brow.

"You'll stay here tonight?" she persisted. "You'll sleep with me?"

"Yes," he said, "I'll stay as long as you like. I won't leave you, I promise you. I love you."

"Oh, Jason," she said in a passion, her arms pressing him closer, "marry me. Marry me tomorrow. Take me to City Hall; talk to your friends. I never want to be alone again."

She felt him tense in her embrace, and then slowly he held her away from him and searched her tortured eyes. "Do you mean that?" he asked, afraid to believe it. "Are you certain that's what you want?"

"Yes, I'm certain, I'm sure. I want to be with you always. I don't want to be alone. It's what you want, too, Jason. You've wanted it for years. Why are you hesitating? Why do you look at me like that?"

The words spilled out swiftly, hotly, disjointedly. Why did he stare at her? Why were his hands on her arms like a vise?

"Adrian," he said, "you know how much I want you to marry me, but I want your decision to be made logically, not out of fear. Wait a few days, a week, until the memory of this night is not so painful in your mind. Marry me because you want to, not because you've been frightened into doing so."

"Why won't you say yes?" she cried, hysterical. "Did the sight of another man touching my body disgust you? Do you think, perhaps, in the back of your mind that I encouraged Crandall, that I enjoyed his advances?"

"Adrian, stop it!" he said sharply, and took hold of her arms and shook her firmly. "You're upset, irrational. None of what you've said is true, and we both know it. Stop it at once! I don't want to hear any more rubbish from your lips."

His severe gaze commanded, but his face was gray with

strain. A tiny spark of sanity quelled Adrian's rage, and with a choked sob she slumped wearily against him. "I'm sorry," she whispered. "Please forgive me. I didn't mean—"

"Hush," he said. "I know you didn't mean it. We're both too emotional tonight to make any sense at all. Let's get some sleep, Adrian, and then tomorrow we can talk all you like."

"Jason." She drew a sobbing breath and looked up at him with anguished eyes. "You must marry me tomorrow. I feel perfectly calm now, I know what I want, and you must not refuse me."

He looked down at her in silence, at her tear-bright eyes, her trembling mouth, her battered jaw. She was fragile in his arms, injured, a pale, helpless, frightened child in the guise of the woman he loved more than life. He knew he ought not to give in to her fear-induced demand, but he loved her so intensely that on this, of all nights, he could deny her nothing.

"Very well," he said quietly. "If I can arrange it we shall be married tomorrow."

She drew another sobbing breath and burrowed closer against him. She felt safe now, truly safe. Jason was here, and she knew now that she could sleep. How good it felt to lean on another's strength, how utterly serene. Jason left her momentarily to undress, then he got back in bed and settled against her under the covers.

Adrian went into his arms with a deep, contented sigh. She kept whispering his name as if to assure herself of his presence. She kept touching him, kissing him, and pressing herself close to the comfort of his warmth. He felt so good against her, so hard, so strong, an impregnable barrier between her and a perilous world. All night long she dozed and awoke intermittently. And each time she awoke she made sure Jason's arms were closed firmly around her.

Twenty-four

THEY WERE MARRIED on their daughter's second birthday. True to his word, Jason called in certain favors owed him by city officials, and on June 10, 1913, in the presence of the justice of the peace and two county employees, Adrian Marlowe and Jason Carradine became husband and wife.

The bare simplicity of the ceremony did not matter to Adrian; its swift completion was her only concern. When she descended the steps of City Hall on Jason's arm, wearing his mother's gold wedding band and the diamond ring he had bought for her two years earlier, she said with great relief, "We're married. Thank God!"

Startled, he turned to her, and at the sight of her flushed cheeks and sparkling eyes, he could not suppress a grin. "I never thought I'd hear you say those words. Surely I must be dreaming."

"It's no dream," she assured him as they settled in the backseat of the waiting Rolls-Royce. "You're stuck with me now, Jason Carradine, whether you like it or not."

"Mrs. Carradine." He smiled, leaning over to kiss her cheek. "I like it very much indeed."

The chauffeur coughed discreetly, awaiting direction.

"To Fifty-ninth Street, Morris."

"No!" Adrian said. "Not there, Jason. I don't want to go home."

"Adrian—"

"Jason, please," she said, determined. "Have all my

things and the baby's sent to your house. Do whatever you think best about my house: sell it or lease it, whichever you choose. I don't want to go back there, not ever again.''

Her face had lost its color, except for the bruise on her jaw. The momentary happiness that had put roses in her cheeks was now dissipated by a memory that would take a long time to forget.

''Very well, darling.'' Jason covered her hand with his. ''Home then, Morris.''

''Jason,'' she said, straightening in her seat and affecting for his sake a semblance of gaiety, ''could we dine with Tessa and Evan this evening? A little celebration would be nice, don't you think? We could go to Rector's or Sherry's or Delmonico's . . . you decide where. I haven't seen Tessa in weeks. Won't she be bowled over when I tell her we're married?''

Her smile was a little too wide, her eyes a shade too bright. Jason's hand tightened on hers and quietly he said, ''Adrian, perhaps it might be better if you rest for a few days.''

''Rest?'' She laughed. ''Don't be silly, Jason. I feel perfectly wonderful. I'm a bride, for heaven's sake. This is a time to celebrate, to share the joyous occasion with family and friends. Of course, we have no close family except for the baby. What we'll do then is have a dual celebration this afternoon for our wedding and for Elyse's birthday, and tonight we can celebrate with Tessa and Evan.''

Again, as on the night before, she was aware that she was rambling, but self-control seemed to have deserted her. Her hands trembled slightly; she felt vaguely unwell. Memories of the night before tried to surface in her mind, but with an intense effort of will she repressed them; she could not face them. She glanced nervously at Jason, and as she had expected, he was watching her gravely, his eyes dark and concerned.

"Please don't worry about me," she appealed to him. "I know I sound like a featherbrained chatterbox. I *am* still upset about last night, but I'm trying my best not to think about it." She turned away from him, and again she felt his hand tighten on hers.

"Adrian, look at me. Look at me, darling. There's no need to pretend with me. I know you're upset. Don't feel you have to hide it. That's why I think it's a good idea if you stay home for a while, spend some time by yourself—"

"No," she said tensely. "I don't want to be alone, nor do I want to be idle. I want to see people, Jason, to talk and to laugh, and I want to be busy every moment I can. I don't want to think, don't you see? Every time I think, I see him. I see his face, I feel his—"

"Adrian." His low voice arrested her racing thoughts. "You're going to have to think about it sooner or later. Wouldn't it be wiser if you face it squarely, deal with it honestly, then dismiss it once and for all from your mind?"

"No," she maintained, swallowing with difficulty. "I can't think of it now. I don't want to."

The car drew up in front of Jason's stately house. As always, when Adrian entered the great hall, she was charmed and comforted by the vibrant beauty of the painted walls and ceilings.

The servants assembled to greet her formally. Jason had telephoned earlier, informing the staff of his marriage. When he and Adrian settled later in Jason's "den of sweet solitude," they found a bottle of French wine cooling, and on a silver tray on a table was a gleaming mound of Russian caviar on ice.

"You think of everything." Adrian smiled, removing her hat and coat.

"This was not my idea," Jason confessed, sampling the caviar. "It must have been Harris," he guessed, referring to his man. "He's been anxious for me to marry since the day I reached the age of twenty-five. I suppose this is his way of saying, 'Well done, sir!' ''

Jason uncorked the wine bottle, poured two glasses, and handed one to his wife.

''To our new partnership,'' he said, raising his glass.

''To our partnership.'' She smiled and tasted the champagne.

The bubbles tickled her nose; the cool liquid soothed her dry throat. She felt oddly unreal standing in Jason's den in the middle of the morning, toasting a union she had vowed would never take place. Her emotions were mixed. She was happy she had married him—the fierce, driving need of the previous night had not left her—and yet, at the back of her thoughts was this disquieting unease, a feeling of things not quite right.

She knew, of course, that Crandall's attack was still strong in her mind, but sensibly she realized that in time the memory would fade. She had not actually been taken by that foul degenerate—for that she was profoundly thankful—but still she could not help feeling filthified, besmirched, unendurably unclean. The long bath she had taken earlier had done little to alter her feeling of contamination. Even now she felt . . .

''What are you thinking about, Adrian?''

''Why, nothing,'' she answered, giving him her brightest smile. ''My mind was a blank just then. Jason . . .'' She put down her glass as a curious lethargy began to creep over her. ''. . . would you mind very much if I took a short nap? All of a sudden I feel desperately tired. I imagine it's all the excitement; marriage is a momentous undertaking. Which room have you put me in?''

''The one adjoining mine, of course.'' He studied her carefully; she was unnaturally pale. ''Come along, I'll escort you upstairs.''

''No, don't bother. Go on down to the bank for a while, if

you like. I'll just nap for an hour or so, and then, when
Molly gets here with the baby, we'll have our party.''

Her pallor concerned him, but he thought it wiser not to
press her. "Sleep well, then," he said, dropping a kiss on
her curls. And as she walked to the door, he asked, "Will
you telephone Tessa, or shall I?"

"I . . ." The lethargy was now so strong that she wondered dully if she would have the strength to climb the
stairs. "Jason, you do it for me. Tell her we'll call for them
at eight. I must get some sleep now. Will you excuse me?"

She trailed from the room and mounted the stairs in a fog
of disorientation. Which room had Jason said he put her in?
Oh, yes, the adjoining bedroom, his mother's old room.
How tired she was; she could not remember ever feeling so
completely done in.

When she entered the bedroom, she kicked off her shoes,
stumbled dazedly across the room, and collapsed on the bed
with a weary groan. She fell asleep instantly, a deep, death-
like sleep—free of dreams, free of fear, and free, especially,
of torturous memories.

While Adrian slept, Jason, instead of telephoning Tessa,
went to see her.

The Colby house was a dignified brownstone on Twenty-
third Street, a dwelling that had been occupied by Evan's father and by his father before him. Tessa heartily disliked the
stuffy, ponderous furnishings, which had been built to Evan's grandfather's specifications, but Evan could not conceive of replacing the pieces, which, despite their outmoded
styling, were just as sturdy and comfortable as they had been
fifty years ago.

"Jason!" said Tessa when her maid showed him into the
red damask parlor. "What a pleasant surprise."

"Tessa, forgive me for stopping by like this—"

"Don't apologize," she said graciously, indicating a

chair. "My goodness, do you know what a treat it is for me to receive an unexpected caller? My days are not the fullest since I've been married. Oh, I have my committees and my charities, and on Fridays I play bridge—" She broke off with an embarrassed laugh. "Listen to me," she said, chagrined. "I sound like a terrible malcontent, and I don't mean to. I have a fine marriage. Evan is the dearest husband, and I'm happier than I've ever been. But if only I had something to *do!*"

She laughed again ruefully and sat opposite Jason in front of the darkened fireplace. "That's enough of my complaints," she said. "Tell me why you're here."

She sobered suddenly at the intensity of his somber blue gaze.

"Jason, what's wrong? Nothing's happened to Evan, has it? There hasn't been an accident at the bank?"

"No, no," he said at once. "It's nothing like that."

"Then what?" she said, disquieted, for in the depths of his eyes there was an ominous stillness.

For a moment he was silent. Then, "Adrian and I were married this morning."

The news, joyous tidings, was announced in a voice that might have been delivering the eulogy of a loved one.

"Married? You were married? Then Jason, for heaven's sake, why do you look like that?"

He did not answer. He took out a cigarette and lit it without thinking to ask his hostess's permission. Tessa, by the same token, could not have cared less at the moment about the social amenities.

"Jason, will you please tell me what's going on? Why did Adrian suddenly agree to marry you? Why are *you* here telling me the news instead of her? Jason, answer me!"

"Tessa, forgive me," he said again, shaking his head as if to clear it. "The fact of the matter is, I'm not thinking too lucidly this morning. You see, last night . . ." A dark look

crossed his face. "Last night Perry Crandall broke into
Adrian's house and tried to"—Jason's voice went very
low— "he tried to rape her."

Tessa drew a sharp breath. "Dear God in heaven! Is she
all right?"

"No. Yes. I mean, Crandall didn't actually . . . Adrian's
all right physically, but her mental state, as you can imagine, is not the best."

Tessa stared at him, incredulous. "Jason, I can't believe
it. Perry Crandall? The journalist from the *World?* Tell me
what happened."

Jason related the facts of the incident as he knew them,
then told Tessa of the accident and of Crandall's death.
"There might be something about it in today's newspapers," he added. "I haven't thought to look. In any case,
the story I gave the police and the press was that Crandall
broke into the house with the intention of burglarizing it. I
mentioned nothing of his attack on Adrian. In her condition
last night I doubt that she could have borne being questioned
by the police."

"Yes, yes," Tessa agreed. "You did the right thing, Jason. With Crandall dead there's no sense bringing up— Oh,
I just can't believe it! My poor Adrian. Jason, are you sure
she's all right?"

"Physically, yes," he said again. "Ned Garvey looked
her over last night, and except for a bruise on her jaw, she's
fine. But I'm worried about her. That's why I'm here today
. . . to solicit your help."

"I'll do anything I can!" she said swiftly.

"Yes, thank you. I appreciate that." He paused, then
said quietly, "You do realize, I hope, that what I've told
you of the attack and what I'm about to say to you now is not
to be repeated to Adrian." And when Tessa nodded, he
went on, "I know how close you and she are. She misses

you at the salon, you know. She's constantly bemoaning the fact that it's not the same without you working by her side.''

"Oh, Jason," she said, swallowing the lump in her throat, "if you only knew how much I miss working with her. And now . . . now that this has happened . . ."

"That's where I need your help," he explained. "Adrian's going to need you now, Tessa, more than ever. I don't want her burdened with pressures at the salon when her mind is already burdened with the memory of . . . Well, you see what I mean, don't you? I want her, at all times, to be with someone who cares for her. At home she'll have me. At work I want her to have you."

"Jason," she said fervently, "I want to do that more than anything in the world. But you know how Evan feels. He would never consent—"

"I shall speak to Evan," he interrupted her. "He will gladly consent to your working again, once he realizes the circumstances. I wanted to talk to you first, though. I wanted to make sure that this is something you want to do."

"*Want* to do? Jason, I owe Adrian so much! Even if I didn't want to return to work I would do it for her sake."

"I thank you again," he said sincerely. "You're a good and loyal friend, Tessa."

He rose to take his leave. Tessa saw him to the front door, and before he left, he said, "By the way, Adrian wants to dine out this evening. Will you and Evan join us for a wedding celebration at Sherry's?"

Tessa nodded silently, her heart too filled with emotion to speak. She bid Jason good-bye, then watched as he descended the front steps and got into his car. She could not help thinking as her eyes clouded over with tears that when he had broken the news of his marriage, a marriage he had been yearning for for so long a time, he had looked anything but the picture of a new and happy husband.

* * *

Adrian wore her prettiest gown to Sherry's, a daffodil-yellow silk with a lace bodice and short lace sleeves. In her shining sable curls she tucked a yellow rosebud, which she had picked late that afternoon from Jason's fragrant garden adjacent to the drawing room.

Her nap had refreshed her, and another long bath had somewhat eased her lingering feeling of contamination. Elyse's birthday celebration, complete with a creamy iced cake decorated with pink-and-yellow rosettes and two lighted candles, had further lifted her flagging spirits.

"This is Papa's house," Adrian had told the bewildered child when they gathered around the gaily festooned birthday table. "We're going to live here now, dumpling."

"Papa's 'ouse," Elyse repeated dutifully, and then snuggled closer in her father's arms and planted a solemn kiss on his hard, curving mouth.

Jason had held his daughter throughout the two-hour festivity. Later, at seven o'clock, he himself had bathed the delighted child, bundled her into her little nightclothes, then had sat by her bed, holding her dimpled hand until, snug and contented, she had drifted off to sleep.

"Jason spoils her totally," Adrian told Tessa at Sherry's over the entrée. She was smiling and vivacious in her pretty yellow dress, but beneath the surface of her gaiety she felt a curious numbness of body and mind. "He's her absolute slave and Elyse knows it. Jason, don't laugh! Tessa, what am I going to do with him?"

"Let him be." Tessa smiled. "He's going to spoil her no matter how you try to prevent it. And now that you're married and Elyse is living in his house, there'll be no stopping him. My goodness, I've never seen a man so wrapped up in a child!"

Adrian turned from Tessa to seek Evan's support. The smile on her lips faded at the sight of his grim, unsmiling face. He was not eating. His fork was in his hand, but his gaze was riveted to the bruise on Adrian's jaw, which a light dusting of rice powder did not fully disguise.

"Evan, what is it?" she asked brightly, suppressing a rising unease. "Don't you like the veal?"

He lowered his eyes quickly, guiltily, and poked at the meat. "It's fine," he mumbled. "I'm just not very hungry."

Adrian looked toward Jason, who was eating unconcernedly. Could he possibly have said something to Evan and Tessa about last night? Tessa was behaving naturally, but Evan had been watching her all evening, and his clear, expressive hazel eyes had been filled with an emotion that to Adrian seemed worried and undeniably pitying.

"Jason," she said, her nerves tightening suddenly, "I'd like more wine."

"Certainly, darling." He signaled to the waiter, who refilled Adrian's glass, then continued to refill it throughout the evening as she swiftly continued to empty it.

"Adrian, don't you think you've had enough to drink?" Jason said mildly when she downed glass after glass of the Dom Perignon, which complemented the fruit baba.

But she had not had enough. She wanted to drink. She wanted to get soddenly drunk, to numb the punishing thoughts that had begun once again to race crazily through her brain. She could still feel Evan's eyes on her, and although she was convinced that Jason had said nothing to the Colbys about Perry Crandall, she felt vulnerable, exposed, as if everyone at her table—indeed, as if everyone in the restaurant—had witnessed the assault on her person the night before.

"Adrian?"

Jason's warm, low, untroubled voice brought a measure of calm to her turbulent thoughts. She looked up at him slowly. His vivid blue eyes seemed a harbor of safety in a calamitous world.

"Jason," she said faintly, "may we go home?"

"Yes, of course."

He rose at once and signaled for the bill. Evan rose also, saying, "Please, let me take care of it."

"Adrian," said Tessa worriedly, taking note of her pallor, "are you all right?"

"Yes, I'm fine," she said with some effort. "Jason was right, though. I shouldn't have had so much to drink."

On the ride to Twenty-third Street, no one could think of anything to say. But after the Colbys had alighted, Tessa bent down at the car window and said to Adrian, "Will you be at the salon tomorrow morning?"

"Yes, why?"

"I'll see you there at nine. I want to talk to you about something."

"About what, Tessa?"

"I'll talk to you tomorrow."

As the car pulled away from the curb Adrian asked Jason, "What do you suppose that was all about?"

"I can't imagine," he said.

If Adrian had not had so much to drink, if her mind had not been occupied with other concerns, she might have pursued the matter further or perhaps questioned the odd flatness of Jason's tone. As it was, she let it pass. A great weariness of body and spirit had taken hold of her. She was glad they were on their way home. She wanted nothing more than to climb into bed and pull up the covers and to succumb to deep slumber, to put an end to all thought. She sighed tiredly and laid her head on Jason's shoulder. His arm went around her, and for the rest of the way home, she surrendered her senses to the physical comfort of his nearness and his strength.

The great house was dim and quiet when they climbed the stairs together. Jason's arm was still around her; he had been silent in the car, and he did not speak until they reached Adrian's room.

At the door he looked down at her for a long moment, then touched her cheek with a caressing hand. "I'll join you shortly," he said softly.

Adrian's maid awaited her, dozing lightly in a chair. Dorothy was the only member of the staff, besides Molly, from her house whom Adrian had decided to keep on at her new home.

"Madam," the girl said, rising as her mistress entered the room. "My best wishes on your marriage."

"Thank you, Dorothy."

Adrian submitted to the girl's ministrations, and before long she was comfortably clad in a soft blue nightdress and a matching cashmere robe. From the adjoining room she could hear muffled sounds of movement. It seemed an interminably long time before Jason joined her, time in which Adrian deliberately closed her mind against all manner of thought. When Jason entered the room, Dorothy bobbed a curtsey and left, and the newlyweds were alone at last.

As Adrian watched her new husband from across the elegant room, she experienced that same feeling of unreality. She was in Jason's house, dressed in her nightclothes. In a few moments he would turn out the light and join her in their conjugal bed. He would make love to her, they would sleep in each other's arms, and she would awaken in the morning in his embrace. She had been daydreaming about this for months. But now that the dream had materialized . . .

"Come," he said softly, holding out a hand as he moved toward the bed.

She complied with a reluctance she did not understand. She loved this man to the depths of her soul. The mere sight of him set her heart thumping like a schoolgirl's. But tonight, in his house, with his wedding ring on her finger, he seemed suddenly to be a man she did not know at all.

"Jason," she said as they settled side by side on the silken sheets, "will you just hold me?"

In silence he drew her close, but in the curve of his loose embrace she said, "No, I mean, will you just hold me . . . nothing else?"

"If that's what you want."

"Yes," she said, puzzled and unsettled by her curious feelings. "I'm so tired. And I did have too much to drink. I'm just not up to making love tonight. You don't mind, do you?"

"No," he said. "I don't mind at all. I'm tired too, Adrian. Why don't we get some sleep?"

"Yes, all right," she agreed, both relieved and disappointed by his easy acquiescence. She was his wife now; she wanted him to make love to her. She could not remember a time when she did not want him to make love to her. Guilty, confused, she reached up to kiss his mouth. "I love you," she whispered. "I love you immeasurably."

"I love you, too, Adrian."

"Jason"—she moved restively in his arms—"you do *want* to make love to me? You haven't lost your desire for me?"

With a soft laugh he took hold of her hips and drew her full length against him. "Does that answer your question?"

She thrilled to his nearness and to the hard proof of his passion. She reached down to caress him, and murmurously he warned her, "If you continue to touch me in that manner I will not be responsible for my actions."

"Oh, Jason," she whispered, feeling now the need for him that he felt for her, "I do want you. Make love to me; I love you so much."

He held her close for a time, only held her, very gently, and when at last his mouth met hers, his kiss was tentative, wary, as if gauging her reaction. But her response was ardent; she pressed close against him and her lips parted, inviting his delicious exploration. As always, when he kissed her, she was swept up in an irresistible tide of passion, a swift, fierce, eddying current of desire from which she had neither the strength nor the wish to escape. He needed only to touch her, to kiss her, and she was totally in his power. Her mind and her will became his to command.

His mouth on hers sent a river of sensation coursing wildly through her veins. His hands on her breasts, on her hips, on her thighs were a master of control that directed her passion to its ultimate goal.

When she lay breathless and ready to receive his ultimate tribute, he slid onto her easily, parting her quivering legs with a touch of his knee. But when she felt him on the point of entry, she stiffened suddenly. The memory she had been trying to suppress all evening flooded back into her mind. Her blood ran cold, her stomach lurched, and she felt again the insult and the horror of another man's body seeking urgently to possess her.

"No," she said, panicked. "Stop it. Jason, don't."

"What's the matter?" His voice was hoarse; he lifted himself on an elbow and looked down at her, trembling with his unfulfilled need.

"Please," she whispered, shamed and revolted. "I cannot . . . Jason, forgive me. I can't."

She, too, was trembling but not with passion. She was thinking of Crandall's hands and of his foul, searching mouth. She was feeling those hands on her skin, and the heat of his body, a vile infamy against hers.

"Jason . . ." Her throat constricted. Hot tears stung her eyes, harsh sobs rose painfully in her breast, and she began to weep bitterly as Jason moved off her body and brought her quickly into his arms.

"Dear God," he groaned, anguished. "Don't cry, darling. It's all right. It was too soon, that's all. We shouldn't have . . ."

He held her close and kissed her wet cheeks. She knew that her tears were a torment in his heart, but she couldn't stop crying; she was too sickened and ashamed. Crandall may not have taken her, but the effect of his actions was the same as if he had. She felt soiled, defiled. And not only did she feel violated, but she felt that Jason, too, in the very worst way, had been brutally dishonored by Crandall's attack on her.

"Adrian, stop it now," Jason said anxiously. "You're going to make yourself ill if you keep on crying. Look at me, listen to me. It was a terrifying experience you had, but it's over now, it's past. You have to realize that it's going to take time to put it behind you, but you *will* eventually forget it. If you give it time, Adrian, and if you don't let it eat at you, it will become nothing more than an unpleasant memory. And, darling, I'll help you all I can. You must always remember that I'm here to support you."

"Jason," she whispered, her bitter tears ebbing, "I really did want you to make love to me. I don't want you to think—"

"Yes, I know," he assured her. "Don't worry about it."

"It was just that I couldn't help thinking of Crandall. . . ."

And when she trailed off and fell silent, he asked her quietly, "Will you feel better if you talk about it?"

"No." She shuddered and burrowed against him. "No, Jason. I just want you to know that my not going through with it had nothing to do with you."

"I do know it, darling," he said, aching for her pain. "And it doesn't matter; please believe me. We have years and years of lovemaking ahead of us. Just remember I'm here when you want me, for whatever reason you want me. It's going to be all right, Adrian. I give you my word. We'll be over this difficulty in no time at all."

Twenty-five

MARRIAGE TO JASON was a good deal more, and unfortunately less, than she had imagined it would be. To live in his house, to dine at his table, to sleep in his arms was a source of joy and contentment undreamed of and unparalleled in her experience. He was the dearest of husbands, the most loving of fathers. Each morning without fail he would go to the nursery, a bright, lovely room that housed the brightest, loveliest child in the world. How he loved Elyse with her charming ringlets of gossamer hair, her pink cheeks, her rosebud mouth, and her delightful blue eyes.

Elyse was always at her most sprightly in the mornings. The moment she saw her father, she would struggle to her feet, clutching the bars of her crib and cooing the word *Papa*.

"Good morning, Miss Prim," he would greet her, and then kiss her tumbled curls and lift her with a smile.

"Mr. Carradine," Molly would say, "she's been chattering like a monkey all morning. It's late you were today and she knew it, and she didn't like it a bit."

"Really?" He would grin as he lifted her, laughing, from the crib. "She's been grumbling?"

"In her own way, yes, sir. Look at her now, though. Butter wouldn't melt in her mouth, the little minx!"

And Jason would laugh as the child snuggled possessively against him and encircled his neck with her arms.

Elyse *was* a minx, a sweet, teasing flirt, and as Adrian

227

had told Tessa, Jason was her absolute slave. Adrian
couldn't have been happier now that she and Elyse were
truly a family with the husband and father who loved them
so completely. Her joy, however, was marred in a way she
had not anticipated. They were not making love, which
struck Adrian as the bitterest of ironies.

Jason, wisely, had decided that Adrian needed time to put
the memory of Crandall's attack from her mind. In part she
agreed with him; she had no wish to repeat the fiasco of their
wedding night. But the absence of physical love was distressing to her. Night after night, as she lay in Jason's arms,
she was painfully aware of his need for her, and she would
say with regularity, "Let's try, Jason. I'm all right now,
really I am." But he knew that she wasn't, and when he
would gently refuse her, she would be more relieved than
disappointed.

It was a trying time for Adrian, an oddly unnatural and
bewildering period. Perry Crandall's attack had awakened
strange fears in her, fears that lurked beneath the surface of
her consciousness: fear of sleeping, fear of dreaming, fear
of crowds, fear of solitude. The list was endless.

The first few weeks of her marriage, she had to force herself to go to work. Only Jason's repeated reminders that she
herself had expressed the desire to keep busy sent her out of
the house and into a suddenly frightening world.

It took a supreme effort just to step out the front door. A
faint trembling would weaken her limbs, and in the Bentley,
as she was driven to Herald Square, a nauseous dread would
grip her, and she would sit ramrod straight in the backseat,
tearing a handkerchief to shreds with shaking hands.

Jason, during this period, could not have been kinder. He
seemed to sense Adrian's underlying fears. With a love and
a patience that brought tears to her eyes he would gently assure her that she was safe now, safe in his home, in his

world, in his loving protection, and that nothing and no one would ever harm her again.

He encouraged her to keep up her social engagements, although even the mere thought of appearing in public made her shudder.

"Darling, you love *Carmen*," he reminded her when she tried to beg off from a night at the opera. "The newspapers say Caruso is magnificent as Don José, and Neily and Grace are counting on us to be there."

So she went to the Met because she could not bear to disappoint her husband. She sat in their box in the Diamond Horseshoe, radiantly beautiful in white silk and diamonds, and as she listened to the incomparable tenor voice of Enrico Caruso, she swallowed her nausea, trembled with her unnamed fears, and tore her program to tiny bits with elegantly gloved hands.

If it had not been for Jason urging her, coaxing her, insisting she keep her engagements and commitments, she might never have left the house. It would have been so much easier if she could sequester herself in the safety of Jason's arms, shut away from a world that had suddenly become intolerable to her. Dimly she would wonder why the memory of Crandall's attack should continue to plague her. It was over, done; Crandall was dead. Her fears were illogical.

But, as secure as she felt as Jason's wife, she also felt trapped, stifled, a prisoner to an unknown captor. It made no sense at all. At the same time it enraged her and frightened her.

In desperation she turned to the ultimate security of her husband's physical love. If he made love to her again surely her fears would fade; surely all the ugly memories that plagued her would cease. But even that was denied her. When Jason tried to make love to her, no matter how gentle his advances, no matter how sweet his loving kisses, Adrian remained unable to surrender herself completely.

He was exceptionally patient during this difficult time. They tried on countless occasions to make love—at Adrian's insistence, not his—but she could not seem to bring herself to go beyond the point of passionate kisses and ardent embraces. Each time he tried to enter her, she froze and pulled away. When the moment of joining came, she was incapable of consummating the act.

Out of guilt, out of love she insisted on satisfying him another way.

"No, don't," he would gasp, shaking with his unrelieved need. "You don't have to do that. Adrian, no . . ."

But she would wave aside his protests and love him in the only way she could. And with Jason's satiation came a pallid satiation of her own. It was no substitute for the love they had previously shared, but it was better than nothing, she would think with little conviction. Jason never complained, but Adrian knew he wasn't happy with the situation. She, too, was unhappy, but she was doing the best she could. In time things would change. In time she would be able to love him. In time, in time; the phrase became her litany. She just needed more time. Jason would have to be patient just a little while longer.

As the weeks and months passed her nebulous fears began slowly to dissipate. It did not enter her mind that Jason's unwavering support was largely responsible for this change. She attributed her new strength to her increased dedication to her work. She began to feel that only in the fulfilling world of creativity could she shut out her fears. So she surrounded herself with the protective barrier of hard, distracting work. When she designed, she did not think; when she chose fabric and color and supervised fittings, her assaulted body and mind began to mend.

Oddly, she had never done better work. Her designs changed, took on a simpler and more classic beauty that was met with enthusiastic approval by her devoted patrons. She began featuring subtle earth colors in her daytime designs: beiges, warm browns and tans, pale rusts, and the gentlest of morning-sun yellows.

She discovered the graceful fluid properties of jersey and designed clinging, comfortable dresses which were at the same time seductive and wonderful to wear. For evenings she relied heavily on the contrasting starkness of black and white. Her black backless jersey gowns were no less stunning than her virginal creations in high-necked white silk, and the combinations she featured—black-and-white stripes, polka dots, or prints—were as readily accepted by an appreciative clientele.

For the spring showing of 1914, she planned to introduce the basque, a Balkan-style tunic bloused below the waist and cinched at the hips with its own sash belt. The basque topped a skirt that was attractively narrow in contrast, and the freedom of torso was repeated at the legs, with either a side or front slit to the knee.

Irene Castle, of the delightful dancing Castles, visited the salon and was given an advance private showing of Adrian's work. Mrs. Castle was so impressed with the liberating features of this design that she ordered half a dozen in varying colors and fabrics. And she was so charmed by Adrian's boyish curls that she promptly had her own hair clipped, and within a matter of months, women by the thousands were sporting the "new Castle bob," a style Adrian had been wearing for years.

Tessa's presence at the salon was invaluable to Adrian. She was grateful for her friend's return, so grateful, in fact, that she made her a partner in Marlowe's. Under other circumstances Adrian might have been suspicious of Evan's change of heart regarding his wife's return to work, but as it was, she accepted Tessa's vague explanations without question.

Evan, during this period, was friendly to the extreme. His previous anger toward Adrian seemed completely forgotten. He was her good friend of old, her surrogate brother. During Jason's frequent business trips abroad Evan would stop at the house on Madison Avenue late at night ("I just wanted to make sure everything was all right"), or he would "accidentally" run into her when she was on her way to the drapers ("Fancy meeting you here!"). Adrian had finally told Tessa of Crandall's attack on her, and she strongly suspected that Tessa had related the incident to Evan. Strangely, though, it did not bother Adrian that Evan knew. On the contrary, it comforted her that he was worried about her and that he should go to such lengths to see that she was safe and protected. She often told Jason of Evan's improved attitude and of his many touching displays of concern. Jason would only nod thoughtfully and make no comment. Adrian was enormously grateful that her relationship with Evan was once more on an even keel.

At the end of April Adrian spent an arduous but exciting day bent industriously over her drawing board, designing a one-piece bathing costume of the softest woven wool. For too long now, she felt, women had been smothering on beaches, wrapped in layers and layers of long-sleeved garments and even black cotton stockings when they ventured into the surf. Adrian's "swimsuit," as she had dubbed it, was much more sensible, styled on the lines of a chemise, leaving arms and legs uncovered for coolness and freedom of movement. When Tessa looked over Adrian's shoulder at the sketch on the drawing board and commented, "Scandalous!" Adrian knew she had created another success.

"Yes, it's marvelous, isn't it?" Adrian smiled, stretching her arms over her head and flexing her aching spine. "In fact, I believe I'll shock everyone by ending the showing with the swimsuit instead of a wedding dress. I'll talk to Flo

Ziegfeld. Perhaps he can give me an idea of how to present it in a dramatic manner.''

"Adrian," said Tessa dryly, "believe me, the swimsuit itself is dramatic enough."

Adrian leaned back in her chair with a feeling of great contentment as Tessa settled behind her desk and lit a cigarette. The past ten months had been like old times. Adrian was even happier than she had thought she would be to have her old comrade working by her side. Two women against the world! It was the great challenge of old. But now it was even better: they had won, they had conquered. The world was now in their hands.

"Tessa," she said, "I thought you gave up smoking when you married Evan."

"I did," Tessa told her, "but since I've been working again, I've been feeling the need for them. I bought this packet days ago, and I only opened it this morning. Talk about self-denial! I hate myself when I do things like that."

"Things like what?"

Tessa exhaled smoke in short, annoyed spurts. "Like giving in to Evan's ridiculous notions about proper conduct; 'Ladies don't smoke; wives don't work.' And now that my income exceeds his, he's really been—" She broke off abruptly, her cheeks reddening.

"Tessa," Adrian said with a groan, "you haven't been quarreling with Evan about your work, have you?"

Tessa looked away, flustered; she would not meet Adrian's gaze.

"Please, Tessa," Adrian insisted, "look at me. Have you and Evan been at odds because of the fashion house?"

Tessa turned to her at last, her expression carefully neutral. She said at length in an unconcerned tone, "Well, we've had a few tiffs, if you want to know the truth, but it's nothing earth-shattering, I assure you."

"Honestly?" Adrian probed. "Is that the truth?"

"Yes." Tessa laughed. "It's the absolute truth. Evan can be a nuisance at times, but believe me, I can handle him. Tell me," she said, adroitly changing the subject, "how are *you* finding married life? Has Jason commanded you to chuck the fashion house yet? Does he tie your apron strings to the stove every morning and forbid you to leave the house?"

"Oh, Tessa." Adrian laughed, diverted. "I was wrong about that. You don't have to rub it in. He's been too wonderful for words. He . . ."

Her laughter faded as she thought of Jason's kindness, his infinite patience, and of how lately she had been neglecting him inexcusably. Jason won't mind, she would say to herself when night after night she worked late at the salon. Jason understands, she would think when again and again she turned away from him in bed.

"Tessa," she said, "it's been awful for him these past months. I don't know how he puts up with me."

"He loves you, Adrian."

"Yes," Adrian said quietly, "I know he does."

And as she thought of her husband in name only, Adrian reflected guiltily that only she knew how much Jason really loved her.

One evening in May, she returned home from work in a towering rage. The spring showing was a few days away. As always before a showing, Adrian was overtired and cross, convinced that nothing would be ready in time or that a major catastrophe would ruin the show. Fortunately for Jason he had been detained at the bank tonight, so it was the hapless servants who were forced to endure the full brunt of Adrian's frustrations.

All the way home in the Bentley she had upbraided Forbes, the junior chauffeur, first for driving too fast, then for braking too sharply, and then, in a fit of perversity, for "driving at the pace of a sleepwalking snail." To Forbes's profound relief they finally reached home. Adrian scrambled out of the car unassisted, stomped up the steps, and pounded on the front door. When she was admitted into the house by the elderly butler, she snapped, "Cronin! There are wet leaves on the front steps. See that they are removed at once."

"Yes, madam," said the servant, startled by her curtness. "I shall attend to it myself."

"You will not!" she contradicted. "I can see by your posture that your lumbago is acting up again. Have Carey do it. Where is that worthless footman?"

"He's polishing the silver, madam, for tonight's dinner party."

"What dinner party?"

"Mrs. Colby's birthday fete, Mrs. Carradine. Had it slipped your mind?"

Tessa's birthday. Oh, no. They were having eight couples to dinner to celebrate the event, and Adrian had completely forgotten.

Ignoring Cronin's question, she told him curtly, "Have those front steps cleaned at once—and don't do it yourself."

"Very good, madam," he said, nodding, and Adrian, defenseless against such submissive forbearance, left the servant abruptly and tramped up the stairs.

"Dorothy!" she said as she entered her bedroom. "Why didn't you remind me of tonight's dinner party?"

"Mrs. Carradine, I did," said the girl, leaping up from her task of placing lingerie in the drawers. "I told you this morning, and you said, 'Yes, yes, I remember.' "

"I don't remember," Adrian said, scowling. But she vaguely remembered the girl saying something to her that morning. What it was she could not recall. She had had so much else on her mind: the showing, the new swimsuit, the demands of the seamstresses for higher wages, the illness of her best cutter, the water damage to her entire supply of Irish lace . . .

"Oh, very well," she conceded grudgingly. "Perhaps you did tell me. But from now on, Dorothy, I want you to make a point of reminding me of such things. I can't think of everything, you know. One person can do just so much."

A bath and washing her hair mitigated her bad temper to some degree, but she was still fuming inwardly when Jason returned home and stopped in her room before changing for dinner.

"You smell wonderful," he murmured, bending to kiss her neck as Dorothy discreetly left the room. "Have you just had your bath?"

"Yes," she said sullenly. As his arms went around her, and his hands, with expert knowledge, began to relax the nerves in her rigid back, she melted against him, her arms crept around his neck, and she said in a voice filled with gratitude and love, "I'm so glad you're home. Nothing is ever so bad when I can share it with you."

"What happened today?" he asked, still holding her close, still relaxing her taut nerves. "The servants are all cowering in corners downstairs."

"Nothing happened," she said, smiling at the image and submitting to the luxury of utter contentment in Jason's arms. "It doesn't matter. Nothing matters as long as I can come home to you." She drew back in his embrace and looked up at him intently. "Jason, you *will* always be here for me? You said you would, do you remember?"

"Yes, I remember," he said with a puzzled smile. "Why are you like this? Something did happen today, didn't it?"

"Not really," she said, and moving away from him, she began to prowl restlessly around the room. "It's just that . . ." She stopped at the window and looked out at the gathering dusk. "Sometimes I feel . . ."

"Tell me," he urged, joining her at the window, not

touching her, yet filling her with the comforting serenity of his nearness. "Tell me what you feel."

She evaded his searching gaze and began to pleat the sash on her dressing gown. "Jason," she said reluctantly, her eyes on the sash, "I don't suppose you've been very happy since we've been married."

"Why do you say that?"

"Why do I say it?" She raised her head and stared at him. "How can you be happy with a wife who won't . . . who can't . . . ?"

"Why don't you let me worry about that?" he suggested. "I haven't complained, have I?"

"No, you haven't," she agreed. "And how do you think that makes me feel?"

"Would you feel better if I did complain?"

"No, of course not!"

"Well, then, what's your problem?"

"Jason, for heaven's sake," she burst out. "I do have a problem; *we* have a problem. I want us to make love, I truly want to be your wife."

"Adrian," he said with a gentle insistence, "you truly *are* my wife. Stop torturing yourself. This problem, as you call it, will work itself out. You're tired now, and over-wrought; that's why you're upset. You need a vacation, darling, we both do. After the showing I'd like us to spend some time at Tuxedo Park. Would you like that?"

"Oh, Jason, yes!" she said at once. "That would be heavenly. And we could ask the Colbys to join us. Tessa's been working like a stevedore on the showing. She deserves a vacation more than I do."

Jason said nothing for a moment. With a dart of remorse Adrian realized that he might have wanted her alone on this vacation. The trip to Tuxedo Park, it occurred to her now, was Jason's wish for the honeymoon that Perry Crandall's attack had made impossible.

"Jason, forgive me," she said. "I didn't think . . . I won't invite the Colbys'. I'd rather be alone with you."

"Don't be silly," Jason said. "By all means invite them. I'm sorry I didn't think of it myself."

"Jason, no," she said, going into his arms and twining her arms around his neck. "I do want to be alone with you. I don't want you to think—"

"Hush," he said, brushing her brow with his lips. "I don't think anything. Of course, we'll invite the Colbys. I know how much you enjoy their company. Get dressed now. Our guests will be arriving shortly."

He kissed her once more and left her to dress, precluding further discussion on the matter. Adrian stood watching his door long after he had closed it. Again, through her thoughtlessness she had hurt the man she loved. This, she vowed silently, was the very last time she would do so.

Twenty-six

WHEN SHE WAS DRESSED and coiffed and subtly perfumed, she went into the nursery to spend some time with her daughter. Jason had given Elyse a spectacular collection of dolls dressed in representative garb of every major country in the world. Reposing on the nursery mantel were a sloe-eyed *señorita* with a *mantilla* of Spanish lace and a Parisian *coquette* clad in Brussels lace and satin. Scattered elsewhere around the room were an Irish colleen in a green velvet cloak, a Swiss miss, an Italian donna, a Scottish lassie, and a creamy-cheeked beauty from Britain dressed in a fine replica of a court presentation gown.

It seemed as if Jason wished to instill in his daughter his own passion for collecting beauty and art. For her second birthday he had given her a stunning variety of Faberge eggs: jeweled and gilt treasures depicting the four seasons, or enclosing minute wild flowers with chalcedony petals, or a gem-encrusted bird within an elegant exterior.

Elyse loved her fabulous collections. And as young as she was she was neither abusive nor destructive of her precious possessions. Like a fine connoisseur, she would handle each piece with an appreciative eye and the gentlest, lightest touch of her dimpled hands. She was truly a Carradine, this discriminating little perfectionist. Adrian would often think fondly that Jason was justly proud of his exquisite jewel of a daughter.

"How's my dumpling this evening?" Adrian greeted her

239

baby, who was already abed, having just lisped her nightly prayers with Molly's help.

"Mama!" the child cried and reached out her arms.

Adrian smiled a greeting àt Molly, scooped up Elyse, unmindful of her ivory silk gown, and pressed copious kisses to her soft apple cheeks.

"What did you do today?" she asked, putting the child down and sitting beside her on the edge of the bed. "Did you have a pleasant day?"

And as Elyse launched into a lengthy narrative about her afternoon in the park Adrian stroked her daughter's silky brown hair and thought yearningly of the love that had conceived this much-loved child. She would have liked another child, a son, a beautiful son, the image of his father; and then, in time, another daughter, because Jason so loved Elyse.

But there would be no more children if Adrian did not overcome her distressing inability to accept her husband's love. There would be no more children—and perhaps, she thought with a sudden and chilling fear, there would be no more marriage. How long, after all, would Jason's patience endure? A man needed physical love; it was essential to his well-being. And yet Jason had gone for several months without the complete physical union and proper satisfaction that was his right as Adrian's husband.

Adrian rose with a start, interrupting her chattering daughter in mid-sentence. "I have to go," she said abruptly, her thoughts racing. "My guests will be arriving at any moment."

"Mama, kiss me first," the child demanded in order to gain a few more precious moments with the mother she rarely saw.

"Oh, my angel!" In a burst of love and guilt Adrian hugged her daughter close and smothered her little face with a passion of apologetic kisses. Here was another member of her family whose needs she had placed second to her own.

"Someday soon," she said, drawing away from her daughter with regret, "I'm going to spend all the time in the world with you. Things are going to change around here, Elyse. From now on I'm going to start doing a lot more thinking about you and Papa, and a little less thinking about myself."

"Mama, honest?" The child beamed, picturing hours and hours together with this vision of loveliness she adored.

"Dumpling, honest!" her mother promised, kissed her to seal the promise, then swept off to the drawing room to look for the man she loved.

All of the guests had already arrived when she reached the drawing room. The Astors, the Vanderbilts, the Morgans, and the Whitneys were grouped clannishly around the fireplace; Anna Held and her newest suitor were sipping aperitifs; and Flo Ziegfeld and his new wife, the Titian-haired actress Billie Burke, were exchanging anecdotes across the room with Charles Frohman and another beauteous actress, Maude Adams.

Jason was with the Colbys, but as Adrian watched from the doorway, she saw that it was Tessa specifically with whom he was engaged in conversation. Tessa's hand was on his sleeve. Oddly, that innocent, friendly gesture roused so fierce a jealousy in Adrian's breast that for a moment she was rendered breathless. From the movement of Tessa's lips Adrian could see that she was talking in that rapid, staccato way of hers when she was endeavoring to press home a point. Evan looked on silently, his hands in his pockets, and Jason, his face still and thoughtful, listened attentively to Tessa's every word.

"I'm so sorry I'm late," Adrian announced, moving gracefully into the room.

She went to each group with a special word of welcome, admiring a lady's dress, inquiring about a gentleman's health. Anna Held captured her close in a suffocating embrace and whispered poisonously near her ear, "Florenz is very happy with that woman, no? I wish him much luck with her—all of it bad!"

Adrian laughed and moved on, reminding some of the ladies of her upcoming showing, then, after a few words with the Ziegfelds and with Frohman and Miss Adams, she went at last to her husband and the Colbys.

"Tessa, happy birthday," she said with a kiss and an embrace. "Many happy returns of the day." She turned then to Evan and reached up to kiss his cheek. "How handsome you look this evening."

His arm, she noticed, surprised, lingered a moment too long about her waist. But even before she could think to move away he released her.

"Tessa's been telling me," said Jason to Adrian, "that you're planning an unorthodox finale for the showing."

"Yes," she answered, though her puzzled gaze remained on Evan. "I must speak to Flo after dinner. I need some suggestions on how to best present the swimsuit."

"Perhaps," Evan commented, his own gaze unreadable, "you should reconsider presenting the swimsuit. Don't you remember the furor you caused with your grand opening showing? The newspapers are bound to react in the same way. They'll likely paint you a scarlet woman, as they did when you presented those undergarments."

With an inward sigh of relief Adrian realized the source of Evan's odd behavior. He was worried about her. How very like him; how very dear.

"Evan," she said with a smile, "I cannot censor my designs in deference to the press. They don't give two straws for what they call 'the preservation of the modesty of the fair sex.' All they're interested in is printing sensational items in order to boost circulation figures.''

He watched her a moment with those disturbingly unreadable eyes. He said then without expression, ''Sometimes, Adrian, you carry your independent thinking too far.''

''Come now, Evan,'' said Jason mildly. ''I think what Adrian needs at this time is our support, not our censure.''

''Dinner is served!'' announced Cronin from the doorway.

Whatever response Evan might have made to Jason's remark remained unspoken. Adrian took Evan's arm as Jason presented his to Tessa, and they and their guests repaired to the dining room.

Dinner, as always at the Carradines, was an epicurean and social delight. Seated on Georgian chairs amidst tapestried walls, the guests partook eagerly of lobster bisque, salmon à la béarnaise, squab cutlets, roast duckling, and Spanish custard cream for dessert. A bronze-and-dore chandelier lit the room and caught the brilliance of diamond brooches and the pale gleam of pearls. The conversation was as sparkling as the gems. The new dances were discussed: the Turkey Trot; the Bunny Hug; and the Tango, that sensuous scandal imported from South America. Jason was telling the gentlemen about the Bugatti automobile he had seen exhibited at the Paris salon on his last trip abroad.

''What a beauty!'' he said, his blue eyes alight. ''Monsieur Bugatti has introduced reverse quarter-elliptic springs this year for the rear of the automobile. The man's a genius. I've decided to invest in his manufacturing firm.''

''Jason,'' said Jim Whitney, a distinguished white-haired banker seated on his left, ''why do you find it necessary to go abroad so often? This is your second trip in less than six months, is it not?''

''My third,'' Jason said. ''I have many business interests in England and Europe, Jim.''

"As have I," Whitney said, somewhat pompously. "But I don't find it necessary to go traipsing over there every other week."

Jason smiled at the exaggeration. "I don't go quite that often. Perhaps four or five times a year is my limit. It's just that I like to keep a close watch on my investments." He caught Adrian's eye at the opposite end of the table. "Isn't that right, darling?"

"Indeed," Adrian agreed, returning her husband's smile. "Jason takes an extremely personal interest in all his investments."

Marla Whitney, on Adrian's left, was the owner of a new Victor talking machine. She was prophesying to the guests that this contraption, as she called it, would soon make opera-going obsolete.

"Why, it sounds like Mr. Caruso is in my very drawing room," she told Adrian. "Why should I waste my time going to the Met when I can hear almost any opera I choose with just the flick of a wrist?"

"But, Marla," Adrian said, laughing, "where would you show off that new sapphire necklace Jim gave you, if not at the Met?"

"There's always Sherry's." Marla sniffed.

Adrian laughed again and turned to her right to ask Evan's opinion. He was not eating; he was watching her with that uninterpretable look that continued to disturb her because of its curious intensity.

"Evan," she said, leaning toward him so that only he could hear, "what's wrong with you tonight? Why do you keep staring at me?"

He said in a toneless voice, "Was I staring? I'm sorry. I'll stop if it annoys you."

"Evan, what is it?" she asked anxiously, for she suspected that it was more than concern for the press's adverse coverage of her designs that was on Evan's mind.

"It's nothing," he said, but his hand gripped his fork so tightly that his knuckles showed white. "I'm tired, that's all. Your husband is a hard taskmaster, Adrian. He keeps me so busy at Carradine's that I barely have time to think. He's given me a promotion, you know; I am currently director of new issues of stock. My salary, of course, has increased commensurate with my duties. I now make a yearly salary that almost but not quite equals Tessa's."

The bitterness in his tone was impossible to ignore. So Tessa had not been entirely truthful. Adrian should have known; she should have realized that Evan was not likely to have changed his fierce convictions. But it was his obvious hostility toward Jason that distressed her. Apparently Evan's feelings toward her husband had not changed, either.

"Evan," she said, "we must talk"—she glanced around the table at her chattering guests—"but not now."

"We'll have plenty of time to talk at Tuxedo Park," Evan said in a hard tone that further disquieted her. "Your husband was kind enough to invite Tessa and me to spend some time with you there when the showing is over. Won't that be cozy, Adrian? The four of us—just like one big happy family. I can't tell you how much I'm looking forward to it."

His eyes were no longer expressionless. They blazed now with every emotion he was feeling. Bitterness and frustration, rage and resentment were most evident to Adrian. But as she searched beneath the surface of this man she knew so well, she saw with alarm that it was his still-active love for her that hardened the contours of his pale, rigid face.

Twenty-seven

TUXEDO PARK, forty miles northwest of New York City, is situated in the graceful Ramapo Hills, which overlook Tuxedo Lake. In 1885, when Jason was twelve, his father, Brendan Carradine, built a two-story summer home in the town that had been developed and designed by his good friend, Pierre Lorillard V, heir to the snuff and tobacco empire.

The likes of the Schermerhorns and Astors, Hollisters and Bowdoins summered in Tuxedo Park and looked down with contempt on the pretentious upstarts who built nouveau riche monstrosities in Newport. In Tuxedo Park one did not flaunt one's affluence with grotesque copies of European castles and with elaborate parties costing hundreds of thousands of dollars. The summer residents here were far too well bred to publicize and sensationalize their immeasurable wealth.

Nevertheless, the aura of money was as manifest in Tuxedo Park as its sweet country air and its lushly scented flora. As the Carradines and Colbys rode through the entrance of the eight-foot fence that enclosed the park, Adrian looked out the car window with admiration on the English-style clubhouse with its wide veranda, and on the charming, lichen-covered cottages. Neat flowerbeds lined the macadam road. Private policemen, handsomely uniformed, strolled around with the holiday air of Parisian gendarmes. Out on the lake pristine white sails could be seen above the sleek hulls of lovely sailboats. The scene was peaceful and bucolic, yet its very perfection gave testimony to the wealth that had built Tuxedo Park and now maintained it.

"It's a fairyland!" Tessa exclaimed as they rode past a block of stores whose thatch-roofed buildings had been patched with moss to give the appearance of great age. "I feel like I'm in medieval England."

"It's a stage set," Jason said, laughing. "Pierre Lorillard believed in leaving nothing to nature. My father's house is quite different from what you see here. It's set amidst a dense wood at the far end of the enclosure. Pierre used to call it the Hermitage."

The house was totally unlike what Adrian had expected. Used to the opulent elegance of Jason's Madison Avenue house, she was surprised to see that the cottage was large but unimposing, and that its furnishings, though obviously costly, were casual and simple. The walls throughout were painted a cool, celestial blue. Gleaming white wicker furniture graced the front porch. Indoors, in the first-floor parlor, sofas and chairs with bright chintz covers looked comfortable and inviting. The second-floor bedrooms were furnished with pretty cherrywood pieces, and the curtains and bedspreads were of white dotted swiss.

"Jason, I love it," she said as they settled in the master bedroom to rest and freshen up before lunch. Tessa and Evan had gone to their assigned bedroom at the far end of the hall. On the entire automobile trip from New York Evan had been exceedingly quiet. Adrian was strongly tempted to tell Jason that she suspected Evan still loved her and that she very much wished he had not acquiesced to her wish to invite the Colbys to join them. But Jason seemed so happy to be on a vacation at last with his wife, she hadn't the heart to spoil his enjoyment.

She stood at the open window, breathing deeply of the

sweet pine and newly mown grass. With a sigh she said wistfully, "I wish we could have brought Elyse with us."

Jason joined her at the window and slipped an arm around her waist. "She'll be here in a few days, darling, as soon as she's over her cold. Do you miss her very much?"

"Yes," she said, then laughed self-consciously, for she had left her daughter only several hours before. "I never thought I'd be a doting mother," she reflected softly, leaning comfortably against her husband. "There are so many things I've been finding out about myself since we've been married, things that really astonish me."

"What things?" he asked, nuzzling her fragrant hair.

"That I love you even more than I thought I did," she answered warmly. "And . . ."

She paused for a moment to collect her random thoughts. She felt happier and more content than she had in a long time. Dimly it occurred to her that this was the first true vacation she had had in years. It was also the first time she had willingly divorced herself from her responsibilities. Adrian loved her work; it was vitally important to her, but her work was not her life as she had once thought it was. Jason and Elyse were her life. Without them her work might sustain her, but it would never afford her the joy and utter completion of sharing herself with the man and the child she loved.

". . . and that I couldn't be happier that I married you," she concluded.

She felt his arms tighten around her and heard him let out a long breath. "I hope you mean that," he said in a restrained voice. "I've been wondering if you regretted the impulse."

She turned swiftly in his embrace and wound her arms around his neck. "Oh, I don't regret it," she whispered fiercely against his chest. "I'm only sorry I didn't marry you sooner."

She pressed her lips to his in a passion of love and longing and remorse. This man was her love, her life, the foundation of the strength upon which her own rested. She was his wife now, a fate she had feared but which she realized at last was the culmination of the love that she would share with him forever.

She leaned back in his arms and faced the troubled look in his eyes. "Jason, I know I've been neglecting you since our marriage. I know our physical relationship is not what it should be. But that's going to change, I promise you."

He looked down at her quietly, his eyes dark and grave. At length he said, "I suppose I am partly to blame. If you've been wrapped up in the fashion house, I've been just as busy with my own work. I've been abroad so much." He paused as if debating whether or not to say more on that subject. Then, choosing another, he mused ironically, "It's odd, Adrian. Since our wedding day, I believe we've spent more time with other people than we have with each other: I with my business associates, and you with the Colbys."

"Oh, Jason, I—"

"Not that I begrudge you their company," he quickly amended. "I couldn't be more relieved that Tessa's working with you again. I know it's what you wanted. And then, of course, Evan has been extremely considerate keeping an eye on you in my absences."

His tone had changed ever so slightly. Adrian wondered if he, too, had his suspicions about Evan's feelings for her. She had not wished to broach the subject—there was always the possibility she might be mistaken—but it occurred to her now that if Jason felt as she did, they were probably both correct in their assumption.

"Jason," she said suddenly, "I think I should tell you something."

A knock at the door stilled her next words.

"Yes, who is it?" she asked, distracted.

"Lunch is ready," called Tessa gaily. "Come along, you two. There'll be plenty of time later to bill and coo."

Tessa. Adrian had not stopped to think what the effect would be on Tessa if she should tell Jason what she suspected about Evan. Nor, she thought uneasily, did she have any idea how Jason would react. He might be so furious with Evan that he might discharge him.

"Adrian, what were you going to tell me?" Jason asked as these thoughts passed disturbingly through her mind.

"It's nothing important," she said, avoiding his gaze. "Let's have lunch," she said brightly, then slipped out of his arms before he could search for and identify the lie in her eyes.

After lunch Jason showed his wife and his guests around the property. Majestic old maple trees surrounded the house. The grass was lush and expertly tended by a year-round staff of gardeners. At the rear of the house was an informal garden where nasturtium, petunias, and fuchsia grew in companionable profusion. But it was the walled formal rose garden that most impressed Tessa. As Jason identified the many species for her Evan took Adrian's hand and said casually, "Let's go for a walk."

Adrian tensed and did not answer.

Jason looked up from his kneeling position at a showy bush.

Tessa said ruefully, "Oh, yes, I forgot. Evan cannot tolerate the scent of roses. His eyes tear, and if he remains near them for any length of time, he begins to sneeze uncontrollably."

"Really?" said Jason, watching Evan with a look that set Adrian's heart pounding. Jason knew; she was sure of it. And yet there was no tactful way to refuse Evan's request.

"Do you two mind?" she said, clutching at straws.

"Mind what?" Tessa asked tartly. "Do you plan to run

off with the family jewels?'' She turned back to Jason. ''What are those gorgeous blooms over there?'' She directed his attention to a dazzling display of variegated pink roses, leaving Adrian no alternative but to submit to the persuasion of Evan's hand tight on hers.

When they were some distance away from the house, in sight of the deep woods, Evan asked her reproachfully, ''What's the matter? Are you afraid to be alone with me?''

''Certainly not!'' Her answer was swift but not entirely truthful. She *was* afraid to be alone with him but only because of the danger she had sensed in Jason's ominous gaze. ''We should not have gone off alone, that's all. If you felt like taking a walk we should have waited for Jason and Tessa to come with us.''

''Why?'' he asked mockingly. ''What's happened to your insatiable need for independence? Must you always have your adoring husband tagging along after you now that you've deigned to submit to holy matrimony?''

His sarcasm hurt, but at the same time it angered her. ''Evan, stop it,'' she said. ''This is not the first time you've sniped at my husband. I deeply resent it, and I want you to stop it.''

His face flushed a fiery red. He released her hand, looked away from her, and sunk his hands deep into his trouser pockets.

A dart of guilt gentled Adrian's next words. ''Evan, listen to me. I know you're unhappy because Tessa's working again, but something else is at the root of your discontent, and I think I know what it is.''

''Do you?'' he said, not looking at her.

''Yes,'' she answered softly as they stopped beneath the shade of a gnarled elm tree. ''I think you want something you cannot have, which is unfortunate because you already have in your possession something that has the capability to afford you unlimited happiness.''

He leaned against the tree trunk, hands still in pockets, and at last, grudgingly, he looked at her. "What might that be?"

"Tessa," she said. "She loves you."

He stared at her for a moment, then his lashes lowered and he stared, in sullen silence, at the ground.

"Evan, you do care for her, don't you?"

His answer was not immediate, but when it came, it was sincere. "Yes, I do."

"Then why do you cling to the past? What you wanted a year ago may not necessarily be what you want now. I thought at one time that I wanted only the fashion house, my independence, to sustain and fulfill me. But I've learned that I want more, that I want to live not only for myself but for the people I love and who love me. If you truly care for Tessa—and I think that you do—don't make the mistake I made; don't hang on blindly to the past while turning away from the reality of the present."

He did not speak; his downturned face was white and tense with resistance. Adrian sensed his inner struggle and impulsively she reached out to him. "Evan, don't fight your feelings for her," she pleaded. "Forget the past. Live for the future and for the woman who loves you."

His head came up, and abruptly he gripped her arms and pulled her close. "I can't forget the past. I still—"

"No, you don't!" she cried. "It's the dream of youth and innocence you still cherish, not me, Evan. Oh, can't you see that you're throwing away what you've always wanted, a woman who loves you with all her heart and soul?"

The crack of a snapping twig turned Adrian's head toward the sound. Approaching her, his dark face hard, was her husband, whose eyes were on Evan's hands possessively holding her arms.

She pulled away quickly, not realizing the action appeared to be an admission of wrongdoing.

"Jason," she said, her throat gone suddenly dry, "we were just—"

"Your wife is worried about you," Jason said to Evan, ignoring Adrian. "I think you had better go back to the house and assure her you haven't lost your way."

His double-edged meaning was painfully clear to Adrian. Oh, why hadn't she told him her suspicions? She had sensed he must be aware of Evan's feelings for her. And now, seeing them together, Evan holding her, he must surely think . . . No, no. He couldn't be thinking *that*.

Evan's face was unnaturally pale. He looked at Adrian as if fearing to leave her. But with her eyes she urged him to comply with her husband's request. Finally Evan turned and reluctantly walked away. Jason's gaze, hard and dark, turned at last to his wife, and came to rest on her lips, which seemed to tremble with guilt.

Twenty-eight

"You were about to tell me what you were doing," Jason said in a low voice that chilled her.

"We were talking." Her own voice shook.

"I'm not blind, Adrian; I could see that. What were you talking about that necessitated his putting his hands on you?"

She swallowed convulsively. She had seen him angry before, but never had his anger been so dangerously icy. "Jason, you can't possibly be thinking—"

"Where you're concerned," he said, stopping her coldly, "I'm never quite sure what to think. I once thought you hated me, but then you gave me reason to believe you love me. You once promised to marry me, but then you promptly ran off to Europe. Since the first night I met you, I've never known what to expect from you. You told me earlier today that you're happy you married me. But if you tell me now that you're having second thoughts about that, it wouldn't much surprise me."

"Jason," she said urgently, "of course I'm not having second thoughts. You're the only man I've ever loved. Surely you know that."

His hand shot out and clamped hard on her wrist. "Then why," he said, enraged, "did you walk here alone with him? Why was he touching you? Do you think I'm a fool? Do you think I don't know he still wants you?"

He dragged her close, one arm going around her waist in a

bone-crushing grip. His face had gone ashen, his eyes were as dark as cobalt yet they burned with a murderous light. "I haven't made sexual demands of you since we've been married. I've been waiting patiently, like an impotent old man, for you to forget that night with Crandall. And yet you permit Evan Colby to put his hands on you—" His arm tightened torturously, and then abruptly he released her. "God damn you," he said in a voice harsh with pain. "God damn you, Adrian."

He turned and strode off into the woods as if fearing if he stayed he would do her physical harm. Adrian tore after him, her heart racing. Everything he had said was true: she had run him a merry chase since the first night he'd met her. But one thing stood to the fore, and of that she must assure him. She loved him, only him. She always had, she always would.

"Jason, wait!" She caught up with him beneath a tangle of overgrown foliage. A chill was in the air like the chill in her heart. "Please listen to me," she said, breathless. "You must know I love you. You can't think otherwise. I have never loved any man but you. Evan thinks . . ." She paused as Jason's hard gaze bore mercilessly into hers. "Evan mistakenly thinks he still cares for me, but I'm trying to convince him that it's Tessa he really loves and wants."

"And is that why he was holding you?" Jason's bitter voice pained her. "Because he loves and wants Tessa?"

"Jason, in the heat of the moment, he took hold of my arms. The situation was innocent, I give you my word. Do you think—" Her voice broke as she realized how dangerously close she was to losing this man. "Do you think for one moment that I would ever willingly permit any man but you to put his hands on me in a gesture of love? Do you know that when Crandall tried to rape me, all I could think of was that if he succeeded, if he took what belonged to you and to no other man, I don't know if I could ever have faced you again.''

She gazed up at him through a veil of tears, trembling with love and with a desperate fear. If she lost him, if she lost what mattered most to her in all the world, she honestly didn't know if she would have the courage or the desire to make a new life without him.

An endless time passed before Jason at last said in an odd, expressionless voice, ''Very well. I believe you. The situation was innocent.''

''Jason, it *was* innocent!''

''I believe you,'' he said in that strange, quiet voice. ''But tell me, Adrian, is it possible that you find yourself happier, more at ease with Evan Colby than you do with me?''

''No!'' she said at once. *''You're* the man I love, the man I married—''

''Yes, you married me,'' he said, stopping her, ''but I can't help wondering if you regret it.''

''Of course I don't regret it,'' she said swiftly. ''Can you be suggesting that I would rather have married Evan than married you?''

''No,'' he said. ''I'm not suggesting that at all. It merely occurs to me that your relationship with Colby is a good one and a happy one. It puts me in mind of our own relationship, yours and mine, before we married.''

''Jason—''

''Kindly let me finish,'' he said curtly. ''It also occurred to me that our physical problem began on the very night of the day we married. I blamed Crandall's attack, naturally, for your sudden aversion to my lovemaking, but when I gave it more thought, I began to think there might be another reason you would not give yourself to me physically.''

Bewildered and oddly fearful, she asked, ''Another reason? I don't understand you.''

"Don't you?" he said. "Well, let me try to put it more plainly then. Ask yourself this question, Adrian: Is it the memory of Perry Crandall's attack that stops you from making love with me, or is it the fact that I'm your husband that cools your ardor?"

"What?" she cried. *"What?"*

"Give it some thought," he drove on coldly. "For years you refused to marry me. Then, when Crandall attacked you, because you were frightened out of your wits, you consented to marry me, but in your heart you regret—"

"That's not true!" she cried. "I don't regret it. I've told you over and over again that I'm happy I married you."

"Yes, you've *told* me," he said bitterly. "But what you say and what you feel have always been two different matters, Adrian. For example, why do you find it so easy to accept my kisses and caresses, but when it comes time for me to make love to you, you turn me away? Could it be that you're punishing me for marrying you? Is there the slightest chance that you're trying to tell me that even though you're my wife, you don't truly belong to me?"

"That's not true!" she cried again. "I *do* belong to you. I belong to you completely."

"And yet you won't let me make love to you." His voice was hard and cold.

"You know I can't," she said painfully. "I've tried, God knows I've tried, but I— Oh, Jason," she cried desperately, "this is all my fault. We should never have asked the Colbys to come here with us. We need to get away alone, away from everything and everyone we know. If we could only be alone, I know our problem would be resolved. Jason, please let's go away together—to Europe, *anywhere*—"

She broke off with a sob and gazed up at him imploringly. How could he have suggested that she was punishing him for marrying her? Dear God, how could she be punishing him when she loved him so deeply and completely?

"Very well," he said at last in that same expressionless voice as before. "We'll go away, we'll go abroad."

"Jason," she said urgently, "we *will* resolve this problem, I know we will."

He said nothing; he only watched her. In his eyes was a fierce pain that increased her own. How much, she wondered, aching, would he endure at her hands? She had fought him for almost as long as she had known him. Had he reached the final limits of his love for her?

Twenty-nine

THE TWO WEEKS in Tuxedo Park were a trial for Adrian. Jason was the perfect host, but beneath his faultless courtesy she sensed a restive disquiet that kept her on edge from breakfast until bedtime. Tessa, fortunately, seemed unaware of the tension that crackled between the Carradines. She delighted in the clean country air, the sailboat rides, the picnics in the woods, and especially in the sudden increased attention paid to her by her husband.

Adrian was at least happy to note that Evan seemed to be regarding his wife in a new light. He no longer looked at Adrian with bitterness and reproach, and he was more openly affectionate to Tessa, a curiously touching affection that conveyed both love and apology.

When Adrian told the Colbys that she and Jason were soon to go abroad, Evan commented, "I suppose that means Tessa will be left in charge of the fashion house again."

"Yes," Adrian said ruefully. "Will you mind very much?"

Evan looked at his wife with a resigned shake of his head. "I'll mind not having her home," he admitted. "But if it makes her happy, I imagine I can learn to put up with it."

While the Colbys' relationship was taking a turn for the better, the Carradines had come to a disturbing impasse. Although Jason was a warm host to his guests, he was undeniably remote to his wife. They slept in the same bed, but he never once attempted to touch her while they were in Tux-

259

edo Park. And when Adrian uneasily mentioned this to him, he only said distantly, "Let's wait until we're alone, Adrian. Let's wait until we're in Europe."

They could not have picked a worse time nor a better time to go abroad. Prince Otto von Bismarck, the German chancellor, through a long succession of small wars and brilliant coups, had managed to coalesce the feuding Teutonic states into one formidably powerful German empire. France, at the same time, still bitter over her defeat in the Franco-Prussian War, entered into an alliance with England and Russia, thus formally drawing the battle line between her own Triple Entente and the Triple Alliance of Germany, Italy, and the Austro-Hungarian Empire.

The seeds of war were slowly germinating in Europe, and yet when Adrian and her husband arrived that early summer of 1914, the social climate could not have been more glorious. At Covent Garden Nellie Melba was singing *La Bohème;* at His Majesty's Theatre, Mrs. Patrick Campbell was playing Eliza to Sir Herbert Tree's Professor Higgins. At the ballet the Carradines were treated to the combined artistry of Stravinsky, Diaghilev, and Nijinsky. At the Palladium and the Palace they saw Little Tich and Nelson Keyes; and at Cliveden, the sumptuous estate of the English Astors, they watched Isadora Duncan, clad in diaphanous white veils, perform an erotic interpretation of Salome's plea for John the Baptist's head.

Their days in London were spent in typical tourist fashion. Like novice sight-seers they took a bus to Kew Gardens and toured the Orangery, the Palm House, and stopped at nearby Chiswick House to view the Palladian manor of the third earl of Burlington.

At Westminster Abbey a guide showed them the wax images of early kings and queens dressed in the brocades and silks and laces of the periods. Adrian found the London

Dungeon interesting but gruesome with its vivid exhibitions
of Tyburn and the Black Plague. She much preferred the
British Museum where they viewed the Elgin marbles and
the black basalt Rosetta Stone, along with Greek, Roman,
and Assyrian antiquities that especially caught the attention
of Jason, the collector.

At night, after dining and "doing the town" in their most
elegant finery, they would return to their suite at Claridge's,
and prepare to retire. Adrian would go into Jason's arms and
press eager kisses to his sensuous mouth. Surely, here in England, away from her work, away from the memories that
had chilled and inhibited her, she would be able at last to
make love with the man she loved.

But night after night the result remained the same. Jason
would return her ardent kisses with a passion that left her
breathless; his warm hands would awake in her a fiery desire
that scorched her very soul. But always, invariably, just as
he would move to claim her, she would tense in his arms,
and turning away from him, she would refuse yet again to
accept her husband's love.

On their fourth night in London, as they lay side by side
recuperating from their latest failure, Jason said in a terse,
low voice, "This has got to stop. It must stop."

He was lying on his back, an arm covering his eyes.
When he spoke, Adrian turned with a start and reached out
an apologetic hand.

"Don't," he said sharply, quivering beneath her touch.
"For the love of God don't touch me."

He swung out of bed, shrugged into his dressing gown,
and went to the window where he lit a cigarette with shaking
hands.

"Jason, I'm sorry," she said miserably, watching him
from the bed. "I really thought that tonight I could—"

"Why?" he snapped, staring fiercely at the moonlit

street. "Why should this night have differed from any other?"

"Jason . . ."

"I'm tired of it, Adrian. I can't take it any longer. I've done everything in my power to bring you around, but by Christ, I've had enough. This is the end of it; I've reached my limit."

She watched in guilty silence as he tossed his cigarette out the window and turned to face her.

"It's been a year," he said quietly, but his quiet voice shook. "Fifty-two weeks, three hundred sixty-five days. How much longer will it take you to forget an experience that lasted only an infinitesimal fraction of that time? How can you lie in my arms and enjoy my kisses yet still be thinking of an incident so revolting that it closes your mind and your heart to my love?"

"Jason, please," she said in despair. "Don't you know how it hurts me to turn you away? Don't you think it tears my heart out to refuse you when I want you so badly?"

"No," he said flatly. "I think nothing of the kind. What I think, in fact, is that you're beginning to derive some perverse pleasure in bringing me to a fever pitch of desire, only to turn away when I most want you. I wonder if it doesn't give you a feeling of power to so manipulate me. I wonder if in your convoluted mind you see yourself as master of a situation few women control."

"That's insane!" she cried. "It makes no sense at all. I'm not manipulating you; I don't want to control anything. I want more than anything for you to make love to me . . . ."

"Do you?" he said, stopping her. "Then prove it, Adrian. Give yourself to me—tonight, now."

"Jason . . ." She faltered as he watched her with narrowed eyes from his post at the window. She wanted him desperately. Why wouldn't he believe her? She fully understood the source of his rage, but to test her in this way . . . it was cruel, it was unfair.

"Please," she urged him in an effort to appease him. "Come to bed. I'll satisfy you in another way."

"I don't want that," he said. "I want you."

"Jason, be fair," she pleaded, and slipping from the bed, she padded across the room and circled his neck with her arms. "I love you so much," she whispered, moving against him, unashamed of her nudity. "How can you accuse me of wanting to hurt you in any way when you know how much I love you?"

He remained motionless against her, but she could feel his hard arousal. With a deft movement of her hand she parted his dressing gown so that the heat of her skin could press freely on his. He still did not stir. She could feel the heavy beating of his heart, and when she reached up to kiss him, his mouth was hot and dry, and he neither protested nor put a stop to her sensuous exploration.

"Jason," she whispered, pressing seductively close to him, "come to bed. Let me make love to you. I want to make you happy. I love you."

With a slow restrained passion his arms went around her at last. He was trembling with his need for her, but beneath it she sensed his smoldering anger. Perhaps she was the one now who was being unfair. Dimly she realized that Jason tolerated too much, that she had come to count on his limitless patience, and perhaps that in itself had perpetuated their problem.

But she could not think of that now. She had to win him back. She had to satisfy him in the only way she could, and then afterward, later, she might be able to think more clearly about her wretched inability to accept her husband's love.

"Come," she said softly, moving with him to the bed. "Lie down. I want to show you how much I love you."

She slipped the robe from his shoulders and let it fall to

the floor. Her own desire was now a fever as she pressed closer against the hard length of his quivering form. He was hot to the touch; his burning skin scorched her hands. And when they sank to the bed, locked tight in an embrace, she thought that there in his arms, with his hard mouth on hers, she would reach satisfaction from just the all-consuming fire of her passionate need.

Every nerve in her body was aflame with sensation. The mere touch of his skin on hers was a rapture she could barely endure. She raised her head and looked down at him with ardent, dark eyes. He was lying on his back; his hands were at her waist. He said in a shaking voice, "Let me love you, let me fill you. Don't be afraid, darling. I love you, I won't hurt you. I want to give you all my love."

She was tempted, but she was afraid. Too often he had thus wooed her, and too often her submission had ended in disaster. No, she thought while her giddy senses spun. She had to love him her way. She must show him her love in the only way she could.

Without a word she bent to kiss him, first on the mouth, then lingeringly, slowly on the throat, on the chest, and then downward to his passion throbbing hot beneath her touch. She felt his sharp intake of breath; she felt the pressure of his hands in her hair and the uncontrollable quivering of his body beneath her lips. With all of her heart she gave him her love; with a velvet-soft touch and the warmth of her mouth she fully gave him the love her treacherous body had withheld. And when he trembled beneath her kisses, she shared his aching pleasure. When he tensed and groaned and released his burning passion, her own passion crested to a rapturous pinnacle of breathtaking ecstasy and overpowering love.

For a long time afterward she held on to him tightly, an arm spanning his waist, her mouth resting warmly near his softly thudding heart. She had won him back, she was thinking dimly. She had loved him in the only way she could. She had satisfied him; she had won him back. That she had angered him, cheated him, did not at the moment concern her. Jason wanted something she was not yet capable of giving. But if he waited just a little longer, if he was patient for just a short while more . . .

"I've been thinking," she heard him say, and his voice was so strange, so astonishingly without emotion that she raised her head and eyed him apprehensively.

His hands, loosely folded, rested lightly on his chest. His face was partly in shadow, and his eyes, a deep, dark blue, were introspective and grim.

"What were you thinking?" She was almost afraid to know.

"Perhaps," he said, "you do regret marrying me. Perhaps you'd be happier if your name were still Marlowe instead of Carradine."

She sat upright with a jolt. Her eyes widened; her breath caught painfully in her throat. "How can you say that?" she gasped. "How can you even think such a thing after what we've just shared?"

He raised his gaze to her suddenly paling face. His eyes were curiously blank, like a calm midnight sea concealing turbulent depths. "Shared?" he echoed in that odd, emotionless voice. "Forgive me, Adrian, but despite the obvious pleasure you gave me, in no way did I feel a participant in that act you say we shared. You see, for ten or twenty-five dollars, depending on the brothel one visits, a man can avail himself of the same service you so generously performed—with a similar lack of involvement on the woman's part."

"Oh, how can you?" she said, wounded. "How can you compare my love to the services of a whore?"

"You flatter yourself," he said quietly. "A whore, at least, is honest in her work."

"Honest?" she cried in outrage. "What are you saying? What dishonesty are you accusing me of? I love you; don't you believe me? And I don't regret marrying you. How many times must I tell you that?"

"You can tell me from now until doomsday," he replied. "It doesn't alter the fact that since the day we were married, you have refused to grant me my conjugal rights."

"But, I've—"

"Don't tell me what you've done instead," he said coolly, stopping her. "I'm all too aware that you have kindly condescended to satisfy my desires in a manner least threatening to your sense of independence."

Her mind reeled against the unexpected cruelty of his soft-spoken attack. Vaguely she realized that she had been fearing such a confrontation. She had known that sooner or later Jason's patience would come to an end, but she had never in her most far-fetched thoughts imagined the bitterness with which he now indicted her.

"I've done quite a lot of thinking this past year," he said when she only watched him in a stunned and dizzy silence. "Mostly, what I've been doing is trying to put myself in your place, attempting to feel what you must have felt when Crandall assaulted you. It wasn't difficult to guess your revulsion, nor was it difficult for me to realize that you needed some time to put the memory behind you and that any sexual overtures on my part would only remind you of what you were desperately trying to forget."

"Jason, please," she said helplessly, "don't look at me like that. And don't talk about it anymore. I'll get over this; I know I will. If you'll just—"

"Be still," he said in that maddeningly quiet voice. "I *will* talk about it. And, for once, Adrian, you're going to listen to me."

"But I don't want—"

"I don't care what you want right now," he said inflexibly. "I've been too concerned lately about what you think you want and not at all concerned with what you truly want."

"What do you mean?" she said in a panic. "Why are you like this? I thought you loved me. I thought you understood how I felt. I know you've been unhappy, but I thought . . ." she trailed off helplessly as he rose from the bed, picked up his dressing gown, and put it on. Adrian watched him in a turmoil, this dark, moody stranger, and he returned her distracted gaze with a severity that chilled her.

"Do you agree I've been a good husband?" he asked at length.

"Yes, yes!" she said readily, afraid to follow where, inescapably, he was leading her.

"Have I proved to your satisfaction that you were wrong when you feared I would deprive you of your freedom?"

"Yes, I was wrong," she blurted. "Jason, come back to bed. Please don't go on with this. I know what you're getting at, but it's not true, I swear it!"

"What am I getting at, Adrian?"

"It's what you said at Tuxedo Park," she said rapidly, erecting a hasty defense. "You think I'm punishing you for marrying me, but, dear God in heaven, that couldn't be further from the truth. I would give anything, *anything*, I tell you, to be able to make love with you properly. Don't you see how I've tried? Jason, what more can I do to prove that I want to belong to you in every sense of the word?"

"Very simply," he said, "you can allow me to make love to you."

"But I can't!" she cried. "You know I can't. Why are you being so unfair? Why can't you be patient just a little while longer?"

"My patience," he said, watching her, "is at an end. Let me say one last word on the subject, and then we need never discuss it again. I want you to be my wife. I want you to give

yourself to me—completely and voluntarily—and until you
do, I prefer that we no longer make love at all. I don't want
to be aroused to no avail, and neither do I wish to be 'ser-
viced' as a concession to your conscience. For some reason,
Adrian, you've gotten it into your head that if our marriage
isn't consummated, then no marriage exists. You seem to
feel that as long as you refuse to accept my physical love
you're still Adrian Marlowe, single woman, free spirit, independent mistress of her own fate."

"You're wrong! You're wrong!" Angry tears blurred her
eyes. "I've done everything possible to make you happy."

"Have you?" he said. "Name one instance, if you
please."

"I married you!" she cried. "I married you against my
will. It was what *you* wanted. *I* never wanted it. I never—"

She broke off in horror and stared at him sickly. Dear
God, it was true. Every last thing he had accused her of was
undeniably true. She had not wanted to marry him. Despite
the fact that her marriage had very probably saved her sanity, she had seen it always, in her deepest heart of hearts, as
a satin-lined prison from which she would never escape.

She continued to stare at him with wide, stricken eyes.
She had not wanted to marry him, but she loved him with all
her soul. How could she make him understand that? And if
he came to understand it how could he ever forgive her for
the cruelty she had shown him in the face of his love?

"I love you," she said hoarsely, her throat tight with
tears. "Part of what you say is true: I didn't want to marry
you, but I don't know if that's the reason I turn away from
you in bed. Jason, I can't bear that I've hurt you. Make love
to me if you wish. I won't stop you this time. I love you
more than I can tell you. I'll do anything you ask."

He watched her in silence with eyes that reflected the burden of her pain. She had hurt him so badly, hurt him, ne-
glected him, deprived him of his rights. Her reasons were

relevant; whether it was the memory of Crandall's attack or the fear of losing her spiritual freedom that turned her cold did not matter. She only knew that she loved her husband: she sorely regretted hurting him, and she would do anything in the world not to lose him.

"Jason," she whispered, her voice a faint plea, "make love to me . . . please. I won't stop you, I promise."

"No," he said, and his own voice shook with an emotion too painful to bear. "Do you think I would take you when you offer yourself like a sacrificial lamb? I love you, god damn it. I want you to give yourself to me freely and without regret. I told you a year ago that I would be here whenever you wanted me, and I tell you the same thing now—"

"Jason . . ." she whispered miserably.

"—but you must come to me of your own accord, Adrian. You must come to me, not in fear or gratitude or obedience or duty. You must come to me in love—in love and nothing else. Only then will you be free of the demons that inhibit you. And only then will you gain the independence you're so desperately afraid of losing."

Thirty

JASON HELD TRUE to his word. He no longer attempted to make love to her. Adrian did not protest. Her mind was still reeling from his accusations. She had to gather her wits about her; she must search her soul, determine once and for all what prevented her from accepting Jason's love. Perhaps, she thought reasonably, it was all to the better that she would have this time to herself without worrying about whether or not she could submit to her husband's love. But, oh, how much easier it would be if she could sort out her jumbled thoughts in the comfort and warmth of Jason's loving arms.

The next night they dined at the Savoy, Jason handsome and aristocratic in evening clothes, and Adrian exceptionally beautiful in a sinuous draping of rose-colored silk. The fare was outstanding: hors d'oeuvres à la Russe, cantaloupe, *noisettes d'agneau*, terrine of pike, and a mouthwatering selection of pastry for dessert. The wine selection was of such a fine and great diversity that Jason, his mind distracted by other matters, had to rely in the end on the judgment of the sommelier, who sniffed haughtily when suggesting the *Côte Rôties* with the entrée, and the Tokai Imperial with dessert.

Seated together, discussing inconsequential matters, the Carradines appeared to the other diners to be the most handsome and carefree of couples. Only on close inspection was the faint trembling of Adrian's lips visible; only the keenest

270

and most searching eye was able to detect the gossamer fine line that creased her husband's brow.

When they returned to their hotel close to midnight, they lingered awhile in the luxurious sitting room, Jason with a glass of Cointreau, Adrian with a delicate Limoges cup of the finest English coffee. Alone now, he could find nothing to say to her. At the Savoy, with the punctilious courtesy of an aloof stranger, he had told her of former trips to England, of visiting Canterbury, Kent, and Sussex. But now he said nothing, and Adrian, half despairing, half maddened by her racing unruly thoughts, could no longer endure the silence.

"I don't see how this is going to solve anything," she said with some heat. "I told you I want you to make love to me. What more can I say?"

"You would be wiser," he said tensely, "to say nothing on that subject."

"Why?" she persisted, her stubborn chin shaking. "What good is ignoring it? You yourself said that one must first face a problem before solving it. I insist that you take me to bed. I won't see our marriage destroyed by—"

She broke off breathlessly, so close to angry tears that to suppress them was agony. Jason watched her with coal-dark eyes, and on his hard, perfect face was a tumultuous anguish that surpassed her own.

"Listen to me," he said roughly. "I don't want to talk about it. It's difficult enough just being with you, looking at you. Do you know how incredibly beautiful you look to me tonight? Do you know that all through dinner I had to physically restrain myself from tearing off your clothes and taking you on the floor in front of the waiters, the diners, and that goddamn supercilious sommelier?"

"Then why don't you make love to me?" she cried. "It's what we both want."

"It's what *I* want," he corrected her. "You want only to show your obedience; and obedience, Adrian, is not what I want from you. I want you to come to me because you wish it. I want you to know without doubt that the love you give me is not a submission but a sharing." He stopped and stared down at her, his eyes ablaze with the passion of wanting her. And when she remained silent and aching beneath his violent gaze, he said in helpless frustration, "Jesus Christ, what's the use?"

And before she could move to stop him, he slammed out of the room.

He was obdurate, adamant; he refused to relent. Despite Adrian's demands that he make love to her and be done with it, Jason would not. Adrian was at her wits' end; she wanted her husband; she wanted his love, his understanding, his limitless tolerance, which in the past she had taken for granted, but which now, she realized dimly, she must work for and earn.

She wanted him so badly; that was the difficult part. With all her heart she wanted to give herself to him, yet as much as she insisted that he make love to her, in the back of her mind she was as afraid as he was, that those "demons" he spoke of would continue to inhibit her.

Perhaps he had been accurate in his appraisal. Perhaps Adrian felt that to submit her body to her husband's love meant submitting her soul to his absolute control. But that was childish, stupid. No man was a better, fairer husband than Jason. Intellectually Adrian knew that he sought no such domination. Why, then, did her fear persist? Why, as much as she wanted him, was she afraid that she was still unable to give him what he wanted?

Every evening for the following week, they dined out at the home of one or another of the county's leading citizens. Jason had many friends in England, friends in high places, which did not surprise Adrian. They dined with the Churchills, the Asquiths, the Balfours, and the Curzons, all

men of government whose wives were the most charming of
hostesses. After dinner Adrian would retire with the ladies
to the drawing room while the gentlemen enjoyed their port
and cigars. They were all lovely, these Dresden-skinned
Englishwomen, and they took a keen interest in their husbands' work. One and all assured Adrian that the war rumors currently circulating were a tempest in a teapot. But
when the gentlemen rejoined the ladies, their faces grave,
their eyes secretive, Adrian received the distinct impression
that the rumors at which everyone scoffed were not to be
taken lightly.

"Jason," she said one night as they were driving back to
their hotel after dining at the home of Sir Edward Grey, who
was Secretary for Foreign Affairs, "what is it you men talk
about after dinner that etches such a formidable gravity on
all your faces?"

For a moment he did not answer. He looked out on the
London streets, then turned to his wife with the same expression she had just described. "Those rumblings about
war we've been hearing," he said carefully, "are growing
louder. The British government is convinced that a conflict
is inevitable. Asquith and Churchill feel that the Kaiser is
simply waiting for an incident to erupt in one of his allied
countries. Germany will then be justified in instituting a
major war in Europe. If that happens the British feel sure
they'll be drawn into the fray."

"What has that to do with you?" she asked. "Do the
British need money? Do they want a loan?"

"Yes," he said quietly. "Among other things."

A nameless fear stirred in her breast. "What other
things?"

"They want me to do some intelligence work for them."

"Intelligent work? I don't understand."

He smiled soberly. "No, Adrian. *Intelligence* work.
Communicating information. You see, I have interests in

Berlin and a good many acquaintances there who owe me favors. Even if war should come I know I'll be able to move freely about the country, first of all because I'm an American and not involved in the conflict, and secondly because Germany, too, will be in need of funds to finance her forces.''

"You mean, the British want you to spy for them.'' Her fear now had a name.

"Yes,'' he said.

"Jason, that could be dangerous, couldn't it?''

"It could.''

"Then why do it?''

"I didn't say I would do it, Adrian. I have to give it some thought. There are several aspects of this project that must be carefully considered.''

"Consider this,'' she said as the fear within her grew. "You have a wife and a daughter.''

"Don't you think I know that?'' His voice was tight with restraint. "If you're assuming I have some hidden heroic tendencies, please disabuse yourself at once. I haven't the slightest desire to risk my neck in a dispute that concerns neither me personally nor my country. But the Kaiser is looking for the least excuse for a war, and who knows where his aggression will stop once it starts. Megalomaniacs dare anything, Adrian. And Wilhelm the Second is thoroughly convinced of his omnipotence.''

"You've met him?''

"Yes,'' Jason said. "On several occasions. The first time was fourteen years ago. He was instructing a shipload of German marines who were on their way to China to put down the Boxer Rebellion. 'Give no quarter!' he shouted. 'Take no prisoners. Kill the enemy when he falls into your hands. As the name of Attila the Hun still strikes fear in hearts, so shall the name of Kaiser Wilhelm resound through Chinese history for a thousand years.' ''

"Dear God," she whispered, horrified.

"Yes, dear God," Jason echoed. "For I fear only God can stop that madman once the wheels of war are set in motion."

"Jason," she said as she sensed the beginning of her husband's resolve, "if you decide to work for the British government, I'm going to help you."

"You?" he said with an indulgent laugh. "What could *you* do?"

"If by that," she said irritably, "you mean 'what could a *woman* do?' let me remind you of a few of my past accomplishments."

"Adrian," he said sternly, his laughter fading, "this is not the world of *haute couture* we're talking about. This is dangerous, deadly work that could involve the loss of thousands of lives, not to mention your own."

"And do you think I'd let you risk your life alone?" she said, determined. "Resign yourself, Jason. If you make the decision to do this thing, you take on a partner whether you wish it or not."

Thirty-one

HE HELD OFF making his decision. Perhaps he was still considering the many aspects of the project as he had said, but Adrian thought it more likely that it was her insistence on joining him in this perilous venture that was weighing most heavily on Jason's mind. On the one hand Adrian felt guilty for burdening him further when she knew how troubled he already was. On the other hand she couldn't dream of letting him go off alone to God knew what destiny while she sat in a luxurious hotel suite, safe as an infant, awaiting his return.

To forestall making a decision, Jason suggested that they go on to Paris as planned. Adrian acceded without a word. Sooner or later she knew his conscience would induce him to comply with the British government's request. When he did, Adrian would be at his side where she belonged. In the meantime let him think, if he liked, that her determination to work with him had been merely a whim.

Their first night in Paris they dined at Maxim's with Gabriel Voison and his enchanting wife Brigitte. Voison was the Frenchman who, with his younger brother Charles, had established an airplane manufacturing company in Billancourt some eight years earlier. This pioneer in his field was even younger than Jason, only thirty-four years old, and his success had transformed him from a scruffy lad with only a few francs in the bank to a wealthy and fashion-conscious boulevardier.

As he lifted his wineglass in a toast to his friend and financier Adrian watched Monsieur Voison in his dandified attire, his diamond-studded shirtfront, his velvet-lapeled tailcoat, and his gardenia boutonniere. His black hair was center-parted and shone with scented pomade. A perfectly trimmed beard and a neat mustache were oddly at variance with the impudent, dark eyes of a mischievous boy. To Adrian's mind he did not hold a candle to Jason, who looked cool and aristocratic in his understated evening clothes with only a small white rosebud in his lapel.

Adrian herself was superbly beautiful in clinging gold lamé with a headband of matching cloth a gleaming foil to her dark curls. Brigitte Voison, a petite blue-eyed brunette in cerulean satin, said with a pretty moue, "Madame Carradine, I waste my time this evening trying to outdo you. You look like a gold-and-sable divinity. When I go home tonight, I slit my throat, yes?"

"That won't be necessary," Adrian said, laughing. "I am green with envy over your gown. Is it by Poiret?"

"*Oui*," the woman said, nodding. "But I am too tiny to give it flair, do you not agree?"

"You are perfectly proportioned," Adrian assured her. "And your coloring puts me in mind of my beautiful daughter. I think you look exquisite."

"You, too, are exquisite, Madame Carradine," observed Gabriel Voison with a Frenchman's admiring eye. "Jason," he added, turning to her husband, "you have found yourself a fine wife. But do you think it wise, *mon ami*, to have brought such a jewel to Europe in such troubled times?"

"In Europe," Jason said, trying to make light of the situation, "all times are troubled. What an excitable people populate this continent! They quite tire me with their interminable border disputes and ideological squabbles."

"We Europeans are of a passionate nature," Voison retorted. "We feel our beliefs strongly and fight for them violently. We are not like the effete Englishmen who always keep the stiff upper lip, nor like your countrymen, Jason, who coolly stand by while other nations do battle, and then afterward swoop down like birds of prey to make feast on the remains of the struggle.''

''Americans are not like that,'' Jason said stiffly. But Adrian, watching him, knew he was taking Voison's remarks personally.

''Eh bien, mon vieux,'' said Voison with a skeptical laugh. ''We shall see what happens if a major war comes to Europe. Perhaps Georges Clemenceau will call on Woodrow Wilson for aid, and we shall see then what your pacifist president has to say in response.''

Some of the sparkle went out of the evening as Adrian watched Jason withdraw into his thoughts. He, like she, knew that President Wilson had no wish to involve his country in foreign disputes. But Jason, with his many European interests and friends, felt a need to help those whom he respected and admired. His eyes were moody as the Voisons ate and drank with Gallic merriment. Adrian sensed in her husband the same stirring of social conscience that had sent his mother parading down Fifth Avenue with placards and banners flying.

He was exceptionally quiet for the next few days, resolving an inner conflict, the outcome of which Adrian felt had already been reached in his heart. They toured the city, strolling on the Champs-Élysée, the Place de la Concorde, and the Bois de Boulogne, but Adrian knew that Jason was finding neither joy nor beauty in the stately monuments and magnificent cathedrals that decorated the city like so many jewels. If anything, Adrian felt, the sights were making Jason even more aware that his responsibilities did not end at the borders of his own country.

In early July the French newspapers blazoned the headline that the Archduke Franz Ferdinand, heir to the throne of Austria-Hungary, and his wife Sophie, had been assassinated by a Serb in Sarajevo, Bosnia. Rumors of retaliation abounded on the Paris streets. A stifling heat wave had kept both natives and tourists indoors for days, but now, with the news of the assassination, the wide boulevards and avenues were alive with people, the Carradines among them, eager to hear all the latest developments.

As the days passed the temperatures dropped, but the rumors continued to spread. Some sources claimed that Austria had charged the Serbian government with plotting the assassination. Others said that German troops were secretly mobilizing in preparation for a war against Serbia, and that Winston Churchill, First Lord of the Admiralty, was dispatching the British fleet to war stations.

But no one in Paris—indeed, no one on the Continent— took seriously any prospect of a major armed conflict. Only Adrian and Jason, who sank deeper into his thoughts, felt a European war was now a frightening inevitability.

On the second Sunday in July a brilliant, sunny day with temperatures pleasantly in the seventies, the Carradines were strolling near the Seine. Jason was smartly turned out in white flannel trousers, a blue and white striped blazer, a stiff-collared shirt, and a handsome straw boater tipped jauntily over one eye. Adrian was a picture of femininity in a white linen walking suit, white kid shoes and gloves, and a broad-brimmed white hat shading her ivory beauty.

As they passed the statue of Henry IV they spotted a group of marchers crossing the Pont-Neuf. The marchers were young on the whole, students likely, with long, shaggy hair, baggy trousers and coats, and flowered cravats spilling gaily on untidy shirtfronts. They were a merry bunch, laughing and shoving one another as if out on a holiday spree. But the placards they carried read: *AUX ARMES!*

AUX ARMES! And one or two serious-faced youths called out with a vengeance, "Long live France! Death to the Kaiser!"

"Jason," said Adrian, puzzled, "why are they denouncing the Kaiser? No hostilities have been declared between the two countries."

"No," Jason answered. "But the French are still seething over their defeat in the Franco-Prussian War. They have only contempt for the Germans to whom they were forced to cede the mining regions of Alsace-Lorraine. Morever, if Franz Ferdinand's assassination is the excuse the Kaiser needs for war, Germany will side with Austria-Hungary, and France will then side with the Serbs, who are supported by France's allies."

He took her arm suddenly and hailed a passing taxi.

"Le Bristol, s'il vous plaît," he told the driver, handing Adrian into the vehicle, then settling back against the seat as she eyed him in bewilderment.

"Jason, what is it? Why are we going back to the hotel? I thought you wanted to see the Conciergerie."

"Not today," he said curtly, peering out the window until the marchers were no longer in sight. "I think we had best return to London."

"Why?" she asked, although the answer was obvious.

"I'm going to talk to Asquith," Jason said. "And I'm putting you on the next ship bound for home."

"I won't go home," she said simply. "I won't leave you."

"Adrian, be reasonable." His voice was terse. "You must go home. Europe is no place for you now that—"

"Jason," she said, facing him squarely, "my place is with you. If you remain here, if you've decided to work for the British government, we shall work together as we've been doing at home. You insisted on a partnership with the fashion house. I'm afraid I'm going to have to insist on a partnership in whatever you do here."

"Think of your daughter," he said roughly and perhaps unfairly.

But she responded with ease, "I am thinking of her. You're the one who said the Kaiser's aggression may not stop at Europe's borders. If I can do anything to prevent that from happening, it's my duty to do it just as much as it is yours."

Ironically, when they met with the prime minister at 10 Downing Street, Asquith could not have been more pleased by Adrian's decision to work with her husband.

"My dear Adrian," he said with his clipped British briskness, "what admirable pluck! Jason," he said to her stunned husband, "with your wife at your side, no one in Germany will even begin to suspect what you're doing."

Jason, who had been counting on Asquith to try to dissuade Adrian, said curtly, "For God's sake, Herbert, what if she's found out? Spies are executed, you know, regardless of their sex."

"But, Jason, don't you see?" the prime minister soothed. "No one could possibly think that an American banker and his couturiere wife were spying on them." He turned with a smile to Adrian. "What a remarkable woman you are. I do believe that Kaiser Wilhelm and his court are in for an exceedingly unpleasant surprise."

Jason, his eyes dark and troubled, regarded his remarkable wife and said nothing.

Before they left the prime minister's office, Asquith said quietly to Adrian as Jason preceded her from the room, "You *do* realize the importance of your task?"

"Yes, of course," she said as Jason entered into a conversation with Asquith's aide in the outer office. "I know what's at stake here. I'm prepared to do anything I can to try to avert a major war."

"Anything?" said Asquith, his meaning unequivocal.

Adrian paused before answering; uneasily she glanced at her husband. "Yes, anything," she finally said. And prayed that Jason had not heard her.

Berlin, when they arrived, was alive with war fever. German reservists paraded down the Unter den Linden in their spiked helmets and *feld-grau* uniforms. Spectators cheered, tossed flowers in their path, and sang *"Deutschland über Alles"* with tears in their eyes.

Adrian said with a shudder as the troops goose-stepped by, "They're only boys, Jason, and yet they shoulder those guns as if they can't wait to use them."

Jason said, his low voice somber, "I fear they'll be using them even sooner than they expect."

They registered that afternoon at the Friedrich der Grosse Hotel. In his excellent German, Jason requested a large suite overlooking the Linden with its stately trees and elegant avenues. The manager, a flaxen-haired Teuton with striking blue eyes, knew Jason well from his many previous trips to Berlin. He welcomed Jason cordially, bowed deeply to "Frau Carradine," and wished her a pleasant stay on this, her first trip to Germany.

They were alone at last in the sitting room of their suite. Adrian removed her hat and stripped off her gloves as Jason stood by the window, smoking a cigarette.

Aware of his mood, she went to him and slipped a hand through his arm. "Are you frightened?" she asked, for the enormity of their task was quite suddenly upon her.

"Yes," he said honestly, his eyes on the swaying trees below.

"I am, too," she admitted. "A little," she qualified. For his fear, she knew, was for her, not for himself.

"What are we to do first?" she asked, rubbing her cheek against his shoulder in a silent gesture of encouragement.

"We wait," he said, and she felt him quiver beneath her

touch. "I cabled General von Moltke that we were arriving today."

"General von Moltke? Who is he?"

"He's the Kaiser's Chief of General Staff," Jason explained. "I met him several years ago through a mutual friend. He's curiously unfitted to his position. He paints and plays the violincello; he's read Nietzsche and Carlyle and is a devout Christian Scientist. I asked him once why he had accepted the top military position in the country when he is so obviously a man of peace. He shrugged and said, 'No man refuses the Kaiser's requests.' "

"What can he do for us?" Adrian asked with another inward shudder.

"He can integrate us into German military circles—socially, of course—which will put us in a position to hear any information that may be useful to the British." Jason tossed his cigarette out the window and turned to her abruptly. "I needn't tell you to be careful? You won't be so foolish as to ask outright questions of the people you meet?"

"Jason, what do you take me for?" she said indignantly. "I'm not a fool."

He regarded her stubborn mouth and her flashing, dark eyes, and in spite of himself, he smiled. "I know that," he said. "I just want to make certain that I'm not going to lose you."

A knock at the door interrupted them. Jason crossed the room and admitted a white-haired gentleman, military cap in hand, whose gentle face and mild gray eyes were a strange contrast to his formidable martial attire, which bristled with battle decorations.

"Helmuth!" said Jason in German, extending a hand. "How are you? I wasn't expecting to see you so soon."

"Am I intruding?" said the gentleman, whose soft-spoken words were slow enough for Adrian to interpret.

"Not at all," Jason said. "Come in, please. I should like

you to meet my wife. Adrian," he said, taking her arm,
"may I present General, Count Helmuth von Moltke. Helmuth, my wife Adrian."

"*Guten tag, gnädige Frau,*" said von Moltke, bending
over Adrian's hand with a click of his heels. And then, in
British-accented English, he added, "I am delighted to meet
you."

Adrian greeted him haltingly, for her German was not fluent. The general smiled at her careful attempt, then said graciously, "If you please, Frau Carradine, let us speak
English so that I may improve my use of your beautiful language."

Adrian readily returned his smile. "I don't see how you
could possibly improve on perfection, Herr General."

Jason telephoned for refreshment. Adrian bade von
Moltke be seated, and as he settled erectly on a chair, she
couldn't help thinking that, despite his military bearing and
the many medals that decorated his uniform, he looked more
a kindly grandfather than premier commander of the Kaiser's armed forces.

"I've ordered schnapps," Jason said, joining his wife on
the sofa. "Helmuth, you're looking fit. How are you keeping yourself?"

As the two men talked of inconsequentials, Adrian
studied the general, trying to associate him with the brutal
concept of war. He was perhaps upward of sixty years old;
his sun-browned face was stern in repose, but at the corners
of his eyes lines of good humor attested to a genial disposition.

Sensing her scrutiny, von Moltke turned to her suddenly
with a charming smile. "Frau Carradine, I understand you
are a designer of women's clothing. My wife would be
thrilled to make your acquaintance. If you and your husband
could make time to spend a weekend at our country house at
Bornstedt, we should be most pleased to have you."

Adrian smiled uncertainly and looked to her husband. Jason said, "I'm not sure how long we'll be in Germany, Helmuth. The reason I'm here is to speak to the Kaiser about the diesel locomotive for the Prussian-Hessian Railways. When I was here a year ago, the tests were disappointing, but I subsequently learned that the Swiss International Railway had good results with their model. When I was last in Switzerland, I undertook to finance the project. The Kaiser, if you will recall, was most anxious for Prussian-Hessian Railways to produce a successful diesel. Perhaps I can be of some help to him in that area."

"That would make him immensely happy," said von Moltke with enthusiasm. "You know as well as I the Kaiser's rabid interest in anything mechanical. Have you an appointment to see him soon?"

"Well, that's my problem," Jason said. "I haven't contacted him yet. I know that with all the war rumors circulating he may have neither the time nor the inclination to see me now."

For a moment von Moltke said nothing. His eyes, so eager and candid a moment ago, had gone curiously blank, veiling his expression. At length he said quietly, "Germany does not want war."

"And the Kaiser?" Jason probed.

"The Kaiser," said von Moltke slowly, "is in a difficult position. His cousin, the Czar, has intimated that he will mobilize his troops if it becomes necessary to protect his allies in the Balkans. The Kaiser, of course, is affronted by such a threat. If the Czar does mobilize against Austria-Hungary the Kaiser will have no recourse but to declare war on Russia."

Jason offered no comment. He reached into his coat pocket, extracted a cigarette, and lit it. His hands, Adrian noted with a catch in her throat, trembled almost imperceptibly.

The waiter arrived with the schnapps and a tray of tea and cakes and set about preparing the serving cart. To relieve the sudden tension that had gripped the two men, Adrian said to von Moltke, "I'm anxious to see the Kaiser's palace, Herr General. Do you think you could arrange to have me presented at court?"

The general's mouth curved into a smile as he regarded Adrian with a gentle, paternal look. "Better than that, my dear Frau. How would you like it if you and your husband were to dine with the Kaiser a week hence?"

"That soon?" she said, surprised. "But how—"

"The Kaiser is having a small dinner party for some members of his staff," von Moltke explained. "I shall inform him that you are looking forward to meeting him—he enjoys a pretty face—and I shall tell him that Jason wishes to speak to him about the diesel. I've no doubt he will welcome your company at his table."

"How very good of you," Adrian said gratefully.

The general finished off his glass of schnapps, then rose. "Now, if you will both excuse me, I must return to headquarters." He bowed to Adrian and shook Jason's hand. "I shall telephone you tomorrow to confirm the invitation."

"Helmuth, thank you," said Jason, seeing him to the door. "I am in your debt."

The general laughed. "Nonsense, Jason. I have not forgotten who arranged to have my son admitted to your Harvard University. I am, and always shall be, in *your* debt, my dear friend."

When von Moltke left, Jason closed the door, slipped his hands into his pockets, and returned to the window to gaze moodily on the Linden. "Christ, I hate this," he said in a low, bitter voice.

"Jason . . ." Adrian went to him at once, but he turned and walked away from her as if too filled with self-disgust to let her see him.

"I hate it," he said again, leaning his hands heavily on the back of the sofa. "That man's my friend; I have no quarrel with him. And yet in helping Asquith, another friend, I may well be destroying the career and reputation of Helmuth von Moltke."

"Jason," she said urgently, pained by his distress, "you must do this. You yourself said—"

"I don't care what I said." Disgustedly he slumped into a chair, leaned his elbows on his knees, and stared at the floor. "I cannot do this; I will not do it."

Adrian knelt at his feet, took both hands in her own. "Jason, what we're doing may avert the destruction of something far more important than a man's career. If war comes—oh, Jason, look at me; listen to me—if war comes, there may be nothing left of these countries you so love. If there is the least chance of avoiding that war, of preserving the peace, we *must* do what we can to—"

"There is no avoiding war now," he said grimly. "Can't you see that? What good is our filtering information from one country to another when it's inevitable that the entire continent may soon go up in flames?"

"Then we must work all the harder," Adrian insisted, holding tightly to his hands. "It's for General von Moltke's sake, too, that we must try to stop his country from starting a war."

Jason looked at her at last, at her fervent, dark eyes, her flushed cheeks, her mouth firm with determination. She was as excited and as vivacious as she had been when she was battling for her fashion house. To Jason's anxiety-ridden mind it appeared that only challenges and daring brought out passion in his wife.

More roughly than he intended, he said, "This is all a great adventure to you, isn't it, another manner of asserting your independence? I daresay you were pleased as punch when Asquith asked for your help."

"Jason," she said firmly, gripping his icy hands tightly, "it's not that at all. This is something we both must do, can't you see that?"

She was right, and he knew it, but his emotions, unlike hers, had temporarily beclouded his judgment. To avoid war at any cost was now of the prime importance. If their mission was a futile one, they would at least have done their duty to the best of their ability.

His forbidding expression softened somewhat. He cupped her chin with a firm, hurting hand and gave her a bitter smile. "I don't know whether you're the bravest or the most foolhardy woman I've ever known." His smile vanished. Abruptly he said, "You *will* be careful? The Kaiser has his faults, but stupidity is not one of them."

"I shall be as careful as I was when I asked you for a loan," she said, smiling up at him.

Jason stared at her for a moment, his hard mouth stern, his gaze intense. Then, with a fierce burst of emotion he had not shown her in a long time, he lifted her swiftly onto his lap and kissed her hard. Adrian's heart leaped as a wild thrill coursed through her. She wound her arms tightly around him and returned his kiss with a passion that dizzied her. For a long time they kissed, straining close to each other as if they longed to become one. At one point Adrian thought he might take her, right there in the chair; she *wanted* him to take her, she wanted him to make her his. But he did not.

Thirty-two

KAISER WILHELM II was the Hohenzollern heir of Frederick III and son of the eldest daughter of the late British queen, Victoria. Despite this English maternal ancestry, Wilhelm's residence in Berlin could in no way be compared with the warm and charming London homes in which Adrian and Jason had been guests. The Kaiser's palace was dark and gloomy and filled with heavy black antique furniture. The rooms were huge, the walls covered with full-length paintings of gory battle scenes. His court was organized on military lines; indeed, all his officials wore uniforms he himself had designed.

When Adrian was presented to him a week after her arrival in Germany, she was surprised to find the Kaiser short of stature and mild of manner. From Jason's description of him and from accounts she had read in French newspapers, she had expected, at least, a seven-foot fire-breathing ogre.

They were in the great reception hall, a cavernous room with high, vaulted ceilings and tapestried walls that were also hung with the heads of stags and boars.

Adrian had already met several of the Kaiser's staff: Count von Bethmann-Hollweg, the German Chancellor who had assured Jason that any hostilities that might erupt would certainly be "localized"; Prince Henry, the Kaiser's brother; Prince Karl Lichnowsky, the German ambassador to England; and Count Frederick von Zeppelin, who had designed the lighter-than-air ship that bore his name. But it was the Kasier who most caught Adrian's interest, the fascination, perhaps, of a bird for a snake.

His English, like General von Moltke's, was flawless. After taking Adrian's hand and grazing it with his lips, he fixed her with his blue-gray gaze and said frankly, "General von Moltke was inaccurate in describing you, madam. He told me you were attractive. I find you exceedingly beautiful."

Adrian did look her best this evening. She had chosen with care the black silk and lace sheath, which gave her an air of both mystery and sophistication. In her hair she had pinned a diamond rosette that glittered and caught the light, and at her breast was a single teardrop diamond Jason had purchased for her at Tiffany & Company in Paris. Jason had told her when they arrived that she far outshone the fussily clad German wives present, and indeed, even the Empress in a white satin gown studded with pearls was no match for Adrian's elegant simplicity.

"Your Majesty is too kind," Adrian murmured, noting with distaste the many rings on his fingers. The man was a fop with his curly blond hair gone gray, his blue uniform liberally trimmed in gold, and his thick brush of a mustache with waxed, upturned ends. And yet, in his steely eyes Adrian sensed an imperious autocrat who brooked no opposition. The Kaiser was not stupid, as Jason had warned her, but much worse than that, he was dangerous.

"Your Majesty," she said with a smile designed to captivate, "I have never been in your lovely country before. Berlin is outstanding, so much more dignified than Paris." She turned to her husband at her side. "Don't you agree, darling?"

Jason nodded silently. The Kaiser said approvingly, "I quite agree with you, madam. The feverish haste and restlessness of Parisian life repels me. I visited the city for the first time in my nineteenth year, and I felt I should not care if I never saw the French capital again.''

A servant appeared at the Kaiser's side and murmured something in his ear.

''*Danke,* Hans,'' said the Kaiser. And then, extending an arm to Adrian, ''May I have the honor of escorting you in to dinner?''

Adrian felt oddly vulnerable as she accompanied him to the Imperial dining room followed by Jason and the Empress and a host of German military men and their wives. From somewhere in the palace an orchestra was playing the prelude to the third act of Wagner's *Siegfried*.

A ghostly unreality pervaded Adrian's senses as the Kaiser murmured social pleasantries in flawless English. In the dining room, as she was seated between the wife of the ambassador and the unmarried Minister of War, she felt that she was a marionette on strings, moving, acting, and speaking as if directed by an unseen force. It occurred to her that fear was the root of her curious feelings. She was frankly apprehensive of what the evening might hold. This was, after all, not the brilliant social occasion it appeared. She was here to garner information for the British government in concert with her husband. But as she looked around at the uniformed guests with their fiercely bristling military mustaches, she began to doubt the success of her impossible task.

Dinner was quite unlike the regal fare Adrian might have expected in an emperor's palace. Although the table was elegantly set with Dresden china, heavy silver, and fragile crystal, the food was less fine. The *weisswurst*, a white sausage mixed with calves' brain and spleen, appalled her. The rabbit, greasy to begin with, had been cooked in lard and was barely edible. The aroma of the cabbage, mingling with the musky perfume of Princess Lichnowsky on her left, threatened to asphyxiate her. Over dessert, a rich torte at which Adrian merely poked, she said to General von Falkenhayn on her right, "How do you military men keep so fit on heavy fare like this?"

The general, a lean, handsome man in his fifties with a boyish crop of fair hair and cool blue eyes, said solemnly, "His Majesty's soldiers eat well, but they vigilantly maintain what they call their 'battle-ready physique.' German soldiers stand ever prepared to defend their country. It is His Majesty's express command, you see."

Adrian nodded, idly moving her torte from one side of the dish to the other. "I daresay the men are now in peak physical condition."

"To be sure," said von Falkenhayn. "Emperor Franz Josef wishes to make war on Serbia to avenge the assassination of his nephew, and His Majesty the Kaiser has pledged every cooperation should this come to pass."

"Really?" Adrian raised her eyes to his with a slow, provocative flutter of her lashes. "How exciting."

The general, not unaffected by her languid gaze, colored slightly and laid down his fork. "You find war exciting, *mein frau?*"

"I find soldiers exciting," she qualified. She leaned toward him seductively, lowering her voice. "My husband is a banker, you know. So dull, so . . . unarousing."

The general's color deepened. Adrian gazed at him appealingly as if waiting breathlessly for his next word. From the corner of her eye she saw Jason watching her from across the table. She glanced at him briefly; his face was stony. He had guessed her intent, and he was warning her to abandon it. She knew he was frightened for her—she herself was frightened—but they had both come too far now to retreat.

"Frau Carradine," said von Falkenhayn, "would you—"

"Please," she murmured, "you must call me Adrian."

"Adrian, yes. My Christian name is Erich."

"Erich." She smiled. "How very . . . virile."

"Adrian," he said, his voice growing husky, "perhaps after dinner I could show you His Majesty's gardens. They are quite spectacular this time of year."

"I should love that," she agreed, laying a light hand on his sleeve. "But"—she glanced again at Jason, whose dark look now alarmed her—"we shall have to find a way to slip out without being noticed. My husband," she explained in a whisper, "is insanely jealous."

"Leave it to me," whispered the general. "The Imperial Army is noted for its evasive tactics."

But it was not an easy matter to evade Jason. For the remainder of the meal he kept a weather eye on his wife and the general. And once, when Jason's gaze met and locked with hers, Adrian felt a momentary qualm of misgiving, a sense of treacherous disloyalty. Here she was deliberately attempting to arouse the sexual interest of a German stranger while her husband, with whom she had not made love in over a year, looked on in open and dangerous warning.

With an immense effort Adrian tore her gaze from Jason's and returned her attention to von Falkenhayn. This was *not* a betrayal, she told herself firmly; she was only doing what she had to do. This was her duty as much as it was Jason's. Her responsibilities were not less than his because she was a woman. Couldn't he understand that? No, obviously he could not, for although Adrian did not look at her husband again during the meal, she was intensely aware of his scrutiny.

At dinner's end the Kaiser claimed Jason's attention as the ladies rose to retire. Von Falkenhayn's departure went unnoticed. Out in the hall the general took Adrian's arm and deftly maneuvered her into a darkened alcove as the ladies passed by on their way to the grand salon. She shivered in his hold, for his arm was tight around her. Mistaking her

fear for anticipation, von Falkenhayn whispered warmly,
"Soon, *liebchen,* soon. We shall be quite alone in the gardens."

Adrian's fear was now compounded a hundredfold. What
had she got herself into? She had flirted with the man in order to gain his confidence. But she realized now that he
wished more from her than she had expected to gain from
him.

"Erich . . ." she said in a shaking voice.

"Shh." He laid a finger against her lips. "Quickly now;
they are all gone. Come along, Adrian."

He took her arm and directed her swiftly to a door down
the hall, which opened on to a vast formal garden. In the
moonlight a neatly patterned design of flowers of every description stretched as far as the eye could see. Interspersed
with the flowerbeds were gleaming statuary and fountained
grottos, everything large—obscenely large—as if it were the
Kaiser's belief that size was synonymous with quality.

"Come," said von Falkenhayn. "There is a bench yon-
der where we can sit and talk."

His hand was warm on hers; his eyes and his golden hair
gleamed in the moonlight. Adrian's heartbeat accelerated.
For one awful moment she thought of Perry Crandall then,
with the greatest effort, dismissed the thought. Erich von
Falkenhayn was not a seedy, vengeance-bent journalist. He
was the Prussian Minister of War, a soldier, a statesman.
And besides, Adrian thought as they settled on the bench
near a gently flowing fountain, she had only to raise her
voice to bring one or more of the many liveried servants she
had seen in the palace rushing to her aid.

"Tell me, Erich," she said in a seductive voice that be-
lied the latent panic that quivered through her limbs, "if war
comes, will you be leading the Kaiser's forces into battle? I
so admire a man of action."

"Do you?" he said, taking both her hands in his and

pressing them ardently to his lips. "You will find, my dear lady, that I am a man who acts always on his deepest feelings."

"Oh, I can see that," Adrian said, flushing with an agitation the general misinterpreted as physical excitement. "When I think of you mounted on a horse, courageously urging your men to attack—"

She broke off abruptly as his breathing quickened and his hands tightened hotly on hers. Her own breathing was a labored constriction in her throat. She opened her mouth to speak, and in the next instant his arms went hard around her, and his mouth came down on hers with a swift, demanding urgency that terrified her.

"Stop!" she gasped against his mouth. But there was no stopping the assault she had so recklessly invited. "Erich, don't!"

She struggled against him and felt the medals on his chest tear the lace at her bodice. He was bending her backward; her spine felt near to snapping. With a sudden strength generated by her great fear, she twisted in his arms, pushed him roughly away from her, and sprang from the bench as he sprawled, openmouthed, at her feet.

"What the devil?" he sputtered, rising at once and indignantly dusting at his trousers. "I thought this was what you wanted."

"I wanted to *talk*," she said, shaking. "How dare you paw me like that? I thought you were a gentleman."

"Oh, I see," he said with a smile that was a grimace. "You're one of those women who like descriptions. Come here then," he said, capturing her again in his arms. "I shall tell you in detail what I'd like to do with you."

"Why don't you tell *me* what you'd like to do with my wife?" said a voice from behind them.

They turned with a start; the general quickly released Adrian. Jason stood at the edge of the fountain, his hands clenched at his sides, his face deadly. Alongside him, in silent, majestic reproach, stood the Kaiser.

"You were saying, General von Falkenhayn?"

Jason's low voice vibrated with a murderous restraint. Adrian watched in fearful silence as he and the Kaiser walked toward the general, who stood waiting as if paralyzed.

"Jason . . ." whispered Adrian, her throat dry.

"Stay out of this," he told her, his eyes on von Falkenhayn. "Well, General?"

"Your Majesty, Herr Carradine," said the general at last. "a thousand apologies. Frau Carradine expressed a desire to see the gardens, and I foolishly assumed—"

"You assumed what?" asked the Kaiser quietly.

"Your Majesty," Jason said tightly, "with your permission I should like to deal with this matter myself."

"With all due respect, Jason," said the Kaiser, "von Falkenhayn is on my staff. His actions, therefore, directly reflect on me. If he has insulted or offended your wife in any way, he is answerable first to me as his sovereign, and then to you as my esteemed guest." He turned to his paling subject. "General von Falkenhayn—"

"Your Majesty," Adrian interjected, fearing this incident might jeopardize their mission, "if you please, sir. This was all a misunderstanding. I was so taken with the general's kindness and courtliness that I may have mistakenly led him to believe my interest was other than friendly admiration."

"I doubt that," said Jason coldly. But when Adrian looked at him with a start, his eyes warned her briefly to follow his lead. "This is not the first time I've had to rescue you from an amorous suitor, my dear. In Austria-Hungary it was from a cavalry man; in Italy it was from a vice-admiral. I grow tired of your fascination with the military."

"Jason, I—"

"Be still!" he commanded her. Then, turning to the Kaiser: "My deepest apologies, Your Majesty, for airing my marital difficulties before you. I think it best to leave now. In fact," he added, glancing darkly at von Falkenhayn, "I think it prudent to leave Berlin at my earliest convenience."

The Kaiser's gaze slid to Adrian, who bristled silently at the indignity of her husband's insinuations. Then he looked at Jason and smiled sympathetically. "I understand," he said, nodding knowingly. "I only regret that you could not have spent more time with us. You *will* go to Winterthur, though, won't you? You will keep your promise to me?"

"Of course," Jason said. "Adrian"—he took her arm—"bid His Majesty good night."

With flaming face Adrian curtsied to the Kaiser as Jason bowed. Behind the Kaiser, General von Falkenhayn stood quietly, in his eyes a curious mixture of relief and suspicion.

Thirty-three

HE DID NOT speak at all on the short ride from the palace in an Imperial automobile with a court chauffeur at the wheel. Jason only held her hand tightly, his eyes turning constantly to the telltale torn lace at her breast.

"Are you all right?" he asked her immediately when they entered their hotel suite.

"Yes," she said gratefully, trembling from the release of nervous tension. "I'm all right. But I can't begin to tell you what a fright he gave me when he—"

"He didn't hurt you?" Jason's voice was hoarse with emotion.

"No," she said at once, submerging her fear in order to allay his. "Jason, honestly, he didn't hurt me. His medals tore the lace. I'm all right, I give you my word."

His eyes strayed to the torn lace again, and he muttered an oath. "We must leave Berlin at once."

"Jason, why?" she asked, her nerves tightening again.

"That little charade in the garden," he said tersely. "I don't know how long it's going to fool them. Once von Falkenhayn and the Kaiser start comparing notes with the other guests, someone is bound to realize that we were both far too inquisitive tonight."

"Jason, you don't think—"

"What I think," he said scathingly, "is that you needn't have gone that far. You didn't have to flaunt yourself like a common tart."

"Jason," she protested, "it was the only way to get information."

"Rubbish!" he said harshly. "It was only another way for you to assert your independence."

"That's unfair!" she cried. "I was performing a duty, that's all. Do you think I enjoyed his advances? Don't you know that your arms are the only ones I want around me, that your mouth is the only one I want on mine? Jason, why won't you make love to me? What are you trying to prove by holding me at arm's length?"

"Prove?" he echoed bitterly. "*You're* the one who seeks constantly to prove. Like your eagerness to do intelligence work—proof of your courage. Like that business with von Falkenhayn—proof of your independence."

Abruptly he took hold of her and dragged her roughly into his arms. "Prove that you belong to me," he said fiercely, his hot breath brushing her lips. "Prove that you want me—*now.*"

His mouth came down on hers with a bruising intensity. All thought was swept away by the unexpected burst of passion that raged through Adrian's body like an inferno. She could feel his hard desire pressing urgently against her. His arms were hurting her, and his mouth was a violent force against which she had neither the will nor the desire to resist. The physical need for her husband was suddenly greater than any need she had ever experienced.

"Jason," she moaned, tearing her mouth from his, "make love to me now."

The telephone rang, startling them both. They broke apart breathlessly, staring first at each other and then at the instrument. Adrian trembled with desire; she gazed at her husband with eyes hot and bright. He returned her passionate stare with an intensity that weakened her knees. But as the telephone shrilled persistently, he turned away from his wife, walked stiffly to the side table, and picked up the receiver.

"Yes?" he said curtly, then glanced out the window with a frown as something on the street below caught his eye.

Adrian's palms began to perspire; she clenched and unclenched her fists.

"Yes, I see," Jason said in German. "That was extremely kind of him. Yes, we'll be ready at eight o'clock. Thank you. Good night."

He replaced the receiver and turned slowly to Adrian. "That was the manager," he said. "The Kaiser is sending his car and a small contingent of men to escort us to Winterthur tomorrow morning."

"Winterthur? In Switzerland? But why, Jason?"

"I told the Kaiser tonight that I would be happy to secure any information he wished concerning the diesel locomotive from the Swiss International Railway in Winterthur. In other words," he explained ironically, "I agreed to spy for him."

"To spy for him? Oh, Jason . . ."

"Yes," he said, extracting a cigarette and lighting it with unsteady hands. "This business is beginning to border on the absurd. At any rate, the Kaiser must either be most anxious for the information or he's starting to smell a rat. Otherwise, why would he be sending his car and an 'escort' for us?"

"Jason, what do we do next?" she asked in a calm tone widely at variance with her racing thoughts. If they were to be escorted to Winterthur, it meant a return escort to Berlin. If war broke out in the meantime—which it was sure to do—when and how would they be able to return to England?

Jason's thoughts must have paralleled hers, for he said, "As soon as we get to Switzerland I'll make some excuse to send you back to London."

"No!" she cried. "I refuse to go without you."

"Listen to me," he said roughly. "I have information for Asquith that can't wait. You must pass it on to him. I'm sure the Kaiser is going to want me back in Berlin as soon as I've completed my business in Winterthur."

"But, Jason," she said desperately, "can't we think of a way to elude the Kaiser's escort and both go to London?"

He smiled grimly and walked over to the window. "Come here," he said. "Take a look down there on the street."

She complied with a fast-beating heart and saw, under the streetlamp, two men in civilian clothing but with the unmistakable military bearing of Prussian soldiers.

"Dear God," she whispered, "we're being watched."

"Yes," he said. "I spotted them when I was on the telephone. Adrian, you must go back to London, with or without me. I learned from von Moltke tonight that Emperor Franz Josef will declare war on Serbia within the next few days. As soon as that happens Russia will mobilize against Austria-Hungary, which will undoubtedly give the Kaiser the excuse he wants to declare war on France. Helmuth told me—though not in so many words—that the Germans intend to attack France through Belgium. If that happens England will have no recourse but to declare war on Germany. We must get this advance warning to Asquith so that he can prepare the British forces as best he can."

"Jason," she said as he drew the curtain closed and extinguished his cigarette, "can't we slip out of the hotel tonight and find our way back to England together?"

He shook his head and promptly lit another cigarette. "I'm willing to wager that all the entrances and exits of the hotel are being watched. We wouldn't get far if we tried to leave now. Adrian, do as I say, just this once. You must go to England without me. I give you my solemn promise that I shall join you as soon as I'm able."

There was nothing to do but to accede to her husband. Adrian knew they were in an extremely dangerous position. For the Kaiser to have sent men to watch them boded very ill, indeed. For him to send a car and an escort for the trip to Winterthur was even more ominous. Ordinarily one traveled such a distance by train. The fact that the Kaiser wanted the

Carradines in an automobile in full view of his men at all
times tended to indicate that he had no desire to risk the
chance of Adrian and Jason escaping along the way.

Adrian went to her husband and laid her head on his
chest. As his arms went around her she wondered in silent
fear if either of them would ever see England again.

It was several hundred miles from Berlin to the Swiss border. They stopped at Leipzig and Coburg to eat and rest, and
spent the night in Stuttgart at a roadside inn, but still they did
not arrive in Winterthur until past four the following day.
The journey had been an ordeal. Adrian and Jason sat in
strained silence in the backseat of a luxurious Daimler,
while in the front seat a liveried chauffeur and a military officer sat in equally stony silence. Behind them trailed another Daimler, three officers within, who leaped out of their
own vehicle every time the lead car stopped, and hovered
around the Carradines as if they were either the most precious cargo or the most desperate criminals.

"I can't bear it," Adrian had said in the privacy of the
Stuttgart bedroom, nearly smothering to death upon a billowy
feather mattress. "They won't let us out of their sight for a
moment. Jason, how are we going to get away from them?"

"I don't know," he said frankly. "But don't worry about
it, Adrian. Once we're in Winterthur I'll think of something.
Johannes Friedl, the manager of the Swiss Railway, is a
friend of mine who owes me a favor. Perhaps he can help us
come up with a way to elude our escort."

"And if he can't?" she was compelled to ask.

Jason kissed her brow lightly and gathered her closer in
his arms. For a long time he was silent, and then he only
said, "Don't think about it."

But try as she might for the rest of a sleepless night, she
could think of nothing else.

Under other circumstances Adrian would have greatly enjoyed the journey through the German countryside. On the last leg of the trip they drove through the Black Forest, passing graceful waterfalls, old castles, and picturesque wine villages. When they skirted the town of Friedrichhafen, Jason said to Adrian in an undertone, "Count von Zeppelin's airships are built here. I daresay the driver has strict orders to avoid the area in order to prevent us from copying the design."

She did not smile at his irony, although the humor of the situation was apparent to her. She was too tense to joke; her nerves felt stretched to the snapping point. But a strange thing happened when they passed over the border into Switzerland. As the Daimler purred smoothly past glossy lakes, serpentine roads, and towering mountain peaks, Adrian experienced a brief but profound feeling of serenity. The Swiss countryside differed vividly from the German. It seemed like a fairyland with its vast open spaces and bright sun-kissed greenery. As they drove through sleepy towns nestled below distant hills dotted with colorful little houses and brilliant summer flowers, Jason said quietly, "Lord, I had forgotten how beautiful Switzerland is. Adrian, smell the cyclamen. It's wonderful, isn't it?"

"Yes," she said, and squeezed the hand he had impulsively thrust in hers. "It's the most beautiful country I've ever seen."

He turned from the window and watched her for a moment, and Adrian smiled at him as that curious sense of serenity again engulfed her. They were together, after all, and nothing was so bad, she felt, as long as they could share it.

Jason's thoughts, however, seemed to differ from hers. As he watched her, unsmiling, a myriad of thoughts reflected bitterly in his eyes. It was obvious to Adrian that he would rather have faced the uncertain fate that awaited them alone. His hand tightened on hers, and then he raised it to his lips. In his look was an apology that banished the smile from her face and brought tears to her own remorseful eyes.

Thirty-four

WINTERTHUR WAS an industrial town, but despite its great railyards and manufactory it was no less bucolic than its neighboring villages. A bustling marketplace occupied the center of town, and just beyond it, an eleventh-century church stood on a hillside. Set back from the roadside were cottages with thatched roofs surrounded by neatly tended gardens.

The hostelry at which the Carradines and their escort registered was as charming an inn as Adrian had ever seen, with its pristine rooms and a view from the bedroom windows of stately fragrant pines.

When they were settled at last in the sitting room of their suite, Adrian worriedly watched her husband light a cigarette. For days he had been smoking almost continuously. His voice was husky; he awoke in the mornings with a rattling cough. Aside from the concern for his physical wellbeing, Adrian was upset because she knew that foremost on Jason's mind was to find a way to get her to England and safety. They were sitting on a powderkeg; their lives now depended solely on how convincingly Jason could act.

"Aren't you hungry?" she asked, assuming for his sake a semblance of normalcy.

Along with his heavy smoking he was not eating well. At every meal Adrian would watch him pick at his food, his mind obviously elsewhere. No matter how she tried to cajole him into eating, he would merely say he wasn't hungry, push away his plate, and then he would light up another of his interminable cigarettes. She had never seen him like this: tense, distracted, he was almost another man. His nerves were stretched to the breaking point.

He might well engineer her escape, her thoughts continued wildly, and not make it himself. She instantly rejected the thought. It just was not possible. She counted on Jason, his support, his understanding, his patience, his being *there*. It was inconceivable that she could live in a world without him.

Yet it *was* conceivable that Jason could walk out of the door of their room and never come back—just on the whim of their armed escort.

This had not occurred to her before, and it made the results of her own actions very real and vital to her; it had been her explicit invitation to von Falkenhayn that set off this chain of events.

And Jason was willing to sacrifice himself for her safety because of it, and do it—dear God, without the reassurance of her love.

She was shaken to the very core by this self-examination. She might never see him again, never have the chance ever again to love him. All the possibilities crowded her mind chaotically as she awaited his answer to her prosaic question. Her whole preoccupation was with her love for the man before her and how she might finally assuage his physical hunger. Her imagination assessed the consequences coldly and boldly, and her body answered its call. She knew what she would do, and she prepared mentally as he turned from the window to answer her question.

"Hungry?" he said, going to the telephone. "No, not really. It's barely five o'clock. I'll have something sent up for you, though. What would you like?"

"I would like," she said firmly, "a partner for dinner. Jason, if you don't have something to eat I'm going to be very annoyed with you."

"Very well." He laughed, picking up the receiver. "What shall we have?"

"You decide," she said, encouraged by this concession. "Make it something very Swiss, very delicious. I have had more than my fill of sausage and sauerbraten."

While Jason ordered dinner, Adrian slipped into the bedroom and changed into one of her most fetching peignoirs. She had purchased it at Poiret's when they were in Paris, unable to resist the creamy confection of clinging ivory satin with a daringly low bodice of frothy Valenciennes lace. She had not yet worn it; there previously had been no occasion to do so. But now, as she dabbed French perfume at the curve of her breast, she realized that for her husband's sake she should have *made* an occasion to give him her love.

When she returned to the sitting room, dinner had already been set out on a linen-covered table completely decorated with two tall candles and a centerpiece of sweet alyssum.

"Jason, it looks lovely!" she said.

"As do you," he murmured, seating her. "Have you any plans for after we dine?"

"A nap, I think," she said, smiling as he took his own seat.

He returned her smile but chose to say nothing.

Dinner was a delight. Jason had ordered *Geschnetzeltes*, tender minced veal with a delicate cream sauce; a fresh vegetable and mushroom salad; and for dessert a spiced honey cake with a thin coating of sugar icing. They drank Neufchâtel wine, a light sparkling drink with a piquant bouquet. Adrian was relieved to note that Jason was eating well, as if he had been momentarily blessed with the underlying sense of serenity Adrian had experienced upon entering the country.

When they were having their coffee, she was tempted to ask him if he intended to see Johannes Friedl first thing in the morning. But he looked so relaxed as he watched her across the table that she decided to say nothing that might spoil his mood.

"My goodness," she said with a pretended yawn. "I can't keep my eyes open. You wouldn't mind, would you, if I took a short nap?"

She rose leisurely, aware of his eyes on her enticing décolletage.

"No," he said, rising, too. "You wouldn't mind, would you, if I joined you?"

"Not at all," she said, a faint tremor in her voice. Would he relent at last? Would he finally end his self-imposed restriction on the physical love Adrian now craved so desperately?

His arm went around her shoulder, and she slipped an arm around his waist as they moved casually to the bedroom. While Jason disrobed in the bathroom Adrian removed the coverlet from the bed and lay down to wait for him. A gentle breeze wafted through the windows, redolent of the pine trees that swayed gently in the distance. The sun's reddish gold glow lit the room, and again that sense of serenity filled Adrian with its peace.

When Jason emerged from the bathroom, clad only in his dressing gown, Adrian turned to him with a sweet, drowsy smile.

"Jason, isn't it lovely here? The clean air, the flowers, the delicious aroma? It's like Eden must have been at the dawn of Creation. Come, my lord Adam," she murmured, holding out her arms to him. "Come share a bed with your devoted Eve."

She was the essence of femininity as she beckoned to him seductively. Her lips, gently parted, were a soft petal pink. The breeze from the window teased her sable curls and blew wispy tendrils across the ivory smoothness of her brow. She had never looked more beautiful, nor more desirable.

Jason looked down at her quietly, his eyes very blue against the sober stillness of his face. Adrian's smile faded; her breath caught in her throat. The stillness of Jason's features was more explicit than language. With a thrilling, erotic slowness he got into bed and took her in his arms. Her heart seemed to stop, for in his eloquent eyes she saw reflected the desire that must surely be in hers.

For a long while he held her, unmoving, just watching her, while the silence that surrounded them became a sensual symphony in her ears. His physical nearness enchanted and enslaved her. She was oddly bemused yet intensely aware of the smallest detail: the texture of his sleeve beneath her hand, the fine hairs at his temple, the thick brush of lashes, the hard curve of his mouth so deliciously close to hers.

"You *are* Eve," he finally said, the timbre of his voice vibrating in harmony with her pleasantly humming nerves. "You're my weakness, my downfall. I cannot look at you without wanting you; I cannot touch you without experiencing the most exquisite torments of love and desire."

"Jason," she whispered as his arms tightened around her and the message in his eyes became a mirror to her thoughts.

She could feel the heat of his passion as he drew her closer against him, and that passionate heat was her own desperate need. She loved him, she wanted him; she had never wanted him more. Her eyes closed, she raised her face to his, and when his mouth covered hers, a thrill such as she had never known sent the blood coursing wildly through her veins.

His mouth moved on hers with a sensuousness that fueled her own desire. He kissed her thoroughly, deeply, his lips a warm insistence, demanding a response she willingly gave him. All else seemed to fade as his mouth left hers and brushed against her cheek, then trailed to her ear.

"I want you," he said, and the soft, whispered words left her breathless and trembling.

She wanted him, too; she wanted him totally. In this beautiful country reminiscent of paradise she felt that he and she were the sole inhabitants of a sweet sun-drenched world, a world where light and color and fragrance heightened the senses so that even the touch of his hands at the base of her spine was an indescribable pleasure she could barely support.

He drew her closer in his embrace. She was conscious of nothing but his strong length against her and a primitive passion she could not control. His hard mouth took hers, creating waves of sensation that engulfed her like a tide. She was drowning in desire, drifting deeper and deeper into the fathomless depths of a sensuous sea that was the force of his will and the all-consuming power of his love.

All conscious thought was erased as she submitted to his kiss and to the slow, erotic movement of his hands. Through the thinness of her peignoir his fingers stoked the blazing fire of her desire. With trembling hands she unfastened the garment to bare herself to his touch. A breeze chilled her skin as she moved aside the fabric, but at once she was warmed by the heat of his mouth as it trailed from her mouth and pressed slow, burning kisses on each quivering breast.

Her fingers entwined in the thickness of his hair, and with a soft helpless moan she surrendered her being to his. She wanted him totally; she wanted to feel his warmth inside her, to receive his full love, to enclose his fiery passion within the hot depths of hers, and to soar with him to ecstasy in a rapturous flight of love.

The barrier of their clothing became a maddening hindrance. In a blur of urgent desire she pushed aside his dressing gown, and though he shuddered at her touch and his mouth at her breast began a more sensuous aggression, he made no move to possess her, and her urgent desire became an agony of need.

His touch was a torment; his kisses were bliss. In her trembling hand she held the promise of fulfillment, but he yet made no move to make her fully his own. Heart pounding, blood racing, she arched close against him. Her legs parted, inviting his hard desire, but still he held back, still he only caressed her—with his hands, with his mouth—still he brought her

closer to the very brink of rapture until she could no longer endure the painful emptiness that only he could fill.

"Jason, now," she begged, breathless. "Take me now. I
want you, I need you, I love you so much."

He raised his head and looked down at her. His eyes were
dark with passion; his warm breath brushed her cheek.
Dizzy with wanting him, she writhed beneath the hard
strength of his body hot on hers. "Jason, now," she begged
again. And with a slow, provocative, sensuous movement,
he grasped her writhing hips, pressed her hard against his
passion, then with one deep, long, loving thrust, he slid
himself fully inside her.

She gasped with pleasure as his throbbing hardness filled
her. She had forgotten the ecstasy of utter possession; she
had forgotten the joy of complete physical union. She belonged to him fully now, and he, enclosed within the confines of her passionate love, belonged to her as well. They
were one, truly one, joined flesh to flesh, heart to heart, soul
to soul. Each stroke of his love was a total commitment; her
acceptance of his love was a pledge in return.

Her arms tightened around him, and she gave herself as
she had never done before. Jason sensed her soul's surrender, and his passion grew fiercer. In accepting her love he
gave her all of his own. His kisses increased her rapture; she
could feel his love inside her, enlarging, expanding, exciting her own. As his slow movements quickened she rose to
meet them. Breathless and shaking she returned his heady
kisses, straining against him, wanting more of him, all of
him, possessing him more fully than he had ever possessed
her.

Every nerve in her body cried out for release, yet in a passionate daze she wished no end to his love. Over and over
again he drove into her deeply, whispering her name, groaning
her name, pressing his mouth to her answering mouth. They
were locked in eternity, bound as one to the ecstasy that joined

them. And when at last he filled her with the essence of his passion, her own passion took flight in a celestial starburst of utter fulfillment and radiant, rapturous love.

The sun had gone down when she stirred beneath him and opened her eyes. They had lain together for what had seemed an endless time, his lips against her breast, her fingers entangled in his hair. Imprisoned beneath him, replete with his love, she wanted never to leave this place where she had at last opened her heart to the man she loved.

How sweet to share love again, how awesomely good. She felt at peace with the world, at peace with herself, and as she luxuriated in the love she had so long withheld from her husband, she felt a sudden sense of freedom that took her breath away.

Her husband, her lover. He was finally and again her lover. Adrian's hands trembled as she relived the moment of joining, felt again the wonderful, smooth warmth of his flesh inside hers. How could she have gone so long without the full measure of his love? Why had she fended him off, using Crandall's attack as the reason for her aversion?

But it hadn't been the attack—not totally—that had turned her away from her husband's love. Perhaps Jason's appraisal of the situation had been an accurate one.

Independence was the keynote. Yes, she feared the mere thought of losing her independence. But she had known for a long time that Jason respected that and would no more deprive her of her spiritual freedom than she would him. Jason had never threatened it, and yet, for the past year the fear of losing that independence had been lurking stealthily at the back of her thoughts.

"Jason," she said as he drew her close and kissed her, "could it be you were right?"

He moved a tendril of hair from her cheek. "About what, darling?"

"About why I couldn't make love with you. Do you really think it was because I was afraid of losing my independence?"

He sighed and stroked her arm. "I don't know," he said. "And frankly, at this moment, I couldn't care less about the reasons. You've accepted my love again, darling, that's all that concerns me. I can't begin to tell you how much I've missed your love. I need it so much, Adrian, *all* of your love, all of *you*. This past year has been a nightmare, a living hell. I didn't know what to do to bring you back to me; I kept thinking I was going to lose you. . . ." His voice shook; he broke off and turned his head away.

"Oh, Jason," she said softly, and embraced him fiercely. "You'll never lose me, never! When we get home again—" Now she was the one who broke off and turned away.

"Listen to me," Jason said, drawing her closer in his embrace, "we *will* go home again. I know it seems that we'll never be free of the Kaiser's surveillance, but I give you my word that we will."

"Jason, I know we will," she said softly. "I know you're trying to protect me, to be strong for me, but we must face adversity together and be strong for each other. You're blaming yourself for putting me in this predicament, but don't you realize that nothing truly frightens me except the thought of losing you?"

He was silent for a long while, then he lifted her chin with a finger and looked deep into her eyes. "Adrian, promise me something," he said quietly.

"Anything," she said, her dark eyes adoring him.

"If something should happen—I know that it won't—but if by chance something should happen to me, I want you to promise me that you won't grieve forever. I want your word that you'll go on with your life, that you'll accept another love if it should come along—"

"Jason," she said, alarmed, "why are you asking me to

do that? Nothing's going to happen to you. We're going to England together. Nothing will—''

"Yes, I know," he soothed softly, "nothing's going to happen to me. But I just want this one promise from you; otherwise, I'll not be able to rest easy."

She looked up at him helplessly as she strove to hold back a sob that rose suddenly in her throat. Why was he saying this now?

"Adrian?" he urged gently.

"Yes, all right," she said, summoning all of her courage. She must not weaken; she must be brave for him. "I'll give you my promise; I'll do anything you ask. Only promise me something in return."

"Yes?" he asked, caressing her wet cheek. "What shall I promise you?"

"Promise me nothing will happen to you," she said in a shaking voice. "Promise me that, and I'll never ask anything of you again for as long as I live."

"It's a bargain." He smiled, but the smile was tinged with sadness.

"Jason . . ."

"Hush," he said, "don't talk, don't say anything. Just let me look at you, let me savor you."

He watched her in silence for a long time, as if imprinting on his brain every line and curve and contour of her face. In his eyes was reflected the same fathomless depth of love she knew was in hers. At length, he bent to kiss her and began to make love to her gently, with infinite tenderness, as if to prolong their loving union for as long as he could. Adrian clung to him tightly, rejoicing in his passion, yet intensely aware of his lingering fears.

He made love to her all night long. When they fell asleep at last, the sun's first rays bathed their entwined figures in a roseate blessing of shimmering morning light.

Thirty-five

THEY SLEPT MOST of the morning away. When they awoke at half past eleven, the sun had disappeared and a light rain had begun to fall. The room was fragrant with the scent of pine and rain-kissed flowers. At the sound of pattering raindrops Adrian opened her eyes, took note of the gray day, and nudged her husband awake.

"Jason, it's raining."

He grunted an acknowledgment and buried his face in the pillow.

Sitting up, Adrian said, "Why don't you postpone your meeting with Herr Friedl until the weather clears, and we can spend the rest of the day in bed?"

"Adrian," he groaned, his face still buried in the pillow, "I couldn't make love to you today if my life depended on it."

"Why don't we try?" she asked, half teasing, half in earnest. If only they could spend the rest of their lives in bed, away from the real world of threatening realities . . .

"We'll try tonight," he said wearily. "Now go back to sleep."

But she was too tense to sleep, and too exhilarated from the memory of the love she had shared with her husband. She snatched the pillow from under his head and pummeled his back with it until he turned swiftly and caught her in his arms.

"You little devil," he said as she twisted provocatively

against him, "I can't make love to you, I tell you. It's a physical impossibility."

"Is it?" she murmured, smiling up at him seductively.

He was lying on top of her. His chest crushed her breasts, and she could feel his desire, reawakened and full, against the insides of her thighs. She had only to move a muscle and he would be buried deep inside her. She imagined his flesh, thrusting deeply into hers; she envisioned her body, a most willing receptacle of his passionate love.

"Jason," she whispered faintly, aroused beyond endurance.

Without conscious will she pressed closer against him and parted her legs. She felt him stiffen with surprise and pull slightly away. With a firm hand she reached down to take hold of him, and as her legs entwined with his, restricting his movements, she drew him easily, smoothly inside her.

He caught his breath, did not move. She felt him, throbbing and rigid, within the confines of her flesh. His slender frame trembled; the pounding of his heartbeat became an echo of her own. She was afraid he might withdraw, but with a soft, aching groan he pressed her close against his body and pushed deeper inside her as his hard mouth closed hotly on hers.

All thought was swept away by the force of his passion. Her senses surrendered to the touch of his tongue and the insistence of his hands. She was wholly in his thrall, his possession, his belonging. She was the instrument of his pleasure, and he, without volition, had fully become the instrument of hers. Satiation was long in coming, but when at last it commenced, he filled her, engulfed her with the full force of his passion and with the overpowering ecstasy of his endless, perfect love.

A long moment passed. She couldn't move, she couldn't speak. Her will dissolved against the onslaught of his, her very spirit submitted to the authority of his physical command. He lay heavily on top of her, her body still tingled from the rapture of his passion, yet all she could think of was that she wanted even more than he had given her.

At last he drew away and lay down beside her. When he spoke, his low voice thrilled her. Her heart, newly quiescent, began a rapid beat once more.

"It's incredible," he said softly, his arm around her waist, his face close to hers on the pillow they shared. "I would have been willing to stake my life on the fact that I couldn't make love to you again, and yet when I was loving you, inside you, I wanted it never to end. You're a sorceress, do you know that? A mystical magical enchantress."

She smiled and snuggled closer. *"You're* the sorcerer," she murmured. "You are the one who beguiled me into loving you, into marrying you. You are the one who taught me to live for others as well as for myself. And you gave me Elyse," she whispered, hugging him tightly. "Jason, you've given me so much more than a wedding ring and a child. I love you intensely and completely. . . ." She wound her arms around his neck and covered his face with a passion of kisses, pressing close to him, touching him, wanting him again.

"Adrian," he said, laughing beneath her ardent aggression, "no more, I beg you! You've done me in completely. I could no more make love to you now than I could swim the English Channel."

She moved back in his arms and regarded him mischievously. "You said much the same thing earlier," she reminded him, "and as I recall, Jason, I managed to convince you otherwise."

He smiled at the memory but slipped out of her grasp and rose from the bed. "That was earlier," he said, pulling on his dressing gown. "But if I had any lingering sexual potency, you have made thorough use of it. Now get out of that bed and let's have some breakfast"—he glanced at his watch on the night table—"or rather, some lunch. And maybe tonight, if I have recovered from your erotic assault, I'll think about making love to you again."

He went into the bathroom and shut the door. Amidst a tangle of sheets Adrian lay back on the pillows, her arms over her head. Her tension had eased somewhat. How much easier it was to face adversity with a loved one. Their situation had not changed; they were in as much danger as they had been, but sharing the fear, sharing love, had lessened the sense of despair that had earlier gripped them both.

Adrian got out of bed and had just slipped on her peignoir when an insistent knocking sounded at the door of the suite. She went to the door with an awakening apprehension and swung it open. In the hall the senior officer of the escort stood at military attention, one hand on the hilt of his saber, the other held stiffly at his side.

"Frau Carradine, may I speak with your husband, please?" The officer's expression told her nothing. She noticed irrelevantly that he must have shaved in a hurry, for there were several small razor nicks on his cheeks and chin.

"My husband is bathing, Colonel Berchtold. May I be of assistance?"

He regarded her dubiously, as if debating whether to entrust his message to a mere woman. Adrian eyed him sardonically and said with an ironic smile, "If you please, Colonel, I am quite capable of delivering a message with complete accuracy to my husband."

"Very well," he said stiffly. "You will kindly inform your husband to make haste with his business with Herr Friedl. We must return to Berlin as soon as possible."

"Why?" she asked as he turned to walk away.

He stopped and turned back to her and for a moment said nothing. Again Adrian's eyes went to the razor nicks on his face, and for some obscure reason those telltale signs of haste suddenly filled her with an icy fear.

"Emperor Franz Josef," said the colonel finally, "has declared war on Serbia. I've had a cable from the Kaiser. He wants all his officers back in Germany at once, which, of course, includes the members of your escort. His Majesty also said," the colonel added significantly, "that it is his wish that you and your husband accompany us."

Adrian went pale. With a few inarticulate words she thanked the colonel and slowly closed the door. War, she thought numbly. The inevitable chain of events was in motion. And she and her husband were at the mercy of the man who would lead the destruction.

"Adrian?" From the next room she heard Jason's voice as if in a dream. "Was someone at the door?"

She took a deep breath and pushed all her fears to the back of her mind. Jason must not know she was afraid. He would have enough to contend with when she relayed Colonel Berchtold's message.

On July 28, 1914, Austria-Hungary formally declared war on Serbia. France, foreseeing the inevitable, readied eight thousand men, while Russian forces began to mass on the eastern border. Soon afterward Belgrade was bombarded and occupied by Austria-Hungary. The Russian czar then summoned his reservists to supplement the troops already mobilized, which meant it was only a matter of time before the Kaiser declared war on Russia and France.

Virtually the entire world was rocked by the news. Fifteen firms failed on the London exchange, and capitals around the globe suffered severe declines. New York remained the only financial center in which there was a free market for securities and in which the workings of the local money market were not interrupted. This fact might have heartened Jason Carradine had not he and his wife been in the very midst of the calamity.

Their stay in Switzerland turned out to be more lengthy

than they had anticipated. Johannes Friedl was out of the country on business, and Jason convinced Colonel Berchtold that he could secure the information the Kaiser wanted from no one else. A cable to the Kaiser elicited a response that directed Berchtold to "allow Herr Carradine all latitude pending future developments." It was clear to the colonel and to Jason as well that Germany's involvement in the war was imminent and that Berchtold should make ready to leave Switzerland at a moment's notice.

When Friedl finally returned to his offices at Swiss Railway, he received Jason and his escort with a measure of surprise.

"But what are you doing here?" he asked while Berchtold looked on silently. Two of the colonel's men stood outside Friedl's office; the third was at the hotel, stationed outside the Carradine suite where Jason had persuaded his reluctant wife to remain.

"I am here to discuss my investment," said Jason carefully. "If you could furnish me with detailed plans of the diesel, I should like to have them examined by my associates in Zurich."

Friedl, a dark-haired Swiss with fine, deep blue eyes, was clearly mystified. Jason's bank in Zurich was already in possession of the diesel's plans. He glanced at Berchtold, who was watching him closely, then he looked at the open door to his office at the two men outside.

"Ah, yes, the plans," Friedl said. "The plant superintendent currently has them. He is on holiday; I expect him tomorrow morning. May I show you the prototype in the meantime?"

"The prototype?" Jason said, surprised. "Is it already completed?"

"Yes," Friedl answered, rising from behind his desk. "Come along, Jason. I'm sure you and your . . . guests would be interested in seeing it."

They left the offices and went out to the railyards where a gleaming locomotive stood in sleek splendor beneath a protective awning. Several workmen were busy at the wheels of the black-and-silver beauty. Friedl said to one of them, "Start it up, Albrecht. I should like Herr Carradine to listen to the engine."

The workman nodded, climbed into the engineer's cab, and with a loud rush, the diesel engine sprang to life. Above the roar Friedl said so that only Jason could hear, "What's going on? Who are those men?"

The soldiers, Berchtold included, were temporarily distracted by the wonder of the powerful engine. Jason said swiftly, "You must help me get my wife away from them and back to England."

Friedl said as swiftly, "Your wife? Where is she?"

And when Jason told him, Friedl asked, "Is she being watched?"

"Yes."

"How many men?"

"One."

Friedl thought for a moment, then said, "Have her pack a few things and be ready to leave tomorrow. I shall arrange to have someone fetch her when you and these men return here in the morning."

But persuading Adrian to leave was another matter entirely. When Jason returned to the hotel later that day and told her of Friedl's plan, she said simply, "I will not go. I refuse to leave you."

"Adrian," he said harshly, his patience at an end, "this is not a choice I'm giving you. You *will* go tomorrow; you must get to Asquith before it's too late."

This appeal to her conscience was futile. "If Herr Friedl can arrange to get me to England," she said stubbornly, "then he can do the same for you."

"He has done," Jason lied, for he knew that nothing else

would convince his wife to leave him. "But we must leave separately, or else his plan will fail."

"Jason," she faltered, "you wouldn't lie to me?"

"Christ, of course not!" he said in his angriest voice. "I told you I'm no hero. I want to save my skin as much as the next man. I'm to meet you at the border, Friedl told me; that's all I know. We couldn't very well have a lengthy chat with Berchtold and his apes breathing down our necks. Now pack your things," he commanded, but when he saw the fearful indecision that drained the color from her face, he almost relented. But he realized that this was no time for sentiment. "Do as I say!" he said sharply. And when she turned away from him, tears blurring her eyes, he had to physically restrain himself from sweeping her into his arms and never, ever letting her go.

Thirty-six

HE LEFT BEFORE the sun rose the next morning. He left after a night of love such as they had never before shared. He made love to her with a heartbreaking gentleness, as if he would never hold her again, caress her, kiss her soft mouth, as if this sweet night of love might be the last they would know.

While he loved her and kissed her and whispered endearments, Adrian gave him all her own love. Yet she was not unaware of the unmistakable feeling of farewell in his touch. How could she go without him? How could she leave him, even for only a little while? But she knew she had to be brave for his sake. She must not let him know how desperately she feared for him.

When he was ready to leave for the Swiss Railway offices, Adrian clung to him at the door. Tall and slender in his impeccable blue broadcloth, he had never looked handsomer nor more painfully unattainable as he did now. His eyes were that exquisite shade of deep Irish blue. Adrian pressed her burning cheek against his chest.

"Be ready for someone to come for you," he said against her hair. "Friedl will not fail us. Whoever he sends for you, make sure that you follow his instructions to the letter."

"And I'll see you soon?" she said against his shirt, barely able to speak.

"Yes, soon, darling," he said softly, his lips brushing her brow.

"Be very, very careful," she whispered, her throat tight with unshed tears. "Take no chances whatsoever. Remember, I'll be at the border waiting for you. If you're so careless as to let something happen to you I will do my best to see to it that you never rest in peace."

He chuckled softly, and his arms tightened around her for a moment, then he released her and stepped back.

His hand cupped her cheek, and he regarded her in silence for a long time. Then: "Wait for me," he said at last, his voice rough with emotion. "Wait for me, Adrian, I love you."

Then after a swift, hurting kiss and a crushing embrace, he turned and left her. When the door closed behind him, she began to weep silently, bitterly, with the taste of his warm mouth still sweet on her lips.

She did not have long to wait for Herr Friedl's man. The "man" turned out to be a boy—Friedl's son, in fact—a slender seventeen-year-old with dark, curling hair and long, dark lashes framing crystal-clear blue eyes.

"Frau Carradine?" the boy said in English. "I am Klaus Friedl, Johannes's son. You are expecting me?"

"Yes," she said uncertainly, taken aback by his youth and by a repressed urgency she sensed in him.

She glanced up and down the hall. It was empty.

"You are looking for your guard?" Klaus asked. And before she could answer, he explained rapidly, "I informed him that his automobile was aflame. He has gone down to attend to the blaze. Now, if you don't mind, Frau Carradine, would you collect your things as quickly as you can and come with me?"

Adrian picked up the satchel she had left by the door and accompanied the boy down the hall and through a door that led to the servants' stairway. As they descended swiftly, she had to ask, "*You* set the car afire, I take it?"

The boy glanced at her and smiled but did not respond.

When they reached the ground floor, he escorted her out the back door where a long, low-slung automobile awaited them, its engine idling.

"Where are we going?" Adrian asked as he assisted her into the car.

"To Lucerne," he said after getting behind the wheel. "We are to wait there for further instructions from my father."

He pushed down hard on the accelerator, and the car took off like a shot. Adrian's hands gripped the seat as she watched the speedometer climb to an incredible fifty kilometers.

"Klaus," she asked, "why are we going to Lucerne rather than directly to the border? Will my husband be meeting me there instead? Has there been a change in plans?"

He glanced at her quizzically, then redirected his attention to the road. "I don't know about that, Frau Carradine. My father only said that we were to wait at Lucerne for further instructions."

They arrived in Lucerne at ten o'clock. By the time they registered at the Schweizerhof Hotel and settled in their respective rooms, it was time for lunch. In the hotel dining room Klaus handed Adrian a thick envelope.

"I forgot to give this to you," he said. "My father knew you'd be needing money."

Adrian thanked him and put the envelope in her purse. Jason had given her several letters of credit the night before, but if she were unable to get to a bank, the cash would come in handy.

The restaurant was very crowded, and war talk was rampant among the diners. As Adrian ate her dessert, a rich *Krapfen* fruitcake, she heard that just that morning there had been a run on the Swiss National Bank and that Swiss trains were due to be immobilized within the week. Gold was at a premium because of the unsettled conditions, and in Bad

Nauheim, the hotels were without waiters, for all the men there had been called into the army.

"I shall have to leave you soon, Frau Carradine," Klaus said upon hearing this. "I must join the army, too."

"Klaus," she said gently, touched by his fervor, "you're only a boy. You cannot fight."

His young mouth hardened, and he faced her squarely. "I am a man," he said quietly, "and it is my duty to respond when oppression threatens my people."

His youthful, fair face and determined blue eyes reminded Adrian so much of her daughter that her throat ached. She reached across the table and covered Klaus's hand with hers. "Let's hope it doesn't come to that," she said softly. But she was very much afraid that her hopes were in vain.

Days passed with no word from either her husband or Johannes Friedl. Time dragged interminably for Adrian. War rumors persisted, yet no one knew which were true. One accurate rumor was that Swiss train service had been limited to troop and supply transport. Another, more frightening, was that the German Lloyd and the Hamburg-American lines had suspended transatlantic service, which meant that many American tourists were now without any means of transportation home. Much to Adrian's dismay, this suspension of service by the German lines tended to indicate that like action would be taken by Cunard and White Star, the British lines. Even if she and Jason did reach England, there would be no way for them to get home.

Worse than that was the news that Germany had finally declared war on Russia. Reports also abounded that there was border fighting between France and Germany. Adrian's fears rose to new heights as she imagined what possible bearing this could have on Jason.

Alone now, without her husband, much was becoming clear to Adrian that before had been only nebulous in her mind. She was on her own here, independent, free, and she could not have been more miserable. Jason was her freedom—oh, why hadn't she seen it? Loving Jason was her freedom; marrying him had been her liberation, the foundation of the independence she so feared to lose. Loving Jason, committing to him, was the first true sharing she had ever permitted herself. Always before she had lived for herself alone. But in loving Jason, in having his child and becoming his wife, Adrian had given completely of herself for the first time in her life, and she realized at last that to give of oneself to the person one loves is not a loss or a submission but the greatest of gains.

She said to Klaus that evening the moment he joined her for dinner, "We must do something; we cannot just sit here and wait. I must know what's happened to my husband."

"Your husband," said Klaus, taking his seat with a wide smile, "will be here in the morning, Frau Carradine."

"What?" she said, stunned.

"Yes," the boy said. "I have just had a message from my father. He is sending a train to transport the stranded tourists to the French border, and your husband, my father said, will be on that train."

Adrian's heart pounded joyously. "Thank God," she said. "Oh, thank God. Klaus, how did my husband elude the German escort?"

"I don't know," the boy answered. "My father's message was brief. But you may rest easy now, Frau Carradine. Tomorrow at dawn you will be with your husband."

But the next morning at dawn, when Adrian raced to the station, she found a crowd of people already assembled, the great locomotive gleaming silver in the dawnlight, and no sign of her husband.

As she frantically searched the milling crowd she finally caught sight of a tall figure standing near the locomotive. "Jason!" she called.

A dark head turned, but it was a stranger who regarded her intently as she pushed through the throng.

"Frau Carradine?" the stranger asked. "You are the wife of Jason Carradine?"

"Yes," she said, approaching him, looking eagerly around for Jason as she tried to catch her breath. "Where is he? Where is my husband?"

"Frau Carradine," he said, "I am Johannes Friedl of the Swiss International Railway." And then, catching sight of his son: "Ah, Klaus. It's good to see you. Please help get the passengers boarded at once." He turned back to Adrian. The gravity of his gaze struck a note of fear in her breast.

"Herr Friedl"—the steadiness of her voice hid the quiver of alarm that shivered through her—"where is my husband?"

"He is not here with me, Frau Carradine."

Her alarm was now paralyzing. "Dear God," she said faintly, "is he . . . ? Did the Germans . . . ?"

"No, no," Friedl said swiftly. "It is not that, Frau Carradine. First of all, your husband was able to convince Colonel Berchtold that you had run off on your own because of some quarrel you had had in the gardens at the Kaiser's palace. A few days later, when Germany entered the war and the colonel was preparing to return home, Jason pretended to suffer an attack of appendicitis, which my physician confirmed. Jason was then rushed to the hospital at Zurich, and after 'surgery' was performed, Dr. Steuben informed the colonel that Jason had died in the operating theater."

"Didn't the colonel insist on seeing his . . . body?" she asked with a shudder.

"Yes," Friedl said, "that was the tricky part. Dr. Steuben administered a drug to Jason, which slowed down all his vital signs and gave the appearance, to an untrained observer, of death. Perhaps if Colonel Berchtold had not been in such a hurry to return to Germany, he might not have been so easily deceived."

"But then, where is he?" Adrian insisted. "Why isn't Jason here?"

"Frau Carradine," he said gently, "after the German escort left I received word from the Swiss government to send a train to collect the stranded American tourists and transport them to the border. Jason told me he would remain in Zurich at his bank until the train came. But when I returned to Winterthur, I had a message from him asking that the train stop at Baden to collect him on the way to Lucerne. At Baden, however, the stationmaster gave me this message." Friedl reached into his coat pocket and extracted a note, which he handed to Adrian.

In Jason's bold hand the message read simply: "Go on to Lucerne as scheduled. Inform my wife that I shall meet her in Paris at the office of the vice-consul at Number Three, Rue Boissy-d'Anglais. Message to Asquith has already been sent."

"But what does it mean?" Adrian asked, frowning first at the note and then at Friedl. "What was Jason doing in Baden? And why wasn't he there when you arrived to collect him?"

"I don't know," Friedl answered.

"You don't know?" she echoed angrily. "Didn't you make inquiries? Couldn't you at least have tried to learn where he is?"

"I did," said Friedl quietly. "But no one knew Jason's whereabouts. I even contacted his bank in Zurich, but his people there could tell me nothing."

"How could that be?" she cried, furious. "A man doesn't just disappear from the face of the earth. Why did he go to Baden? And how does he intend to get safely across the border? There is no transportation out of the country except on your train."

"Frau Carradine," said Friedl in a low voice that chilled her, "I know that."

Thirty-seven

IT WASN'T TRUE, it was a nightmare. She mustn't think about it. If she did she would go mad. Jason was missing on a continent at war. Anything might have happened to him. He might be sick or injured. He might be in enemy hands, recaptured by the German escort. Or, knowing of his great wealth, a band of kidnappers might have plotted to hold him for ransom. If Jason had resisted or if he had tried to escape, he might now be lying dead on some cold, distant field in German territory.

The train left Lucerne just as the sun rose. From her window seat next to Johannes Friedl, Adrian had a spectacular view of the valleys and mountains growing rosy with first light. The sky was pale mauve; the clouds were puff balls of creamy pink confection. But Adrian was blind to all she saw. She could think only of Jason. How could she go on if something had truly happened to him? A remnant of logic told her that her fears were likely groundless: Jason was alive and well and on his way to Paris to meet her. Yet, try as she might, she could not stop herself from thinking the worst.

She dozed for a while on the long trip to Bern. The train stopped at each station along the way to take on any other tourists who were stranded without transportation. When they finally arrived at Bern, Friedl and his son went at once to the French embassy to have Adrian's passport validated while Adrian had rolls and chocolate at the depot café. When Friedl returned two hours later, he had bad news.

"We're going to have to spend the night in Bern," he told Adrian. "The train is to be shunted onto a siding to allow the mobilization trains to pass through. I have sent Klaus home. There is no telling how long we'll be here."

Adrian's heart sank. Another delay. How long would it take them to reach Paris? How long would it be until she could assure herself once and for all that Jason was safe?

"Well, no matter," said Friedl briskly, taking note of the look on Adrian's face. "Why don't we register at the hotel and then spend the rest of the day sight-seeing? Are you game, Frau Carradine?"

In truth, Adrian was game for nothing more than to stamp her foot in frustration. She wanted to get to Paris! She had to know if her husband was safe.

"Frau Carradine," Friedl urged, "will you come with me?"

Adrian roused herself with an effort. She had two choices: she could hide in the hotel room, brood alone, and conjure all sorts of catastrophes that might have befallen her husband; or she could tour the town of Bern with this thoughtful, caring man.

"Yes, all right," she said finally. "I'd be happy to go with you."

Jason stayed on her mind throughout the day, but touring the quaint twelfth-century town with its fountains and arcades and its colorful Clock Tower was a distraction she sorely needed and for which she was appropriately grateful.

After an early dinner with Friedl Adrian retired for the night and slept dreamlessly until four the next morning. One day closer, she thought as she rose and dressed and prepared to board the train. One day closer to seeing Jason. I *will* see him. He's probably waiting for me now at the consulate office in Paris.

The train left Bern at five A.M. As they neared the French border Adrian saw many soldiers on foot and horse-drawn carts bearing artillery and implements of war. On trains that passed by, soldiers were being transported in cattle cars, jammed shoulder to shoulder with no room to sit, and on their weary young faces Adrian saw a lonely fear that surpassed her own.

When they were a kilometer away from the border town of Pontarlier, the passengers were discharged and changed to a third-class train, and there Adrian said good-bye to Johannes Friedl.

"Courage, Frau Carradine," he said, holding firmly to her hand. "I know Jason is safe, and in your heart you must convince yourself that this is so."

Adrian could not answer. She only nodded silently and watched Friedl leave with an agony in her throat that kept her dark fears unspoken.

At Pontarlier there was a rigorous customs examination. Bags were searched first, and then people. Adrian bristled at the indignity of having her clothing and person searched for concealed bombs or letters. But her own inconvenience was quickly forgotten when she boarded the French train for Dijon and saw sick and wounded soldiers lying head to foot on an unprotected field as far as the eye could see.

Now the war was real to her: the awful grandeur, the bloody truth. Young men lay dying before her horrified eyes, young men who had not yet begun to live. This scene, she realized grimly, was only a small portion of what was occurring throughout Europe. And then she thought with a sudden surge of terror, Was this what had happened to Jason? While she traveled to Paris in hopes of joining him, was he lying, bloodied and near death, on some foreign field?

No, no, no. She refused to let herself believe such a thing. Jason was in Paris, most likely at the Bristol. At this very moment he was enjoying an apéritif, and shortly he would be dining on consommé Imperial and filet of beef Napolitaine. She imagined him in evening clothes; he looked ever so elegant in his impeccable black broadcloth and gleaming white linen. She imagined herself on his arm, clad in white peau de soie, a proper complement to his dark and perfect beauty. And, with these sweet, hazy images filling her thoughts, Adrian managed to close her mind, for a little while at least, to the possibility of an unfaceable reality.

The train reached Paris at last. The streets were deadly quiet; all of the cafés were shut and boarded, and no one was around, for martial law had been declared.

After dispatching her luggage to the Bristol Hotel Adrian took a taxi to the consulate office. The deserted streets did nothing to bolster her courage, and the shops she passed, empty and forlorn, merely echoed the desolation of her dark and fearful thoughts.

The consulate building was a stately white edifice with a great golden eagle perched atop the colonnaded entrance. Adrian was reassured by the American flag fluttering grandly in the breeze, but after she paid the cabbie and entered the building, her heart began an uncontrollable pounding.

As she stopped at the reception desk and asked the whereabouts of the vice-consul's office, she was vaguely reminded of the day she had gone to Jason's bank to ask for a loan. Now as then, she felt a terrible trepidation, the dread of venturing blindly into unknown territory.

She followed the young adjutant to the vice-consul's office, looking around at the silk-curtained windows, the white, painted walls, and the portraits of President Wilson and Vice-President Marshall. This unexpected touch of home on foreign soil brightened her outlook to a small degree. When she entered the vice-consul's office, it was with a measure of renewed optimism that she gave her hand in greeting and told him her name.

"Mrs. Carradine," he said as the adjutant left, "please sit down. I've been expecting you."

His face and his voice told her nothing. He was a man of middle years, Franklin Henning by name, stockily built, with iron-gray hair and the most piercing dark eyes Adrian had ever seen. After seating her he returned to his chair, folded his hands before him, and faced her across the desk.

"Now, then," he began. "I know you've come in hopes of joining your husband, but I'm afraid he isn't here. As you may know, he was recently in Baden, and from there he—"

Her heart leaped; every nerve in her body went rigid. "Mr. Henning," she said, stopping him, her voice sharp with alarm, "I know my husband was in Baden, but I don't know why. In fact, I know nothing of his activities for the past few days. Will you therefore please tell me at once why he's not here?"

Her dark eyes were hard, but it was fear that blazed in their depths. Henning noted the fear, and gently he told her, "To begin with, Mrs. Carradine, your husband went to Baden when he learned that the wife of an employee at his bank in Zurich was about to give birth. The couple are Americans, and when war was declared, it was their intention to leave Switzerland and go home. The wife's time, however, came a month sooner than expected. When Jason heard of their plight, he went to Baden, where the couple live, and sent a message to Johannes Friedl, asking Friedl to send the train there."

"Yes," she said distractedly, "I know about the message. But what happened? Why wasn't Jason at Baden when Friedl arrived? And where is he now?"

"Mrs. Carradine," Henning said in a tone designed to calm her, "let me relate everything I know from the begin-

ning, if you please.'' And when she nodded helplessly, he
went on. ''I heard from Jason while he was in Baden. It
seems the wife of his employee was in labor when the train
arrived. Jason then somehow managed to secure an automobile, and shortly after the woman gave birth, they started out
for Pontarlier in hopes of catching up with the train. Jason
told me in his message that if he missed the train at the border he would get here to meet you by other means.''

''And then?'' Adrian urged him, her hands digging into
her purse.

''And then,'' said Henning slowly, ''I received word
from the Swiss border patrol of an automobile accident at
Rheinfelden.''

''An accident?'' She felt suddenly dizzy; her hands
gripped the sides of the chair.

''Yes, an accident,'' he said, his tone low and somber.
''The automobile had run off an embankment. Apparently it
burst into flame, and all the passengers''—he paused and
looked away from her—''were burned beyond recogni-
tion.''

Adrian's stomach lurched; the room spun dizzily before
her eyes. By a supreme effort of will she forced herself to
speak. ''Are you saying that my husband is dead?''

Henning's dark, piercing gaze turned reluctantly to hers.
''I can only assume—''

''Assume?'' she echoed hoarsely, her throat tight with
pain. ''You're *assuming* my husband is dead?''

''Mrs. Carradine,'' he said patiently, ''some personal effects were discovered near the scene of the accident; your
husband's coat, for one thing, containing his passport and
other papers. Again this is an assumption, but I can only
conclude that he had removed his coat in the automobile,
and at the time of the accident, it was thrown clear of the
wreckage. Among his papers, by the way, was my name and

the address of the consulate, which is why the border patrol contacted me.''

She wanted to scream. She wanted to leap to her feet and scream, but she was too numb to move, too horrified to even utter a sound. Jason was dead. It was not an assumption; it was not a bad dream. This was reality, the reality she had feared to face.

She stared blindly at the floor, unwilling and unable to believe the awful truth. Jason couldn't be dead. But she knew that he was. Somehow, she thought, she had known it all along. When she had told him good-bye in Winterthur, she had known she would never see him again. When she traveled from Lucerne to Paris, outwardly hopeful and secretly afraid, she had felt in her deepest heart that their brief separation would prove to be permanent.

At length, in a toneless voice, she heard herself ask, ''Will I be permitted to bring his . . . body home?''

''I'm very sorry,'' said Henning regretfully. ''It's out of the question. With so many sailings cancelled, and with the exceptional number of people leaving the country . . . I'm sorry, Mrs. Carradine.''

She looked up at him slowly, her face without color. ''A funeral service then?'' she asked brokenly. ''Can that be arranged?''

''If you wish,'' he agreed with a compassionate nod. ''Your husband's remains are now on their way to Paris. As soon as they arrive I'll arrange for burial.'' Henning paused for a moment, then went on with some reluctance. ''Mrs. Carradine, I don't wish to seem callous, but everything must be done with all possible haste.''

''Why?'' The word was barely audible.

''At Jason's earlier request,'' Henning told her, ''I booked passage for you on the *Arabic*. It sails on Thursday from Liverpool. All Southampton sailings have been diverted for the time being, and since you now have that added traveling distance, I suggest we hold the funeral just as quickly as we can. I hope you don't mind.''

"No, I don't mind," she said dully, and rose to take her leave.

What difference did it make? What difference did anything make now? Jason was dead. What did it matter if he was buried in haste or at leisure? The farewell she must bid him would be just as final in either case.

Was this how love ended then, with some soft-spoken words? "I can only assume . . ." "His personal effects . . ." "The accident . . ." "His remains . . ." Words, soft yet final. Was this how love died?

She buried her husband on a drizzly August morning in the same cemetery where years earlier she had buried her aunt. The scene had a feeling of eerie familiarity. A gray mist hung over the mournful monuments; the casket gleamed dully beneath a blanket of white roses. An Episcopalian minister read the service. Franklin Henning stood at Adrian's side much in the same manner Armand Mitterand had stood by her at Aunt Meg's funeral.

Adrian, heavily veiled and in deepest mourning, was dry-eyed and composed. She had wept for two days in her hotel room, harsh, bitter tears, so fierce and filled with anguish that when she finally rose from her bed, she felt drained to the depths of her soul. It was so much worse than the grief that had torn her when her aunt had died on foreign soil. She was alone again, alone and desolate and bereft of her love and strength.

Ironically when she had arrived at the hotel, she had found a letter from Tessa waiting for her, a letter filled with such optimism and joy as to drive home more deeply the agony of Adrian's grief.

"I'm going to have a baby," Tessa had written. "I couldn't be happier, and Evan is ecstatic. You'll have to find a *temporary* replacement for me at the fashion house. Believe it or not, Evan said that if I want to return to work when the baby is a year or two old, I may do so. Can you believe it? He's changing, Adrian; slowly but surely he's changing. Confidentially, when we were first married, I wasn't quite sure he loved me. But in the past few months or so he's been an absolute angel.

"Hurry home! I have so much to tell you. Sales couldn't be better; I've had to employ more dressmakers. I hope those rumors of war we've been reading about have no truth in them. Give my love to Jason. . . ."

Love to Jason. It was reading those words that had started Adrian's tears. Her husband was dead, and with him had died all the joy and love of living that was the hallmark of their love.

But she had a promise to honor—or part of one at least. She would go on with her life as Jason had asked. She would continue with her work, and she would raise her daughter with love enough for two.

As to the rest of his demand—that Adrian accept another love—she smiled bleakly at the thought. Another love after Jason? To what end? What other man was as warm and as loving and as understanding as he? How could she even consider giving her love to someone else when her whole mind and heart were inextricably committed to the man who had taught her the meaning of love? She was content with his memory and with the child he had given her. For the rest of her life she would need nothing else.

"Mrs. Carradine?"

The service had ended. Franklin Henning touched her arm. Adrian looked up slowly from her deep meditation, and her gaze came to rest on the rose-covered coffin.

She moved to the catafalque as if in a dream. Now was the moment of parting. Now she must leave her husband for the last time, never again to see his dear face, never to touch him, to kiss him, to hold him in her arms.

She looked down at the casket, her eyes blurring with tears. She was leaving her love for the last time. She touched a trembling rose, velvet-smooth like his skin. She remembered his touch, the sound of his voice, the clasp of his arms, the tender love in his eyes . . .

Oh, how could she bear it? How could she go on?

But she had to go on; she had given him her promise. He had given her so much: he had taught her to love; he had allowed her always the precious freedom that he knew she prized so highly. And because she loved him, because her love and her gratitude were greater than the pain of losing him, she knew she must find the strength to live the rest of her life without him.

She picked up the rain-kissed rose, pressed it gently to her lips. The sweet fragrance was reminiscent of the love she had shared with him in Switzerland, the love she would share with no other man. "Jason," she whispered, giving him a final promise, "I'll never stop loving you as long as I live."

Epilogue

IT WAS COOL on the deck of the R.M.S. *Arabic*. The August night was clear; a silver-white moon and a brilliant array of stars cast a phosphorescent glow on the ebony surface of the North Atlantic sea. A lone passenger stood at the rail, a woman in mourning, a portrait in black, the only contrast her cameo face upon which a recent and profound grief was most intensely, exquisitely etched.

Nearby but apart stood a gentleman watching her. He had boarded the ship an hour earlier at Queenstown; he had been, in fact, the last person to board, having arrived in Queenstown only minutes before the great ship hoisted anchor. Without luggage, in need of a bath and a shave, he had imposed upon the captain for the use of his cabin and a fresh change of clothes. Now, as he quietly watched the woman at the rail, he was impeccably turned out in a dark blue uniform with gold braid, a sober blue tie, and a crisp white shirt redolent of soap and starch.

For the past quarter hour he had been watching the woman in black, watching her and waiting, fearful of approaching her, for his unexpected appearance would surely cause great shock to her. He knew she was grieving: her pain was most evident on the perfect contours of her ivory face. It was therefore of the utmost importance to him that he spare her further pain. But after a few moments more of waiting, no longer able to remain apart from her, he decided at last on a manner of approaching her.

"Madame." He spoke in French. "Your pardon if I disturb you, but I believe we once made love in a pine-scented bedroom in Switzerland."

The woman turned from the rail slowly, as if in a daze. Her eyes, dark and lustrous, widened in disbelief.

"Jason," she whispered, swaying slightly as she spoke. "Dear God, Jason . . ."

"Darling, don't," he said, taking her swiftly in his arms. "Don't faint on me, whatever you do. You're not seeing a ghost. I'm real and alive, I promise you. I wasn't in the automobile—"

"Jason," she said again, hardly daring to believe that she was awake and not dreaming. But she knew she was awake, for his arms around her were hurting her, thrilling her. His eyes, midnight blue, were alive with love and happiness, and his fresh, clean male scent enveloped her blissfully as his hard mouth closed firmly on hers.

Alive! He was alive! Her heart was close to bursting. His touch was an ecstasy; his kiss was a rapture she had thought never to know again. She wound her arms around him, pressing close to him, breathless with loving him, faint with the joy of holding him. She was holding him, kissing him, touching him, loving him. She wanted to sing with the joy of it; she wanted never to leave the blessed haven of his wondrous perfect love.

At long length he drew away from her, but she would not let him go. "Stay," she said, trembling, holding fast to his arms. "Don't let go of me; don't ever let go of me again."

He smiled down at her. He was trembling as she was; his dark-lashed blue eyes were a radiant light in his sunbrowned face. "Poor darling," he said shakily. "Was it very bad for you? I can't tell you how sorry I am for having caused you such pain."

"Jason, what happened at Rheinfelden?" she asked. But

she truly didn't care. He was alive, in her arms. Nothing else mattered but that he was back where he belonged.

"It was nothing more than an unfortunate mix-up," he said, releasing her and leaning back against the rail. "I started out for Pontarlier with the Wallaces—"

"The Wallaces?"

"The couple in Baden," he explained. "George and Edith Wallace and their new baby. When we got to the train crossing at Rheinfelden, we were stopped by men I thought were railroad guards but who turned out to be a trio of thieves bent on robbing us at gunpoint and taking the automobile, which they did. My coat, as you already know, was in the auto, along with my passport and all my money."

"Then it was the thieves who were—"

"Yes," he said. "Their bodies were discovered by the border patrol. In any case, shortly after we were left stranded, a munitions train passed by on its way to Paris. The Wallaces and I scrambled aboard the last car and were promptly discovered by an extremely nervous young soldier. The soldier arrested us at once despite our protests that we could hardly be German spies, traveling as we were with a newborn baby."

Jason paused to light a cigarette, and Adrian watched him hungrily, hardly able to believe that she was actually next to him, within a hairsbreadth of touching him. Her excitement was such that his words had almost no meaning. He was alive; he was here. That was the only thing now that mattered to her.

"When we finally arrived in Paris," he went on, "the soldier turned us over to the military authorities who eventually allowed me to contact the vice-consul."

"But, Jason, I was at the consulate office," she said, puzzled. "How is it we didn't meet? When did you get to Paris?"

"I got there," he said with a grim smile, "on the day after you buried me."

"Oh, Jason," she shuddered.

"Darling, I'm sorry," he said at once. "That wasn't very amusing. It must have been torturous for you. Dear God, if there had only been some way to let you know I was alive."

"Oh, don't," she cried softly, circling his neck with her arms and pressing swift, loving kisses on his warm cheeks and mouth. "Don't blame yourself for something that couldn't be helped. It doesn't matter. Nothing matters now except that you're here and we're together."

She stepped back abruptly and gazed up at him with a fever of love and passion. Why were they wasting their time up here on deck? Why weren't they in her stateroom, lying together on a gently swaying bed, pressing close to each other, telling each other with their lips and their hands and their bodies how much they loved and had missed each other?

"Jason, let's go inside," she said breathlessly.

He looked down at her, easily guessing her sensuous thoughts, and he laughed softly. "Good Lord, Adrian, aren't you even interested to know how I managed to board the ship in time?"

"Tell me in bed," she said, tugging impatiently at his sleeve.

"Very well," he said with a grin as he tossed away his cigarette.

But when they were in bed in the luxurious suite on the A deck, no words were necessary between the two of them. They came together as if they had been parted for decades. Their mouths clung together hungrily; their hands explored and caressed with an urgent and delicious intimacy. They could barely wait to join. When they did, satiation was immediate, yet they remained as one, kissing, touching, moving in sweet harmony, reaffirming the love that they both knew would last until the end of eternity.

They were of one mind, one body, one heart. Locked in each other's arms, the adversities that had separated them were vanquished by their passion. Jason was hers, and Adrian was his as she had never been before. When satiation came again, it was swift and fierce and all-consuming. Adrian clung to him tightly; Jason's arms crushed her closer. For a long time they did not speak. The silence hummed with the strength of their utter unity.

An hour passed, and then another, and still she held onto him, an arm spanning his waist, her cheek resting warmly on his chest. She could feel the soft thudding of his heart; his warm breath on her lips seemed a gentle caress. At length he said softly, "I wish it were possible for me to convey how much I love you."

Drowsily she murmured, "You've just done that—and very thoroughly, I might add."

He chuckled and pulled her ear, then sat up against the headboard and drew her up with him. "Well," he said, "now that we've got that out of the way, let me tell you how I managed to catch up with the ship."

"Yes, do," she murmured, and snuggled comfortably closer.

"Adrian!" he said in mock injury. "You don't sound very interested to know how your brave husband risked life and limb to join his grieving widow."

Adrian raised her head abruptly and glared at him. "Jason," she threatened ominously, "if you make one more reference to—"

"Very well," he said, laughing. "I shall never again mention my untimely demise. But listen to me, Adrian," he said excitedly, hugging her closer. "I want you to know how I got to Queenstown so quickly. After I talked to Henning and he told me you had left for Liverpool, I knew that no power

on earth could get me there in time to board the *Arabic*. It
was only last night that I remembered the airplane factory at
Billancourt.''

"The one you invested in!" she exclaimed.

"Yes, that's right.'' He grinned. "So off I went to Billancourt, unbathed, unshaven, with only the clothes on my
back; and when I got there, I talked to Gabriel Voison—you
remember him, don't you, Adrian?''

"Yes.'' She laughed. "We dined with him and his wife
in Paris. But don't tell me what happened when you got to
Billancourt; let me try to piece it together myself. Gabriel
flew you over to Queenstown in one of his airplanes because
he's a friend of yours and owes you a favor, am I right?''

"Yes! How did you know, darling?''

"I don't know," she said, smiling, reaching up to embrace him in a warm surge of love and happiness. "I suppose it was just a lucky guess.''